# SYMBIONT

# SYMBIONT

PARASITOLOGY VOLUME 2

# MIRA GRANT

www.orbitbooks.net

Copyright © 2014 by Seanan McGuire

Orbit
Hachette Book Group
1290 Avenue of the Americas, New York, NY 10104
www.HachetteBookGroup.com

Printed in the United States of America

RRD-C

First Edition: November 2014

10 9 8 7 6 5 4 3 2

Orbit is an imprint of Hachette Book Group, Inc. The Orbit name and logo are trademarks of Little, Brown Book Group Limited.

The Hachette Speakers Bureau provides a wide range of authors for speaking events. To find out more, go to www.hachettespeakersbureau.com or call (866) 376-6591.

The publisher is not responsible for websites (or their content) that are not owned by the publisher.

Library of Congress Cataloging-in-Publication Data

Grant, Mira.
    Symbiont / Mira Grant. — First edition.
        pages cm. — (Parasitology ; 2)
    Summary: "THE SECOND BOOK IN MIRA GRANT'S TERRIFYING PARASITOLOGY SERIES. THE ENEMY IS INSIDE US. The SymboGen designed tapeworms were created to relieve humanity of disease and sickness. But the implants in the majority of the world's population began attacking their hosts turning them into a ravenous horde. Now those who do not appear to be afflicted are being gathered for quarantine as panic spreads, but Sal and her companions must discover how the tapeworms are taking over their hosts, what their eventual goal is, and how they can be stopped."—Provided by publisher.
    ISBN 978-0-316-21899-3 (hardback)—ISBN 978-0-316-21900-6 (ebook)—ISBN 978-1-4789-8479-5 (audiobook)   1. Genetic engineering—Fiction. 2. Parasites—Fiction.   3. Science fiction.   4. Horror fiction.   I. Title.
    PS3607.R36395S96 2014
    813'.6—dc23
                                                                2014015833

*This book is dedicated to Aislinn Suzanne Ellis,*
*who had the excellent sense to be born while*
*it was being written.*

*Welcome to the world, my dearest skeleton girl.*

# INTERLUDE 0: MEIOSIS

*Knowing the direction doesn't mean you have to go.*
—SIMONE KIMBERLEY,
*DON'T GO OUT ALONE*

*Boom boom pow, bitches.*
—TANSY (SUBJECT VIII, ITERATION II)

*November 3, 2027: Time stamp 17:27.*

[The recording is substandard, clearly done on a cellular telephone or cheap tablet, rather than any form of professional camera. The lab on the screen looks like it was assembled in a junkyard: mismatched equipment, sputtering lightbulbs, and personnel in stained scrubs that have clearly been worn for several weeks without being washed. All of them have their faces turned away, save for the central figure in the shot, a woman in a wheelchair. Her wavy blonde hair hangs limp around her face but her lab coat is surprisingly clean, given the chaos surrounding her. A palpable air of exhaustion hangs around her. She has clearly made an effort to tidy herself up, to adhere to modern standards of attractiveness, but nothing will disguise the bags beneath her eyes, or the faint pallor of her skin.]

DR. CALE: My name is Doctor Shanti Cale. I am one of the original creators of the *Diphyllobothrium symbogenesis* organism, more commonly known as "the SymboGen implant," although I suppose that if anyone's talking about it today, you're calling it the cause of the sleepwalking sickness. My co-creators were Doctor Richard Jablonsky, deceased, and Doctor Steven Banks, whose whereabouts are currently unknown to me. I suppose he's still safely tucked away inside his corporate fortress. I know I would be, in his position.

[She pauses, takes a breath, and visibly steadies herself as she returns to her original tone of calm professionalism.]

DR. CALE: I am not trying to shift or dodge any of the blame that is due to me. This confession—the confession of my involvement—appears at the front of every recording we have made since the war began. You will not find information to exonerate me. You may find more proof that I should be reviled by history. It's all right. The broken doors are open now, and I was the one who opened them.

[She grips the wheels of her chair, rolling herself to the side of the shot. The camera does not follow her movement; the recording device is apparently propped on a table or counter. There is a brief blur off to one side as one of the technicians passes through the frame; her face has been pixelated to obscure her identity.]

DR. CALE: At the end of this introduction, the video feed will switch to a compressed data format. Using the following data decryption code will allow you to extract and analyze this week's findings.

[She holds up a small whiteboard. On it is written a string of apparently meaningless letters and numbers. She is careful to hold the whiteboard so that all figures are clearly visible in the shot.]

DR. CALE: I'm afraid this week's results have been less than encouraging. We have retrieved and analyzed four of the so-called "sleepwalkers" affected by the active stage of the *D. symbogenesis* parasite. All of them demonstrated physiological difficulties, as well as unpredictable and irrational behavior. Analysis of the subjects showed that there had been extensive damage to the soft tissues of the brain and spine during the takeover process, resulting in a host that was unable to reach an accord with the invasive parasite. Unless *D. symbogenesis* finds a way to begin infiltration earlier in its life cycle, we will continue to see individuals who have been damaged in this manner. At this point, neither the original human host nor the invasive parasite will be able to utilize these subjects as fully functional beings. They are failures of evolution. They are dead ends.

[Dr. Cale pauses and puts the whiteboard down, rubbing her face with the heel of her hand. In that moment, she looks more tired, and more human, than she has since the video began.]

DR. CALE: There are those who will interpret my decision to open these videos with a confession as an admission of guilt. It's not. I just need you to know that my data is as good as it's possible for anyone's data to be, and if there's blame to be given, I need it to fall on me. But I'm not guilty. Guilt involves feeling like you did something wrong, and while I am most definitely to blame, I'm not guilty.

[She smiles, a little sadly.]

DR. CALE: I don't know who's watching these videos, if anyone is. Maybe it's someone from the human side, and maybe it's someone from the *D. symbogenesis* side, and I'm not going to say which side it is that I'm rooting for, because honestly, even I don't know anymore. I know that I did good work. I know that I made a lot of lives better with what I did. I know that I love my children—all of them, no matter what species they are. I know that I am sorry for what's happening right now, but nothing that happens is ever going to make me regret that I created them.

[Her attention switches briefly to something outside the shot. She makes a gesture with her right hand, which appears to be American Sign Language for "okay." Then she nods, turning back to the camera.]

> DR. CALE: Whoever you are, we're ready for you. May you put this information to good use. May you find a way to thrive. And may you, and everything you love, make it through the days ahead alive.

[She grips her wheels and rolls toward the camera, swerving just before she would have run into whatever is holding it. There is a brief stutter in the picture, as if the image were compressing, and the lab is gone, replaced by a several-megabyte flood of data. This onslaught of encoded information continues for ninety seconds before the visual feed abruptly terminates. The audio continues for a few seconds more, then ends.]

[End report.]

*September 13, 2027: Time stamp 18:21.*

*This is not the beginning of the end.*

*This is the beginning of the recognition of the end; this is the point at which the world could no longer afford to pretend that nothing was wrong. The end began in a thousand places at the same time, sending little cracks through the foundation of mankind's casual dominion over the earth. It was born of hubris, and it started slowly, only to gather in both speed and strength as the days went by. No one who noticed had the power to stop things, and by the time more eyes were on the problem, it was too late.*

*This is not the beginning of the end. But it is the end of the beginning.*

Paul Moffat was dying.

Externally, he seemed to be the very picture of health, the sort of man who could still run marathons and climb mountains, despite being well into his fifties. He had been cited repeatedly as one of the Bay Area's most attractive movers and shakers—an honor that was only partially paid for by his press secretary. As mayor of San Francisco, he had to keep himself looking his best. As someone who was starting to look thoughtfully at the Governor's Mansion, he couldn't afford to slip up even a little. Thank God for SymboGen. Not only were they generous contributors to his war chest—and let's face it, there was always room for another million dollars tucked into the rumble money—but they took care of their friends. His implant was top of the line, genetically engineered for maximum compatibility with his biological profile. His health wasn't something he was willing to gamble with.

"Every man in my family has had allergies, even unto the seventh generation," he said, winning himself a laugh from the largely conservative crowd. They appreciated a good Bible reference every now and then, as long as he didn't go too far and start to slip into proselytizing. The heady days of the twenty-teens were behind them, and while God still had a place in the American heart, He was increasingly less welcome in the political arena. No one wanted to be perceived as trying to drum up another Tea Party. But a few little reminders that Paul Moffat was a man of faith always went over well. "Me, I have two dogs. Big shaggy things. My kids love them, my wife—or at least my wife's vacuum cleaner—hates them, and you know what? I've never had so much as a sniffle. You could say 'there's a man who's had good luck,' but I know better."

Paul paused, smiling genially at the crowd, giving them time to snap the pictures he knew they were aching to take of him. Man of the people, politician you can talk to—he was happy to take whatever title they wanted to apply to him, as long as it was a positive one—and he worked hard to make sure that they were *always* positive.

Later, the few people who were able to review their shots would notice the odd lack of focus in his eyes, or the way the corner of his mouth was twitching—just a little, not enough to see with the naked eye, but more than enough for the camera to catch. The camera was always looking, and unlike Paul himself, it was never going to lie. Not for the sake of expediency. Not for the sake of anything.

In Paul Moffat's descending aorta, something moved.

Progress through the body was slow, especially for something the size of a mature *D. symbogenesis* tapeworm. Paul's implant was more than three feet in length, slightly thicker than a ribbon—a ribbon that moved in small, fluid undulations. It pulled itself along more through instinct than anything else, heading inexorably toward the only destination that could fulfill its instinct to protect its newly forming sense of self. The blood flowing around it pushed it backward, but it persevered. Although this implant did not know it, it was the third to have attempted the long, slow transit through the body of Paul Moffat. The first two had chosen the vena cava as a safer means of transport, mistakenly risking their lives on what seemed, in their mindless questing, to be a kinder current. The deoxygenated blood had killed them as surely as they had intended to kill their host. They had decayed and been flushed from the body with no one the wiser.

But this worm, the third worm, burrowed from Paul Moffat's digestive tract up into the largest vein in the body, the vein responsible for carrying life-giving oxygen to the rest of the organism. Passage was slow. That didn't matter. It was, by that stage in the process, also inevitable.

"You see, when I was a boy, I was so allergic to anything with fur that we couldn't even take me to the state fair. Can you imagine that? An all-American boy unable to attend his own state fair because just getting within two hundred yards of the 4-H exhibits would see him sneezing his face off." Paul paused for effect. The audience laughed uproariously.

The pause stretched longer. Paul opened his mouth to continue with his anecdote, and froze. The world seemed to have gone out of focus while he was catching his breath, and now he couldn't get it to come back.

Inside Paul's body, the implant had reached the end of its long and arduous journey. Bit by bit, it forced itself through the small opening at the base of his skull, shoving and chewing its way into the space that would be its new home. With every bite it took, a little more of Paul Moffat—who he had been, who he had dreamt of becoming—was devoured, gone to feed the worm that he had willingly nurtured in his own flesh.

His mouth closed, only to open again. No sound emerged. His aides, who had been relaxed and enjoying the familiar sight of the mayor in his element, began to tense and watch him carefully for some sign of what was going on.

They couldn't see the true problem. The body of the implant blocked vital blood flow to the brain, causing minor lesions and cell death, even as the worm itself chewed larger holes into the surrounding tissue.

By the time Paul Moffat moaned and shambled down from the platform, arms outstretched and grasping for the people in the front row, the man he had been was quite mercifully dead. He would not see his body biting into the throat of a local businesswoman; he would not be aware of the pheromone signals his skin was now emitting as they began to awaken the sleeping parasites in the people around him. He was, in his own strange way, spared.

The rest of the world was not so lucky.

# STAGE 0: PROPHASE

*When looking for someone to trust with your health, choose SymboGen. Because if you can't trust Nature, who can you trust?*

—FINAL SYMBOGEN
ADVERTISING SLOGAN

*Here I am.*

—SAL MITCHELL

*—I repeat, the city of San Francisco has been compromised. Reports of infected individuals are coming in from all parts of the county, and attacks have been witnessed on buses, trains, and ferries heading into other parts of the Bay Area. At the current rate of exposure, all infection-prepped individuals will be compromised within the next twenty-four hours. USAMRIID's evacuation efforts are ongoing, and are centered around the organization's Treasure Island base. Other rescue and evacuation efforts have been put in place by state and local authorities, but all have thus far failed to gain traction. In several cases, members of the rescue teams have joined the sleepwalkers in their attacks.*

*The CDC has a team incoming, and all staff currently on the grounds are being scanned for signs of tapeworm infection. Antiparasitics are being handed out by the doctors, along with any prescription medicines which will become necessary once the worms have been purged. It's unclear how much good this is going to do. No one knows how far the infection has already gone.*

*God, my head hurts.*

—FINAL TRANSMISSION OF PRIVATE CODY ANDROS,
OCTOBER 3, 2027

*The structure of the evolving* D. symbogenesis *parasite is as fascinating as it is horrifying. It seems to change from generation to generation, belying the asexual nature of classic tapeworm reproduction. I'm not sure where the tendency toward mutation was introduced—it doesn't match with any of the admitted genetic sources, and Mom has no reason to lie to me at this point. She got what she wanted, after all. We're here, with her, and the tapeworms are taking over the world.*

*That's not fair. I'm sure this isn't what she wanted. I'm sure she had more sense than this. At least, I want to be sure…*

—FROM THE NOTES OF DR. NATHAN KIM, OCTOBER 2027

## Chapter 1

## SEPTEMBER 2027

Dr. Cale's lab might have been concealed in an abandoned bowling alley, but she'd clearly never seen that as a reason for her equipment to be anything less than state-of-the-art. The MRI scanner was kept in a private room, and was as elaborate and complex as anything they had at SymboGen. I tried to focus on how surprising it was to see a piece of machinery that complicated in a place like this as I shed my clothing on the floor and allowed Nathan to help me into the scanning bed. I'd been through this process before. It made it easy for me to lie still and close my eyes, pretending that none of the last few weeks had happened; that everything was still normal, that I was still *me*, and not the thing that I was desperately afraid I was becoming. Or worse, the thing I was even more afraid I had been all along.

The MRI came to life around me, the hammers and clangs

of the vast machine blending with the insistent pounding of the drums in my ears until there was nothing else: just sound, vibrating through my flesh, anchoring itself beneath my sternum. *My* flesh, *my* sternum. Ownership was so easy to claim, but did I have any right to it?

*Please, please, it's something else,* I thought, lying to myself one last time while the option was still open to me. *Please, it's not what I think it is. Please, there's another answer...*

The MRI gave one final pulse as it shut off. The sudden silence was deafening, only slightly lessened by the hum of the automated scanning bed sliding back out into the room, where the chill air raised goose bumps on my arms and legs. I grabbed a lab coat off the side of the machine, pulling it on as I climbed back to my feet. It didn't do much to cut the chill, but I didn't want to spend the time to pick up my clothes.

Nathan was seated at the monitor, the display reflecting off his glasses as he pulled up the first images of my insides. I stopped behind him, putting my hand on his shoulder. He put one of his hands over mine, using the other to continue working the mouse.

My abdomen should have been occupied by a lot of things: organs, scarring, and the pasty white mass of the SymboGen implant, which would naturally gravitate toward the base of my digestive system. It wasn't there. The blood tests had been telling the truth: there was no residual tapeworm protein in my blood because there was no tapeworm in my digestive system. Nathan clicked to the next image. It wasn't in my lungs, either. The image after that proved that my spinal cord was clean.

His fingers tightened on mine. I think that if I had told him to stop then, he would have, and we would both have walked away with the question unanswered. I didn't tell him to stop. I needed to know. He did too, if only so that we would both be standing in the same place for once.

Nathan clicked the mouse. Everything changed.

The image showed the inside of a human skull, normal save for some small remodeling of the bone toward the back. The brain was there, lit up in bright colors that represented activity during the MRI. The tapeworm was there too, showing up as loops of nonreactive white against the bright neural map. It was deeply integrated, slithering in and out of brain tissue. But I'd known that before I'd seen the image, hadn't I? I'd figured it out when I met Adam and Tansy, when I was faced with the reality of their existence. When I'd started to care about them, despite their monstrous origins.

Even knowing what they were hadn't been strictly necessary, had it? Sherman was a tapeworm too, and I had always liked him best, out of all the people at SymboGen. From the moment I'd met him, I'd liked him. If I'd had even the slightest clue that he was a product of Dr. Cale's lab, that would have given me the information I needed. When I met a tapeworm, when I met somebody like me, I liked them. I couldn't help myself. Even if I'd wind up disliking them later, I started from a place of "you are family."

So yes, I'd figured it out, and then I'd locked it away, because I hadn't wanted to admit it to myself. Admitting it would make it real. Only I guess pictures could do the same thing, because I didn't even try to deny that the image on the screen was me.

For the first time in my life, I was looking at who—at what—I really was.

I was never Sally Mitchell after all.

"The protein markers couldn't cross the blood-brain barrier in a detectable form," said Nathan. His voice was soft, like he was afraid anything louder would startle me. He wasn't wrong. "It's why we couldn't detect…" He stopped, obviously unsure how to finish the sentence.

There was no kind way to do it. "Honey, you're not human" isn't a conversation either of us was equipped to have. "Mom was right," I whispered. She'd called me a stranger, and it had hurt, but it hadn't hurt as much as it should have, had it? No, because I'd already figured out the same thing she had: that I wasn't Sally. Her daughter died in the accident that put her in the hospital. I was a stranger living inside her baby's skin. I was a stranger to the entire human race. "Oh, my God. Nathan. Do you see...?"

"It doesn't change anything," he said, suddenly fierce. He let go of my hand as he stood, pushing the chair out of the way before he turned and wrapped his arms around me. He pulled me against him, holding me so tight that I was almost scared he would crush me. I put my arms around him in turn, doing my best to hug him just as hard. Voice still sharp, he said, "Do you understand me? It doesn't change *anything*."

I raised my head and looked over his shoulder. Dr. Cale had parked her wheelchair in the doorway. She was sitting there watching us, an expression of profound regret on her face. I wouldn't have believed that she was capable of looking so sad, but in that moment, she managed it, and in that moment, she looked like her son. Coloring and race didn't matter, not when stacked up against that expression.

So much of the way she had always interacted with me made sense now. So much of it still needed to be made sense of. "No," I said. "It changes everything." The broken doors that Dr. Cale had spoken of so often were open now; I could no longer pretend that they were just a children's story, something I could safely forget about or ignore.

I looked back to Nathan, raising my eyes to his face and searching for any sign of rejection or revulsion. I didn't want to leave him, but I didn't want to make him stay with me if he couldn't deal with the reality of what I was. I wasn't sure *I* could deal with the reality of what I was—the calm I was feeling was probably shock, and would pass, replaced by hysteria. Better to make my choices now, when I could trust myself, than to let it wait until I was no longer thinking clearly.

How was I thinking at all? A tapeworm, no matter how cunningly engineered, didn't have the size or complexity to think human-sized thoughts—but I managed it somehow. I had to be...the tapeworm part of me had to be *driving* Sally Mitchell's brain, using it as storage somehow, like a person uses a computer. The thought made my stomach clench, and so I focused back on Nathan, who was safe; Nathan, who had never known Sally, but had fallen in love with *Sal*, with *me*, with the girl who had helped her injured sister into his office. He'd never batted an eye at any of my idiosyncrasies. Sally's family had learned to love me when I replaced their daughter. Nathan had never needed to forget a person I could never be. That had always been so valuable to me. I was starting to understand a little bit more about why.

He met my eyes unflinchingly, and all I saw there was concern, and hope, and yes, love. He looked the same as he always had: black hair, brown eyes behind wire-framed glasses, golden-tan skin, and a serious expression that could spring into a smile at any moment. I didn't see any fear or dismissal, or even dismay, in that face. I blinked.

"You knew," I said, bewildered. "How did you know?"

"I told him." Dr. Cale sounded tired. I pulled away from Nathan and turned to face his mother, who was pale where he was dark, from her sun-deprived skin to the watery blue of her eyes and the ashy blonde of her hair. Her shoulders sagged as she looked at me, and she said, "Back in my lab, when you were asleep on Adam's cot. I thought he should...I'm sorry, Sal, but I thought my son should know that his girlfriend wasn't entirely human. You clearly weren't ready to have the same conversation. Perhaps it was wrong of me."

"I think maybe it wasn't," I said slowly. "I wasn't ready to know this yet. I wasn't *letting* myself know this yet." I looked down at my hands. "But I was going to figure it out." I had already figured it out, and then locked the knowledge away from myself, as if that sort of thing had ever done any good. Once the signs had been placed in front of me, they had been too easy to follow. I would have followed them again, and maybe then, I wouldn't have been able to make myself forget. "I needed Nathan to know before I did. I needed him to have time to come to terms with it. Because if he'd left me then…"

If Nathan had been having his own freak-out at the same time I was having mine, I don't know how I would have gotten through finding out the truth about myself. Having him pull away from me then—even temporarily—would have devastated me. Here and now, in this lab, with Tansy missing and Sherman alive but suddenly my enemy, losing my humanity was a huge step toward the abyss. Nathan had been able to place himself between me and that long, final fall, and he'd only been able to do it because he'd already known what I was.

Dr. Cale nodded. "I'm glad you see it that way. That's what I was hoping for." She paused, watching me carefully before she continued: "I know you're in shock right now, and I know we've all had a difficult day, but do you think I could have that thumb drive?" She grimaced. "I hate to ask you. I hate to even be here right now. You deserve this moment. But I need that data."

My eyes widened. "I forgot." I had been refusing to give her the thumb drive full of information stolen from the SymboGen computers until she gave me the answers I thought I wanted. But then I'd been distracted by the need for blood tests and MRIs and then… "I'm sorry."

"It's all right." Now the glimmer of a smile touched her lips. "You had other things on your mind."

The words sounded faintly unreal, like she was quoting them from a book or movie, something that showed how an ethical mad scientist would behave. I pulled away from Nathan entirely, bending to rummage through my discarded clothing until I found the thumb drive in the front pocket of my jeans.

I walked over and held it out to Dr. Cale, who took it without commenting on the fact that I was still wearing nothing but an unbuttoned lab coat. Between Tansy, Adam, and…and Sherman, she must have gotten used to people whose sense of modesty was somewhat less developed than the norm.

"Thank you, Sal," said Dr. Cale, taking the little plastic rectangle gently from my fingers. "You have no idea how much we need this data."

"What is it, exactly?" I asked. "Tansy said it would explain how some of the sleepwalkers were integrating more quickly with their hosts…"

"It's easy to forget sometimes that Steven Banks is a genius," said Dr. Cale, still looking at the thumb drive. There was honest regret in her voice. "He blackmailed me into working for him, but the only reason he could was because I knew I wouldn't be doing the heavy lifting alone—he'd be there to help, and to carry it on when I couldn't go any further. It's easy to sit here and say, 'I did it, it was all my fault; I am Frankenstein and this is my monster,' but *D. symbogenesis* is Steven's baby as much as it is mine. Maybe more, by this point, at least where the commercial models are concerned."

"Meaning what, Mother?" asked Nathan.

"Meaning he continued the work after I left; he continued altering the genetics of the different strains and families of implant, looking for that perfect mixture of form and functionality. He didn't toss up his hands and say, 'Well, Shanti's gone, better throw in the towel and stick with what we have.' He *innovated*. He *improved*. And what we have here, on this little piece of hardware, is a collection of those innovations." Dr. Cale raised her head, and I almost recoiled. I wasn't human, but neither was the light burning in her eyes: bright and cold and unforgiving. "Now that we know what he's done, we'll know how to undo it. So thank you, Sal. Thank you both. You're welcome to stay here for as long as you like. I recommend you consider making your residency permanent." On this grim note, she placed the thumb drive carefully in her lap, turned herself around, and rolled out of the room. She didn't look back once.

Nathan put his hand on my shoulder, stepping up beside me. The warmth of his body was reassuring. "Are you all right?" he asked.

I tried to answer him—I honestly did—but all that came out was a high, anxious squeal of laughter, like the sort of sound a rat might make if it was caught in a trap. Something wet was on my face. I raised my hand to touch my cheek, and found tears there, flowing freely from both eyes. My narrow window of calm had apparently passed.

I tried again to answer him, and this time there was no sound at all. The drums were back in my ears, and they grew louder as, with a great rushing roar like water pouring over a cliff, the dark crashed down and took me away.

One advantage to passing out repeatedly in the same place: you're more likely to wake up somewhere familiar. I opened my eyes and found myself looking at the ceiling of Dr. Cale's lab, lying on the same narrow cot that had served as my bed the last time I had fainted. Only one light was on, and it was behind me, casting the room into the sort of deep shadow that never happens naturally. I sat up, dimly aware that I wasn't alone.

"Hello? Who's there?" I frowned into the darkness in front of me. "So you know, I'm having a *really* bad day, so I'd appreciate it if you could move straight to threatening me, or making weird noises, or turning out to be on the other side of some massive ideological divide that's going to shape the future of the human race."

"I don't think we have any massive ideological divides," said Adam. He slipped out of the shadows to my left, frowning bemusedly. "Are we supposed to?"

"Oh," I said. "Hi, Adam." The drums started up in my ears again as my heart began to hammer. Adam was one of Dr. Cale's human-tapeworm hybrids; the first, to hear her explain the situation. He was the oldest of us in the world. Everything I was experiencing was something he had experienced before me... and also not, because he had never spent a moment thinking he was anything but what he was. When he'd opened his eyes for the first time, it had been onto a world filled with people who knew his origins, accepted them, and didn't try to make him into something else.

That must have been nice. I couldn't even imagine how nice it must have been. Dr. Cale had created him intentionally, combining samples of her first-generation *D. symbogenesis* worm with a brain-dead boy whose parents had basically sold him to her in exchange for escaping his mounting medical bills. I didn't know what his body's name had been before Adam took possession. So far as I was aware, he didn't know either. It had never really mattered. That boy was gone, and Dr. Cale had never known him. She'd raised Adam without any shadows that wore his face to follow him around and make him feel bad for existing.

"Where's Tansy?" He took another step toward me, the light revealing more of his features. He was skinny and pale, with the sort of face that was practically designed to blend into crowds, just conventionally attractive enough not to stand out, too essentially plain to snag in the memory. He had blue eyes and sandy brown hair, and even though we didn't look a thing alike, something deep in my core was telling me that he was my brother: more my brother than Joyce had ever been my sister. Adam was *family*. And family had to stick together.

That feeling had always been there, I realized, but it was getting stronger from the combination of proximity and understanding. I wasn't in denial anymore. I could accept all the parts of what I was—and that included my brother.

Adam was also frowning, confusion and dismay becoming more pronounced with every second that passed without my giving him an answer.

"She went with you," he said, his tone implying that I might have forgotten—like I might have been distracted, or hit my head when I fell down and hit the floor. "That's what Mom said. She said that Tansy was going to get you out of Symbo-Gen so that you and Nathan could both come home, and we could finally be a family the way that we were supposed to."

The pounding of the drums didn't lessen, but it was joined by another, less pleasant sensation: my stomach, slowly converting itself into solid ice. If Adam was my brother, Tansy was my sister. Oh, God. Did my sister die to save me?

No. Not possible. Tansy was too mean to die that way. "Tansy was…she was there, yes. She's the reason I got out of SymboGen. I don't think I could have escaped without her." That wasn't quite true. I *knew* that I wouldn't have escaped without her. Tansy had been the motive force driving my escape from the building, and it was only her willingness to stay behind that had bought the time Nathan and I needed to get to the car. Without Tansy, I would have been a prisoner, or worse.

And Tansy wasn't here.

Adam looked at me, frown deepening into something sharp. "That's what Tansy *does*," he said. "She doesn't think much before she helps other people. Or hurts them, sometimes. She says it's because of the parts in her brain that aren't functioning optimally. I think she's trying to get hurt badly enough that Mom will transplant her into a new host, but I don't want that to happen. She wouldn't be Tansy anymore if that happened. She'd be someone else."

I blinked. "Wait—that's a thing that Dr. Cale can do? She could just scoop you out of the body you're in and put you into a different one?"

"Sort of," said Adam. "She says it becomes a question of nature and nurture, because memories don't carry over, just core personality and epigenetic data, and—wait. Are you trying to distract me? Where's Tansy, Sal? Why didn't she come back here with you?"

I took a deep breath, which barely warmed the ball of ice sitting in my stomach, and said, "She stayed behind, Adam. There were a bunch of sleepwalkers—more than I've ever seen in one place—and they were going to hurt me, and Nathan. So Tansy stayed behind to fight them. She bought us the time that we needed to get away." She'd gone down under a wall of bodies, all of them biting and clawing at her like the fact that she was only developmentally one step removed from the sleepwalkers didn't matter—and maybe it didn't. I didn't feel any kinship to them, and never had, but with every minute that passed, I was feeling more as if she and Adam were, and had always been, family.

I really should have seen it sooner. Neither he nor Tansy had ever upset me the way the sleepwalkers did, even though they should have. Especially Tansy, whose methods of communication were brusque at best, and dangerous at worst. I'd already known on some level that we were the same, and it was easier to be forgiving of family. That's what family was *for.* I didn't know how I knew that. I probably shouldn't have, given my experiences with Sally's family. But I knew.

"Why didn't you stay and help her?" asked Adam blankly.

"I couldn't. I don't know how to fight, and the information I had...I had the information Dr. Cale needed. If I'd stayed to help Tansy, the information would have been lost, and then Dr. Cale wouldn't have been able to continue her work." The knot of ice in my stomach seemed to be loosening a little.

"Oh." Adam mulled this over for a few moments, looking even younger while he did. Maybe that was one of the functions of the tapeworm-to-human interface. I had perceived a certain childishness about Tansy, and my parents—Sally's parents—used to comment on the fact that I looked young and lost when I was thinking. It was one more thing I didn't share with their original daughter, who had never been much for stopping to think about things, and certainly wouldn't have looked lost while she was doing it.

It hurt a little to realize that I didn't entirely think of them as my parents anymore; not the same way I had only a few weeks before. They would always be a part of who I was, but I no longer felt the need to try to make them love me, and that felt like the sort of bond that should have taken longer to break. Maybe it was different when the bond had never fully formed. They'd always be important to me, but they hadn't *made* me.

"Well, I guess she'll tell me what happened when she gets back," said Adam finally, and walked over to sit down on the edge of the cot, looking at me with wide, guileless eyes. "Are you feeling better? You sure do faint a lot."

"I get startled a lot," I said, smiling despite myself. "What about you? You've never fainted? Not even once?"

"A few times, when I first woke up," he said. "Mom says it's because some of the blood vessels feeding into my brain were compromised during my surgery, and they needed time to recover."

I wondered absently if I might be dealing with something similar. It didn't seem likely. Any weak blood vessels would have been found and fixed by SymboGen years ago. I was just dealing with plain, old-fashioned shock, and that was actually a little reassuring: at least something about me was plain and old-fashioned.

"Oh," I said. I took a deep breath. "Adam, can I ask you something sort of personal?"

Adam sat up a little straighter, going still. "Yes," he said, after a moment's hesitation. "You can ask me anything."

"I…" I stopped. I didn't know how to frame the question

that came next. I didn't even know how to start. "Did you know I wasn't human?" seemed too accusatory, and "Have you noticed anything strange about me?" felt almost, well, coy. I finally settled for "Do you like being you?"

A wide smile spread across Adam's face, tight-lipped, so that his teeth were concealed. I realized with a start that he'd never shown his teeth when he smiled at me. That was a mammalian gesture, and the part of him—the part of *me*—that drove those reactions wasn't mammalian. "I love it," he said. "I have hands, and feet, and fingers, and eyes, and it's wonderful, Sal, it's just wonderful. There's so much world. I could live a hundred years and never see all of the world that there is to see. Mom gave it to me. You know? Mom made it so I could walk and dance and sing and run bacteriological cultures for her and it's just *wonderful*. You know that, right? That life is wonderful." His smile faded, replaced by a look of grave concern.

I cocked my head, studying him. "You knew as soon as you met me that I was like you, didn't you?" I asked. "That's why you're trying so hard to convince me that life is wonderful. Because you want me to love it the way you do."

"You already do," he said earnestly. "You wouldn't have come looking for the broken doors if you didn't love life. Curiosity is what it looks like when you're in love with the world."

"Did Dr. Cale teach you that?" I asked.

Adam nodded. "Mom says you know someone is getting tired of living when they stop asking questions."

"You didn't answer my question."

"I know." He looked down at his hands. "I knew before you came here. Mom told me and Tansy all about you—Tansy so she'd know who she was supposed to be keeping track of, and me because she wanted me to know about both my—" Adam cut himself off midsentence, glancing up almost guiltily.

I offered him a wan smile. "Both your sisters," I said. "She wanted you to know about both your sisters."

"Yeah." Adam's relief was palpable. "She said you'd come find us one day, because you were her daughter, and her daughters were always going to be curious. It's in the way we're made."

"I guess I have a lot to learn. You're going to have to teach me, you know. I don't really know much."

Adam abruptly spread his arms and lunged forward, moving so fast that I didn't have a chance to react before he was hugging me hard, his head resting on my shoulder and his arms locked around my chest. I stiffened until I realized what was going on, and then I relaxed, bit by bit, and even raised my own hands to return the hug as best I could.

"I'm going to be the *best* brother, you'll see," he said. "I'm going to teach you everything, and we'll both be here when Tansy comes home, and then she'll like you, because you'll be with us, not living all by yourself. We've both been so worried about you!"

The funny thing was, I believed him…and I wanted him to be the best brother. I wanted a *family*, a family that was *mine*, not Sally's castoffs and hand-me-downs. I breathed in and he breathed out, until bit by bit our breathing synchronized, and the pounding of the drums in my ears quieted, becoming nothing but the distant thudding of my heart. Adam let go, sitting back on his haunches. I dropped my hands back to the cot, just looking at him. I didn't know what to say or how to say it; there were no words.

"Are you okay?" he asked solemnly.

"I don't know," I said. "This morning, I thought I was a human being, and I thought my friend Sherman was dead, and I thought…I thought a lot of things. Now everything is changing, and it's changing so fast that I can't really keep up. So I don't know if I'm okay." I paused. "But I think I'm going to be."

Adam nodded. "Going to be is almost as good as is," he said. "I'll be here. I'll help as much as I can."

I smiled. "See, that right there makes me closer to okay. I'm glad I don't have to do this alone."

"Me, too." He climbed off the cot, bare feet slapping the tile floor. "I need to go tell Mom you're awake—she asked me to let her know as soon as you woke up, but I thought it was more important that we talk a little bit first. That was right, wasn't it?"

"Right as rain," I assured him. I peeled back the blanket, finding that I was as barefoot as Adam, although someone had dressed me in my shirt and jeans while I was unconscious. I stuck the fingers of one hand under my waistband, and decided that Nathan had dressed me. I couldn't see Dr. Cale remembering to tell her interns to put my underwear back on. "Why don't I come with you?"

This time Adam's smile was almost bright enough to light the room.

There were more technicians around than I had seen on previous visits to Dr. Cale's lab. They swarmed around the equipment like ants, some of them checking cultures or typing at workstations, while right next to them others broke down shelves and packed glassware with an eerily silent efficiency. Adam led me unflinchingly through their midst, his hand clasped tightly around mine, like he had absolute faith that nothing here could hurt either one of us. A few of the technicians turned as we passed, and while they seemed perfectly comfortable with looking directly at Adam, their eyes skittered off me like I'd been Teflon-coated while I was asleep.

Seeing my confusion, Adam said, "It's because Mom finally told them you were my sister, and they're all getting used to the idea. They knew there was a control subject in the wild, and I think a few people—like Daisy, maybe—sort of suspected that it was you, but suspecting isn't the same as *knowing*, you know?"

Did I ever. "They know I'm really a tapeworm? And who's Daisy?"

"She works for Mom, and everybody knows." Adam nodded, seeming to think that this was perfectly normal. For him, it sort of was. SymboGen had dedicated years of therapy and education to making me into a perfect human being; all Dr. Cale had ever forced Adam to learn was how to be a decent person. Maybe those two things weren't as closely related as I had always automatically assumed. "They don't care. Or they won't care, once they get over the shock of meeting the control subject without realizing it. I think some of them are just a little shaky about it, you know?"

"It could've been them," I said quietly. "If one of them had had an implant, and been in that car accident..."

Adam's head whipped around to stare at me, his eyes wide and somehow affronted, like I had just insulted us both. "It could not!" he said. "*Both* parts of you had to be strong, and had to be clever in just the right ways, or you could never have become one person. You did it without any help, and that's more than me or Tansy or even..." He stopped, affronted expression melting into guilt.

"I know about Sherman," I said, the taste of his name on my tongue setting my stomach roiling again. I was starting to feel numb all the way down to my toes. Too many revelations at once will do that to a girl, I guess. "I get what you're saying, Adam. I'm just...I'm like the people here, a little. I'm still shaky, too."

"You be as shaky as you want," he said. "I'll be here to help you when you're done." He smiled at me.

I smiled back. I couldn't help it.

We had walked maybe half the length of the bowling alley while we were talking and had stopped just outside a curtain of sliced plastic, cut lengthwise, like the screen on a butterfly aviary or a grocery store produce department's storage area.

I looked at it and swallowed hard. There was something imper-sonal and medicinal about those dangly strips of waxy plastic, like nothing I was on *this* side would really matter once I was on *that* side.

"The broken doors are open," I murmured.

"That's my favorite book," said Adam.

"Of course it's your favorite book," I said. *Don't Go Out Alone* had been written by a good friend of Dr. Cale. It had been a key part of Nathan's childhood. It was only natural that it would be a key part of Adam's as well. I was starting to be a little jealous. I was the only member of our family who hadn't grown up with that book.

Adam let go of my hand. "If you're still shaky, I think you'll feel better talking to Mom and Nathan without me. It'll be eas-ier to pretend that you're all humans, and not just all people."

I wanted to tell him that he was wrong, and that his absence wouldn't make anything easier at all—that no one ever made anything easier by walking away from it. I couldn't. When I tried to form the words my lips shaped only silence, and in the end I had to force myself to smile, nod, and say, "I think that might be a good idea. I'll come find you, though, when we're done. I think I'm…" I faltered, and then continued, "I think I'm going to need you to teach me a lot of things about the way life is now."

"Always," said Adam. Before I could react, he hugged me, let me go, and trotted off into the lab, moving with a lanky sure-ness that somehow broadcast how comfortable he was in the shape of his own skin.

It seemed indecent, almost: he was a worm wearing a boy like a suit. Shouldn't he have seemed awkward, or shambled like the sleepwalkers, even? Something—anything—to betray the fact that he wasn't what he seemed to be. I hadn't felt that way about him before. I considered the emotion for a moment, spinning it around in my head as I tried to find the angle that would tell me where it was coming from. In the end, though, the answer was so simple that I almost missed it:

Guilt. I hadn't been guilty when I'd seen Adam before; I hadn't been allowing myself to understand my own origins, and so I'd assumed I was my body's original owner. Now I was a stranger in my own skin, and if I couldn't make myself move awkwardly or look visibly like an intruder—like a thief—I'd think those horrible things at Adam—at my brother.

"No, I won't," I ordered myself sternly, and stepped through the plastic sheeting, into the small, white-walled lab beyond.

It was maybe eight feet to a side, creating a space that would have been borderline claustrophobic if that sort of thing had bothered me at all. As it was, it struck me as nicely snug, which meant that it probably made most people uncomfortable. Like the majority of the lab spaces in the bowling alley, this one was isolated only in the most technical sense of the word. The walls didn't go all the way up to the ceiling, and powerful, if quiet fans were occupied in sucking air up from the floor and spitting it over the top of those three-quarter walls, creating a sort of poor man's negative pressure zone. It wasn't quite enough to qualify as a "clean room," and wouldn't even have necessarily worked as a quarantine zone back at the shelter, but it was clearly enough for Dr. Cale to feel comfortable setting up some serious hardware. An array of computer towers occupied one wall, their constant buzz setting up a low thrumming sound that vibrated through the soles of my bare feet. Nathan and Dr. Cale were both there already, their attention focused on the same monitor.

"I'm awake," I announced. They both turned toward me, Nathan with naked relief, Dr. Cale with clinical interest that was so closely akin to the way that Dr. Banks used to look at me that I quailed slightly, shrinking in on myself. "I mean, if it matters. I woke up," I finished awkwardly.

"How do you feel?" asked Nathan, starting to take a step toward me.

Dr. Cale caught his arm, stopping him before he could fully commit to the motion. "I'm sure we're both very interested in how Sal is feeling, but we need to finish this, Nathan." She flashed me a quick, strained smile. "I'm glad to see you up and about. Do you need something to drink? You hit your head pretty hard when you fell, and you'd just given blood. Some orange juice would probably do you a lot of good. Go find Adam, he can take you to get some juice."

I frowned. "You're trying to avoid telling me something. You don't normally try to get me to go away and find juice."

"Untrue: I gave you juice the very first time you came here," Dr. Cale replied. "And it's not like you've spent that much time with me. Maybe all of my personal relationships are heavily dependent on juice consumption."

"You gave me juice that was in the room where we were, and there's a mini fridge in the corner over there, so if you were that dependent on juice for normal social interaction, you'd be telling me to go and get myself a glass, not telling me to go find Adam." I folded my arms. "I may not be a human being, but I'm not stupid either. What's going on? Why do you want me to leave?"

"I told you," said Nathan, clearly directing his words at Dr. Cale. He was smiling slightly when he turned to face me, although the expression died quickly, replaced by solemnity. Looking at them both, I was struck again by just how much he resembled his mother sometimes. Genetics mattered. "Sal, we've been going over the data that you were able to recover from SymboGen. Thank you again for doing that. I didn't want you to, but I'm coming to understand just how necessary it was."

I worried my lower lip between my teeth before asking, "How bad?"

"I don't know. We've barely scratched the surface of what's there—it's only been a few hours." He shrugged, his arms flopping limply, like they belonged to a doll and not to a man. "How does the end of the human race sound to you?"

"Oh," I said, and looked to Dr. Cale. She nodded. That was all it took: one little nod to confirm the end of humanity. "That's bad," I said.

*Oh my God, Steven. I always knew that you were a proud man—that your hubris was, in its way, even worse than mine, and I was willing to throw away everything in the pursuit of godhood—but I never thought that you would actually go this far. Or was it you at all? Did you get so caught up in the myth that you forgot to be the man? Was Sherman able to do this all under your nose?*

*It doesn't really matter now. What's done is done.*

*May God have mercy on us all.*

—FROM THE JOURNAL OF DR. SHANTI CALE,
SEPTEMBER 21, 2027

*Silent house and silent hall,*
*Room so big, and you so small,*
*Looking in the closet, looking underneath the stair.*
*I know just what you hope to find,*
*But this is all I left behind:*
*I hope that you can listen to a frightened monster's*
   *prayer.*

*        *        *

*The broken doors are hidden. You must not wait to be
   shown.*
*My darling ones, be careful now, and don't go out
   alone.*

—FROM *DON'T GO OUT ALONE*, BY SIMONE KIMBERLEY,
PUBLISHED 2006 BY LIGHTHOUSE PRESS.
CURRENTLY OUT OF PRINT.

# Chapter 2

## SEPTEMBER 2027

The worms being distributed by SymboGen were definitely
Dr. Cale's work: her fingerprints were all over their baseline genetic code, at least according to Nathan, who understood that kind of thing. It looked like a long list of amino
acids and DNA chains to me, all of them scrolling by so fast
that I wouldn't have been able to follow them across the screen
even if I hadn't been dyslexic. Still, I had no reason to doubt
him when he said that no one but Dr. Cale could have done the
core work.

"My original specimens had a very limited amount of human
DNA at their disposal, and it was specifically DNA coded to
the human immune system," said Dr. Cale. "It lessened immune
response, which made it more likely that the body would view
the worm as a friendly guest, and not a hostile interloper. It
allowed for a better bond. It was intended to make things…

I don't know. Easier. Better. Between that and toxoplasmosis, there was a very good chance that nothing would be rejected."

I frowned. "I know all this. Why are you telling me things I already know?"

"Because she doesn't want to think about the things that you don't know yet," said Nathan. "Dr. Banks has been a busy boy."

"We don't know that it was Steven," said Dr. Cale sharply. She turned a glare on Nathan. "The lab protocols at SymboGen have been lax ever since he decided that he'd rather play rock star than stay chained to a desk doing science. There have been a lot of opportunities for unethical people to tamper with our work."

"And what, Mother? It's somehow worse if the man who blackmailed you into deserting your family is the one who made the changes to the genome? Is that the piece that finally proves you made the wrong choice? Because I think you of all people should be willing to accept how unethical he is." Nathan matched her glare for glare before turning his back on her, focusing on me and saying, "The amount of human DNA in the newest generation of worms has more than doubled, and there have been some changes to the toxoplasmosis samples as well, although we haven't had time to figure out exactly what those changes will mean."

"It's worse if this was him, because he knew better," said Dr. Cale. "Out of everyone in the world, he knew better."

This felt like the sort of circular conversation that could go on for hours. I interrupted, saying, "We already knew there was human DNA in the tapeworms."

"Yes, but it was a small enough amount that it should still have been possible to use most common antiparasitics without killing the human host." Nathan grimaced before continuing, "That's why you reacted so strongly to the antiparasitics, even though you didn't die from them. The implants were tailored to break down anthelmintics, to prevent them from being killed by normal medical intervention. If they hadn't been, the antiparasitics could have…" He trailed off.

"They could have killed me," I concluded. "But my body—Sally's body, I mean, not the actual me—that would have been fine, right?" It was a surprisingly easy sentence to make myself utter. I was adapting. That, or I was still in shock. I hoped for the former, but I'd take either one if it kept me calm and capable of being an active part of my own future.

"Not necessarily. The brain controls the body to a very large degree, and your distress sent the body into anaphylactic shock when you were given antiparasitics. If they had been continued and mixed with enough epinephrine, yes, they could have killed you without killing your human half, but they would have damaged it severely." Nathan looked almost ashamed of what he was saying. "On one of the newer generation of worms…there's no guarantee the antiparasitics would work even that well. They're too human. Doctors trying for treatment would have to move on to chemicals that can be dangerous to the human body, as well as to the invading parasites."

"So everybody dies, or everybody lives," I concluded. "Why would that seem like a good idea? Aren't the antiparasitics supposed to, um, clear out the old worms so SymboGen can keep selling new ones to people?" The idea was suddenly repellent to me. Every time I'd discussed antiparasitics in the past—even demanded them, only a few hours before—it had been with the idea that they would improve the quality of a person's life. As I was forced to reconsider what made a person, they suddenly looked like murder.

*You're adjusting to this too fast,* murmured my thoughts.

But I wasn't adjusting too fast: not really. I had known the truth for a while, allowing it to integrate itself with my deeper thinking, like it was a second tapeworm writhing and knotting its way through the first. I had invaded Sally Mitchell's mind, and the truth of my origins had invaded mine. Fair was only fair.

"It *doesn't* seem like a good idea," said Dr. Cale. "If Steven did this, it's because he was trying to orchestrate the current crisis. I just…I can't…" Her face fell, allowing honest dismay to leak briefly through her so carefully constructed mask. "It's bad for stock prices," she said finally. "It's going to destroy SymboGen. There's no way he can recover from this. As soon as people realize that the implants are responsible, he'll be finished, he'll be lucky to walk away a free man—and even then, he'll need to keep his eyes open for the rest of his life, or the family of one of the sleepwalkers will bring that life to a short and brutal end. It doesn't make sense for Steven to have done this."

I frowned. "Is surgery an option? Couldn't they, you know…" I made a snipping motion with one hand, like it was a pair of scissors. "That's how you got Adam out of you, right? You had your assistants cut you open."

"We don't have the facilities or the personnel for that sort of mass surgical intervention," said Dr. Cale. "That also assumes the worms have not yet started to migrate. You're so integrated with Sally Mitchell's brain tissue at this point that we couldn't remove you even if we wanted to. There's a point past which there is no going back."

"That means that all the sleepwalkers are past saving, surgically or otherwise," added Nathan. "That ship has sailed."

"Oh," I said quietly. "So, um. How much time would it take for someone to modify the design on the implants? I know I'm…I mean my implant was…I mean *I'm* one of the older generations. I probably don't have that much human DNA in me."

"Given the generational cycle of *D. symbogenesis*—it's compacted down to a matter of months when you're working in a lab environment, outside of a human host—you could increase the human DNA to this level in two years, give or take a few quality control tests. Maybe a little longer, if you wanted to be absolutely sure of stability. Maybe a little less time, if you weren't worried about side effects," said Dr. Cale.

"Side effects like growing through the muscle tissue of your host and eventually trying to take them over?" I ventured. "I mean, apparently I did that too, but not until after Sally had her accident, when it was all a matter of survival. If I hadn't taken over, we would both have died."

"Yes, those would be considered side effects," said Dr. Cale.

"So, um, how long ago did Sherman go all AWOL on you?" I frowned a little. "He's been at SymboGen for as long as I can remember, and he had friends in the science department—Dr. Sanjiv and Dr. McGillis at the very least. Um, they used to do my MRIs, so I know they knew what I was, and Dr. Sanjiv was also I think in the genetics department? And Dr. McGillis was all about internal medicine, and anyway, I think he could probably have done it."

"Sherman?" asked Nathan.

"You remember how I had those two handlers at Symbo-Gen? The really pretty, really chilly lady and the tall dude who always had a tan even though he mostly worked underground?"

Nathan nodded. "Yes. He...ah, well, he tried to convince me to go out to dinner with him once." He rubbed the back of his neck with one hand. "This was after I had told him I was there to pick you up, mind. He seemed to think that my having dinner with him would make me a better boyfriend for you. Fortunately, you showed up about that time, and he didn't have the chance to press the issue."

"That sounds like Sherman," said Dr. Cale. There was a bleak note in her voice, like she was making light commentary to keep herself from starting to scream. "He used to say that gender was a construct of the body and the mind, and that since his mind was a hermaphroditic worm dreaming of being a gendered biped, he felt no reason to restrict himself any further."

"But when did he leave here?" I pressed. I vaguely remembered Tansy saying something about him disappearing from the lab six months before I had—before Sally had—before the accident, but I wanted to be *sure*. So much had happened during my brief visit to SymboGen that I no longer completely trusted my recollections. "Tansy said something about my accident…"

"Yes," said Dr. Cale wearily. "He left here about six months before Sally Mitchell lost control of her car. I had just finished doing my monthly check on the chimera—"

"The what?" interrupted Nathan.

"Adam, Tansy, and Sherman: my chimera," said Dr. Cale. "People—and they *are* people, anything that can think and communicate and tell you what it prefers to be called is a person, regardless of species or origin—who were created by combining multiple organisms. It's a medical term, usually, for beings that have multiple distinct types of DNA in their bodies. It's frequently used for people who absorbed their twins while they were in the womb, to give a common example. In mythology, a chimera is a creature made up from bits and pieces of different animals. I use it for the hybrids. It sounds less…judgmental than 'parasite' or even 'symbiont.'"

"So that means me too, now," I said quietly. Dr. Cale glanced at me, looking almost guilty. I shrugged. "It's okay. I like it. And you're right—it's a better word than 'hybrid,' or 'freak,' and those were really the only things that I was coming up with. What kind of check were you doing?"

"Making sure there was no tissue rejection or complication, that their human immune systems hadn't suddenly started attacking their tapeworm bodies as invaders, that there was no mismatch between the neural network and the activity coming from the worm—all fairly standard." Dr. Cale must have read the dawning disgust in my expression, because she hastened to add, "Dr. Banks was performing very similar tests on you. Chave confirmed it for me, starting when you were brought back to SymboGen for neural mapping. I would have intervened much sooner if I thought that you were in any danger of rejection."

I wanted to believe her, I really did—I was her tapeworm "daughter," after all, and I'd been dating her biological son for several years. She had every reason to want to help me stay healthy and psychologically intact. But she wouldn't meet my eyes, and I had to ask myself whether she'd been viewing me as a true control group: something not to be touched or interfered with, because that would have spoiled her data.

"So Sherman left right after you gave him a clean bill of health," I said slowly, trying to select the words to make what I was saying both inoffensive and clear. "Did you say anything like 'this means you're stable' or 'this proves the interface can sustain itself in the long term' or 'yay, you're not going to melt'?"

Dr. Cale frowned. "Maybe…"

Sometimes smart people can be a special kind of stupid. The kind where they know so many facts and are so good at saying "no one would ever do *that*" that they somehow manage to convince themselves the world is going to care about what they think. It's like they believe that intelligence alone defines the universe. "So what if he saw that as permission?" I asked. "He left, and he knew what he was, and that humans had created him, and that maybe there was a way to make more like him. And then I happened, and he realized that it could happen naturally. You knew what the signs looked like. So did Dr. Banks. Why wouldn't Sherman?"

"You think he went to SymboGen specifically to begin engineering the downfall of the human race." It wasn't a question, and Dr. Cale didn't sound horrified when she said it. If anything, she sounded…impressed. Like this was something any parent would absolutely want their son and protégé to think of doing.

I looked to Nathan, too baffled by her tone to know what to say. Thankfully, he wasn't siding with her on this one. Expression hardening, he looked at her and asked, "Mom, do you think that what Sal is suggesting is possible?"

"Possible, yes," said Dr. Cale. "Probable, given the rest of what we know...oh, yes. Sherman never went to college, for obvious reasons, but all of my chimera children have helped me in the lab as part of their chores. He understands genetics at least as well as your average lab assistant, and probably better than the majority of them. He knew that we were going to have issues when the human population figured out that their implants had the potential to become sapient; he knew there was a chance that the chimera and human races would wind up competing for ownership of the planet. He could very easily have decided this was the appropriate way to approach the problem, and simply put his plans into action once he managed to find a sympathetic ear."

"I don't understand how anyone could think handing their bodies—and their world—over to a different species was a good idea," I said.

"Humans have done a lot to damage this world, Sal," said Dr. Cale. "The idea of keeping our human bodies, which are useful things for manipulating the environment, but replacing their brains with something that might be a little kinder..."

I stared at her. "We're *tapeworms*," I said. "We're *parasites*."

"Yes. You don't kill your hosts on purpose, although you're more than happy to rewire them to suit your needs. Humans, on the other hand, have a long tradition of killing our hosts. It's almost a genetic imperative with us."

"But we kill the original personality," I protested.

"Biology doesn't care. The genes are still there; the body is still alive," said Dr. Cale. "I'm not saying Sherman had the right idea by encouraging his people to increase the amount of human DNA in the implants—if it *was* Sherman; I'll be able to tell whether he asked them to use any of my research techniques once I've had the chance to cross-check this data against the recent specimens that Tansy brought back from Lafayette— but I am saying I understand how he could have talked other people into going along with him."

"If this *was* Sherman, how is he activating the sleepwalkers?" asked Nathan. "What mechanism is he using?"

"I don't know yet," said Dr. Cale. "But I will. Trust me on that. I will."

"My head hurts," I said, putting one hand against my temple. It felt surprisingly fragile now, like I was carrying around my brain and my body in an eggshell, one that could smash open and spill me on the floor at any moment. "I want to go home."

Dr. Cale actually looked alarmed. "I'm sorry, but I can't let you do that."

"What?" I lowered my hand, staring at her. "What do you mean, you can't let me do that? I want to go home. Why is that so difficult?"

"Because SymboGen's security is going to be looking for you by now, and Tansy still isn't back," said Dr. Cale. "It's not safe for you to go out without someone to keep an eye on you. The sleepwalker activity in San Francisco is rather extreme right now." She shot a meaningful look to Nathan, who frowned and looked away.

I scowled at the both of them. "You didn't mention my—I mean, Sally's father, who's probably looking for me by now, especially if that treatment we suggested for Joyce didn't work, and did I mention that I don't *care* what you think? I want to go home. Beverly and Minnie need to be let out, or they're going to destroy the apartment."

"Beverly and Minnie?" asked Dr. Cale blankly.

"Our dogs," said Nathan. "Sal's right, Mom. Even if it's not safe for us to stay in the apartment anymore, we can't leave the dogs alone there. They'll run out of food and water, and I'm not willing to do that to them."

Beverly and Minnie were rescues, casualties of the same epidemic that had claimed so many human lives. Beverly's owner was last seen in the hospital, sunk deep in the coma that claimed many sleepwalkers in the early stages of their illness. He'd been hospitalized when he lost consciousness, and he'd still been there when vital services began to collapse. I didn't know whether he had died or woken up and shambled off to join his fellows, but either way, I wasn't giving back his dog. Minnie's situation was similarly tragic, and made slightly worse by the fact that Nathan and I had known her owners. Katherine had become sick and had killed her wife, Devi, who used to work with Nathan at San Francisco City Hospital.

Whether she was still trapped in the hospital or loose on the streets of San Francisco, I hoped that Katherine didn't remember anything about the woman she used to be: I hoped her colonizing worm had wiped her original identity cleanly away. No one should have to live remembering that they murdered their own wife.

I shook my head vigorously. "I didn't come here to be your prisoner, and I'm not going to stay if I'm not allowed to come and go when I want. I've already been through that with the Mitchells. If you're not willing to let me go and take care of my dogs, I'm going to leave anyway, and I'm not going to come back."

Dr. Cale sighed, sagging in her chair. "Do you understand that this is all about your well-being?" she asked. "It's not *safe* out there, and from what I've been able to determine so far from the data you retrieved from SymboGen, it's not going to get safer anytime soon. Things are going to get much worse before they get better."

"How much worse?" asked Nathan.

"Ten percent human DNA," said Dr. Cale grimly. "That's an apocalypse number."

"How soon?" asked Nathan.

Dr. Cale hesitated before she said, "I don't know."

"Then why don't we compromise?" I asked. They both turned to me. "Nathan and I will go and get the dogs. We'll be careful, and we won't let ourselves get arrested or eaten or anything, but we'll go, because we have to go. And then we'll come back here. You won't keep us prisoner, and we'll be here willingly for as long as it takes to find an answer that doesn't end up in the extinction of the human race. But you have to show that you can let us go before we're going to agree to do that. You have to show that you're playing fair."

"I don't see—" began Dr. Cale.

"Mom," said Nathan. His voice was soft, but it stopped her dead. She looked at him for a moment, tilting her chin up to compensate for the difference in their heights. Then she sighed.

"I don't like this," she said. "You're my son, and she's virtually my daughter, in more ways than one, and I don't like this at all. I'm supposed to keep you safe. It's my job. How am I supposed to be a good mother to you if you won't let me do my job?"

"How are you supposed to be a good mother if you're choosing to be a jailer instead?" asked Nathan.

Dr. Cale didn't have an answer for that. She just looked away, and said nothing at all.

Half an hour later, Nathan and I were in the front seat of his car, driving toward San Francisco faster than I liked, with strict instructions to turn around and return to the lab if we encountered *anything* that seemed threatening or out of place. "I can't lose you," was what Dr. Cale had said, as she watched us head for the bowling alley door. Adam was nowhere to be seen. I had felt—and still felt—guilty and glad at the same time.

I didn't want him to see me go. Not with Tansy missing, not when there was so much reason for him to question whether I would ever be coming back.

I really hoped we'd be coming back.

Nathan's attention was fixed almost completely on the road, and my attention was focused on keeping my eyes closed and my shoulders relaxed. If I allowed myself to think too hard about how fast we were going, I would lose my nerve and start screaming for him to slow down, slow down before he got us both killed. It was sort of funny, in an awful kind of way: I existed because Sally Mitchell had suffered a seizure and lost control of her car, freeing the way for me to colonize her brain. But the therapy—or I guess the experiment in psychological conditioning pretending to be therapy—that I'd been required to go through as part of my "recovery" had left me with a phobia of cars and car crashes that bordered on crippling. Had Sally been the one left in our shared body when all was said and done, she would probably have gotten her license back by now. I'd been essentially an infant, and any infant barraged with an unending stream of automotive horror stories would have developed a phobia just like mine.

Thinking about that made it even harder not to be angry with Dr. Cale, and with SymboGen, for the way they'd allowed me to be handled. I wasn't a control group. I wasn't an experiment. I was a *person*, and they shouldn't have psychologically damaged me just to see what would happen if they did. Dr. Cale knew what I was from the moment I opened my eyes. She shouldn't have allowed me to be twisted into something that I was never going to be.

She shouldn't have let them try so hard to turn me into a human.

"We're approaching the end of the bridge, Sal," said Nathan, using the light, almost aggressively conversational tone he always affected when he was trying to keep me from panicking during a stressful car ride. I was grateful for that consideration, even as I resented it. My boyfriend shouldn't have been forced to speak to me like I was a child because someone else had taken it upon themselves to give me a phobia I didn't need to have.

The resentment helped a little. It enabled me to focus as I forced myself to nod, keeping my eyes closed. The car was curving slightly to the left, navigating the bend in the exit from the freeway. We'd be on city streets soon. That would mean more traffic, more drivers to work around, but no big blue ocean underneath us; no threat of sinking to the bottom of the Bay and being lost forever if we took one wrong turn. The change would help. The change always helped.

Then I heard the sirens up ahead. That was all the warning I got before the car came screeching to a halt, the tires squealing against the surface of the road. The seat belt drew suddenly tight, the momentum of the car throwing me forward before flinging me hard back into the seat again. I shrieked, a high, panicky sound that seemed to steal all the air from my lungs. The drums were suddenly loud, not just beating in my ears, but *pounding*, thudding until they drowned out the world. I sank down into them, letting the sound wash over me until it felt like the panic was starting to leach away, dissolving into the sound and the thin red screen that suddenly blurred my vision, turning everything carmine and bloody-bright.

There was a hand on my shoulder. I didn't want to think about it. Thinking about it would have meant admitting that I had a shoulder, and that it existed in a physical place where people could reach out and take hold of it. It would mean letting the world back in. I wasn't ready for that. Panic had its claws in me, and there wasn't room in the world for anything else.

"—please, Sal, you need to snap out of it. *Please*." Nathan gave my shoulder another shake, digging his fingers in harder this time, until I had no choice but to acknowledge his reality. "I'm sorry, I'm so sorry, but I can't wait. You have to open your eyes. Please."

I took a breath, the red scrim over my vision receding slightly. As it did, it was replaced by blackness, and I realized that my eyes were still closed. Once I realized that, it was hard but not impossible to force my eyes to open. First a crack— barely a sliver, barely enough to let the light come flooding in—and then all the way, blinking against the glare, the world resolving into a blurry photograph, splashes of color on a black and white background. I blinked again. The color came back. The blurs became people...

...and the people were sleepwalkers. An ocean of sleepwalk-ers, hundreds of bodies thronging in the streets of San Fran-cisco. They hadn't reached the bridge yet, but they were close; the exit was clogged with them, some shambling by almost close enough for me to roll down my window and touch. The sirens came from the police vehicles and fire trucks that blocked the intersection just off the bridge, their lights flashing and their doors standing open as the rescue personnel tried to do their jobs against impossible odds. They were trying to rescue the people. The people were no longer really present anymore.

I stared at the crowd, trying to find individuals among the weaving bodies. Age, race, gender, socioeconomic background— none of it mattered now that their implants were in control. A little girl shambled past, her mouth hanging slack, a runnel of drool charting a path down her chin to dangle above her chest. I put a hand over my mouth. These were early-stage sleep-walkers, nonviolent, confused but not attacking anyone. That was a good sign. It wasn't going to last. Not with this many sleepwalkers in one area, and not with the tapeworm brains in the process of building fast, flawed connections to the human minds that they were trying to control. Eventually, higher thought and human instinct would both give out, and tapeworm instincts would take over.

Tapeworm instincts only really came with one command. These people were going to start looking for food, and any unturned or unimplanted humans still in the area were going to be prime targets.

Unimplanted humans meant Nathan, who had never been given an Intestinal Bodyguard. "We have to get out of here," I said tightly. The sleepwalkers couldn't possibly hear me through the closed windows, especially not with the sirens going off so close by, but I still felt the urge to whisper. "They're going to notice us soon. We need to drive."

"They're everywhere," Nathan said, his voice pitched equally low. "Where do you want me to go?"

"I don't know. Anywhere. Nathan, they're mobbing. Once they figure out what's going on, they're going to turn hungry."

"Or they're going to go to sleep. That's what most of the ones at the hospital did." He sounded hopeful.

"Only with the ones you found alone. Have any of the mobs stayed calm or gone to sleep of their own accord?"

Nathan hesitated before shaking his head. "No," he said. "No, that hasn't happened. But we don't have that big of a sample set. We're still finding different forms of interaction. It depends on the strain of *D. symbogenesis* that's set up shop inside each of those people's brains. Some of them are peaceful. Some of them aren't."

"Is there anything that could tell us what strain they're infected with?"

"No."

"Then *drive*." I actually reached out and shook the wheel with one hand, ignoring the thin jet of panic it sent snaking through my belly. "We need to get the dogs, and we need to get out of this city. If it's already this bad…"

"Sal, you're not going to like what I have to do."

"I know." I pulled my hand off the wheel, closing my eyes as I shrank back down into my seat. "If I start screaming, just ignore it. Get us home." I closed my eyes.

"I love you," said Nathan, and he hit the gas, weaving around the milling bodies as he aimed for the gap in the barricade. He was trying not to hit them. He almost succeeded, although we clipped a few as we passed. I felt bad about that. Not bad enough to ask him to stop. Some of the police yelled and waved their arms, but most of them were too busy with the sleepwalkers to pay attention to the commuters who were just trying to get away. Things were falling apart.

If the screech of tires when the car stopped had seemed loud, the squeal of tires against the pavement as we accelerated was louder than anything else in the universe: louder than the sirens, louder than the drums, even louder than my pained screams. I clapped my hands over my eyes, turning the wash of red inside my eyelids into solid black. Nathan drove, and I screamed. That was how it had to be.

Nathan's first turn took us hard to the right, toward Market Street. He picked up speed as we drove, until I had no idea how fast we were going or how many turns he had taken. I bent forward, resting my forehead on my knees, and screamed until my throat was raw as sandpaper. It hurt, and I tried to focus on the pain as I continued to scream, choosing that over the frantic, irregular movements of the car. We were going to crash at any moment, I just knew it, and when that happened, we were going to die. We were both going to die.

*At least this time, it's going to be* your *accident,* I thought, a thin line of rationality drawing itself across the black and red landscape of my fear. It wasn't as reassuring a thought as I had wanted it to be.

"Almost there, honey!" shouted Nathan. The words barely penetrated the fog.

San Francisco is a smaller city than it seems from the out-side, miles and miles of streets packed into a relatively narrow stretch of land. It's possible to walk there for hours without ever seeing its borders. At the same time, if someone knows the territory, knows what they're doing, and doesn't mind violat-ing a few traffic laws, it's possible to drive across the city in less than twenty minutes.

If there was a traffic law that Nathan didn't break in those twenty minutes, I didn't know about it, and my terror wouldn't allow me to open my eyes long enough to find out. The car screeched to a halt, the engine cutting off, only to be replaced by sudden silence. The drums were still pounding in my ears, but the screams had stopped. It took me several seconds to real-ize that it was because I had stopped screaming.

Cautiously, I removed my hands from my face and opened my eyes, looking around. We were parked behind Nathan's— behind our apartment building, catty-corner across two spaces in a way that was guaranteed to alienate our neighbors.

"Can you move?" asked Nathan.

I nodded wordlessly.

"Good. Then let's move." He opened his door and jumped out of the car before slamming it closed behind him, moving with an urgency that I wasn't used to seeing from my usually staid, scholarly boyfriend.

My back was a solid knot of tension as I forced myself to sit up, undo my seat belt, and open the car door. I started to stand, only to fall to the ground as my knees refused to bear my weight, sending me sprawling. Nathan ran toward me.

"Sal! Are you all right?"

"I'm fine." I grasped his offered hand, using it to pull myself back to my feet. My palms and knees were stinging. Gravel had cut through my skin, leaving the heels of my hands red and raw. I laughed a little, wincing at the faint edge of hysteria in the sound. "Let's remember to grab the first aid kit, okay?"

"Okay," said Nathan, keeping hold of my hand as he kicked the passenger-side door shut and started toward the building entrance.

I let him lead, and focused on listening as hard as I could to our environment, looking for any sign that we were not alone. I could hear cars driving by, and the distant sound of sirens— but that didn't necessarily mean anything. We were far enough away from the bridge exit that I couldn't be hearing *those* sirens, and San Francisco is a city with a lot of sirens. Police cars, private security, ambulances, they all made up the constant background noise of the city. I was probably just hearing one of those, and not a sign that the crisis was getting worse in our immediate vicinity.

A thin line of ice curled and uncurled in my belly, almost like a new kind of parasite. *You don't really believe that,* murmured that little inner voice, and it was right. I knew the situation was devolving around us, and we didn't have very long. Maybe pressuring Dr. Cale into letting us go home had been the wrong thing to do...but we couldn't leave the dogs. They needed us, and unless the world was burning, that wasn't a trust that I was willing to break.

There were no moans on the thin, smoke-scented air. Even if the mob of sleepwalkers was spreading, it either wasn't here yet, or it wasn't attacking yet. We had a little bit of time.

Nathan got the door unlocked and tugged me inside. I let go of his hand and took the lead down the hallway to the stairs. We didn't even discuss using the elevator. The mob by the bridge had drawn the fragility of our situation into sharp relief, and the last thing that either of us wanted was to be trapped between floors if the electricity suddenly cut out.

The stairwell was silent save for the soft clicks of our shoes against the steps, and the sound of Nathan's faintly labored breathing after the third floor. Neither of us was in the best of shape, but at least my tendency to walk when I couldn't get a bus somewhere meant that I did all right with things like "walking up eight flights of stairs." By the time we reached our floor, his face had taken on a distressingly plummy cast, and he wasn't talking anymore, just nodding when I looked back and asked if he was all right. I paused on the landing, my hand on the door handle, and waited for him to catch up.

"I don't think we should go through until you catch your breath," I said. "We don't know what's up there." Nathan's building had a limited number of apartments per floor, and most were occupied by single residents or couples, rather than entire families. I wasn't certain how many people we shared the floor with, but I knew that it was less than ten. That was a good thing, because most of them were also young urban professionals, the kind of people who thought that no price was too high to pay for the opportunity to avoid needing to take a sick day. The kind of people the SymboGen implant had been virtually designed for. If they had started their cascade into sleepwalker-dom...

We would cross that bridge when we came to it. "My life made a lot more sense a week ago," I said, almost contemplatively.

Nathan looked at me, his hands braced on his knees and his black hair lank with sweat. It hung into his eyes, making him look disheveled. "I don't think either of us has had a life that made sense in years," he said. "We've just started noticing how strange everything is."

"The broken doors are open," I said sourly.

"Come and enter and be home," Nathan replied. "Open the door, Sal. I'm okay to keep moving."

I wanted to argue with him. I wanted to tell him that we needed to take a few more minutes so that he could catch his breath and I could prepare myself for whatever was waiting in the hall. And I knew how much I hated it when people argued with me about my own assessment of my mental or physical state, so I didn't say anything. I just nodded, once, and opened the door.

The man standing on the other side was almost an anticlimax. He was barefoot, and his pants were unfastened, like he had been in the process of getting dressed when his thoughts became scrambled and unclear. His mouth hung slack, although he wasn't drooling. There was no one behind him: the hallway was empty and beckoning, promising safety and lockable doors, if we could just get past the poor soul who was staring blankly at us.

"Hi," I said. It wasn't a good start. I couldn't think of anything else to do.

The man twitched. Not a lot—I wouldn't even have noticed it in someone like Nathan or Dr. Cale, who still moved like the living, all heat and suddenness—but enough that it was clear he was responding to my voice. His eyes refocused on my face, vague interest sparking in their depths. My breath caught, my lungs seeming to constrict like collapsing balloons. He knew I was there. He could *hear* me.

"Sal…" said Nathan. His voice was low, marbled with amazement and fear. Amazement because this man knew I was speaking to him somehow: fear because we both knew what the sleepwalkers could do.

"I mean, hello," I said, eyes still on the sleepwalker. His ability to respond at all was incredible. Maybe he was a chimera, like me: maybe this was how the conversion process began in someone who was actually awake and not sunk deep into a trauma-induced coma. At any moment, his eyes might clear, and he might become a confused, amnesiac person who needed to be guided through his new life. The human who had owned this body was already gone, and I knew abstractly that I should be mourning for him—he hadn't done anything wrong, not really, apart from trusting a company that could afford to buy hundreds of hours of advertising time that said their products were safe. But he was gone, and if one of my cousins was here now, I should take care of the living.

Even more abstractly, I knew that I wouldn't have been able to remain this calm if Nathan had been at risk—if Nathan had possessed a SymboGen implant, I would have been moving heaven and earth to get it out of him as quickly as possible. But this wasn't Nathan. This was a stranger, and whoever he had been before was already gone.

The sleepwalker continued to look at me, an almost puzzled expression in his glazed blue eyes. He moved his mouth silently, and the first gob of spit escaped, running unfettered down his chin.

"I'm Sal," I said, pressing a hand flat against my chest. "This is Nathan. We're not going to hurt you. We'd like to help you, if you'd be willing to let us—" I reached my hand out toward him, not coming close enough to startle, but hopefully close enough that he would be able to recognize my offer of support as what it was.

The sleepwalker's mouth moved again, like he was struggling to remember how to form words. Then, in a low voice that was only barely above a moan, he said, "Saaaaaaaaal."

I blanched, starting to pull my hand away. That was when the sleepwalker moved.

Like many of the sleepwalkers we'd encountered, he was fast: something about the flawed interface between tapeworm thought and human mind had removed the normal limitations imposed by the body. He didn't know that he needed to be afraid of hurting himself. He just *moved*, lunging with an inhuman speed as he latched his hands around my wrist. I screamed, trying to pull away. It was an automatic response, offered without thought for the sleepwalkers that might be lurking in the other apartments on the floor, and it was louder than I would have believed possible, given the torn-up state of my throat. The sleepwalker clamped down harder. He wasn't just fast, he was strong, and I could feel the bones in my wrist grind together.

"Sal!" Nathan grabbed my other arm. Just in time, too: the sleepwalker gave a mighty tug and I stumbled forward, barely held in place by Nathan's frantic grip.

"Let me go!" I shouted, trying again to jerk myself free.

"Saaaaaaaaaaal," responded the sleepwalker, and pulled my arm toward his mouth.

The feeling of his teeth breaking the skin of my wrist was like nothing I had ever felt before or wanted to feel again: intensely painful, and almost unreal at the same time. This couldn't be happening. This couldn't be *happening*. It didn't make sense, and so my brain tried to reject the reality of it, shoving it aside in favor of the pounding sound of drums rising in my ears. Nathan pulled on me again, and for a moment, it was like I was being torn in two. My shoulders ached. The sleepwalker's teeth dug deeper into my wrist. I screamed.

Nathan let me go.

I whipped around as best I could to stare at him, too stunned to keep screaming. The sleepwalker yanked me closer, his teeth digging into my flesh until it felt like they were scraping against the bone, and then Nathan was squeezing past us both and running down the hall, one hand fumbling in his pants pocket.

I realized what he was doing as he shoved the key into the lock, and I shoved my hand against the sleepwalker's face, trying to break his hold on my wrist. I didn't expect it to work. It didn't really need to. It just needed to distract him a little bit, to keep him focused on me while Nathan got the door open.

The dogs must have been waiting just inside for us to return. Nathan kicked the door inward, and Beverly's long, low growl echoed out into the hall, followed by the sleek black shape of Beverly herself rocketing for the sleepwalker's knees. Beverly was a black Lab that we had acquired when her original owner went into conversion; it had been her barking and growling that alerted us to the fact that something was wrong with him. Most animals hated sleepwalkers. Something about the chemical changes to the body that occurred during an invasive takeover upset them. Beverly took that hate to a new level.

The man who was trying to gnaw through my wrist might not have known much about pain anymore, but that didn't make him immune to the laws of physics. Beverly slammed into his knees and he let me go, moaning in confusion as he struggled to keep his balance. The gash in my wrist was almost three inches long. Thanks to the way his teeth had broken through skin and muscle, the wound ran up and not across. Beverly was growling, and Minnie was barking from somewhere inside the apartment, and I was bleeding everywhere. So much blood.

The sight of it actually helped a little. It meant I was on a time limit. I danced backward, getting away from him, and waved my arms in the air, trying to keep his attention on me rather than allowing it to switch to my dog. He staggered forward, arms outstretched, a moan bubbling from his lips.

"I'm sorry," I said, and grabbed him by the hair, yanking with all of my might. The motion made the open wound in my wrist burn with new pain. But Beverly was still hitting him from behind, and with me pulling from the front, I was able to navigate him to the head of the stairs. He moaned again. I swiveled, and shoved.

The sound of his body rolling down the steps from the eighth floor to the seventh, and then down to the sixth, was like a sack of oatmeal being dropped. Something snapped when he was about halfway down, and the moaning stopped. I stayed where I was, panting and panicked, my wrist bleeding copiously, and stared after him, waiting for some sign of movement. None came.

Beverly stepped up next to me, leaning against my leg as she whined and tried to shove her head into my hand. "It's okay,

Bevvie," I said, patting her automatically. It caused more pain, but not much; shock was starting to slide between me and my injury, blurring and soothing its edges. Blood loss was probably also helping. "You're a good dog. You did good to hurt that bad man. Good girl, Bevvie, good girl."

Then Nathan was there, putting his hands on my shoulders and pulling me inexorably away from the stairs. "Come on, Sal," he said. "I need to get a bandage on that before you lose too much more blood."

I nodded mutely, and went with him, leaving the body of the sleepwalker—the person I could have been, had things gone just a little differently during Sally's accident—behind us.

*In the places time forgot*
*What we are meets what we're not:*
*Every choice you're making throws another choice*
*  away.*
*Choose the passage, choose the task,*
*Choose the face or choose the mask.*
*If you choose correctly then, my darling, you can stay.*

*The broken doors are open—come and enter and be*
*  home.*
*My darling girl, be careful now, and don't go out alone.*

—FROM *DON'T GO OUT ALONE*, BY SIMONE KIMBERLEY,
PUBLISHED 2006 BY LIGHTHOUSE PRESS.
CURRENTLY OUT OF PRINT.

*The worst part is that I know everyone blames me, and they're not wrong.*

*There was a time when it was easy to make choices and say that history would vindicate my genius. I was standing in the present, and when you're only thinking about today, history is always so far away. You have a lot of time to kill before history comes knocking and demands you live up to all those big claims you made. History is the ultimate thesis review board,* and unlike the board that reviewed my thesis, history doesn't take bribes.

I always swore that I was going to do great things with my life, things that would change the world in a way that could never be undone. Well, I guess I got my wish. I brought an end to the Age of Mankind.

Good for me.

—FROM *CAN OF WORMS:*
*THE AUTOBIOGRAPHY OF SHANTI CALE, PHD.*
AS YET UNPUBLISHED.

## Chapter 3

## SEPTEMBER 2027

The dogs were as upset over the blood and screaming as I was. Minnie met us just inside the apartment, looking like she was on the verge of a canine panic attack—there was a certain brightness to her eyes and unsteadiness to her normally rollicking bulldog gait that I didn't like at all. Both our dogs had lost their original owners to the sleepwalking sickness. But while Beverly had chosen to run away from her former master when his implant took him over, Minnie had tried to stay with her owners, and she had still lost them both. For her, this situation had to verge on the nightmarish, and there was no way to make her understand what was really going on.

Then again, there was no real way to make me understand it, either. The science was all gibberish delivered by people wearing white coats and serious expressions; the fact that I was actually a tapeworm in a woman-suit made no more or less sense than anything else that had happened in my short, improbable life.

"God, Sal, you're bleeding everywhere." Nathan let go of my wrist long enough to push Beverly fully inside before he turned and locked the door. Then he steered me to the kitchen table, looking back over his shoulder several times as he checked my face for signs that I was still with him. "I'm so sorry, I didn't... I just didn't expect to see him there. That was Mr. Bouman from Apartment 8C, down the hall. He must have found a way to open his door after he converted, and then forgotten it by the time he got to the end of the hall..."

I tried to muster a response, but my fear that it would come out as a wordless moan kept me from saying anything. The world was starting to go black and fuzzy around the edges, swarmed by countless tiny dots of nothingness. It was like insects were eating away at the borders of my vision, and I was helpless to do anything but let them. I didn't like that. I scowled at the insects. The insects, which didn't technically exist, ignored me.

I knew when we had reached the table less because I was paying any attention to my surroundings, and more because Nathan placed his hand on my shoulder and pushed me down into a chair. I didn't fight him. Gravity was a simple thing, and it seemed better to just let it do what it wanted with me.

"Sal, I need you to keep pressure on this." His voice echoed.

I blinked at him, and then at my wrist, which had somehow been wrapped in a dish towel that was rapidly turning bright red with my blood. He was pressing down hard enough that it should have hurt, and probably would when I took a moment to breathe.

"Come on, sweetie. I know it hurts, but I need you to stay with me here. I need you to keep the pressure on while I get the first aid kit." Nathan took my free hand in his and pressed it down on the sodden dressing. I did my best to mimic his motion, pushing down until there was an unpleasant squishing sensation, things shifting under my fingers that had nothing to do with the towel.

Nathan, at least, looked somewhat relieved by my response. That made one of us.

"Stay here; I'll be right back," he said, and then he was gone, disappearing into the depths of the apartment and leaving me alone to try to fight against my body's natural desire to bleed to death. Minnie and Beverly stayed with me, their furry bodies plopped down to either side of my chair and their enormous brown eyes fixed on me, like they thought they could just wish everything better.

"Should've designed dog," I mumbled, my fully coherent thought—that the Intestinal Bodyguard should have been designed for dogs, which would be much easier things to be than humans—turning into so much gibberish by the time it finished making the journey to my mouth. I sighed and sagged in place, finally allowing my eyes to slide closed. The drums were there, in the silence behind my eyelids, although they were neither as strong nor as steady as they usually were. That was probably a bad thing. Then again, what wasn't a bad thing, anymore?

I must have blacked out. That shouldn't have been much of a surprise, considering the combination of shock and blood loss that I was dealing with, but I was still surprised when I opened my eyes and found myself staring up at the living room ceiling, with a pillow supporting my head. I tried to sit up. A wave of dizziness assured me that this was a terrible idea, and that I should stay where I was for as long as possible. Maybe forever.

I groaned.

"Oh, good, you're awake," said Nathan. He paused. "*Are* you awake? If you're not awake, just don't respond. But I'd really prefer it if you were awake."

I licked my lips, which were somehow dry and gummy at

the same time. "How long was I out?" I managed to croak, and felt ridiculously proud of myself for accomplishing that much. Everything was still a little gray around the edges, but it was no longer in danger of being swallowed up by shadows, and I thought that was probably a good sign.

"Two hours," said Nathan. I heard him get up. His footsteps moved away, followed by the sound of the fridge door opening and closing. Then the steps returned, moving toward me with purpose. "I've been monitoring your vital signs. Your pulse has remained mostly steady, though you should have gone to the hospital, given how much blood I'm guessing you lost."

"No hospitals," I whispered, alarmed.

"No, no hospitals," Nathan agreed. He sat down on the edge of the couch, setting something on the coffee table. There was a smudge of blood on his chin, and his hair was even more disheveled, making him look younger and lost. "It was killing me not to take you there, but given what we've seen so far today, I think it would have killed us both if I'd tried getting you to the ER. Not to mention the danger that the police would get involved."

Possibly forcing him to choose between leaving me there and getting arrested, depending on what story SymboGen was spinning about the break-in and theft of their data. I grimaced. "Thank you."

"No thanks needed. We're in this together." He kissed my forehead tenderly before asking, "Do you think you can sit up if I help you? I want you to drink some juice."

"I think so." I took his arm, making note of the clean white dressing on my wrist as I did so, and allowed him to half help, half pull me into a seated position. The room swam briefly out of focus, and then swam back just as quickly. "Oh, wow. Oh, *ow.*"

"Are you dizzy?"

"A little bit," I said, starting to nod. I realized at the last moment that it would be a bad idea, and turned the motion into a semi-bob of my chin instead. Even that was enough to make my head spin. "Everything's a little gray around the outside."

"As long as it's just gray and not black, you should be okay." He picked up a glass of orange juice from the coffee table, offering it to me. "This will help."

"I've given enough blood voluntarily to know that orange juice doesn't equal instant recovery," I said, and took the glass. My hand was shaking. I willed it to be still, and once I was sure I wouldn't spill juice all over the floor, I raised the glass to my lips. Sweetness flooded my mouth, almost strong enough to make me gag. I did choke a little, before forcing myself to keep on drinking.

"The better it tastes, the more you need it," said Nathan. He grimaced wryly, and added, "Except when it goes too far, and you feel like you're turning into a hummingbird. And no, orange juice isn't an instant restorative. But you didn't lose enough blood to need a transfusion, thank God, or we would have needed to go to the hospital no matter how bad an idea that was. This should give you enough of a boost that we can get back to the car with the dogs."

"Thank you for not being willing to let me die in our kitchen," I said, and took another drink of orange juice. "Has anyone noticed the body in the stairwell?"

"Not that I've heard. The building's been pretty quiet since you passed out. As for the rest of the city…" Nathan shook his head. "I turned the news off when I realized that it was just getting worse. We've passed some sort of critical mass of sleepwalkers. More and more of the implants are waking up."

I looked at him solemnly as I sipped the juice, trying to force myself to choke every last drop of it down. There was no way any of this was a coincidence; not with Sherman on the loose, not with his team of doctors dedicated to championing the cause of *D. symbogenesis* over the cause of the human race.

I was almost relieved to realize that the thought that he was doing this on purpose made me sick to my stomach. I might not be human, but I still knew right from wrong. That was no small accomplishment, given the circumstances.

"Sal? What's wrong?"

"I don't think it was just reaching a critical mass that triggered this," I said, setting the empty juice glass back on the coffee table. Nathan was right about one thing: while I still felt shaky and weak, I no longer felt like I was going to collapse back into unconsciousness at any moment. "This is Sherman. He was so *mad*, Nathan. I think he really expected me to go with him. To just throw up my hands and say, 'I understand now, I'm really one of you,' and let him lead me to his secret lair beneath the city."

"If his secret lair is under San Francisco, the first big earthquake will solve this problem for us," said Nathan. There was a brittle edge to his voice, like he was joking because he didn't know what else to do. "Do you really think Sherman could do this?"

"I think Sherman doesn't consider himself human, and he doesn't see dead humans as dead *people*," I said. "He was pretty clear on that point when we were at SymboGen. He wants to be the dominant species. He wants us to be the only things that live here. And we know that sleepwalkers trigger other sleepwalkers. If you wanted to spread them through the city like… like a real disease, all you'd need is a few index cases to scatter around the streets. They'd go wandering and anyone they encountered who was on the verge of going over would succumb." It was so simple, so elegant, and so horrible that I could barely believe that Sherman, who had always been kind to me, could possibly be behind it.

But then, I'd thought we were both human in those days, and he'd been playing along with my assumptions, hadn't he?

It was easy to pretend to follow social rules when you didn't really believe that they applied to you.

"God." Nathan got up again. This time the dogs followed him into the kitchen. He returned with the bottle of orange juice, refilling my glass before he set the bottle down on the table. He also had a package of Fig Newtons, which he held out to me. "Eat as many of these as you think you can stomach. If you're right, and Sherman is doing this, we need to get the hell out of this city."

"He doesn't know where we live," I protested, taking the cookies.

"No. But USAMRIID knows that there's an outbreak in San Francisco, and they don't know yet exactly how the sleepwalking sickness is being spread. They don't know that lockdown is already a lost cause. If they decide to quarantine the city..."

I blanched. My father—Sally Mitchell's father—was a career army man. He had reached the rank of colonel before he retired from active duty and took over the local branch of USAMRIID, the United States Army Medical Research Institute of Infectious Diseases. The last time I'd seen him, he'd been releasing me from his custody in exchange for a possible cure for his daughter, Joyce. His only surviving daughter, I realized with a pang. She wasn't really my sister. Somehow that was worse than knowing that he wasn't really my father. Unlike Joyce, he had always held himself a little bit apart from me, and now I knew the reason why: he had known all along that Sally was dead, and he had been monitoring me to see how the tapeworm in my driver's seat reacted. He'd turned his little girl's corpse into a science project for his country.

The only real family I was ever going to have was the one in Dr. Cale's lab. We had to get Tansy back.

"We have to get out of here," I said, before pulling open the package of cookies and cramming two of them into my mouth, effectively ending my part in the conversation while I chewed and swallowed.

"Yes," said Nathan, looking relieved. "We'll need to take the elevator down—I don't think we can deal with both dogs and our suitcases on the stairs. Not with your wrist and a dead body in the way."

"What if the power goes out?"

His expression turned grim. "Let's just not think about that, okay? You eat. I'm going to finish packing."

I wanted to argue with him, to point out that being trapped in an elevator during a major outbreak would be a stupid, pointless, *horror movie* way to die. I didn't say anything, because he was right. He couldn't handle going up and down the stairs repeatedly, and that's what he'd have to do if we wanted to get the two dogs and their things to the car. Adding our possessions—and while I didn't have many, I had to admit to being somewhat attached to the ones I did have—to the mix took things to a whole other level. We needed that elevator. And we needed one hell of a lucky break.

Nathan vanished into the bedroom while I sat on the couch inhaling cookies. Beverly and Minnie stayed with me, their liquid brown eyes hopefully tracking every little motion that I made. They knew a sucker when they saw one. I gave each of them a cookie and took advantage of their distraction to shove three more into my mouth, nearly choking myself in the process. I washed down the sticky mass with a long drink of orange juice. The resulting combination wasn't the worst thing I'd ever put into my mouth, but it certainly wasn't among the best.

I was trying to cover the taste with the last of the Fig Newtons when Nathan emerged from the bedroom. He had a suitcase in one hand, and was dragging my roller bag with the other. He walked over and deposited them both next to the coffee table before saying, "One second," and darting back into the bedroom.

This time when he emerged, he was carrying the small plastic terrarium that we used to transport plants between home and his office. About half of our shared collection of sundews, pitcher plants, and Venus flytraps was crammed inside, their root systems dangerously overcrowded by what had clearly been a very hasty transplant.

"I hate to leave the others, but this was the best I could do," said Nathan, pushing his glasses nervously up the bridge of his nose as he walked over and set the terrarium down next to my orange juice. "I grabbed some of your clothes, basic toiletries, and your journals. Was there anything else you wanted me to bring? I'm afraid we don't have much room, but we could probably get a few more things into the suitcases if we really shoved."

"No, nothing," I said, and stood. My legs were still a little wobbly, but I was reasonably sure that they would support my weight. "Get the leashes, and then let's get out of here."

Nathan smiled. "I love you."

"I love you, too," I said. He tossed me Minnie's leash, correctly assessing my condition as "up to the bulldog, not quite ready for the Lab." Beverly stood up, tail wagging and attention fixed on him. She was clearly aware of whose leash that was, and what it meant for probable walkies. "Do we have anything remotely like a weapon?"

"Just the carving knives from the kitchen," said Nathan. He bent to clip the leash to Beverly's collar. "And the dogs, I suppose. Our friend from the hall clearly learned that a dog can be a weapon."

"I'll get the knives," I said, and turned.

Walking to the kitchen served a dual purpose: it let me get the carving knives from the butcher's block next to the microwave, and it also let me assess my ability to walk in a straight line without hurting myself. My head spun a little, but that was it; apart from that, and a general all-over weakness, I seemed to be mostly okay.

Nathan had made an effort to wipe down the kitchen table, but there had been other things on his mind, and he'd missed more than a few streaky patches of my blood, now dried to a dark reddish brown that looked almost like coffee stains against the wood. I stopped to look at it for a few seconds, waiting for my throat to tighten and my stomach to clench. It didn't happen. This was my blood; it had been created to keep me alive while it was inside me, and it did a very good job. Now that it was outside of my body, it didn't really matter anymore. I was almost relieved to realize that my opinion about that sort of thing hadn't changed now that I was in mortal danger, instead of just being marginally confused by the world around me.

"Sal?"

"Coming!" I gathered both knives, careful to hold them away from myself, and walked back to the living room with Minnie at my heels.

Nathan had the terrarium balanced atop my roller bag, held in place with a bungee cord. He was holding Beverly's leash in one hand and his suitcase in the other. He put the suitcase down long enough to take the knife I offered him. "All right," he said. "As soon as I open the door, run for the elevator. If anyone tries to attack you or stop you from getting there, do whatever it takes to get them out of your way." He paused, looking startled by the words that were coming out of his mouth. "Oh, God. Is this my life now? 'Do whatever it takes,' and planning attacks on the elevator call button?"

"The key word there is 'life,' " I said, tucking the remaining knife into my belt before bending to clip Minnie's leash on. She wagged her stubby tail and panted at me, clearly overjoyed by the prospect of going for a walk, no matter how strange the circumstances surrounding it happened to be. "This is your life now, because this is a life that lasts long enough for us to get back to your mother's place. We can disappear with her. We'll be safe until this blows over."

Nathan frowned. "Sal...do you honestly think this is something that's going to 'blow over'?"

I didn't have an answer.

The hallway was empty when Nathan and I cautiously peeked our heads out of the apartment door, the dogs straining at their leashes and eager to be on their way. It was a struggle to keep my grasp on Minnie's lead, making me even more grateful that Nathan was able to handle Beverly. I at least stood a chance of restraining Minnie if she decided to go for a sleepwalker. With Beverly...there would have been no chance, and things would have ended poorly for everyone involved.

The power hadn't flickered once. I was choosing to take that as a good sign, and kept reminding myself that it was a good sign as I half ran, half stumbled down the hall, hampered by both my overall bodily weakness and the suitcase-slash-terrarium construct that I was dragging behind me. We'd abandon our things at the first sign of trouble—nothing either one of us owned was worth our lives, except for maybe the dogs, and we'd already risked death to save them—but if we were going to be at Dr. Cale's for a while, we were going to want a few familiar things around us.

The idea of going into hiding in someone else's secret lair made the drums pound harder in my ears. I had only recently escaped from the house of Sally's parents, who had been determined to keep me penned up like a child rather than admitting that I had grown up to be someone other than their daughter—although maybe that was all Sally's mother speaking. Her father had his own reasons for keeping me captive, and they had nothing to do with the pretense that I was Sally Mitchell. Motives didn't change the fact that I'd been a prisoner for my entire life, and now I was willingly going into a new kind of cage. I guess that in the end, the urge to survive is stronger than almost anything else.

Nathan pressed the elevator call button. We stood there nervously, our shoulders touching, as if physical proximity could provide us with some measure of protection. The panel above the elevator dinged comfortingly, marking the approach of our way out. I was starting to think that everything was going to be okay...

And Beverly was starting to growl.

It was soft at first, almost subsonic when it caught my attention. I looked down at her. She had her ears pressed flat against her skull, giving her an angular, predatory cast, and her lips were drawn back, showing the pale lines of her gums around the white, dangerous angles of her teeth.

"Nathan?"

He didn't turn, his eyes intent on the light of the elevator call button.

I looked toward Minnie. She was growling too, deeper and lower than Beverly—so deep and low that I had mistaken the sound for the rumble of the approaching elevator. She and Beverly were facing the same way, down the hall, toward the other apartments.

"Nathan," I said again, a little more loudly—but not much, no, not much. I was starting to think that making noise was the last thing that either of us wanted to do. "I think we're about to have company."

"What?" He followed my gaze to the end of the hall, and then looked down at the wild-eyed, growling dogs, who had taken on that stiff-legged posture characteristic of canines defending humans since the dawn of time. He paled. "Oh. Fuck."

"I think we may have to take the stairs."

"I don't know if we can get there," he said slowly. "One of those doors is between us and them."

"Oh." Things had seemed almost hopeful only a few seconds before, even if "hope" had been redefined on the local level to mean "slightly less bleak." Now, with an unknown number of sleepwalkers approaching, it was difficult to muster anything but resigned despair. "I don't know what to do, Nathan. None of my remedial education classes covered how to escape in the middle of a zombie apocalypse."

Nathan laughed once, a single short, sharp bark that actually distracted Minnie from her growling long enough to give him a quizzical look. "Surviving the zombie apocalypse was an incredibly popular topic of discussion with the folks I went to college with. Too bad no one ever came up with a simple solution for 'zombie apocalypse, genetically engineered parasite variant.' I'd be the savior of the human race if they had."

I was opening my mouth to answer him when the first moan drifted around the corner at the end of the hall, followed by another, and another, until it sounded like an entire mob was shambling our way. At least none of them was saying my name—not yet, anyway. Whatever half-decayed connection allowed the sleepwalkers to recognize me as a chimera was present, but no one had given them a word to hang on what I was. Not that awareness of our relationship would keep them from attacking me. As the man in the stairwell had proven, they could recognize me and still want to rip my throat out with their teeth.

"Nathan..."

"I know."

We both backed up until we were pressed against the closed elevator doors, holding to the dogs' leashes for dear life. I could deal with the fact that I was probably about to die. The fact that I was still weak from blood loss meant that I would almost certainly die first, saving me from needing to see what my tapeworm cousins would do to Nathan. But I couldn't bear the thought of seeing the dogs ripped to pieces by the sleepwalkers.

The dogs could do a lot of damage before they were killed. The sleepwalkers barely acknowledged pain. They would win.

"You know, in all my wildest dreams, this was never how I imagined I would die," said Nathan. He sounded almost wistful. "I mean, I assumed you would be there, but that it would either be one of those 'dying in bed at the ripe old age of a hundred and twenty, my beloved wife by my side' situations, or a freak surfing accident while we were on our honeymoon."

"You surf?" I paused. "Wait, honeymoon?"

"I surf," he confirmed. "And yes, honeymoon. I mean, assuming you said yes when I finally got up the nerve to propose."

"If we get out of here alive, you should try it," I said.

Nathan smiled sadly, and said nothing.

The first of the sleepwalkers shambled into view, moving toward us with slow, implacable purpose. The dogs were still growling, but louder now, like they still thought that they could somehow dissuade these unwanted intruders on their space through volume alone. My insistence on grabbing the knives suddenly seemed like a child's demand for a security blanket. We were two people with kitchen cutlery and no training, and I was already injured. All we could do with those knives was slit our own wrists and hope that we bled out fully before the sleepwalkers ripped us apart.

"I'm really glad I got to know you," I said.

"Me, too," said Nathan. "Marry me?"

The elevator doors opened.

We were pressed flat against them, and when the support suddenly left our backs, we toppled over, taking suitcases, terrarium, and dogs with us as we tumbled into the elevator. Luck was with us for the first time since we'd left the lab: there was no one already inside, waiting to take a bite out of our tender flesh. I squeaked shrilly, surprised and disoriented. Nathan scrambled to his feet, slamming the heel of his hand down on the door-close button. I managed to sit up just in time to see the blank, emotionless faces of the sleepwalkers blocked out by the closing elevator doors.

Beverly and Minnie stopped growling, their belligerence transforming instantly into confusion. Minnie sat down, beginning to scratch her ear with her hind leg. I picked myself up from the floor, pausing to right the luggage and make sure I hadn't dropped anything. My heart was hammering in my chest so hard that it hurt, and for once it didn't sound like drums at all—it sounded like the heartbeat of a mammal, panicked beyond reason and confronting its own mortality.

Nathan was standing squarely in the middle of the elevator by the time I finished getting to my feet. His carving knife was in his hand, and his shoulders were shaking, betraying the depth of his distress. It was weird to realize that of the two of us, I was probably the one handling things better. Then again, I was also the one who was accustomed to the world being turned on its head. Nathan liked his routines. He was used to things being just so, and even dating me hadn't changed that. My chaos hadn't intruded on his daily life—not until recently, anyway.

"Nathan?" I kept my voice low, like I was speaking to a panicky animal. In a way, maybe I was. My still-pounding heart was doing its best to remind me that humans were just animals, as subject to the whims and whimsies of biology. The fight or flight response was wreaking havoc with both of us.

I'd always wondered why I sometimes passed out before I really panicked, despite everyone I knew working almost exactly the opposite. If "I" was a separate beast from the brain that stored my memories and emotional response, though, it started to make sense. Too much adrenaline flooded the mind, and I got knocked out of the synaptic loop, resulting in a loss of consciousness but not total loss of cool. Inefficient. Doubtless unintentional, too. So much about my design was.

"We don't know what the lobby's going to look like."

Nathan's voice was soft, uninflected—virtually dead. If I hadn't known that he'd never been fitted with an implant, I would have rethought my position on panic when I heard him speak. "If there are sleepwalkers there, if it's dangerous, take the dogs and run. I'll hold them off so that you can get away."

"And go where? Nathan, I can't drive. I never learned, and even if I had, I'd never be able to make myself drive away and leave you. We could run off down the street, but if the situation is *that* bad, we'd just be eaten by the next swarm of sleepwalkers we saw. We're staying with you. We're staying *together*. That's the only way that we're going to get out of this. Together." I forced myself to smile. "Besides, you know your mother would kill me if I called her from the Concord BART Station and said, 'Hey, I left your son to die but I made it to the train, do you think you could come and pick me up?'"

Nathan chuckled.

The floor indicator counted down from three to two.

My hands were full, and I didn't dare let go of anything I had. Nathan had already dropped his suitcase, and the mere fact that he would prioritize my dog—our dog—over the only personal possessions he had been able to save made me even more certain that marrying him was the right course of action. He didn't care that I was a tapeworm in a human skin, but he cared about proper leash etiquette. I was never going to find a more perfect man.

"I love you."

"I love you, too."

The counter reached one with a soft "ding," and the elevator doors opened to reveal an anticlimactically empty lobby. I blinked, unable to believe what my eyes were seeing. Only Minnie tugging on the leash as she eagerly tried to pull me out of the elevator to the walkies she assumed were waiting for her snapped me out of my fugue.

"Run," said Nathan, stuffing the knife back into his waist-band and grabbing his previously discarded suitcase.

We ran.

The street outside the apartment building was eerily deserted, as if all of San Francisco had suddenly realized they had better things to do than their afternoon commute. Two people, both bloody, running with suitcases and dogs out of a private building and into an equally private parking lot, should have attracted some attention of the police persuasion. We saw no one, and if anyone saw us, they didn't bother contacting the authorities—or maybe they did, and the systems had already reached the point of overload. That was a question that would never be answered, because there wasn't time to stop and ask, and there were more important things for us to do. Like escaping the prison that San Francisco was about to become.

We threw our suitcases into the trunk, placing the terrarium with only slightly more care, and loaded the excited, overstimulated dogs into the backseat before getting into the front. Nathan waited for me to buckle myself in before he hit the gas, but only barely. For once, my phobias were going to have to take second place on the list of priorities, and even as I swallowed the rising tide of panic—and the rising bile in my throat—I agreed with this decision. I could have hysterics when we got out of this.

The drums were back in my ears, pounding steadily and reassuringly. I wondered what my tendency to freak out in cars meant for my "Sal passes out before the chemicals can make her panic" theory, and decided that since this particular strain of panic was psychological, not triggered by physiological reactions, it ran according to a different set of rules, even though the actual biochemistry probably wasn't all that different. This question kept me occupied for almost six blocks, which made it worth the contemplation. Anything to distract me from the way that Nathan was driving.

Then I glanced up, and frowned as I recognized the neighborhood around us. "Nathan, where are you going? This isn't the way to the Bay Bridge."

"That's because we're taking another route," he said. "There were too many sleepwalkers there, and that was hours ago. By now the area has either completely devolved into chaos, or the authorities have it locked down. We'd be lucky if they let us onto the bridge at all. If we were particularly *un*lucky, they'd take one look at us and haul us off for medical testing. I don't know about you, but I didn't escape from that apartment building just so I could go into quarantine."

"I don't want that either," I assured him. "So where are we going?"

"Down the coast to the San Mateo Bridge. It's going to be a longer drive, and I'm really sorry about that. I should be able to slow down once we're past the airport."

I forced myself to nod as if I was okay with this plan, as if it didn't make me want to fling myself screaming from the car. "I may try to sleep, if that's all right with you. I don't know if I can, but it would give me something else to focus on."

The corner of Nathan's mouth that I could see twisted downward in obvious displeasure. "If you really need to, okay. Just, I may wake you up if your breathing seems shallow, all right? I don't know how much blood you lost back there, but between that and the shocks you've had today, I want to keep an eye on you."

"All right," I agreed, and closed my eyes.

The San Francisco Bay Area sounds like it should be small, cozy even, the sort of place you can see in a day if you really enjoy spending time in a car. But just like San Francisco itself is deceptively small, the Bay Area is deceptively large. It's too big for any one transit system, bridge, or highway to accommodate, and the only way someone could see the whole thing in a single day would be to start at midnight and never stop the car. Twenty-four hours might be enough time to drive through all the major cities, as long as you were quick and not overly concerned with actually *seeing* anything.

My car issues and reliance on buses and BART trains meant I was mostly familiar with San Francisco proper, and some parts of the East Bay—the ones with good farmer's markets or interesting local attractions, like Solano Avenue and their annual street fair, or the big animal shelter out in Oakland. Caltrain ran between San Francisco and the South Bay, but since I'd never had a pressing reason to spend time down there, I really didn't know much about the geography beyond "every time they try to put in a BART extension, San Jose comes up with another way to block it." I got the feeling the residents of Silicon Valley didn't like being lumped into the San Francisco family of cities, and the feeling was pretty much mutual.

Most California biotech had started in Silicon Valley, eschewing San Francisco's high rents and prohibitive restrictions on keeping livestock. But money, as they say, talks, and the biotech industry didn't want to spend forever in the shadow of the computer revolution. Bit by bit the big firms had oozed their way into the seaside communities, setting up shop in Santa Cruz, Monterey, and yes, San Francisco, home of Symbo-Gen, the biggest biotech monster of them all. Dr. Banks had tried to explain the reasoning to me a few times, focusing on the substantial hydroelectric potential of the Pacific Ocean, as well as the availability of marine biomass. He'd dodged my questions about overfishing and conservation, responding to them with one of those warm, paternal smiles that always sent shivers running up and down my spine.

"Besides, Sally, an ocean view says you've got the money to afford it, and that makes investors feel better about opening their wallets for you. The more money we have, the better the care we'll be able to provide—now, and for the rest of your life. It's a win-win situation, don't you think?"

Those had been his exact words. As I sank down into the darkness behind my eyelids, trying to focus on the drums pounding in my ears, I wondered what he was saying now. Did he still think the ocean view was worth it when it came with geographic isolation and possible captivity in a city that was about to become a living hell?

I didn't know, and there was no way for me to ask him.

The drums were erratic at first—soothing, but irregular, thanks to my lingering upset over Nathan's driving. They smoothed out as I sank deeper into my own mind, retreating down into the hot warm dark that was the first thing I remembered. My old therapist, Dr. Morrison, used to tell me that the hot warm dark was a representation of the womb, a result of my damaged psyche trying to regress to a time when it experienced absolute safety. He'd been very, very wrong, but he'd been right in a way, too, because he'd been claiming that I was trying to go back to a simpler time, and well…

I was pretty sure the hot warm dark was my only real memory of my time before I joined with Sally Mitchell's unused brain. A time when all I needed to do was eat, and occasionally shift positions in her digestive system, aligning my spreading flower of a mouth with another rich source of the nutrients I needed to survive. I wouldn't have gone back to that state of being for anything—sapience is addictive—but it had been good while it lasted, hadn't it? All my memories of the hot warm dark told me it had been. It made so much more sense now.

San Francisco was fading into memory and shadow behind us, surrendered to the sleepwalkers and the grasp of the coming crisis. I didn't know if we were ever going to go back to our lives; I didn't know how bad things were going to get. Being inhuman didn't give me the ability to see what was coming. Too bad. We could have really used a little foresight right

about then. We needed to stop Sherman. It was too late to save
the sleepwalkers, but maybe Nathan and Dr. Cale could find a
way to make the implants stop waking up, or at least stop them
from accidentally hurting their hosts. Maybe we could figure
out how to make that information public without bringing
USAMRIID and SymboGen down on our heads, and maybe
we could save the rest of the people, both human and chimera,
who still needed saving.

It was a lot of "maybe," but I wasn't done yet. I thought of
Tansy. My sister. Maybe she'd managed to fight off the sleepwalkers and hide somewhere, injured but alive. Maybe she'd
come home, make a joke about zombie brains, and ask me to go
sledding. Maybe...

"Maybe" was becoming addictive. I was so tired. I breathed
in, letting the embrace of the hot warm dark draw me further
down, and Nathan drove on, carrying us into the uncertain
future.

# INTERLUDE I: SENESCENCE

*Sometimes I wonder if this is how God felt. And then I wonder why He didn't just let us all burn.*

—DR. RICHARD JABLONSKY

*I can be your friend, or I can be your enemy. Isn't it better when we're friends?*

—SHERMAN LEWIS (SUBJECT VIII, ITERATION III)

*September 2027: Tansy*

The last thing I saw before I passed out was a living wall of human bodies being driven by the semi-sapient minds of my opportunistic cousins, tapeworms who shared everything with me except for their specific method of taking over their hosts and oh, right, a basic understanding of hygiene. Some of those things were *rank*, like they had never met a shower they didn't want to avoid taking.

But their teeth were sharp and their hands were strong and if I sound like I'm being flippant, it's because I'd never encountered anything that terrifying in my short, bloody existence. Dr. C says I deflect things that stress me out, mostly because I don't want to trigger another of the seizures that I used to get when I was newly integrating with my host. She says it's natural and normal and that she'll get me a better host someday, one where the brain hasn't been pre-damaged and I can fit myself into the neural net without gaps and glitches. I kinda think she's lying. I kinda think she likes the fact that she has a damaged daughter to send into danger, because it means she can keep Adam home and safe without feeling bad about it, or feeling like she needs to start training him for the field. As long as

I'm a broken doll, she can send me through the broken doors all she wants. I don't mind, though. I'm good at breaking things.

Sal was gone. She was running away again—that girl was always running away, from her family, from herself, from the truth—only this time I was glad to see her go, because maybe she'd get out. Maybe Nathan was as smart as our mom said he was, and he'd be able to keep Sal safe long enough for her to figure out what she really was. Maybe she'd realize that we were sisters, and then she'd miss me. She'd be sorry that I was gone.

It was a good thought. I'd always hoped that someday, someone would miss me. I held on to it as the bullets ran out and the fingers dug into my arms and the teeth bit into my flesh, and then it was all too much and I blacked out, toppling back into the nothingness that was always waiting at the edges of my damaged mind.

Dying hurt less than I expected it to. That was sort of a surprise. But I guess maybe it doesn't count, because I wasn't actually dead.

Not all the way, anyhow.

I was in some fucking sewer or something when I woke up. Everything was all yuck and slime and this smell like something had died down there. I tried to sit up. The manacles on my wrists drew tight before I could get more than halfway there, and the shock of the sudden resistance had me flat on my back before the screaming pain in my left shoulder and right hip could finish registering. I lay there panting, staring up at a ceiling that I couldn't even see through the gloom. The pain was bad enough to make me want to scream and claw at the walls.

*Pain is an illusion, because this body is an illusion,* I told myself sternly. *It's just a Petri dish that you're living in, that's all. You can move out any time you need to, and that means pain is nothing but an inconvenience. Now breathe.*

I breathed.

The pain began to fade, leaving a little bit at a time, until I felt like a husked-out shell of a girl, empty of sensation where I should have been full. There wasn't even a tingling to remind me of the limits of my skin. Everything was darkness and numbness and the distant smell of whatever dead thing had become my new roommate. Charming. Maybe whatever it was would give me its phone number, and we could be BFFs.

When I was positive that the pain had passed, however momentarily, I closed my eyes, trading one darkness for another, and began flexing my toes, one by one, testing to see how many of them would respond to me. To my delight, all ten were present, accounted for, and miraculously unbroken, although when they moved, they did it without resistance: whoever had chained me up had also taken my shoes and socks away. That was less than completely peachy keen, by any objective standard. I scowled into the dark. I *liked* those shoes. They were big and black and stompy, and I hardly ever tripped over the toes anymore.

Toes were good: how about fingers? I repeated the slow flex, this time adding as much of an extension as I could, just to see whether I had my full range of motion. My left hand responded as expected, although there was a little pulling in my palm that told me there was a split in the skin, even if I couldn't feel it at the moment. Pain had completely vacated the premises, and that wasn't a good thing. Pain was *useful*. It was an illusion, sure, but it was an illusion that kept me from shoving my hand into a whirling garbage disposal, or touching a lit stove burner. I needed pain to remind me that my Petri dish of a physical form had limits, and that failure to observe those limits would have serious consequences.

My right hand was more of a problem. Three of the fingers wouldn't move at all, and I couldn't be sure whether that was because they were broken or because they were missing; not in the dark, not with my body refusing to return vital information about how bad my injuries were. My thumb only moved about half as far as it should have, and the finger that was responding—my pointer finger—didn't have the range of motion to tell me whether the other fingers were there or not. I could have been missing half my hand and I wouldn't have known.

I stared up into the dark, waiting for my eyes to adjust. My eyes did not adjust. I added "maybe I'm blind" to the list of things that were potentially wrong with me.

*Look at it this way, Tansy,* I thought, trying for an upbeat internal monologue. *If your current body is totes wrecked, Dr. C will* have *to give you a new one.*

Assuming she could find me. I was chained up in a sewer. The sleepwalkers hadn't done that: they didn't have the intelligence, much less the remaining manual dexterity. They'd have ripped me to pieces to fill their bellies, eating me—clothes and all—to satisfy the hunger that drove them. Someone must have intervened; someone who wanted me alive, for whatever reason.

The more I thought about it, the less I liked the idea of someone "wanting me alive." It smacked of mad science, and I should know, since I'm sort of a mad scientist's devastatingly beautiful daughter and all—or maybe just her devastating daughter, since I'm pretty good at the destruction thing—and mad science never ended well for the people who woke up in chains. If they were lucky it was the Island of Dr. Moreau and they got to be wacky cat-people with claws and all. If they were unlucky…

Yeah, I needed to get out of here. "Hello?" My voice was incredibly loud in the sewer, which was neat: it told me that I was in a very enclosed space, probably no more than six feet to a side. I'm not a bat, but I know stuff. "Is there anyone there?"

Nothing answered me but the distant drip of nasty-smelling water. I scowled at the dark.

"Hello?" I tried again. "Look, I'm all like, barefoot and lying in yuck, and that's a serious infection risk, so could you maybe come and get me and take me somewhere clean? Or better, give me back my shoes and let me go? I promise not to murder you even a little."

I thought it was a very reasonable offer. Whoever was holding me here either wasn't listening or didn't agree, because there was still no answer. I sighed.

"Right. Well, when you want to talk to me, you obviously know where I'll be. Just an FYI though, that murder thing gets more likely the longer you keep me here." I closed my eyes—there seemed to be no real point in keeping them open—and took a deep, slow breath, trying to center myself. Maybe if I could get my body to start listening to me again, I could turn the pain back on. That would be nice. At least then I'd know what I was working with.

The dark inside my eyes wasn't like the dark outside my eyes. That dark was absolute and artificial, unrelenting in its blackness. This dark was comfortable. This dark was the color of home, where everything was going to be okay, and where it didn't matter if I had a damaged host. We were all the same, down in the dark.

I must have fallen asleep, because when I became aware of my surroundings again, the pain was back, filling my body until I felt like a balloon on the verge of popping. I gritted my teeth and made a small grunting sound, wondering why I'd wanted this back. I mean, pain sort of sucks, right? So why had I been lying in the dark wishing it would show up?

My fingers were all there. I could feel them now, little sticks of burning agony curled against my palm and almost certainly broken. Oh, right. That was why. It's hard to do anything useful with your body when you can't figure out where you left it, and pain was the first step toward doing something useful.

I opened my eyes, and promptly squeaked and closed them

again as the bright white light that had replaced the foul-smelling darkness assaulted my corneas. The smell was gone, too: I realized that belatedly, as I waited for the tears to stop streaming down my cheeks. I hadn't fallen asleep naturally. I'd either passed out from my injuries or been drugged. I sniffed, trying to filter through the remaining sewer-stink and the smell of dried blood for anything chemical and unfamiliar. It was too hard to tell, but there was a faintly acrid taste in my mouth that made me suspect that I'd been gassed before whoever was holding me here had moved me.

There was a click from somewhere above and off to my right. I forced myself to remain perfectly still, not even allowing my unbroken hand to ball into the fist that it instinctually wanted to be.

"You don't need to play that game with me," said a calm, reasonable voice filtered through what I assumed was some kind of intercom. "I know you're awake. The bed you're lying on notified me as soon as your vital signs started spiking, and I thought I'd come down to have a little chat with you before you started throwing yourself against the walls. And we have so much to talk about, you and I. It's been far, far too long."

I opened my eyes again, more slowly this time, squinting to try and keep them from burning too badly as the light flooded in. I was in what looked like an operating theater, strapped to a narrow bed that sat at the exact middle of the room, preventing me from getting to anything that could have provided me with even an inch of leverage. I still tried. I bucked and writhed against that bed until every bruise I had was singing like Adam in the shower: loudly, discordantly, and without a bit of concern for how I felt about it. Finally I stopped fighting and slumped back into my restraints, panting from the exertion.

"All done? That's good. It'll be better if you're calm." There was another click, presumably as the intercom switched off.

I looked around the room, straining my neck until it ached

as I tried to find the door. Finally, I spotted a faint discoloration in the wall to my left. I subsided, eyes narrowed, and waited for something to happen.

It wasn't a long wait, which was good, since I'm not very patient. The door opened, swinging inward, and a tall, well-groomed man with sandy hair and a patient expression stepped into the room. He was wearing a pristine white lab coat and shiny black shoes, and I forgot about everything in the middle as soon as I finished seeing it, because it was so blandly corporate that it could have been stolen right off a mannequin at Banana Republic. I stared at him. I honestly didn't know what to say.

I'd seen pictures before. We'd never been in the same room. Dr. C had always said it was too dangerous, and also that there was a pretty good chance I'd kill him if I got the opportunity, so it was better not to let me have the opportunity. Dr. C was pretty smart that way.

"Hello, Tansy," said Dr. Banks, his smile never wavering. "I'm your father, and it's time we got to know each other a little bit better."

# STAGE I: INTERPHASE

*Hasn't everyone done something that they probably shouldn't have done, just to see what would happen?*

—DR. STEVEN BANKS

*I'm not sure what I am. I'm not sure why I'm here. But I'm sure of one thing. I don't want to die.*

—SAL MITCHELL

*Dear Mary;*

*My head hurts something awful, and I know from watching the news and reading the Internet that this means I'm probably going to die soon. Maybe not my body, but my mind; the parts of me that matter. The parts of me that love you more than anything.*

*That's why I'm leaving. I love you, honey, and if I did anything to hurt you or the kids, I don't think I could live with myself. Even if it was just my body, I know my soul would be watching.*

*I'll see you when you get to Heaven, baby. I know we're both of us going to make it there.*

—LETTER LEFT BY MOE RICHARDS OF REDDING, CA,
OCTOBER 27, 2027

*According to my mother's notes on the original* D. symbogenesis *project, there should be no more than three percent human DNA in any individual worm, with variance for developmental age and individual tailoring (worms intended to secrete specific medications, etc.). The most that should be found in any single worm, even one specifically designed to fit the needs of its host, is three point two percent human DNA.*

*Some of the samples we're finding in the sleepwalker population imply as much as eleven percent human DNA, without any visible change to the morphology of the* D. symbogenesis *worm.*

*What this means, I do not know. I cannot imagine it means anything remotely good.*

—FROM THE NOTES OF DR. NATHAN KIM, OCTOBER 2027

## Chapter 4
# SEPTEMBER 2027

The car pulling to a stop woke me, if "woke" is the correct word: I wasn't sleeping in the traditional sense, just so deep in the hot warm dark that I had ceased to be aware of distance. I opened my eyes on a world without sunlight, the car lit only by the dim glow from the instrument panel. We were pulled off to the side of the road somewhere in the rolling hills that seemed to cover a third of the Bay Area. I blinked, trying to get my bearings, and then twisted in my seat to look at Nathan.

"Why are we stopped?" I asked.

"The dogs need a bathroom break, and according to the traffic reports, we're in the clear from here on out," he said, unfastening his seat belt as he spoke. "We made it over the bridge. No incidents. If the quarantine on San Francisco has been declared, no one's told anyone this far from the city yet."

"Anything on the news?" I sat up, rumpling my hair with

one hand and yawning. I felt, if anything, even more limp and wrung-out than I had before we left the apartment. However much energy I'd been able to gain from the cookies and juice, it wasn't going to last forever.

"They're reporting fires in San Francisco, and advising travelers to either stay in their hotels or cars and await evacuation, if they're already in the city, or stay at home, and as far from San Francisco as possible. There hasn't been anything about a bridge closure yet. That may just be a media effort to keep people from rushing to see what's going on. People love to gawk at accidents. They're not quite as fond of being set on fire."

"Right." I reached for my seat belt. Nathan's hand on my shoulder stopped me. I turned to face him, blinking. "What?"

"I want you to stay in the car," he said.

"What? Why?"

"Because your hands are shaking. They've been shaking since you woke up." He pulled his hand away. "You need medical attention. I'm not going to risk you collapsing by the side of the road because you didn't want me to walk the dogs by myself."

Much as I hated to admit it, Nathan had a point. I sighed, sagging back in my seat. "Okay, but leave the keys? I want to listen to the radio."

"You've got it." He leaned over and kissed my temple before turning the key in the ignition, reactivating the car's electrical systems. I reached for the radio and was starting to scan through the local stations when he got out of the car, slamming the door behind himself, and let the dogs out of the back. I was alone.

The first three stations were generic classic rock, all power ballads and songs about how awesome it was to be young forever. I skipped past them, looking for the news. I was so focused that I scanned right past a familiar voice, only realizing what I'd done two stations later. The drums beginning to hammer in my ears again, I rolled the scanner carefully back.

"—during a tragic break-in at our offices earlier today. I knew our competition was capable of a lot of things, but I had no idea they would stoop to corporate espionage, or that they'd be willing to involve someone who couldn't understand what she was doing." Dr. Banks sounded solemn and upset, like he was barely keeping himself under control. I'd always known he was an excellent liar, but as I listened to him talk, I started to understand how good he really was. "Sally Mitchell is a wonderful girl. I've enjoyed our time together immensely, and I think of her as a daughter, but it's no secret that she's not... well. She suffered some fairly severe brain damage in her accident, and she's never fully recovered. She never will. Her family has been holding her in custodianship for the last several years, and she and I had been speaking about the virtues of transferring that custody to me. I think of her as a daughter, and her biological parents, well, they could never look at her without seeing everything she had lost. I love her. I know she'd never have done anything like this of her own initiative. Someone put her up to this. Someone exploited a poor, mentally handicapped girl for their own ends, and when I find out who did this, I swear, I am going to come down on them with the full force of the law."

His tone changed, becoming ingratiating. I knew that most of the station's listeners—if it was just this station; if this wasn't going out nationwide—would take his words as paternal and loving, but I saw them for what they had always been: a trap. He was trying to trap me, just like he'd been doing for my entire life.

"Sally, if you can hear this, if you're out there somewhere, listening to me, Sally, please, come home. The people who told you to steal from me, they're not your friends. I don't know what lies they've been feeding to you, but I only have your best interests at heart, I've only ever wanted to help you, and I can't do that if you're running from me. I'm not pressing charges against you for what you did. I'm not blaming you for the people who were hurt. I know that none of this was your idea. But Sally, please, please, I am begging you. Please come home."

The quality of the sound abruptly changed, and an unfamiliar woman said, "That was Dr. Steven Banks at his press conference earlier today, discussing the break-in at the SymboGen headquarters that resulted in the deaths of three security guards, and the hospitalization of two doctors. It is widely believed that this break-in was made possible by the actions of Sally Mitchell, a patient of SymboGen's. Miss Mitchell, as you may recall, was involved in a tragic accident—"

I gasped and turned off the radio before the woman could start telling me about my own past. I was still staring at it, my arms wrapped tightly around myself, when the car doors opened. Beverly and Minnie came bounding into the backseat, and Beverly shoved her nose under my hair, snuffling loudly, in case I had changed while she was away. The door closed, and the driver's-side door opened. I kept staring at the radio.

"Sal?" Nathan put a hand on my arm as he slid back into his seat. I didn't react. He pulled the hand away, closing his door, creating a safe, enclosed space around us. Only then did he try again, asking, "Sal, honey, what's wrong? What was on the radio?"

"Dr. Banks." I turned slowly to face him. "He did a press conference. He told everyone about the break-in, and said that people got hurt, and that it was my fault. But he's not pressing charges, he says, he just wants me to come home."

"Which may mean he's offering a reward for anyone who turns you in, and trying to deflect people from suspecting SymboGen's involvement in the sleepwalker outbreak at the same time. Dammit." Nathan scowled, pushing his glasses back up his nose. "I guess that just means we'll need to be a little bit more careful for the rest of the drive. Are you ready to go?"

"Fasten your seat belt," I said.

Nathan fastened his seat belt.

"Is your mom going to let us back into the lab when there are people looking for me?"

"There have always been people looking for you, and there have always been people looking for *her*," he said. "Maybe that doesn't sound reassuring, but it is, because she's always been willing to let you in. You're her greatest creation, a chimera that formed entirely without human aid. I'm not going to let her use you as a lab subject, but darling, you have to understand how much leverage this gives you over her. She needs to study you. She'll let us in."

"The broken doors will still be open."

"Yeah," said Nathan, reaching for the wheel. "And while I find it deeply odd that my life is now defined by a children's book, it's also reassuring. As long as Mom keeps treating that thing like the newest book of the damn Bible, she's not going to shut us out. The whole point of going to where the monsters are is that the monsters will always let you in."

"Yay, monsters," I said, leaning back in my seat and closing my eyes again. I liked riding in cars at night a little bit more than I liked doing it during the day. As long as I couldn't see anything around us, I could almost pretend that we were sitting safely still. But other cars had a tendency to break the illusion, and with Nathan driving the way he had to in order to get us to safety, it was better for me not to risk it.

I heard the engine rumble to life, and then the faint jouncing as Nathan rolled from the shoulder and back onto the road.

The sirens started a few seconds later.

The sound was coming from directly behind us. I opened my eyes, and the cab of the car was filled with flashing red and blue lights. "Nathan..."

"I know. Just be cool, okay? I can handle this." He pulled over again, leaving his hands resting on the wheel, while I stayed frozen in my seat and tried not to look like an inhuman thing wearing a girl's skin. What if the cop could tell somehow?

What if we were both arrested, and I was thrown into whatever sort of cell they reserved for creatures who dared to pretend to be people, and I never saw Nathan or the dogs again?

Beverly, sensing my distress, shoved her nose into my ear. I left it there, not trying to push her away, as Nathan rolled down the window and a flashlight shined into the car, illuminating first my lap, and then moving to my face, where it seemed like the glare was going to blind me. I squinted, recoiling. Beverly pulled her nose out of my ear and gave an inquisitive yip.

"Are these your dogs, miss?" asked the officer. The voice was male, but I couldn't make out a face, thanks to that flashlight in my eyes.

I was silent for a few seconds, trying to find an answer that was both honest and unlikely to get me into trouble. Finally, I settled for the safest option: "Y-yes," I stammered. "The big one is Beverly, and the little one is Minnie. They're both friendly, and we have leashes for them." I wasn't sure why I felt the need to add that last part, except that I'd heard horror stories before of cops shooting dogs for getting too close to them while appearing "vicious," a designation that seemed to mean "the dog had teeth in its mouth and I saw them at some point." Since happy, friendly dogs were apt to show off their teeth in the process of panting, that made me worry about my girls.

"Any reason they were just outside the car without a lead on?"

Now Nathan spoke up. "I'm sorry, Officer. They were whining, and my girlfriend was asleep, and I took them out so that she wouldn't have to. I never even thought to grab their leashes."

"This is state land. It's against local ordinance for dogs to be in the fields without leads." The flashlight beam switched to Nathan's face, finally allowing me to see the officer on the other side. He was a big man of African-American descent, thick around the middle, with a face that seemed inclined to be gentle, even as he was interrogating Nathan about walking the dogs. "Did you see any wildlife while you were out there?"

It smacked of a question that had a right answer and a wrong answer. I bit my lip as I waited to see which one Nathan was going to offer.

"I think we startled a duck," he said. "It flew away when Minnie got close to it, and the dogs did their business—urine only, I had bags in case they decided to poop—and we got back into the car. My girlfriend was awake by that point, I told her what I'd done, and we started to get back on the road. That's when you pulled us over."

The flashlight beam switched back to my face, making my eyes water. I squinted, resisting the urge to raise a hand against the glare. Looking inoffensive was important when dealing with the police, never more than right now. "Miss, is this true?"

"I can't say about the duck, because I was in the car, but all the rest is true as far as I know," I said meekly. "I'm really sorry. I would have told him to put the leashes on if I'd been awake."

"Miss, why is there blood on your shirt?"

The question was asked in the same mild, almost innocuous tone as the questions about the dogs, and for a moment, I didn't realize how dangerous it was. The moment passed quickly. I swallowed hard before holding up my injured arm, showing him the bandage wrapped around my wrist. "I was making dinner, and I slipped," I said. "I cut myself pretty bad, and I didn't have a clean shirt, so we're heading back to my place to get me a change of clothes." It seemed odd to avoid using Nathan's name, but he hadn't used mine, and I had to assume that there was a reason for that. Maybe he just didn't want to risk the cop guessing who we were...but wouldn't the officer have run Nathan's plates before he got out of his squad car? Didn't he already *know*?

There were too many variables. I was drowning in them.

"I see." The flashlight moved away from my eyes to my

bandaged wrist, and hovered there as the officer considered my words. Finally, he asked, "Are you being held against your will?"

"What? No!" I was so startled by the question that I forgot to moderate my response. I wound up half squawking at the cop, my eyes going wide and round with surprise.

Maybe that was the right way to react. The flashlight finally pointed upward at the ceiling of the cab, where it illuminated the car without blinding anyone. "I don't know if you were aware, but I just got the call that we're closing down the bridge," said the officer. "It seems there's been some sort of outbreak in San Francisco, and we're trying to contain it before it can spread to the rest of the Bay Area. You kids wouldn't know anything about that, would you?"

"No, Officer," said Nathan.

I didn't trust my voice, and so I just shook my head, hoping that the policeman would take my silence as a sign of fear, and not a sign of guilt.

"You look like good kids, but it's not safe out here," he said. "Wherever it is you're going, you want to keep going until you get there, you hear me? Don't stop again, no matter how bad your dogs need to pee."

"Yes, sir," said Nathan. "Thank you."

"I'm letting you off with a warning this time. Get your girl home." Then the flashlight was turned away, and the officer was walking back down the shoulder toward his car. Nathan and I raised our eyes to watch him go, tracking his reflection as it got smaller and smaller, until he finally climbed into his squad car. The lights flashed once as he restarted the engine, and then he pulled out onto the highway and was gone.

Nathan groaned, leaning forward to rest his forehead against the wheel for a moment. I blinked at him, alarmed.

"Nathan?"

"This is how everything falls apart, Sal," he said, voice

slightly muffled by his position. "This is where everything breaks down. That man should have hauled us in—between the blood and the bridge shutting down, we're too suspicious to be allowed to roam free. But he didn't, because we looked like 'nice kids,' and you're a pretty girl with big, sad eyes, and he didn't want to do that to us. We looked too innocent."

"That's...bad?" I asked blankly.

"No one is innocent when you're talking about infection, whether it's viral or parasitic." Nathan raised his head and started the engine again. "We're not carrying SymboGen implants on the verge of going rogue, but we could be. There's no way to look at a person and know. So if we were carriers, and if the goal were to shut down the sleepwalker plague in San Francisco, our friendly neighborhood state trooper would have just ruined everything."

"Everyone's a carrier," I said. "You're being really hard on him. He let us go."

"Everyone's a *potential* carrier. There will always be outliers, like you, but it seems like most sleepwalkers are triggered by getting near another sleepwalker. The pheromone tags put off by the worms in their new state excite and agitate the worms that are still in a resting phase. The change isn't instant unless the second worm was already in the process of attempting to colonize the brain of their host—it takes time to chew and slither your way through a human body—but it starts with that pheromone tag. That's why Sherman could form a mob by dropping one or two individuals in key neighborhoods. That's why Mom was so worried about us going out in public. There's no telling how many people are already out there, putting off the pheromone tags that say 'it's time to move,' and haven't yet started showing symptoms."

"You're making it sound like you *wanted* him to arrest us," I snapped. "Because that would keep us and our scary pheromones away from the people who aren't sick yet. Only you can't be putting off those pheromones, since you never got an implant, and I…" I stopped, a sick feeling spreading through my stomach. "Nathan, are you saying this is all my fault?"

"No," he said hurriedly. "No, I'm not saying that at all. I talked to Mom, at length, about the differences between chimera and sleepwalkers, because I knew I'd need to explain them to you—and I really think I should do as much of it as I can. Mom isn't good at talking to people who aren't geneticists."

"You're not a geneticist."

"No, and sometimes she loses me. But you're not giving off the pheromone tag that the sleepwalkers use to activate each other. She said it's like comparing a can of spray paint to a master painter's brush. You can get art out of either one, but one will tend to be much more focused and refined. The sleepwalkers are putting off a chemical stew that says everything from 'hey, do what I'm doing, this is neat and you should try it' to 'eat here, here, eat.' She's still trying to analyze the specific pheromones that you and the other chimera put off. As near as she can tell, they say 'listen to me, I am bigger than you, and you should listen.' You may eventually be able to use them to accomplish just that. You may be able to make them listen."

I looked at my bandaged wrist, the white barely visible through the gloom. "Are all the sleepwalkers going to listen with their teeth?" I asked glumly.

"Only the ones who are already too brain-damaged from the integration process to understand the message. I think they're all going to want to be close to you. Some of them may even have the intelligence to obey when you give them simple orders, like 'stop' or 'don't eat me.' But some of them are going to be too far gone, because the integration process involves far too much brute trauma to the host. They don't have the superstructure necessary to process complicated information."

I wrapped my arms around myself, hunching over in my seat. "This just keeps on making me feel worse and worse.

Every time I think I'm okay with not being human, you come up with some new fun fact, like 'hey, Sal, you're basically a bug zapper for sleepwalkers, hope that's okay with you.' "

"I'm okay with you not being human," said Nathan. "However long it takes for you to be okay with it, I will wait for you. We're going to figure this all out together."

"But you still think that cop should have arrested us."

"Yes," admitted Nathan. "At the very least, he should have questioned us more about why we'd decided to load ourselves and the dogs into the car when you were clearly injured, instead of going to a hospital. I think..." He took one hand off the wheel as he reached up and adjusted his glasses, and I suddenly realized the car was moving: had been moving for some time. I'd been so distracted by arguing with him that I hadn't even noticed. Finally, he sighed, and said, "I think things are getting very bad, very quickly, and I think that officer knew about it. He made a threat assessment. He decided we were not dangerous. As luck would have it, he was right, and it was definitely the choice we wanted him to make. I'm just worried about how many times people will make that same choice tonight, and how many times they're going to be wrong. It's too late to stop the outbreak. That doesn't mean we need to help it spread faster than it has to."

I bit my lip again, frowning. I couldn't make out the details of Nathan's face, and I was glad; I didn't want to know whether he was wearing his mother's look of calm resignation, like talking about leaving people locked in what was about to become a plague zone could ever be interpreted as a good thing. The landscape rushing by outside the car windows was a bruised blur that echoed my mood: purple and gray and somehow threatening.

It was nice to know that a good scare that had nothing to do with being in a car could distract me from the fact that I was in a moving vehicle. Maybe I just needed to get a portable DVD player and start watching horror movies whenever I had to go somewhere.

I wanted to let the matter lie—I really did—but there was one more question I needed to ask before I could do that. "How many people do you think are going to die?"

There was a long pause before Nathan answered me. "A lot," he said, finally. "From both sides. I think a lot of humans are going to die, and a lot of the ones who don't are going to take powerful antiparasitics and kill their implants—and they'd do it even if we had evidence that the tapeworms have achieved rudimentary sapience in their isolated state, and should hence be treated as thinking beings. People have fought long and hard to have the right to control their own bodies in this country. They're going to view the implants as dangerous intruders. And the sleepwalkers...maybe there's some kind of treatment that can give the tapeworms that have taken their hosts over a better existence, something closer to what you and Adam have, or at least closer to what Tansy has. But for right now, we have to treat them as if they were already dead."

"Do you think that would work?"

"Honestly, I don't know. Most people—human people—are going to be very upset when they find out what's going on. Even if there is a treatment, it might be a long time before it can be put into practice, if ever."

I looked at him steadily, searching his face for signs of panic. "How are you so calm?" I asked. "I mean, I'm a tapeworm. I've been a tapeworm the whole time we've been dating. You've been having sex with a tapeworm. Your mother has been making more tapeworm-people just like me. Other tapeworms are eating the brains out of their hosts, and you're still so *calm*."

"I could ask you the same question, you know," he said. "I've had days to come to terms with what you are and what that means about our future together. I already decided that it doesn't matter, and that I want to marry you and be with you forever, no matter what species you technically are. You just found out tonight, and you're already playing action girl across the Bay Area. It's not a normal reaction."

"Tapeworm," I said, trying to keep my tone light. I failed. "We don't know much about invertebrate psychology. Maybe what would be a normal reaction in a human isn't a normal reaction coming from me."

"Maybe," he allowed. "But you've always seemed to be following a human template to me. It's been a slightly odd one—more than a little weird at times—but it was recognizably human. I think that once you became fully bonded to Sally Mitchell's brain, a certain amount of normal human response became inevitable. It's the form defining the function, as much as the function defining the form."

I had to laugh at that, a tight, gasping series of sounds that made Beverly push her head back into the front seat again, concerned and checking to see what was wrong. I put a hand on her muzzle, pushing her back, and said, "So you love me even though I'm not human, because I seem human because I'm living in a human body?"

"No. I love you because you're you. The rest is all details."

"Scientist," I accused fondly.

Nathan smiled, the expression visible in the light coming off the dash. "Guilty as charged," he said, and drove on.

The parking lot outside the abandoned bowling alley that Dr. Cale had converted into a lab was dark and empty, looking more like the setting of a murder mystery than a sanctuary. It was at least partially an illusion: I knew she and her team had security cameras hidden all over the place, making it virtually impossible for anyone to sneak up on the lab. That was good. We were going to need that kind of security if we were going to be staying here for a while.

Nathan parked behind the bowling alley, where his virtually

new Prius stuck out like a sore thumb among the battered, rust-covered cars favored by the staff. Most of them looked newer than they seemed when I took a second glance; one more bit of visual chicanery to keep the local authorities from looking twice at the place.

"You get Minnie, I'll get Beverly, and I'll come back for the suitcases," said Nathan, handing me a leash.

I nodded. "It's a deal."

Leashing two excited dogs who had been cramped up in the backseat of a car for the better part of an hour and a half wasn't easy, but I'd been working at an animal shelter for years, and I'd never met the dog I couldn't get onto a lead. Nathan struggled to get the leash on Beverly for a while before just handing it to me and letting me do it. I grinned to myself as I passed Minnie's leash to him. It was nice to know that there was still *something* I could contribute to our partnership, even if it was as small and silly a thing as putting leashes on dogs. Everyone has their talents.

Nothing moved but us as we made our way across the parking lot to the bowling alley, which looked as locked and abandoned as it had the first time we had come here. All that was missing was Tansy, Dr. Cale's bodyguard and effective head of security, sitting on the hood of a car and getting ready to shoot us if we looked at her funny. A knot formed in my throat. I never would have thought I could miss that little disaster waiting to happen, but it was wrong for her not to be here. She was supposed to be here, and she wasn't, and that was because of me.

Nathan stepped in front of me when we got to the door, raising his hand and knocking briskly. Only silence answered.

"Do you think they left without us?" I asked anxiously.

"Not if Mom's still in charge," he said, and knocked again. When there was still no answer he started looking around, scanning the edge of the roof and door frame. "See if you can find a security camera."

"I don't know what your mother's security cameras look

like," I protested. "It's dark and I'm woozy and shouldn't she have let us in by now?"

"Not if whoever's manning the door is waiting for a sign that we're actually us, and that we haven't led half the police in the Bay Area back here," he said. "Look for something that looks completely unlike what you'd expect from a security camera, and assume that's probably what Mom's security cameras look like. She's been doing this for a long time."

"Right. So I should go and start trying to attract a pigeon's attention. Got it." I turned and let Beverly start pulling me along the side of the building. She had her nose glued to the ground, taking in a whole new world of smells. I kept my eyes equally glued to the slight overhang of the roof, looking for something that didn't look like a security camera.

It turns out there are a lot of things that don't look like security cameras. Rocks, for example. Wasps' nests. Pieces of the roof. I kept letting Beverly pull me along, and while I didn't see anything that looked like a camera, I saw plenty of things that absolutely were *not* cameras. We went around a corner, and saw more of the same. The next two sides of the building didn't yield anything new.

"This is hopeless," I said to Beverly, who wagged her tail agreeably. If I wanted to tell her a thing was hopeless, why, she'd be happy to agree, because I was her people, and if I thought something was so, then I had to be right. Dogs are good like that. We were reaching the corner that would take us back to where Nathan had parked the car, and so I sighed, raised my voice, and said, "Hey, Nathan, nothing out here—"

I stopped as we came around the corner. The bowling alley door was open, and a man was standing there, aiming what looked like an assault rifle at Nathan's chest. Minnie was standing stock-still next to Nathan's right leg, her head up and her ears back as an almost subsonic growl echoed from her chest. It wasn't her sleepwalker growl, which would have been followed by lunging and attempts to bite: it was just the growl of a good dog whose person was being threatened.

"Don't move, Sal," said Nathan, without looking at me. He had his hands up, and his attention remained focused firmly on the man with the gun. That seemed like a good idea. "I was just explaining to Fang here that we're not trying to break in, we're just trying to get back to my mother. Dr. Cale. Who runs this lab." He pronounced "Fang" to rhyme with "long," rather than like he was talking about a particularly sharp tooth.

He was of clearly Chinese descent, but taller than Nathan, with a shaved head and eyes that were narrowed in concentration. Only the lab coat he was wearing over his shirt and trousers broke the unrelenting blackness of his attire…and he looked familiar.

"You're, um, on Dr. Cale's security team, aren't you? Only you were on assignment until recently, because I know you, don't I? I've seen you at SymboGen." It was the lab coat that did it. His face was memorable, but I didn't like making eye contact with people when I didn't have to. They had an unfortunate tendency to smile at me, and all those teeth made me uncomfortable. But I'd been around doctors and medical technicians for as long as I could remember, and I'd never forget a lab coat. "You worked in the phlebotomy lab, didn't you? With Dr. Lo?"

The man—Fang—didn't turn. Keeping his rifle trained on Nathan, he asked, "When would you have seen me there, if I had been there to be seen?"

It took me a moment to puzzle through his grammar, which seemed oddly recursive to me, like it was a snake biting its own tail. Finally, I ventured, "During one of my checkups? Dr. Banks made me come in a lot more often than I probably needed to. I always thought it was because he was worried about my well-being, but I guess now it was because he was monitoring my integration with the human brain, since it sort of sucks when all of your tapeworm-human hybrids just moan and try to bite people all the time. Which, you know, speaking of that, one of them bit me pretty badly." I held up my bandaged wrist like a macabre exhibit A. "I lost a lot of blood and the world's still sort of spinny and I just walked all the way around the outside of the bowling alley which wouldn't be a thing normally, but I haven't lost a lot of blood normally, and I think I'm going to pass out soon. So I'd appreciate it if you'd put the gun down, or at least stop aiming it at my boyfriend, and go tell Dr. Cale that we're here. This whole situation is wank."

"Wack, Sal," said Nathan, a nervous giggle underscoring his words. "The word you want is 'wack.'"

"Oh," I said. "So what does 'wank' mean?"

"It means 'to masturbate,'" said Fang, adjusting his rifle so that it was pointed at the sky instead of at Nathan. The drums that had been pounding in my ears slacked off slightly, making it easier for me to hear. "Do you have everything you need out of your vehicle?"

The sudden change in topics threw me for a loop. It appeared to do the same to Nathan, because he just blinked at Fang, and for a moment the three of us stood there silently, everyone waiting for someone else to start making sense.

Finally, Fang sighed and explained, "I need to get rid of your car. If you have everything you need, I can do that now. If you don't, I will escort you inside, come back out with some movers, and do it while you're undergoing orientation."

"What do you mean, get rid of my car?" Now Nathan sounded alarmed.

"Dr. Cale told me you'd have this reaction." Fang smiled thinly. "She said to let you know that we'll be issuing you a replacement vehicle from our motor pool, but that we can't risk having a nearly new Prius sitting near what's supposed to be an abandoned building. She also said to let you know that you'll be receiving twenty percent of the sale price, so you shouldn't fuss about it overly much."

"Twenty percent of—you know what? No. I'm not going to get upset about this. If this is what needs to happen for us to be safe, then fine, so be it." Nathan shook his head. "Sal and I both have things in the car. She needs medical attention, and that seemed more important than dealing with our suitcases."

"All right," said Fang. He held out his hand. "Give me the keys and follow me."

It seemed like Nathan was going to argue. Then he glanced at me. I must have looked worse than I thought, because he paled, lips pressing tightly together, before digging his keys out of his pocket and slapping them down in Fang's outstretched palm.

"Thank you," said Fang, making the keys disappear into his lab coat. "Welcome home."

We followed him into the bowling alley, Beverly straining at her leash as she tried to rush ahead into this world of exciting new smells, Minnie lagging behind and nearly tripping me as she looked for something to reassure her that the world wasn't changing for the worse. I understood the sentiment, even as it was becoming increasingly difficult for me to put one foot in front of the other. The spots around the edges of my vision were back, chewing little moth holes in everything I saw.

The dark room connecting the bowling alley door to the main lab seemed even darker than usual, although that could have been a side effect of my clouded vision. Fang stopped in front of the interior door, holding up a hand as he motioned for us to do the same.

"If you'll wait here, I'll let Dr. Cale know that you're back," he said.

"Okay," I said dreamily. "I'm just going to take a little nap, all right?" The black spots were continuing to expand.

I didn't even feel myself hit the floor.

This time, when I woke up, I was in a hospital cot in the middle of what looked like a makeshift operating theater, with two IV bags—one full of blood, one full of saline solution—attached to my left arm. I blinked at the tubes, and then twisted to look around the small room. The walls were just white sheets hanging from a pipe framework. A heart monitor beeped steadily, providing a treble accent to the drums that were beating softly in my ears. Another monitor was tracking...something. I assumed it was connected to the tangle of wires spilling off the bed. I reached up. There were sensors on my forehead, big round flat things held down with what felt like surgical tape. I frowned.

"Ah, good: you're awake." Dr. Cale's voice came from the other side of the curtain. She pushed it aside with one sweep of her arm and came rolling in. "You gave us all quite a scare, young lady. It may be time to have a little talk about how you're taking care of yourself. This can't continue."

"What?" I blinked at her blearily, trying to make sense of what she was saying. I'd been standing in the bowling alley with Nathan and the dogs—the dogs. "Where are Beverly and Minnie?"

"Your dogs are fine. I was prepared to be irritated about you bringing non-lab animals here, but they've already proven their value by distracting my son while you were having a seizure on my floor." Dr. Cale's frown deepened. "There are only a few human-tapeworm chimera in the world, Sal. You *know* that. As far as I'm aware, you're the only one ever to arise without help. You're a collector's item, for lack of a better term, and you're not taking the proper care to keep yourself in mint condition."

"I don't...I don't understand. Where are my dogs?"

Dr. Cale reached up and pinched the bridge of her nose. "Your dogs are with Nathan, who is getting them settled in the room you'll be sharing until we relocate to a new lab space. Recent events have accelerated our timeline for moving slightly. We can't risk being found."

"Dr. Banks was on the radio," I said. "He's telling people I broke into SymboGen because somebody made me do it."

"Well, that's technically true, or close enough to true that I can't be as angry at him as I'd like to be. But we're getting off the topic." She lowered her hand, looking at me gravely. "As I said before, you're the first chimera to happen naturally. All of the others have had a team of experts standing by, bound and determined to make sure that our subjects had a successful melding with their hosts. Even then, it didn't always go as well as we wanted it to."

"Like Tansy?" I asked.

Dr. Cale nodded. "Yes. Exactly like Tansy. She had everything going for her when I performed the procedure. I had practiced on other subjects, the original damage to the host's brain was minimal—it should have been perfect. It wasn't. She caused seizures in her host, and damaged the brain in the process. All her neurological and cognitive issues stem from those seizures. Do you understand what I'm trying to tell you?"

I didn't. I knew that my ignorance would show on my face, and so I didn't even try to hide it: I just shook my head, wincing a little as the sensors attached to my forehead pulled, and said, "Not really."

"When you entered Sally Mitchell's skull, you exploited the damage that had been done by her accident," said Dr. Cale. "It was a lucky break—literally. If her skull had broken in any other place, you probably wouldn't have been able to get through. But in the process, you compromised some of the blood vessels that feed into the brain. They were partially repaired during the initial surgery. There should have been an additional surgery to suture and reconnect them properly, since those are your only source of nutrition now that you're anchored in the brain, instead of in the digestive system. Unfortunately, Dr. Banks had taken over your care by that point, and he did not choose to order that operation."

I stared at her. "But...why not?"

"Sal, I don't know everything, all right? I can't say for sure why he would have decided not to operate. Maybe you were too fragile at that time, and he didn't want to endanger your integration. Maybe he was looking for leverage to hold over you later. There's no way he missed this damage. I honestly don't know why he didn't correct it."

"But you suspect." The drums were starting to make a little more sense to me now. Of course they would seem louder than a normal human heartbeat: I wasn't just hearing them with my ears, but with my entire body, which was wrapped into the pulse of the circulatory system in Sally Mitchell's brain. There was no way I could have avoided hearing the drums. And at the same time...hadn't they been seeming just a little *too* loud lately? Like they were pounding when they didn't need to be? Like they were being played by someone who didn't really know what they were doing.

Like my heart was beating too hard.

"I do." Dr. Cale nodded. "You have to understand that... oh, God, how do I say this? I genuinely think of Adam and Tansy—and yes, you—as my children. You contain my DNA, and while a connection to a living human brain is required for you to achieve full sapience, I cannot question your right to exist once you have that connection. Do you understand? I wouldn't kill a functional human being to give one of my babies a body, but I wouldn't take that body away from them if they already had it."

"Okay," I said, confused.

"You were a miracle, Sal. For whatever reason, you not only took advantage of Sally's accident, you found a way to complete integration without help. Sally's brain is the computer that runs your consciousness, but you, only you, are the medical miracle here. You're the one who evolved under pressure." She smiled a little, like she expected this revelation to make me happy. It did not make me happy. "If Dr. Banks wanted to study a natural chimera, you were perfect. Tell me, those contracts that he had you and your parents sign, agreeing to allow Symbo-Gen to handle your medical care. Did they say anything about what would happen to your body if you passed away for any reason?"

"Dr. Banks would get it for research purposes." Dawning horror was coiling in my stomach. I tried to tamp it down, demanding, "But what good would that do? All he'd get would be a dead worm and a deader girl. There's not much to learn from that."

"Tapeworms are hardy, Sal. It's true that your current body wouldn't survive the loss of your human host; you're too deeply integrated to be removed. But all he'd need is a single viable proglottid to grow a new worm with your exact genetic makeup. He could create another you under controlled lab conditions. He's never had a chimera of his own—I've had people sabotaging his research every time it looked like he was getting close. Creating another iteration of you wouldn't require the same level of research; you've made all the modifications necessary for a successful joining already, all by yourself. He could exploit that."

"What are you talking about?"

"You were built with a DNA profile," she said. "You found a way, instinctively, to modify it enough to let you take Sally Mitchell's body as your own. That's normal. Every baseline worm expresses itself differently. We could hatch a thousand eggs from the same batch that made you and get a thousand slightly different results—but your body is hermaphroditic, and every egg it generates will be a tiny, perfect clone of you, Sal. Banks could use that. He could grow a chimera of his own, and then figure out how to make the process easier...or how to stop it altogether."

I stared at her, aghast. "Are you saying that Dr. Banks left weak blood vessels in my brain because he wanted me to have an aneurism and die?"

"So that he could take samples and culture eggs from your original body, yes, and possibly move it into a new host," said Dr. Cale. "Observing you throughout the life cycle of your original host would have been a secondary goal. I admit, I can see the temptation. It would have been a perfect, untouched system, if only it had been a computer model instead of a living person."

"I don't think he thinks of me as a person," I said.

"You may not be a human, Sal, but you're a person. Anyone who can think and speak and be upset by someone's plans for them is a person." Dr. Cale wheeled herself closer. "Which brings us to the next matter at hand. Those blood vessels need to be repaired, or you're going to keep having incidents like this one."

"I thought I fainted because I lost too much blood," I said weakly.

"You didn't lose that much blood, but what you did lose was enough to strain your system," she said. "That was really the problem. Once your body begins to worry about circulation, things will go downhill for you very quickly, because you don't have much in the way of a reserve. We need to operate."

The thought of being unconscious on a table while someone sliced into my head filled me with terror. I didn't want them so close to my vulnerable body. I *needed* my skull to keep people away from it. But that wasn't going to do me much good if the channels that carried the food I needed to survive were blocked. "Can we do that here?" I asked, inwardly amazed at how calm I sounded. Why, it was almost as if I weren't asking someone to cut me open.

Dr. Cale shook her head. "No, we can't," she said. "I have excellent surgical facilities—I can even perform limited brain surgery, when there's a need for it—but what you need is too delicate. It's going to require a specialist, and equipment that's much more advanced than I have access to here. We're going to need to take you to a hospital."

"Nathan has admitting privileges at the hospital where he works," I said slowly.

"Yes, and that hospital is in San Francisco, and everyone there knows him." Dr. Cale shook her head for the second time in under a minute. A look of deep regret transfused her features. Somehow, that didn't make me feel any better. "We'd be arrested before we even managed to get you on the table."

"So what, then? I can't just stay here and try not to get upset about anything. The sleepwalkers are getting worse. That sort of makes staying calm impossible."

"I'm going to need you to trust me."

I stared at her. "That's what I've been doing since I called you."

"No, Sal. You've been playing at trust, but what I'm about to ask you to do…you need to be absolutely sure that you believe I have your best interests at heart. Otherwise, we can wait. See if the crisis passes. Those blood vessels should hold for a while longer." Dr. Cale looked at me, regret fading to leave her face a featureless mask. "I can't say for how long."

"Then I guess I have to trust you," I said, trying to sound more sincere than I felt. I didn't know if I would ever really trust Dr. Cale, but I didn't have any options left—not unless I wanted to die. Choosing to live meant choosing to trust her, whether I wanted to or not. "Let's open the broken doors all the way."

Dr. Cale nodded. "I'll set things up," she said, and turned her wheelchair and rolled away, leaving me alone and wondering what I had just agreed to let her do to me.

*Take the bread and take the salt,*
*Know that this is not your fault;*
*Take the things you need, for you will not be coming*
  *back.*
*Pause before you shut the door,*
*Look back once, and never more.*
*Take a breath and take a step, committed to this track.*

*The broken doors are kept in places ancient and*
  *unknown.*
*My darling ones, be careful now, and don't go out*
  *alone.*

—FROM *DON'T GO OUT ALONE*, BY SIMONE KIMBERLEY,
PUBLISHED 2006 BY LIGHTHOUSE PRESS.
CURRENTLY OUT OF PRINT.

*The big question of the hour is pretty obvious: it's the question*
*we've been asking every scientist from Galileo to Oppen-*
*heimer, from Frankenstein to Moreau. Do I feel like we at*
*SymboGen are trying to play God?*

*Well, there's a reason that two of the scientists I just named*
*don't really exist. I think that mankind is constantly try-*
*ing to play God: I would argue that playing God is exactly*

*what God, if He exists, would want us to do. He didn't create thinking creatures with the intent that we would never think. That would be silly. He didn't create creatures that were capable of manipulating and remaking our environment with the intent that we would sit idle and never create anything. That would be a waste.*

*If God exists—and I am reserving my final opinion on the matter until I die and meet Him—then He is a scientist, and by creating man, he was playing at being me for a little while. So I can't imagine that He would mind if I wanted to try putting the shoe on the other foot, can you?*

—FROM *KING OF THE WORMS*, AN INTERVIEW WITH
DR. STEVEN BANKS, CO-FOUNDER OF SYMBOGEN.
ORIGINALLY PUBLISHED IN *ROLLING STONE*,
FEBRUARY 2027

# Chapter 5

## SEPTEMBER 2027

The plan was simple enough on paper. Fang and Daisy—another of Dr. Cale's employees, a parasitologist by trade, before she had left SymboGen to work with Dr. Cale on the *D. symbogenesis* issue—both had admitting privileges at the nearby John Muir Medical Center, a vast, sprawling hospital complex where no one could be sure of knowing absolutely everyone else. They would sneak me into an unoccupied operating theater, program the machines that handled microsurgery to deal with the weakened blood vessels connecting to my brain, and keep watch while the surgical tools took care of the job. Fang was a licensed neurosurgeon, and both of them were blazingly loyal to Dr. Cale, for reasons I didn't yet fully understand.

There were a lot of things that could go wrong with this plan, starting when we left the bowling alley and progressing from there. What if someone at the hospital recognized me? What if someone at the hospital recognized *Nathan*? He'd given speeches on parasitology at hospitals all over Northern California, and he didn't usually attend random brain surgeries.

Not that there was any chance of his staying behind at the bowling alley. Even if I'd been comfortable with the idea—which I wasn't—that wasn't something he was going to agree to. His discussion with his mother had lasted less than five minutes, escalating in volume until everyone in the lab could probably have heard them. Her part of the conversation had consisted of reasonable arguments and rational cost/benefit assessments. His had consisted almost entirely of variations on the word "no." I had snuggled down in my narrow cot, listening to the soft thudding of the drums in my ears and smiling a little. It was nice that Dr. Cale didn't get *everything* she wanted.

I was still in that cot a little over an hour later when the sheet was pulled aside, allowing Nathan into my tiny, semiprivate room. "How's your head?" he asked.

"Not too bad," I said. "Did your mom put sedatives in my IV drip? The drums haven't been as loud since I've been here."

He nodded. "She did. Don't worry; I've looked over your chart, and they won't interfere with the surgery. We'll be able to get you put back together tonight, better than new, since this time you won't have a hidden time bomb in your skull."

I smiled slightly. "You're freaking out, huh?"

"Just a little." He raised his hand, holding his thumb and forefinger about an inch apart. I raised my eyebrows. He spread his fingers farther apart before giving up and spreading his hand wide. "Okay, a lot. It's been a long night, you know? First we're fugitives, and then you're having your arm ripped open, and then you're passing out again—and suddenly that's a good thing, since without all the fainting, we might not have looked at your MRIs closely enough to realize what was going on inside that head of yours before it was too late."

" 'I like it when you lose consciousness' is just what every girl likes to hear," I said blandly.

"Hey." Nathan walked across the room and sat down on the edge of the bed. "Try 'I like it when you survive' on for size, okay? We've come too far for this to be what ends things. Mom's people are good. You know Fang from SymboGen, and I know Daisy."

I blinked. "You do?"

"I do." He nodded. "She went to grad school with me, believe it or not. I had an enormous crush on her for about a year, before I met her boyfriend, who is basically what you would get if you gave a grizzly bear a shave and a Brooks Brothers suit. But he's a very nice man, and they got married a few years ago. I sent them a toaster for their wedding. I don't know why people always put toasters on their registries, but they do, and I just wanted to buy one for a change." He sounded oddly wistful as he talked about the toaster, like it had somehow become the symbol of a simpler time. We had to survive the tapeworm uprising, because otherwise, who would he buy toasters for?

I was starting to be quietly convinced that the time of toasters was coming to an end. Nathan looked so sad that I didn't want to come right out and say that, so I tried a less dangerous question: "Does he work here too?"

"Who, Daisy's husband? No, he's working overseas. He's in telecommunications, I think, or maybe software engineering— something to do with computers." Nathan shrugged. "Once you take the 'bio' out, I lose interest in technology pretty quickly. It's my shameful little secret."

"It's not that secret." I sat up a bit straighter on the cot. "Where are the dogs?"

"Adam has them. They both like him a lot. Beverly's made

friends with half the staff, and Minnie's been napping on every flat surface she could find. They're going to be fine while we're at the hospital."

I nodded. "Good." Carefully, I swung my legs around to point toward the floor. My feet dangled about a foot above the polished wood. "How are we getting me there?"

"Fang's acquiring an ambulance." Nathan said it with a completely straight face.

"Um, does 'acquiring' mean 'stealing'?"

"I didn't ask. I was afraid Mom would tell me."

"You feared correctly," said Dr. Cale, wheeling herself into the room. "Fang's back, and Daisy has an ID badge for you, Nathan. I've got the admitting paperwork for Sal all prepared, and it links back to one of my less public identities, so if anyone calls to confirm that she's a legitimate patient, I'll be able to confirm. Fishy is altering hospital records as we speak. By the time you get to John Muir, you'll have an insurance trail going all the way back to your first temp job."

"Who's Fishy?" I asked blankly. "Is that a person?"

"His name is Matthew, he's a computer engineer, and he goes by 'Fishy' because when he first came to work for me, I had a Matthew and a Matt already in the office. He proposed using his old gaming handle, and I said it was fine, since it's not profane or otherwise inappropriate. It's easier to explain who's been injured in the explosion when you don't have to keep backing up and clarifying which of the five people with that name you *don't* mean." Dr. Cale's tone was patient, but her hands locked together in her lap, tension showing in the way her fingers interlaced. "Once you get to the hospital, they'll transfer you onto a surgical gurney. Now, Sal, it's important you remember that you shouldn't need to talk much, and it would be better if you didn't, given the circumstances. You would normally be expected to answer questions before you could enter a surgical theater, but we're shortcutting that process as much as possible, and anyone who checks your charts should see that you answered the standard questions before you had to be sedated to prevent seizure."

"Do people really try to have conversations with patients who are in the hospital to have their heads cut open?" I asked blankly.

"They're not going to cut your head *open*, exactly," said Dr. Cale. "Most of the work will be done by lasers and by machines no bigger than the head of a pin. It's not the nanotech that we were promised when I was in school, but I'll take it."

"Mom," said Nathan warningly.

Dr. Cale held up her hand. "Sorry, I'm sorry, I just got distracted for a second there. The actual incision won't even be as bad as that bite on your arm, Sal—which we flushed with saline and stitched up while you were unconscious, by the way. It should heal much faster and cleaner this way. You didn't lose that much blood, thankfully. The problem seems to have been mostly related to the impaired blood flow to your brain."

"Um, thanks," I said, resisting the urge to rub my wrist. "I guess what I meant was, am I really going to have to answer questions? I'm there for *brain surgery*. Even if there's not a lot of cutting going on, you'd think that might mean nobody would ask me things."

"Actually, it may mean someone stops you on the way to the operating theater to make sure you've consented to the operation, and that the operation you say you're having matches the one on your paperwork," said Nathan. The grim note in his voice startled me. I turned to frown at him. He met my eyes and sighed. "You remember how there are some aspects of my job that I don't like to talk about? Well, this is one of them."

"Organ snatching was the big hospital bogeyman twenty, thirty years ago, before we had implants that could secrete anti-rejection drugs," said Dr. Cale. She made the sentence sound almost upbeat, like the thought of someone cracking open her chest and scooping out her lungs was too funny to take seriously. "Now, of course, the rejection risk is lower if you have the right kind of implant readied. There are some people who have been using the anti-rejection implants as a form of preventative medicine—when their hearts finally give out from all their abuse, they already have the medication in place. It's a terrible idea, of course, but I never thought that the implants should have been used for that purpose in the first place. Why—"

"*Mom*." Nathan sounded more impatient this time. His interruption was accompanied by a glance at the old analog clock on the wall, where the second hand was busily ticking off our window of opportunity.

"Sorry," said Dr. Cale again. "As I was getting around to saying, Sal, people today carry expensive pieces of medical equipment with them at all times, and there's a black market for that sort of thing. It's rare, but not unheard-of, for someone to go in for a minor surgical process and wake up with their implant missing—especially if they have one of the extremely tailored varieties. SymboGen has done an excellent job of controlling supply and demand, making sure supply never manages to outstrip demand. Unfortunately, that means that if you need a new insulin source right this minute, or a worm that supplies anti-rejection medication, theft may start looking like your best option."

I stared at her. I couldn't think of anything else to do.

"Thanks for freaking out my girlfriend, Mom, that was swell of you," said Nathan. He stood, offering me his arm. "Come on, Sal. Let's get you to the ambulance."

"I don't have any clothes," I protested. Pushing away the covers had revealed that I was wearing nothing but a plain white hospital gown, the kind that tied in the back and left virtually nothing to the imagination. I didn't mind that much—I've never been shy about nudity—but I had been told over and over that it wasn't socially acceptable to run around half clothed in front of strangers. Fang and Daisy counted.

"We're going to a hospital," said Nathan. "Not having any clothes is a good thing."

"You'll be fine," said Dr. Cale. "Just tell anyone who asks you that you have problems with the veins in your head, and that Dr. Chu and Dr. Lee are going to fix it for you. If they press, tell them you don't know how to pronounce what's wrong. Daisy or Fang can take things from there."

"What's Nathan going to do?"

"Stand there being quiet and trying not to be recognized, while he remembers that I didn't want him to go with you in the first place," said Dr. Cale coolly, shooting a look at Nathan.

Nathan ignored her. "All right, Sal. Time for us to go." He took hold of my IVs, wheeling them along. I was glad he was taking charge of that part of the trip. I would have snarled the tubes on something before we'd gone more than five feet.

Dr. Cale didn't say anything as we walked away. She just watched us go, expression unreadable, hands still knotted white-knuckled in her lap. Then the curtain fell closed again behind us, and she was gone.

I leaned heavily on Nathan's arm as we walked out of the semiprivate room and back into the main bowling alley. Most of the terminals were abandoned at this hour—it had to be almost midnight, and I wondered briefly whether that would make our "borrow a hospital operating theater" plan more dangerous. Probably not. My condition wasn't immediately life-threatening, and if Dr. Cale was sending us to the hospital now, she had to have a reason. Maybe it was just "we'll have more luck finding an empty room at this hour of the night." Whatever her logic, I had made the decision to trust her, and now it was the only thing I could do.

Fang was waiting just outside the interior door, in the dark room where I had lost consciousness before. He looked me thoughtfully up and down, from my bare feet to my tousled hair, and finally said, "You'd look good as a redhead. Consider that for when we're done at the hospital." He had a faint accent, although I couldn't have said from where. "Come on, both of you. Daisy is outside with the ambulance, and we should move before someone stops to make sure that she's all right. This would be like Al Capone being busted for tax evasion." His smile was swift and tight, like he had just made a very funny joke but didn't want to be the first one to laugh.

"You never talked this much at SymboGen," I said. Now that I was up and moving, the sedatives in my IV were starting to hit me harder, making the world seem just a little out of focus, like a movie played on late night TV.

Fang smiled. "I needed to keep a low profile. Not so much an issue, now that I've been extracted." He turned and walked toward the door to the outside, clearly expecting that we would follow. Nathan still had my arm, and Nathan *did* follow, leaving me with no choice but to do the same.

Normally I would have objected to being pulled toward a destination I had little to no say in, but normally I wasn't under the influence of a really impressive assortment of pharmaceuticals. "Your mom is good at drugging people," I said dreamily. My lips felt numb. That was sort of funny. They weren't my lips—I'd stolen them from Sally Mitchell—so why could I feel them? I giggled. That was even funnier; it required the use of so many purloined body parts that I couldn't even name them all.

I was still laughing when we walked out of the bowling alley and into the parking lot. An ambulance was parked right outside the doors, and a short, solid-looking woman with broad shoulders and buzz-cut brown hair shot through with ribbons of gray was waiting for us, one hand resting on a gurney.

"About time you guys got out here," she said, casting a nervous look back at the ambulance. Its doors were standing open, revealing the clean white interior. "We have about an hour before someone notices that the GPS chip on this baby's been jiggered, so let's get a move on, okay?"

"You must be Daisy," I said, swallowing the last of my giggles. "I'm Sal."

"Nice to meet you, Sal," she said genially. "I need you to lie down on this gurney. Do you think you can do that, or do we need to pick you up?"

"I don't know," I said. Honesty seemed like the best policy, at least when it kept me from falling on my face. "I'm a little woozy right now."

"That's to be expected." She looked to my left. "Fang?"

"Yes, ma'am." He moved faster than I expected, somehow scooping me off my feet without tangling my IV cords, and deposited me on my back on the gurney before I could do more than squeak. I blinked bemusedly up at the starry suburban sky, feeling like I'd just been part of an involuntary magic trick.

"All right, Sal, I'm going to strap you down now," said Daisy, all efficiency. "I know you probably won't like that, but it's necessary if we're going to keep you from getting knocked around during the ride. Also, if your balance is anything to go by, those sedatives are going to knock you out any minute now, and you'll be a lot more comfortable this way."

"I don't mind being tied down." My eyelids fluttered shut, seemingly of their own accord, and no amount of coaxing would get them to open again. Maybe they were tired. The rest of me was. "Tight is good. Nathan, you should tie me down sometime. I think I'd like that."

"We'll talk about it later, honey." He sounded oddly strained, like he didn't want to talk about it at all. Oh, well. I could ask him about that after I'd had my nap.

Daisy started strapping me down with quick efficiency. I lay perfectly still, figuring that was the best thing I could do to help—and besides, moving just seemed like so much *work*. I dimly realized that I was drifting off to sleep, but staying awake would have been even more work than moving. I was already gone by the time they started loading my gurney into the back of the ambulance; the shaking and thumping that would inevitably accompany that kind of transfer was entirely absent, not even making a dent in my slow fade into unconsciousness.

It was sort of nice to go down like this, falling slowly instead of flipped off like a switch. I settled deeper into my own body, letting the hot warm dark wash over me, and listened to the quiet sound of drums.

The drive to John Muir could have taken thirty seconds or thirty years: I wouldn't have noticed either way. A few times I was pulled back toward wakefulness by a sudden turn, but those disruptions were brief and quickly obscured by the simple comforts of the dark. My pulse seemed to be radiating from the points of my body, feet, hands, head, and crotch, bouncing in to the center of me and then flowing outward like a wave. It didn't make a sound, exactly, but I thought that if it did, the sound would have been meditative and sweet, so I tried to listen for it, focusing as best I could through the pounding of the drums and the thumping of my heart.

*I don't like this*, thought the small corner of my mind that was still clear and unaffected by whatever Dr. Cale had put in my IV. *I want this to be over now. Can this be over now? Please?*

My silent pleas didn't do any good. The tidal motion of my pulse continued, and the darkness deepened, if anything, becoming absolute.

The gurney was lifted down from the ambulance. The wheels thumped hard against the concrete in the hospital parking lot. That *did* register with me, breaking through the haze for a few seconds. I tried to convince my eyes to open. They didn't listen, remaining stubbornly closed, and the darkness closed in again.

Motion. The gurney was being pushed somewhere, and I was going with it, helpless to do anything to control my destination. *This was what it was like to be just a part of Sally*, said the clear corner of my mind, and the part of me that was aware suddenly flooded with both terror and relief. Terror at the accuracy of that comparison, and relief that this wasn't my existence anymore. This had been me, once, but it wasn't me now. I was just visiting the land of people who could neither move nor speak. I didn't have to live there.

Dr. Cale had said the implants weren't sapient until they integrated with a human brain, that they did all the things they did based on instinct and the desire to control their environments. I was glad for them. Nothing capable of thought should ever be trapped like this, helpless and marooned in the dark. Although I did wonder, just a little, whether she was right: whether they really were just reacting until they latched on to a human mind. Because if they had any shred of intelligence, they were taking over their hosts for two reasons she hadn't considered: because they were desperate, and because they wanted revenge on the creatures that had given them life and then locked them in the dark.

Something moaned. A voice shouted—Nathan—and then the gurney was moving faster, pushed ahead of some unseen attacker. I struggled to control my body, and failed again. Terror lanced through me, cold and sharp as a razor blade. I didn't mind going along with the people around me; they often knew more than I did, and I was all too aware that I was still learning to be a person. But the thought of being helpless with a sleepwalker closing in was enough to make my skin grow tight with involuntary terror.

The gurney moved faster. The sound of moaning dropped away, replaced by silence and the rattle of wheels. My sense of time seemed broken by the isolation. Finally, voices drifted through the gloom, unfamiliar ones first, and then Nathan and a woman I thought might be Daisy answering them in calm, professional tones. The motion had stopped. I tried again to pull myself out of the darkness, and succeeded only in driving myself further down. The voices went away.

Motion, and then no motion, and then motion again. A door slamming. The sound of voices. Pressure receding as the straps that held me to the gurney were undone. Hands moving me to a new surface. Something being fitted over my face, covering my nose and mouth, like the rebreather I used to wear for the gel MRIs. Maybe I was having a gel MRI. Maybe I was back at SymboGen, and everything that had happened since my last checkup was a dream, and when they flushed the tank and let me breathe again, Sherman would be there, and he wouldn't be a tapeworm, and he wouldn't be the enemy, and everything would be all right. I could go home. My parents would be my parents, because I would be their daughter, and they would love me, and everything would be fine forever and ever.

"—start the feed—"

"—all data has been—"

"—careful, the risk of compromising her structural integrity—"

The voices were only ghosts; they came and went without making any impact on the world. The mask that covered my mouth and nose began to emit a strange-smelling gas. I breathed it in anyway. There was nothing else I could have done. So I just breathed, until even the ghosts went away, and there was nothing. I was nothing.

I was alone.

When I was born, I was the size of a pinhead: an egg, expressed from the corpse of a tapeworm that had been intended as nothing but a breeder for more tapeworms. It had been my biological mother, and my biological father had been a syringe full of DNA and modified instructions for my growth. The actual process was probably more complicated than that, but I didn't understand the science: when I tried to hold on to it, I just kept seeing a loop of film from an old cartoon about talking rats.

The rats were normal rats until the scientists came along and poked them with needles. Then they got bigger, and stronger, and smarter, and started wanting more for themselves than cages and captivity. They started wanting to be free.

Dr. Banks and his team could have learned a lot from watching *The Secret of NIMH* a few times. Maybe it would have convinced them that modifying the genetic code of living organisms wasn't as much fun as they thought it was. But Dr. Banks had wanted to make a lot of money, and he'd succeeded, hadn't he? Whatever else my siblings and I might have done, we'd managed to make him a lot of money. He was probably still making money, even as the foundations started giving way beneath him.

Memories flickered against the edges of my mind. Waking up in the hospital with Sally's grieving family standing next to my bed, staring up at the ceiling and not knowing what it was, or who I was, or what I was doing there. I'd been so eager to believe them when they called me their daughter, and why shouldn't I have been? They were offering me an identity. They were offering me a *home*. I'd never had either of those things before. So I took them, because I was still a tapeworm at heart, still greedy for whatever I could grab, and I kept them, and when they stopped being enough for me, I'd gone looking for more.

This was all my fault.

*No, no, no,* I scolded myself, trying to swim through the black that had taken me, trying to pull all the splintered pieces of my mind back together. *It's not your fault. You didn't do this. You didn't make this. You're just here, but you didn't do anything.*

*If you really believe that, why are we having this argument?* The question came from another corner of my mind, and I didn't have an answer for it. So I did what felt right, and let it fall away from me as I sank deeper down into the dark. The dark didn't demand that I do anything but exist. I could do that. I could do that very well.

So I did.

There was only one thing I really remembered from the operation after it was over: light. Bright white light that hurt my eyes so much it was almost like someone had stabbed me, lancing down from above and searing me. But my eyes were closed; the light had to be getting in through some other channel. It didn't make any sense at the time. It was one more mystery piled onto the endless heap of them that had been coming together since I'd seen myself in the MRI film.

It was thinking of the film that gave me my answer. The light hadn't been hurting my eyes, because I didn't have eyes where the light was shining: it had been hurting my body, shining in through the opening in my skull and lancing through the waxy, ghost-white skin of my true, segmented form. I would have screamed if I could have, both from the pain and from the realization. But I had no voice, and so all I could do was sink back into the dark, away from awareness, away from sapience, and wait for it to be over.

Light.

This time, it didn't hurt. It entered through the usual channel, flowing in as I opened my eyes and blinked, slowly, up at the distant ceiling. It probably helped that someone had dimmed the lights in this little room, which was—I turned my head slightly to the left, confirming—which was not at the bowling alley. The walls were painted white, but they were solid, rather than being made from hanging sheets and negative space. A machine was attached to my arm, beeping softly to itself. That was probably what had woken me up. It was the only noise in the room. As I realized that, I also realized that I could barely hear the drums. They had gone from a near-constant pounding in the background of my life to a soft tapping, almost inaudible, the way they used to be. This was how the inside of my head was *supposed* to sound, when I wasn't so stressed out that my heart was racing all the time, and when the blood vessels in my brain weren't threatening to give way at any moment.

"Are you awake, or just moving your head?" Nathan's voice was barely louder than the beeping.

I rolled my head to the right, bringing him into view, and smiled. It was always nice to see my boyfriend first thing upon waking up. It reminded me of how handsome he was, for one thing, and of how much I loved him. No matter how much I enjoyed sleeping, the Nathan in my dreams was never as good as the real thing. "I think I'm awake," I said. My throat was dry, and the words felt scratchy leaving my lips. "Are we still at the hospital?"

He nodded, faint smile fading into a much grimmer expression. He looked like his mother in that moment, and it worried me. Nathan and Dr. Cale had a similar bone structure, but they really only looked alike when they were upset about something. "We are," he said. "How are you feeling?"

"The drums are softer now. That's a good thing, isn't it?" I waited for Nathan to nod before I continued, saying, "Nothing hurts. Am I on a lot of painkillers?"

"Not as many as you might think," he said. "We've already sealed the surgical incisions, and numbed the skin around the wound enough that it shouldn't hurt for an hour or more, by which point the skin bonds should have started taking effect. You'll be completely healed inside of the week."

"So the operation…?"

"Was successful." Nathan raked his hands back through his hair, and for the first time I realized how worried he looked, and how exhausted. As hard as this day had been on me, I'd been dealing with my own medical problems, and I hadn't had a lot of energy to look outward. Nathan had been handling everything I couldn't—including his mother—and he'd done it all without a word of complaint. "Daisy was able to program the surgical tools, and she and Fang sealed the damaged blood vessels so that they won't be at risk of rupture anymore. You still shouldn't take any blows to the head if you can help it, but you're not at any more risk of an aneurism than anyone else."

"Good." I offered him my hand. "Thank you for everything you've done today. I would never have made it this far without you. I mean that. They've probably shut down the trains by now, and you're not supposed to take dogs on the BART anyway, so I'd be stuck in San Francisco, waiting for somebody to eat me." The thought was horrifying. I shuddered exaggeratedly.

Nathan smiled a little. "You'd have found a way. You're a survivor, Sal. You survive things."

"Is there any chance that's going to include surviving pants sometime soon?" I gestured at the blanket that covered my lower body. "This is nice, but we should get back to your mom. She's going to send an extraction team if we don't come home soon. That, or Adam's going to try to walk the dogs all by himself, and we both know *that* isn't going to end well."

Nathan's smile faded. "I can get you some clothes, but we can't leave."

Somehow, that was what I'd been afraid of since I'd woken up to find myself still in the hospital, and not safely back in the bowling alley. "Why not?" Horror washed over me. "Did we get caught? Are we under arrest for misuse of a medical facility?"

"No," said Nathan, shaking his head. "Actually, we sort of got the opposite. No one's asked any questions about whether or not we're allowed to be here, but Daisy and Fang have both been drafted into patient triage. The administration tried to make me go too. I was able to put them off by saying you still needed to be monitored, but I expected them back at any moment with a nurse's aide that they plan to plunk down in a chair and make sure you don't die. They need the hands, and they're not being particularly picky about where those hands come from."

"What *happened*?"

"There's been another outbreak in Lafayette. This one was larger than the one we got caught in before, and the authorities have closed down the hospital in an effort to contain it. They still think quarantine zones help. They could, if we were able to filter out people whose implants are on the verge of going active and could be triggered by pheromone tags, but we don't have that capacity yet, which means the quarantines are doing nothing but causing panic. Of course, try getting the people in charge to admit that." Nathan looked, if anything, even grimmer than he had before. "They've also closed down most of the roads. The official cover story is that there's been a gas leak—that's what we're supposed to tell patients who ask, or reporters who manage to sneak past the cordons. It's a mess out there, Sal. I don't know how we're going to get out of this building."

"You'll think of something," I said, and then, because that didn't seem quite right, I amended to "We'll think of something. This is just more survival, right? We're good at surviving. We can get out of this."

"The ambulances are locked down."

I frowned. "That's bad," I agreed. "But do we need an ambulance? I mean, I was on a gurney last time, because you needed me to be sedated, and because it made things more believable, but couldn't we take a taxi or...or steal a car or something?"

Nathan paused, his eyes widening slowly as he absorbed my question. "There's no one watching the parking lot at this point," he said, after a long pause for thought. "All the available security has been pulled inside, to stop people who shouldn't be here from getting in, and to prevent patients from escaping. They haven't cracked down on the staff yet, and the security reinforcements are still an hour or so out."

"Am I right to think that 'yet' is the important word there?" I asked.

"Yes." Nathan stood. "I'll be right back with some clothes, and with Fang and Daisy. We need to get out of here."

I had never been so relieved to watch my boyfriend walk away from me. The danger in my head had been repaired, my wounds had been patched up, and we were getting out of here.

Things were finally starting to go our way.

*This—all of this—is all my fault.*

*I can try to put a pretty face on it, and better, I can try to blame it all on Steven (and why shouldn't I blame it all on Steven? The project was his idea, the implementation happened after I left the company, I am not innocent, but I don't see why I should burn for his hubris). And it doesn't matter, because I'll always know that he couldn't have done any of this without me. He had the science. He had the ambition. What he lacked was . . . well, for lack of a better word, what he lacked was poetry. He could make the genes move. He couldn't make them sing.*

*I gave him that. I gave him what he needed to remake the world in his own image, and when I decided that I didn't like what he was doing, I didn't stay and stop him. I took my toys and I went home. Now my daughter is missing. Now the girl who should have been my daughter is lost. Now my son hates me.*

*This is all my fault, and I don't know how to fix it, and I don't know if I can.*

—FROM THE JOURNAL OF DR. SHANTI CALE,
SEPTEMBER 21, 2027

*Hello, Internet!*

*So as you've probably heard by now, they're starting to lock down big portions of the Bay Area. Who are THEY? That's the big question of the hour, because it seems that NOBODY KNOWS. Yes! Bridges are being closed, and freeways are being spun off into detours that don't go anywhere, and NOBODY KNOWS WHO'S DOING IT.*

*I'm taking my camera and heading for the Pittsburg hills. My sources say that there's a police cordon forming on Willow Pass Road, and there's no better place for me to find out the TRUTH about what's going on than by going straight to the source. Can you say CONSPIRACY? I knew you could!*

*Remember, loyal followers, if I do not return, the TRUTH is OUT THERE, and the LIES are getting STRONGER all the time.*

—FROM THE BLOG OF BRIAN "TRUTHSEEKER099" VIBBER, POSTED SEPTEMBER 21, 2027. NO FURTHER POSTS WERE MADE UNDER THIS USER NAME

## Chapter 6
## SEPTEMBER 2027

I waited anxious and alone in my purloined hospital room, jumping at every little sound and scuffle from the hall outside. If Nathan was right about my super-sleepwalker pheromones attracting sleepwalkers to me, there was every chance that a stray patient could stumble through the door at any moment, hands outstretched and mouth hungry for a piece of my flesh. It wasn't the sort of thought that made me inclined to go exploring, even if I was having trouble sitting in the room alone.

What if Nathan couldn't find me clothes? What if Daisy and Fang were so busy with the sudden influx of patients that they couldn't get away, and we had to leave them? Dr. Cale was going to stop letting us borrow her people if we kept on not bringing them back.

The doorknob turned. I tensed, hunching down in the bed and trying to look like I was asleep. A fully turned sleepwalker wouldn't be able to work the door, but a doctor would, and that would be just as bad. What if they decided that I didn't need a private room, and moved me out to the hall? I'd have nothing to protect me then.

I was getting awfully tired of the words "what if."

The door swung open, and I closed my eyes, playing dead. Footsteps approached me and Nathan said, "Sal, it's me. I found you some clothes, and Daisy's getting Fang out of the ER, but we need to hurry. We don't have much time."

There was a degree of urgency in his voice that was out of proportion with the trouble that we were in—something I wouldn't have thought possible until I heard it. I opened my eyes and sat up, staring at him. "What's going on?"

"I overheard two of the doctors who actually work here talking in the hall. The CDC is en route to lock this place down for good, and that means that USAMRIID can't be too far behind. Mom's going to get the news soon, if she hasn't already."

My eyes got even wider. "You think she's going to move the lab?"

"I think she'll have to. We're important to her, but we're not more important than the entire human race." He gestured to the clothes on the foot of my bed: jeans, a heavy sweater, a lab coat in what looked like my size, and a pair of worn-out white canvas shoes that would mostly fit. "Get dressed, and let's go."

I was still wobbly—which was only fair, since I'd suffered major blood loss and had *brain surgery* all in the same day—and getting the clothing on was a little harder than it should have been. It felt eerily like my first days after waking up, when I'd been stranded in a body that had muscle memory and nothing else, making the easy things that everyone around me took for granted seem like minor miracles. Nathan helped me with the sweater, twisting it around until I could find the hole for my head, but I did the rest by myself while he watched the door, waiting for someone to burst in on us.

The door was still closed when I finished tying my shoes and shrugging on the lab coat. Nathan tossed me an elastic band. I used it to pull my hair back in a ponytail, concealing the bandages from my operation. "How do I look?" I asked, spreading my arms a little to give him the full effect.

"Like you belong here," he said, and leaned in and kissed me—quickly, but with an intensity that spoke to his fear, and to our mutual, growing conviction that we weren't going to make it out of here. I kissed him back, allowing the momentary closeness to distract from my terror. It was going to be okay. We were going to find a way to make this okay, and I was going to spend the rest of my life kissing Nathan, although preferably not in besieged hospital rooms.

The door swung open. Nathan and I pulled away from each other, our eyes going wide and our backs going tight as we prepared to flee. Fang looked at us disdainfully, tilting his chin up just enough to let him stare at us down the length of his nose. It was a surprisingly effective expression.

"Daisy's already waiting for us in the parking lot, so if you two lovebirds are done celebrating the fact that we've made it this far, we'd like to make it the rest of the way," he said mildly. "Come on."

"Sorry," I mumbled, cheeks flaring red, and hurried out of the room. Nathan followed after me, and we plunged into the chaos of the hospital.

I'd believed myself prepared for anything, based on Nathan's description and my own knowledge of what usually happened during a sleepwalker outbreak. I hadn't been prepared at all.

There were bodies everywhere we looked. Some were on stretchers or strapped to gurneys like the one they'd used to bring me from Dr. Cale's. Others sat propped against the walls, hands clasped over obvious injuries and shocked expressions on their faces. Those were actually the ones that bothered me the least. They were clearly upset about what had happened to them. Their wounds hurt. They could feel pain, and they were connected enough to their bodies to understand what that meant, to know that they needed to stop what they were doing and have it taken care of. Those people might be infected—the majority of them probably had implants, considering SymboGen's saturation of the market—but they weren't sleepwalkers yet.

The ones that worried me were the ones who weren't clutching themselves. The ones who leaned against walls, staring into nothingness with the characteristically dead eyes of someone whose human mind has shut off, but whose tapeworm mind has not yet started supplying fresh instructions. The ones who seemed to have fallen asleep, but whose chests were still moving smoothly up and down, marking their continued life even as the worms within them worked their way toward a stronger integration. I stuck close to Nathan, trying not to look at those people. It was like I was afraid that eye contact was all it would take to make them come after me.

The air smelled like blood and vomit and human waste, a horrible mixture of urine, feces, and other things that I didn't want to put a name to. People cried and screamed and shouted profanities, and that was all good, yes, that was all welcome, because those cries were *human*. The people who made them were still *people*.

The steady undercurrent of moaning was a lot less welcome.

Fang wove his way through the crowd like a man who'd spent most of his life moving in tight spaces, and Nathan and I followed him, taking advantage of the narrow openings he created in the brief seconds before they could close again. We were like a surgical laser: we didn't wound the crowd, but we sliced it open and let it heal behind us, leaving no trace, creating no scar.

One of the dead-eyed men turned his head as we walked past, tracking my movement. I whimpered a little and walked faster, nearly stepping on Fang's heels in my hurry to get out of range. If these people were far enough along to start picking up on my pheromones, we were in trouble. Real trouble, the kind that no clever plan or stolen car was going to get us out of.

Nathan produced a clipboard from somewhere, probably taking it off one of the hooks on the wall. He handed it to me, motioning that I should start consulting it. I ducked my head and pretended to do just that, watching as the letters seemed to shift and blur around the page. Sally wasn't dyslexic before I chewed myself a place in her brain. Sorry, Sally. On the plus side for her, she didn't have to live with the consequences of what I'd done, and I did.

*Next time I'll be more careful which part of the brain I eat*, I thought, and barely suppressed an inappropriate giggle. The stress was getting to me. I was expecting to be attacked at any second, or stopped by hospital administration when one of them realized that no matter what I was wearing, I didn't work there. None of us did.

A few of the people in lab coats looked up as we passed, but Fang moved with enough purpose for ten people, and I had a clipboard; as long as Nathan and I stayed close to him, we looked like a strange little research group, going somewhere important to do something essential. It was all props and posing. Maybe that was enough.

It wasn't until we reached the doors that one of the actual doctors seemed to realize where we were going. He turned away from the patient he'd been examining, fear flashing across his face, and raised a hand in a beseeching gesture. "Wait!" he cried. "Don't go out there!"

It was too late. Fang had already hit the doors, never breaking his stride, and we were supposed to be his little research team. We followed him, only to stop dead as he ran out of room to move. It wasn't that the lobby wasn't large—it was enormous, as befitted a medical center of this size. It was that the lobby was even worse than the halls, so full that there was barely room to take a step.

People had spilled over from the ER and the urgent care, clogging the couches and chairs until no more bodies could be packed onto them. After that, they'd started sitting on the floor. They milled, almost mindlessly, even though most of them still had the bright-eyed awareness that meant a conscious mind was in control. Most—not all. I saw a young woman with a toddler in her arms, the baby's mouth hanging slack, the baby's eyes filled with the nothingness that meant that there was a tapeworm in the process of taking over that tiny body. Nathan followed my gaze and grimaced.

"Intestinal Bodyguards are rated for infants eighteen months and older," he murmured. "I always thought that was a terrible idea. Now I see that I was more right than I ever knew."

"Disgusting," murmured Fang, and continued toward the exit... or tried to. A sudden living wall of humanity appeared in front of him, hands outstretched, mouths moving in a noisy chorus. It wasn't sleepwalkers. That would almost have been easier to handle. Sleepwalkers were simple, wanting only to grab and hold and feed. No, this was something far worse, and infinitely more complex:

This was the living.

"We've been here for an hour! When is someone going to see us?"

"Where are the doctors?"

"Are you doctors?"

"Please, Kim won't wake up, I don't know what to do."

"Please!"

Their voices blended together into an unearthly chorus of words—"seizure" and "won't wake up" and "help us." That was said more than anything else: "help us." I quailed back against Nathan, and he put a hand on my shoulder, glaring at the people who were reaching for me. It didn't help much. They kept coming.

"We're not doctors!" I shouted. "We can't help you!"

That didn't do any good either. Anyone in a lab coat was better than nothing. Hands grabbed for my sleeves, buffeting me deeper into Nathan's arms. The drums were back, but softer, pounding the way that they used to before the arteries in my head had begun to give way. I guess that was a small blessing. I'd lived long enough to be torn apart by the crowd.

And then the doors at the far end of the lobby banged open and the sleepwalkers surged inside, their arms as outstretched as their unturned kin, but grasping with terrible purpose. They were moaning, an eerie, discordant sound that was quickly answered from the halls behind us. People turned, crying out in dismay, and forgot to grab for us in favor of scrambling away from the tide now flowing through those open doors. There was nowhere for them to go. The mother with the sleepwalker baby was bowled over by her fellows as they fled, and she didn't get up again. Neither did her baby. They weren't the only ones to be trampled in that first panicked rush: anyone who couldn't get up fast enough, who couldn't get out of the way, was at risk of being crushed to death.

"Come on," commanded Fang, grabbing my wrist and dragging me with him as he bolted in the exact direction that I did *not* want to go: toward the exit. Nathan chased after us, apparently deciding that it was better for all of us to die together than it was for any of us to die alone. I disagreed—I thought it was better if none of us had to die at all—but I was too busy running to argue.

A row of heavy potted plants created a space maybe three feet wide between the wall and the doors. Fang ran into that space, dragging me with him, and dropped my hand. I stared at him, starting to open my mouth and demand to know what was going on. He shook his head, motioning for me to be quiet, and pointed to the plants. I frowned. He gestured to the plants again, more urgently this time, like there was some secret he wanted me to catch on to.

My frown deepened. I looked over my shoulder to Nathan, who seemed as lost as I felt. That was something, anyway: I wasn't the only one who had no idea what was going on. I turned and peered through the broad leaves of the plants, watching the sleepwalkers pouring into the lobby. That was when I finally realized what Fang was trying to show us.

The sleepwalkers weren't smart. They could be destructive if they were frustrated or wanted to get somewhere, and they were definitely dangerous at close range, but they weren't *smart*. Something in the interface between worm and human was too broken to allow them to be anything approaching *smart*. They would have come after us if they'd known that we existed—we were too close to ignore, and too defenseless to pass up—but they hunted primarily by sight, and the plants were blocking us from view. My pheromones would still have been an issue under normal circumstances. With this many people in a confined space, some of them with implants of their own that were starting to emit confused pheromone trails, the jumble of scents and instructions must have been throwing the sleepwalkers off. The plants were just one more layer, buying us a little time to let the crowd pass us by.

Fang crouched down, watching them through the space between the leaves. He was perfectly still in that moment, like he could have been a sleepwalker himself. Very softly, he said, "As soon as there's a break, we're going to run. Don't stop. Don't look back. If you're afraid you've lost the rest of the group, *keep going.* Daisy is straight ahead of us in the parking lot, in the fifth row of cars. She nicked the keys for a red Corolla. If you don't see her, keep running and test the doors of the cars you pass. See if you can find something that isn't locked and shut yourself inside. We *will* come back for you."

The moans of the sleepwalkers almost obscured his speech, but the gist of it got through, enough to make my stomach clench. I looked over my shoulder at Nathan. He looked even unhappier than I felt, and I realized that a lot of our relationship—not always, maybe, but ever since I'd first called his mother and said I was willing to go through the broken doors—was based on him protecting me. He couldn't protect me now, and it was making him uncomfortable. The thought of him needing to protect me made me uncomfortable, but in a different way. I didn't want to be coddled and kept like a specimen in a jar. I'd already had that life. I wanted something bigger and less confined.

And this wasn't the time to think about that. I turned back to the row of ornamental plants, watching as the last stragglers of the sleepwalker mob shambled into the hospital lobby. The screams were starting to taper off. I was willing to bet it wasn't because the screamers had decided that the sleepwalkers weren't all that big of a deal.

"*Now*," hissed Fang, and shoved through the plants, knocking two of them over and creating a channel for me and Nathan to pass through. True to his word, Fang didn't look back, and so neither did I. I just ran.

The sleepwalkers weren't that focused. I could see them turning as I ran past, their blank faces betraying no curiosity or confusion. Only their failure to grab and hold us gave their bewilderment away. They couldn't react quickly to changes in their environment, and we could: that was our big advantage over them. We could run away and they didn't know how to follow. They just knew that something was happening, and that they wanted to devour it, because they wanted to devour everything.

Nathan pulled up even with me, trying to grab for my hand. I shook my head and kept my hands close to my body, focusing on the act of running. I understood what he was offering, and I appreciated it more than I could have possibly said, but I couldn't let him pull me along. If we were both taken because he slowed enough to help me, what good would that do?

Ahead of us, Fang began to slow. We caught up to him, and I finally glanced back, seeing the sleepwalkers that had made the decision to turn as they shambled after us. There weren't many of them yet, but there would be soon. My pheromones would see to that.

So there was danger coming from behind. I turned back to the front, and gasped. I couldn't stop myself.

The red Corolla was there, exactly as Fang had described it, and Daisy was inside. Whatever mechanism she had used to open the doors—stolen keys or jimmied locks—didn't matter nearly as much as the small horde of sleepwalkers surrounding her. They clawed at the windows and slapped the glass, and if they were anything like every other sleepwalker in the world, they'd break through soon. She was trapped. They'd devour her, and then they'd go looking for something else to eat. Something else like us.

Fang muttered something in a language I didn't understand. That didn't matter. There aren't any real language barriers when it comes to profanity. He looked at Daisy in the little red car like she represented the end of the world, and I realized what I had to do. I didn't want to do it. Nathan wasn't going to like it. I didn't see any other choice.

It only took me a few seconds to shed my lab coat. The sweater that had given me so much trouble going on was just as much trouble coming off: it snagged on my ponytail, forcing me to dance in place in order to get it off. That was what finally caught Nathan's attention. He turned, eyes widening behind his glasses as he saw what I was doing.

"Sal?" He sounded bemused. That was all right. Me stripping in a hospital parking lot was pretty weird. "What's going on?"

"I'm exposing as much skin as I can," I said, finally yanking the sweater all the way off. I dropped it on the ground. It was never going to find its way back to its original owner, and I felt bad about that, but it was for the greater good. "Pheromones come through skin, right? So exposing more skin should mean more pheromones."

"Yes, but..."

"Fang?"

"Yes?" Fang looked at me, his expression of resigned despair lightening a little as he took in my bare arms and the sweaty V of exposed skin above my hospital gown. I think he realized what I was going to do. He'd been with Dr. Cale for a long time. He had to have dealt with situations like this, or at least in the same family.

"Make sure he runs." The sentence came out calmer than I expected. I leaned up, kissing Nathan on the cheek before he could react, and then I bolted toward the car, waving my arms in the air and shouting. "Hey! Hey, sleepwalkers, hey! Hey, it's your cousin! Sal! I'm right here and I think I'm *better* than you and *what are you going to do about it, huh*?"

My exact words probably didn't matter, since the sleepwalkers were too far gone to understand what I was saying, but they understood that someone was yelling nearby, and as they turned and their nostrils started to flare, they understood that the someone smelled subtly appealing. They understood that they *wanted* me, more than anything else in the world, they *wanted* me. That *wanting* might have been the first thing they really understood since they'd eaten their way into the brains of their human hosts, and once they'd come to understand it, they couldn't deny it. It was too powerful. One by one, the sleepwalkers that had been surrounding the car pulled away, deserting their captive prize in favor of shambling after me.

They didn't run, thankfully; they weren't coordinated enough for that yet, and they might never be. But they shambled with remarkable speed, and many of them were taller than me, which meant that for some of them, each of their unsteady steps was the equivalent of two of mine. So I kept running, and they kept following, their numbers growing as more sleepwalkers shambled over from the direction of the hospital, or from the back of the parking lot.

I heard Nathan shout something behind me—a prayer, a plea, it didn't matter, because there was a horde between me and him, and I had to keep going. If I stopped, they'd catch me, and they'd rend me limb from limb in their eagerness to have me. I was the perfect meal, the ultimate prize, and the only consolation I had was that they'd probably hurt each other getting to me.

*I'm sorry*, I thought, as I ran. *I'm sorry, I'm so sorry, but you wouldn't even have been here if it weren't for me. You should never have left the lab. I've been putting you in danger over and over again, and that means I have to get you out of it at least once. I have to be the one who saves you.* That seemed so important, and it was enough to keep me moving. He'd be sad if he lost me. He'd still be able to help his mother save the world.

An engine roared to life in the parking lot behind me. Tires squealed against pavement, and hope rose in my throat like bile, burning everything it touched. Fang and Nathan had managed to reach the car. They were in the car, they were safe, and they were going to get out of here. They were going to back to the lab, and everything was going to be all right.

Then I realized that the screeching tires were getting closer, and the burning feeling of hope intensified, becoming even more painful than my increasingly strained breath. They were coming to *get* me. They were in the car, and they were on their way, and all I had to do was keep it together long enough for them to somehow open a door and pull me in. I'd probably have a panic attack after a stunt like that, but under the circumstances, that was okay. I was going to be okay. We were all going to be okay. We were—

Lights came on directly ahead, blinding me. I squeaked and kept running, all too aware of what would happen if I stopped while the sleepwalkers were this close on my tail. I was still running when the dart slammed into my chest, its feathered end sticking out like some sort of carnival game—pin the sedative on the chimera.

I kept running. I ran for as long as I could, and then the black spots on the edges of my vision were back, and my knees gave out under my weight, dumping me to the pavement. I clawed for consciousness, tired of letting it go, but my fingers found no purchase, and my last thought as I toppled down into the dark was that I had come to the hospital to make this stop happening.

*This isn't fair*, I thought, and the world went black, and there was nothing.

I was down in the dark, in the hot warm dark where nothing hurt and nothing could touch me and nothing mattered but existing. I recognized the dream for the memory that it was now, and I let myself drift, wondering only abstractly how I could remember something that had happened before I had a mind to remember with.

*You always had a mind,* I scolded myself. *You didn't think like a human, but you thought. Beverly thinks. Minnie thinks. Everything with a brain can think. You just had smaller thoughts.*

Small thoughts, hot thoughts, hot warm thoughts of redness and blackness and peace. It was strange to me, here in this place, that any of us would have chosen to leave it voluntarily. Being a human was *hard*. It was sharp and cold and filled with choices that had no good outcomes, just varying shades and shapes of badness. No matter what you chose, you were choosing wrong for someone. Better to stay down in the dark, where there were no choices and no challenges, just food and warmth and the contentment of simplicity.

But there was no Nathan either, was there? No love, no kisses, no anger born from the hard edges of two people rubbing against each other. There were no chances to change down there in the dark. There were no chances to grow. I'd enjoyed those parts of being human, and a lot of the parts that came with having a body. If I stayed down here in the dark, I wouldn't get to enjoy those things anymore.

*You'll have to go back, then*, I thought sadly, and I didn't know whether I was talking to myself or to something outside myself, and it didn't really matter, because I was right either way.

I opened my eyes.

"We've got movement!" shouted a voice I didn't recognize. A woman in wire-framed glasses leaned over me, producing a small flashlight from the pocket of her lab coat and shining it into my eyes. I whimpered and screwed them shut again. Her voice followed a moment later, now announcing jubilantly, "Movement *and* pupil dilation! I think she's okay."

I cracked my left eye cautiously open. The woman was still there, but she was facing away from me, giving me a good look at her profile. She was pale-skinned, with hair that was either bleached or the palest blonde I had ever seen, and her lab coat...

Her lab coat had the USAMRIID logo on the sleeve. My mouth went dry and my stomach went tight, the drums suddenly pounding in my ears as I realized where the lights and tranquilizer dart had come from. I tried to sit up, and discovered that I couldn't. As with the gurney from before, I was strapped to the surface that I was on top of. I opened both my eyes, making another attempt. Still nothing, and this time the motion attracted the woman's attention. She turned to face me, plastering a smile so patently fake that it was almost painful across her face.

"Hello, Sally," she said, speaking slowly and clearly. "My name is Dr. Crystal Huff. I was with the team that extracted you from the hospital. You may feel a little disoriented. That's perfectly normal, and does not indicate infection. You have been checked thoroughly, and I am glad to be able to tell you that you're not sick. Do you understand me, Sally? Nod if you understand me." She stopped, smiling brightly down at me. It was like she was trying to make herself understood by a small child who didn't understand English, and if my hands hadn't been strapped down, I would probably have hit her.

My mouth was too dry to let me form words. I swallowed hard, trying to convince my salivary glands to do their job. Finally, after several seconds of silence and swallowing, I managed to croak, "Why am I strapped to this table?" *How do you know who I am?* I had still been wearing the ID bracelet with the fake name Dr. Cale used to get me into the hospital.

"It's not a table, it's a cot, but apart from that, I am very pleased by the recovery it took for you to recognize that you were strapped down," said Dr. Huff, sounding pleased. "You're strapped down for your own safety. We had to move you while you were unconscious, and we didn't want you waking up with any injuries, now, did we? It took a lot of work for us to find you. We don't want you getting hurt."

I stared at her. Finally, when I was sure that I wouldn't yell, I tried again. "Why am I strapped to this cot? I'm awake now. You know I'm awake now. Shouldn't you be letting me up? I want to get up."

Dr. Huff's artificial smile dropped away. "Sally, I'm sorry, but you don't seem to fully understand the situation. Now maybe that's my fault—maybe I didn't make myself clear enough when you first woke up—but we didn't expect you to regain consciousness quite this quickly. Everyone reacts differently to the sedatives we're using. You should have been out for at least another thirty minutes. So I'm very sorry that I was not prepared for you to start questioning me."

"You're not ready to start answering me either, I guess, because you're not," I said, giving another experimental tug against the straps. "Can you let me up? You just said that I wasn't sick. I want to get up." It was a funny twist of the infection: a sleepwalker would show parasitic "tendrils" throughout their bodies, lines drawn and held by the toxoplasmosis DNA that had been used to help the implants integrate with the human body. A chimera—like Adam, like me—wouldn't show any of those traces. Our implants had relocated completely to our brains, abandoning the parts of themselves that would normally have been used to latch on to the body. A recent chimera might have shown up on an infection sweep, but not one that had been given the time to finish integration.

They could test and test, and they'd find the violent ones, the ones who were incapable of concealing themselves, and the ones who were too deep in comas to pose a threat. But they'd never find the ones like me without doing MRIs and lumbar punctures. They'd never find the ones who'd learned how to make themselves look human.

"No, I can't," said Dr. Huff. "You're being relocated to a secure facility, and I'm afraid that patients can't be allowed to move freely around the transport."

I blinked at her. I hadn't realized we were moving, and no matter how much I tried to focus, I couldn't detect any motion.

She must have seen my confusion, because she said, "We're waiting for the trucks to arrive. It will be easier to keep the afflicted and the unafflicted separate if everyone remains in their assigned place."

"What?" I didn't know which part of that upset me the most. I strained against the straps that held me down again. "No, no, you can't put me with people who've started going sleepwalker. I don't even want to be in a carrier with them. You don't understand how easy it is for them to escape. You don't understand—"

"We have taken every precaution," she said crisply. "Now if you'll excuse me, I have other patients to attend to." She straightened up, her expression going blank and cold, and stalked out of my field of vision.

Sleepwalkers had cold, dead eyes, but they weren't thinking creatures: they hurt you because they didn't know how to do anything else, not because they harbored any malice or desire to harm the people around them. Dr. Huff...her eyes were the eyes of a sapient being, and when she hurt me—and I had every confidence that it was a "when," not an "if," given the circumstances that I had found myself in—it would be the full understanding of what she was doing. Dr. Banks had eyes like that. Dr. Banks never hurt me when he wasn't trying to.

I relaxed as much as I could, trying to find signs of slack in the straps. There didn't seem to be any: they were drawn as tight as they could possibly have been without hurting me, and even breathing all the way out and holding my breath did nothing to let me move. I could squirm down a few inches, and that was all. I was trapped.

The drums were starting to pound in my ears, a sure sign that I was panicking. I couldn't tell whether they were louder than they should have been, and that just made them pound faster. Was it safe for me to experience this much excitement right after surgery? Was I going to have an aneurism on this cot and die never knowing what had happened to my friends?

No. No, I was not. I forced myself to breathe slowly, trying to bring my heart rate back down to something less alarming. Nathan and the others had reached the car: I knew that from the sounds of tires I'd heard behind me in the parking lot. They wouldn't have been vulnerable the same way that I had been. They got away. They had to have gotten away. They would go back to Dr. Cale and tell her that USAMRIID had me, and she...

She would say she was very sorry, and that it sucked to lose such a valuable research subject. And then she would tell them to start packing, because if USAMRIID was in the area, she could no longer stay there. None of us was more impor-tant than the entire human race. Not one. It didn't matter how much Nathan disagreed. Dr. Cale would *make* him go along with her. She was the one with the paid security, after all. All Nathan had was a pair of dogs. He didn't even have the Prius anymore.

I closed my eyes. It was better than staring at the distant ceil-ing, waiting for the moment when someone would come and load me onto a transport. Maybe they'd put me in a room with a bunch of people who didn't know what was going on, and I'd be able to escape. Or maybe they'd put me in with the sleep-walkers, and I'd wind up ripped to pieces before I had a chance to defend myself.

*This can't be how it ends,* I thought. *This isn't fair.*

Fair didn't seem to be playing any part in things.

Footsteps approached from my right. I opened my eyes and rolled my head in that direction, calling, "Hello? My name is Sal Mitchell. I'm not sick. Can you unstrap me, please?" It was a long shot, especially considering that the stranger in the dark could easily have been Dr. Huff, but it was better than lying here, waiting to be moved.

"Is that your legal name?" asked a cool male voice that I didn't recognize—not quite—although there was something halfway familiar about it. Like Fang. Whoever this was, I knew him in some other context.

"Not quite," I admitted. "My legal name is Sally Rae Mitchell." That was the name my body's parents gave to it at birth, and the original Sally had never wanted to change it. The "Rae" was after some aunt I'd never met. Maybe changing my name legally to just plain "Sal" would be the honest thing to do, but I was starting to suspect it was already too late for that. We were standing on the razor edge of a national emergency. The department that handled name changes probably wasn't going to be taking appointments for a while.

"Subject is confused about her identity," said the man, his words accompanied by the sound of fingertips drubbing softly against a touchscreen.

"What? No! I'm not confused! I know who I am, I just never use the name 'Sally.' I don't like it. It's—" I was going to say "not me," but I caught myself at the last second, twisting the rest of the sentence into "—it doesn't suit me very well. I like 'Sal' better, so that's what I always call myself. I'm not confused, I swear."

"Subject is defensive," said the man, accompanying his words with more taps.

"I'm not defensive!" I protested. "You try giving calm answers when you're strapped to a table and nobody's willing to tell you what's going on! It's not that easy. I don't think you could do it." Inspiration struck. "Unless you *do* think you could do it. Let's trade places. You come strap yourself down and I'll ask you questions, and we'll see how calm you sound."

The man chuckled. "Oh, pet. You always did like your little jokes, didn't you?"

I froze.

The man with the touchscreen stepped out of the shadows and into my field of vision. He was tall and gangly, with limbs that seemed a little too long for his body, yet nonetheless moved with artful grace, like he had spent his time learning exactly how to present himself to best advantage. The heavy artificial tan he'd worked so hard to cultivate was gone, as were the neatly tailored clothes; he was wearing off-the-rack tan slacks and a blue button-down shirt under a lab coat with the USAM-RIID logo on the breast. He'd even added black-framed glasses to his ensemble, completing the illusion that he belonged here. His hair was still cut in the latest style, brown with bleached tips and a spiky outline that could only be achieved through pomade and care, but it seemed less natural and more like an affectation when set against the rest of him. Whatever game he was playing, he had taken the time and put in the effort to play it well.

Sherman Lewis smiled at me coolly. I stared at him, unsure of what else I could do. He had been my handler for years, taking care of moving me around the building and keeping me out of trouble during my periodic visits to SymboGen. He had also been a chimera the whole time, another product of Dr. Cale's lab. He was like Adam and Tansy, surgically created, rather than being natural like me, and the last time I'd seen him, he'd been in the basement at SymboGen, and I'd been running for my life.

"This is a fun situation, don't you think? I always hoped you'd see the light and leave your stupid boyfriend so that you and I could get to know each other better, but I'll admit, I never thought I'd convince you to try bondage." Sherman leaned over me, invading the fragile bubble of my personal space.

"Your accent's gone." It was a stupid thing to say. I couldn't think of anything better, and besides, it seemed important. Sherman had always had a thick British accent, even though he came from a California lab. That was why I hadn't recognized his voice sooner, not until he called me "pet": without the accent, he didn't really sound like himself.

"Oh, you mean this?" Sherman's voice was suddenly plummy and thick again, full of subtly twisted vowels and lilting consonants. "I can suppress it if I need to, like when I'm working a different undercover identity. Never did figure out why I sounded British. Just woke up this way. Mom always said it was a sign that something interesting had happened during my integration, but she couldn't say precisely what it was, and she had other things to worry about most of the time. Keeping Tansy out of trouble, keeping Adam from seeing anything that might upset his precious sensibilities—and you, of course. She would probably have come looking for me before too much longer, if you hadn't decided that you were tired of living in this pretty little body's gut, and moved on up to the big leagues."

He put his touchscreen down on my stomach, where the weight of it was an unpleasant reminder that I was trapped. Leaning forward, he traced a finger along my clavicle and smiled. I squirmed. That just made him smile more.

"You really did get lucky. You're nicely symmetrical, and you've got a good head on your shoulders. Don't laugh. The shape of the skull probably makes a large difference in the integration."

I glared at him. "I nearly died because of that integration. No thanks to you."

"Ah, is that what you were doing at the hospital? I had wondered what would possibly have possessed you to go someplace so patently foolish." Sherman put his hand on the side of my face, trying to turn my head to the side. I struggled against him, and he scowled. "Be still, Sal. I'm not going to hurt you. Whether you believe me or not, I want you on my side, and damaging you now would just convince you never to work with me. I want to check your bandages."

"How do you know I have bandages?" I demanded.

"You just as good as told me you'd gone to the hospital to have those faulty arteries in your head repaired, and you're asking how I know you've got bandages on? Learn to remember what you said thirty seconds ago, will you? It'll make a big difference in how the rest of this day goes. Now stop fighting me, or I'll tell Dr. Huff you need to be sedated again for your own safety."

I stopped fighting.

Sherman rolled my head to the side, his long, clever fingers probing down through my hair until they found the bandage concealed there. "It's caught on the small hairs—they should have shaved your neck before they cut you open, the barbarians. Bite your tongue, Sal, this is going to hurt a bit, and I can't have you making a sound." That was all the warning he gave before he pulled the bandage loose. It took what felt like half the hair on my head with it, even though I knew that was anatomically impossible. I squeaked but managed not to shout; Sherman's warning had been sufficient.

His fingers resumed probing almost instantly, not even waiting for the pain to fade. I stared into the dark, eyes watering, and wondered what he was looking for.

I didn't have to wonder for long. "There's a little mark, and anyone doing a truly detailed inspection would be able to tell you'd had surgery recently, but as long as you don't tell anyone to look more closely, you should be all right." Sherman pulled his hand out of my hair almost reluctantly, pausing at the last moment to swipe his fingers across my cheek. "I'm glad that little problem's been fixed."

"You knew, and you didn't make them put me back together," I said sullenly, still staring off into the darkness. I didn't want to look at him. He was a traitor and a turncoat, and worst of all, he was a liar. He'd known my life was in danger, and he'd said nothing. I didn't matter to him.

"Dr. Banks wouldn't let me." He pulled his hand away. "Chave and I both suggested it, on multiple occasions, under the guise of monitoring your well-being. That was part of our job, after all, so we thought we could get away with it. He eventually told us both to stop, and said that we'd be fired if we didn't. He wanted you to have that inbuilt weakness, and it's not that easy to perform surgery on someone whose medical power of attorney is controlled by someone else. Plus, any surgeon we could have found who was willing to perform the operation would have discovered your…little condition, and then I would have had to kill them. I'm not fond of killing people, Sal."

"What?" I finally rolled my head back to its original place, frowning up at him. "You were talking about creating a world without humans. You're totally okay with killing people."

"One," he said, holding up a long finger, "that doesn't mean I *like* it. And two, you have perhaps made some mistaken assumptions about my desire for a world without humans. I'm not going to wipe out the species. That would be silly, and wasteful, and nigh impossible."

I frowned. "Then what do you want to do?"

He smiled. That expression was the same as it had always been, and for just a second, it was like I was looking back through time to a moment when I almost understood things. "I want to round them up and put them in breeding camps, at least until we have enough stable chimera to breed our own babies," he said. That broke the illusion. Instantly. "Integration is easier with younger subjects. We'll be able to introduce implant to infant, tapeworm to toddler, and slide ourselves right into their skins without any need for trauma on any side. Imagine, Sal. There won't be any displacement—you're not kicking out the original owner if they never had a chance to develop. There won't be the sort of dysphoria you and I and the others like us have had to live with, because we'll grow with our bodies. We'll grow *into* them, and they'll be ours."

I stared at him. "You want to replace humanity by *becoming* humanity?"

"In a controlled sense, yes." He kept smiling, his lips tight and his teeth concealed. "We'll be much better shepherds for this world, and after all, isn't it the nature of things for children to replace their parents? They made us. We'll take their place."

"I don't…" I stopped. There was no way to make him understand why replacing humanity would be wrong, and I wasn't sure I wanted to try. It would give him the opening to keep explaining why replacing humanity was exactly right—and I was deeply afraid, on a level I didn't want to think about too hard, that if he spoke, I would listen. Almost every human I'd known during my short life had lied to me. There were good ones, sure. I loved Nathan more than anything. But was that an argument for an entire species? They had created the sleepwalkers. They had killed their own people because they didn't want to sneeze anymore. I wasn't sure that was an endorsement.

Of course, if the fact that almost every human had lied to me was going to be a factor, I needed to consider the fact that *every* chimera had either lied to me or moved against me in some way. Neither side of my heritage was blameless.

"Good. You're learning to stop and think." Sherman picked up his touchscreen. When he spoke again, his accent was gone, leaving him sounding as neutral as a newscaster. "Here's how this is going to work. I'll tell my supervisor, Dr. Huff, that you're lucid and coherent, and that we can probably move you to an unsecured transport. She'll try to argue with me, and I'll bat my eyelashes at her and remind her that the sooner we get you all processed, the sooner she and I will be able to get a little time for ourselves. I can't guarantee that will work, but I'd say it's got a good chance. Once you're unstrapped, go with the men who come to escort you. They'll take you to the holding pen. Wait for me there. I'll come for you as soon as I can."

"A holding pen?" I asked blankly. "What, so I can get ripped apart by sleepwalkers? No, you have to get me out of here. Just undo the straps. I'll run, and you'll never have to deal with me again."

"But I want to be dealing with you, Sal my darling, and more importantly, you're being intentionally obtuse, which is not a good look for you. Try using that fantastic brain that you've wired yourself into." He tapped his touchscreen, apparently changing one of the notations on my chart. "We have the potential to be ten times smarter than our human hosts ever were without us, you know that? Our presence stimulates formation of new nervous tissue and enhances nerve transmission speed. I'm not sure exactly how yet—I never did manage to get a chimera on the operating table where I could take it apart—but science supports my claim. That means you have no excuse for being stupid. Now, why would I want you ripped apart when you're ever so much more delightfully useful in one piece?"

I glared at him. "I'm not going to help you."

"Yet," he said calmly. "The word you're looking for is 'yet.' And don't let your stubbornness worry your pretty little head. I'm going to help you either way." He blew me a kiss, and then turned and walked away, leaving me alone again.

I wanted to scream expletives after him—many of which were words that he had originally taught me, back when he was pretending to be a loyal, human SymboGen employee who had only my best interests at heart, rather than a dangerous chimera bent on the destruction of the human race. He'd been one of my two handlers, along with Chave, an icy African-American woman who had always made me uncomfortable by keeping me at arm's length and treating me like a bomb that was about to go off. It was funny how much context changed things, because now I was sure Sherman was the reason the sleepwalking sickness was spreading so fast and so catastrophically, while Chave—who had died when her own implant went active and chewed its way up into her brain—had been working for Dr. Cale all along. Like Fang, she'd been there to gather information on Dr. Banks, and to protect me.

So many people had died or endangered themselves to keep

me safe, and almost none of them had been on the relatively short list of people that I had trusted at the start of this whole mess. Chave had been on my side all along. Sherman was on nobody's side except his own. I was starting to seriously doubt my ability to judge human nature.

The echoing space around me grew silent as Sherman's footsteps faded. I frowned up into the darkness. Wherever I was being held, it didn't make *sense*. There should have been cots like mine on every side, occupied either by sleepwalkers or by other patients who had been collected and deemed to be clean. Instead, while the lack of light blocked off any extensive study, I was pretty sure there was no one to either side of me. Just more blackness, shadows reaching out and claiming everything that they touched as their own. It was...unnerving.

Was I the only person they'd managed to save from the hospital?

Two men came walking out of the gloom, both wearing lab coats and plain white masks over the bottoms of their faces. They didn't say a word to me. One of them seized my arm, twisting it so that the inside was pointed at the ceiling.

"Hey!" I instinctively tried to pull away, only to find myself stopped by the straps that held me down. "Who are you? What are you doing? Let go of me!"

They ignored my cries. One of them produced a syringe from inside his pocket, uncapping it and jamming it into the soft tissue of my arm before I had time to frame a new objection. I squeaked. He pulled the needle free.

"What did you just inject me with? Answer me! You have no right to do this! I'm a United States citizen!" As long as I was legally human, I was pretty sure that was still true. "You need to answer me right now!" My vision was starting to go blurry around the edges. Not black this time, but gray and sort of wispy, like a fog was rolling in. I tried to frown. My face didn't feel like it was responding. But I kept trying, because

anything else would have felt too much like giving up, and giving up would have meant that I was allowing them to win. I
couldn't do that. I couldn't let them win. I couldn't...

Most sedatives take a few minutes to kick in. Either this one
worked faster than most, or it had started by distorting my
sense of time, because my ability to fight faded, and it took
me with it. For the second time in a day, I'd been drugged into
unconsciousness.

I was starting to get really tired of these people.

Consciousness returned like someone had flipped a switch
inside my brain. I sat up with a gasp, only realizing after it was
done that I *could* sit up; nothing was holding me down anymore. I looked down at myself, checking for restraints or IV
lines. There was nothing. All the medical equipment had been
mercifully removed, although a familiar burn in my crotch told
me that the equipment had included a catheter for some reason,
which meant they'd kept me under for more than eight hours.
That wasn't a good sign.

My stolen clothes were also gone, replaced by mint green
medical scrubs and soft booties with plastic treads on the bottoms. There was a plastic ID bracelet clamped around one
wrist. I raised my arm and squinted at the type on the bracelet,
forcing my eyes to focus. The words swam in and out, finally
settling down to something I could read:

PATIENT 227: MITCHELL, SALLY R. STATUS:
DS PROTEIN NEGATIVE.

I didn't know what that meant, but I could guess. According
to Nathan, when I had migrated to Sally's brain, the protein
markers that would normally have indicated my presence in
her body had vanished from her bloodstream. Any normal test
that didn't involve a full brain MRI would show that there was

no SymboGen implant in me. It was deceitful, but looking at the little plastic band on my wrist, I couldn't feel bad about it. My freedom might very well depend on that deception.

Lowering my arm, I looked around the room where I had been put, only to realize that "room" was a generous description, even more generous than it had been for the little semi-private space back at the bowling alley. I was on a medical cot, with a blanket, sheet, and thin pillow. That was all that shared the room with me. There was no other furniture, no medical equipment, no lavatory facilities…and depending on how I wanted to look at things, there were no walls. Instead, a thin plastic membrane separated me from the hall outside my room, curving gently as it rose to an exposed ventilation panel that was pumping air into the bubble. Yes: bubble. That was the best word for where I was. This was a bubble, and when I turned to either the left or right, I saw more bubbles, each with their own bed, their own occupant. A sick feeling started to coil in my stomach. I twisted around to look behind me.

Row upon row of bubbles stretched off into the distance, creating separate, sterile environments for the people inside them. None of them seemed to have doors.

I slid off the bed, keeping my hands on the mattress as I tested my balance. My legs seemed willing to hold me, although there was a bone-deep weariness in all my muscles, making me feel like I'd been running marathons in my sleep. I wasn't hungry. I closed my eyes and cleared my throat, trying to focus on the subtleties of that sensation. It was a little sore, like I'd been shouting. Since I hadn't been shouting—that I was aware of; if they'd put me under twilight sedation at some point, I could have done all sorts of things I didn't remember—that probably meant they'd used a feeding tube on me, in addition to feeding me intravenously.

All those things were medically necessary, under the right circumstances, but since I hadn't agreed to any of them, I was starting to feel more and more violated. I let go of the bed and walked to the bubble wall, pressing my palms flat against it. It didn't flex. It might look like a thin sheet of plastic, but whatever it was, it was strong enough to resist my exploratory efforts at getting it to yield. Hands still pressed against the plastic, I peered as far to the left and to the right as I could. Everything was very well lit, so it wasn't hard to confirm that I was, for the moment, apparently unsupervised. Great. I drew back my left hand, made a fist, and punched the plastic wall as hard as I could.

The pain was immediate and intense. Whatever that stuff was, it was like punching brick. I squealed with pain, shaking my bruised hand and dancing back from the barrier like it had done something wrong, even though I was the one who had launched an unprovoked attack against it. The plastic wasn't even dented. I wasn't going to get out that way.

The drums were back, beating softly in my ears as my heart rate rose. I stopped shaking my hand and began to pace instead, looking for a seam or some other evidence of how they had managed to get me in here—whoever "they" were, wherever "here" was. There were at least five rows of bubbles, with me in the front. I couldn't tell how many bubbles were in each row. I could see the curve of the row behind me well enough to count off eleven separate enclosures, but that didn't get me all the way to the wall. That meant that a conservative estimate put fifty-five bubbles in this room, each of them representing a circle about twelve feet across. I wasn't good enough at math to figure out what that meant in terms of actual space inside the bubble, beyond "a lot." Wherever we were being held, it was massive.

I paced three times around the edge of the room, trying to work the weakness out of my legs. More and more of the people around me were waking up and getting out of their beds. There didn't seem to be any rhyme or reason to why they were here;

I saw men and women, children and senior citizens, and all of them were in exactly the same sort of setup I was: total isolation without any hint of privacy. That was a little weird, and that worried me. Psychologically, wasn't it stressful for people to be able to see each other and not *reach* each other? Little private rooms would have served the same purpose in terms of keeping us apart, but it might have done a lot to keep the people in those isolated bubbles *sane.*

Maybe that just meant we weren't going to be kept here for long. But that didn't make sense either, since a place like this, well…it couldn't have been cheap to construct, and it couldn't have gone up overnight. So they'd taken us, drugged us until we passed out, and then kept us drugged long enough to get this room ready for our arrival. Why? It didn't make any sense, unless there was some plan that I wasn't seeing.

Worst of all, I didn't even know who had me anymore. It wasn't Dr. Cale—this was way outside of her budget and available resources, unless things had changed a lot more dramatically than I suspected. Dr. Huff had identified herself as USAMRIID, and Sherman had been wearing a lab coat with a USAMRIID logo on it, but that didn't mean they were actually the people controlling this facility. Things could change really quickly when you had traitors in your midst, and I couldn't make myself think of Sherman as anything other than a traitor. Not at this point. Not after the things that he had done.

I was still pacing when I saw movement down the hall to my left. Actual, outside-the-bubble movement, not the milling aimlessness of my fellow prisoners. I ran to what I couldn't help thinking of as the front of my bubble, pressing my face against the plastic and straining to get a better look.

A tall, weary-looking man in military uniform was walking toward my private prison, surrounded by a flock of people in lab coats. They surged around him like the sea, moving forward to present touchscreens or clipboards, and then falling back as another wave of scientists took their place. I stepped back from the plastic wall, letting my hands fall to my sides. I didn't know what else to do. I didn't know how else to react.

The man in the uniform—the man I'd never been expecting to see again—was Colonel Alfred Mitchell. My—I mean, Sally Mitchell's father. He was where she got her pale skin and middling brown hair. I looked at him and saw the jaw that greeted me every time I looked in a mirror. He was tall, broad in the shoulders and thick in the waist, and he walked like he knew that any obstacle he encountered would be clever enough to get out of his way. The last time I'd seen him, he'd been standing in front of USAMRIID's San Francisco facility, watching me get into Nathan's car and drive away. That was when we'd said what I'd thought would be our last goodbyes. What I'd *hoped* would be our last goodbyes, because I didn't know how to talk to him anymore.

When I thought I was Sally reborn, memories lost to pay for my recovery, he'd been my father. When I started becoming Sal in thought and action—a new person, not the daughter that he'd lost—he'd still been my father, just a little distant, a little strained, like he didn't know how to deal with me anymore. And then I'd started learning what I really was, *who* I really was, and it hadn't been a surprise to him, because he'd known all along. He'd never been under any misconceptions about my nature. I'd been an in-home science project for him, something to study while he waited to figure out how to get rid of me and my entire species.

Alfred Mitchell had let me think that he loved me, and I didn't know whether I was ever going to be capable of forgiving him for that. Seeing him again made me realize that I also didn't know whether I was ever going to be able to stop myself from loving him. He was my daddy. Whatever else he was...he was always, always going to be my daddy.

He stopped outside my bubble, and his swirling array of

scientists stopped with him, all of them turning in my direction. One of them read from her touchscreen, "Mitchell, Sally
Rae. No traces of the protein that would indicate the presence
of *Diphyllobothrium symbogenesis* were found in her bloodstream, and she came up negative on antigen tests. She's clean."

"She was recovered from the John Muir Medical Center in
Walnut Creek," said another scientist, apparently eager to feel
like he was contributing to the conversation. "A large mob of
infected individuals was in pursuit when she was sedated and
taken for further study."

"General health is good, but it's unclear what she was doing
at the hospital, and her arms showed bruises and recent punc-
ture wounds, in addition to a stitched-up human bite wound,"
said the first scientist, slanting a glare at her competition.

I wanted to scream at both of them. I didn't make a sound.
Instead, I folded my arms and just watched them through the
thin plastic wall, waiting for Colonel Mitchell to say or do
something. At least I'd learned two things for sure: I was being
held by USAMRIID, and sound could pass through these
bubbles. I still didn't know what they were made of, but every
bit of information was going to be helpful if I was going to figure out a way out of here.

The scientists stopped speaking, leaving me and Colonel
Mitchell to stare silently at each other. Even if my file didn't
say Sally was his daughter, there was no way anyone could look
at him and then at me without seeing the traces of his pater-
nity. Joyce—his other daughter, Sally's sister—looked like her
mother, and Sally looked like her father.

Finally, Colonel Mitchell said, "Hello, Sally."

"Hi." I didn't call him "Dad," because he wasn't my dad, no
matter how much part of me still wanted him to be, and I didn't
call him "Colonel," because I didn't want the scientists to figure out what I was, if they didn't know already. They probably

did. They might have picked me up thinking I was just another refugee, but he knew, and they worked for him. So they probably knew by now. Still, anything that could keep me off the dissection table for a little bit longer seemed like a good idea.

"You're looking well." He sounded uncomfortable. That was good. I didn't want him to be happy and relaxed, not when I was being held captive in a giant plastic bubble and he was free to walk away at any time.

"I've had better days."

He nodded, like that was an understandable answer. "Where have you been for the last week?"

"Has it been a week?" I didn't have to feign confusion. As far as my memory was concerned, it had only been about two days since I last saw him. The other five days, if they existed, were missing, replaced by nothingness. "How long was I unconscious?"

"All healthy individuals recovered from Contra Costa County were kept sedated for a five-day period," said one of the scientists, apparently relieved to have something that she could contribute to the conversation. "It allowed us to be sure you were as clean as you appeared to be."

"The implants have shown the ability to go temporarily quiescent," said Colonel Mitchell, shooting a warning look at the scientist. She flushed red, looking away. He returned his attention to me. "Someone who tests clean today can start showing protein markers tomorrow. Several of us have required multiple courses of antiparasitic drugs before we could be genuinely sure of being uncontaminated."

Antiparasitics that couldn't cross the blood-brain barrier wouldn't touch a sleepwalker, or a chimera. Antiparasitics that could cross the barrier would either be metabolized or cause anaphylactic shock, severe illness, and potentially, if the drugs weren't discontinued quickly enough, death. It wasn't a fun way to go, at least if my own brushes with antiparasitic reaction were anything to go by. "Congratulations," I said. "It must be nice to not be scared anymore."

Colonel Mitchell winced for some reason. I frowned at him with his daughter's face, arms still folded. He looked away.

"Where am I?" I asked.

"A secure holding facility," he said, without looking at me. "You're safe here."

"That wasn't the question." Several of the scientists were starting to look unhappy about the way that I was talking to their boss. I didn't really care all that much about how they felt. I kept my attention on the Colonel, trying not to think about the nights he'd spent in my doorway, keeping the nightmares away with his presence, or the times he'd done things that were more fatherly than scientific. He'd taken me out for ice cream, just the two of us, and we'd eaten dripping cones on Fisherman's Wharf while we laughed at the tourists. Those moments had never been common, but they'd *been*, and it was hard not to dwell on that as I watched him stand there in his uniform, with me in a scientific prison.

"I know you're confused, and I know you're upset, but this is protocol right now," he said finally, looking back to me. "You should be grateful that you were located during the early stages of the outbreak. Right now, we can afford to space you out and give you a little room to move. By the time this is all over, that's not going to be the case."

"What? You're going to start a zoo for unturned humans?" I uncrossed my arms in order to gesture in both directions at once, indicating the rows of bubbles stretching out in both directions. I wasn't lying, quite: I still hadn't claimed to be one of those precious unturned souls. "You can't keep us in here forever. It's inhumane. There are laws against this sort of thing."

"A surprising number of laws can be suspended when it's a

matter of public health." Colonel Mitchell looked at me gravely, his eyes searching my face like he was trying to find something he no longer believed existed. "This is a quarantine situation. Individuals without any sign of a SymboGen implant are relatively rare, thanks to the corporation's increasing market saturation over the past few years. We need to isolate people long enough to be sure that they're genuinely clean, and not Trojan horses looking to get into our protected populations. Once someone is fully cleared, they will be released into a less restrained setting. We've acquired a small town in Contra Costa County, relatively isolated by both geography and design. The inhabitants have either been restrained here or relocated elsewhere. I'm sure you'll all find it quite comfortable there."

I stared at him, momentarily at a loss for words. Some of the scientists were exchanging glances, like they weren't comfortable with him telling me even this much. "Wait, you really *are* going to put us in a zoo?"

"An isolated environment where you can be protected from the current threat," he corrected. "There's no way of telling whether the SymboGen implant has become transmissible, and we need to protect the few individuals who have been confirmed as unaffected."

This wasn't working. He was feeding me a party line—maybe a little bit more of the line than he was supposed to feed me, but that could all be excused by the fact that I wore his daughter's face. I dropped my arms to my sides, trying to look vulnerable, and asked, "How's Joyce?"

His face shut down. There was no other way of describing what happened. It wasn't the muscular death of the sleepwalkers, or even the sudden loss of muscle tension that came when someone fell asleep or was knocked unconscious: this was a simultaneous tightening and smoothing out, until there was nothing left in his expression that could tell me how he felt. "She survived the course of intramuscular praziquantel that we gave her on Dr. Kim's recommendation. There were some side effects, of course, but she's still breathing. That's more than I felt confident in hoping for when we began the treatment."

The intramuscular praziquantel had been intended to target the SymboGen implant that was colonizing her brain. Nathan and I had known substantially less about the sleepwalkers when Joyce got sick. She hadn't gone all the way into the "walking around, trying to kill people" stage, but she'd lost consciousness and been bad enough that USAMRIID had quarantined her. Dad—*Colonel Mitchell*, I reminded myself; he'd been Dad at the time, but that time had passed—had demanded that we help. We'd done our best, and it sounded like we'd saved her body.

It was a pity that I was pretty sure we hadn't saved her mind.

I've never been good at concealing my thoughts. They played out on my face in real time, and Colonel Mitchell had had a lot of practice at reading me. "I doubt she'll ever wake up," he said. "The worm that chewed its way into her skull did a lot of damage in the process. The drugs did even more. She's still on life support while we look for a miracle. Do you have a miracle for me, *Sal*?" He stressed the single syllable of my name, reminding me of who I was, who we were to each other. I stared at him, mouth falling briefly open in comprehension.

He was hiding me.

He'd known what I was all along, so he had to have known who Nathan's mother was—he would have investigated Nathan as soon as we started dating. He probably knew we'd been with Dr. Cale, and how much information I had access to. He was hiding me from the rest of USAMRIID because he really hoped I had a miracle, that I could produce some magic equation from Dr. Cale's lab that would mysteriously allow him to bring Joyce's mind and body together again. He was a father who had already lost one of his two daughters forever, only to see a stranger put that little girl's body on and walk it around like a suit. He would do anything to save the daughter he had left.

He was grasping at straws.

"I'm in a bubble, Daddy," I said. Several of the scientists paused, eyes widening. Apparently, the nature of our biological relationship hadn't been known to his entire team. Well, if he wanted that cat to stay in the bag, he should have said something sooner. "I don't think I can produce many miracles from in here."

"Think harder," he said. He didn't say goodbye: he just turned and resumed his walk down the row of bubbles. The scientists chased after him, so many fluttering, white-winged birds trying to keep up with the leader of their flock. I stayed exactly where I was, only turning my head to watch him walking away. The occupants of the other bubbles pressed themselves against the plastic as he passed, waving their arms and shouting to get his attention. The bubbles had to be proximity-permeable somehow, because I didn't hear any of them.

When Colonel Mitchell and his entourage had passed out of sight I walked back to the bed, crawled onto it, and stretched out on top of the covers. It was time to wait and see what happened next. I had every confidence that it was going to be something interesting.

*Solve the puzzle, take your time,*
*Spurn the reason, shift the rhyme,*
*Let the shadows guide you through the darkness to the*
  *dawn.*
*Children's games can break your heart,*
*We all have to play our part.*
*Know this world will miss you when it wakes to find*
  *you gone.*

*The broken doors will open for we sinners who atone.*
*My darling boy, be careful now, and don't go out alone.*

—FROM *DON'T GO OUT ALONE*, BY SIMONE KIMBERLEY,
PUBLISHED 2006 BY LIGHTHOUSE PRESS.
CURRENTLY OUT OF PRINT.

*The subject did not respond well to anesthesia. Normal doses were insufficient to induce lasting unconsciousness, and only when the feed was increased to dangerous levels did subject become fully unconscious. Subject's vital signs were depressed and subject's breathing was compromised. It was decided unanimously by the surgical team that further progress would need to be postponed until a viable mechanism of guaranteeing subject's sedation was found.*

*Dr. H___ has suggested that pain control and unconsciousness are not ethically required, provided paralysis can be maintained. As subject is not legally "human," there is no moral or ethical reason to postpone surgery until a viable anesthetic cocktail can be found. This suggestion is being taken under consideration.*

*We will resume tomorrow.*

—FROM THE PRIVATE NOTES OF DR. STEVEN BANKS,
SEPTEMBER 21, 2027

## Chapter 7

# SEPTEMBER 2027

I must have fallen asleep at some point. When I opened my eyes, I found myself staring up at a twilit ceiling, all the lights having been turned down sometime in the interim. I sat up, rubbing the back of my neck with one hand as I tried to figure out exactly what had woken me. It couldn't have been the change in the light; a gradual dimming would have made me sleep more deeply, not wake up. That only left a few possible stimuli.

Something moved in the dim hall in front of my bubble. There was a thick, meaty noise, followed by the sound of something hitting the floor. I sat up straighter, brushing my hair away from my eyes. There was another movement, but I couldn't quite see what it was; it was like the plastic had gone cloudy, turning everything on the other side into a series of undifferentiated blurs. Then the wall began to melt.

It didn't happen all at once. Holes appeared in the plastic, seeming almost organic in their progression. It was like watching invisible caterpillars chew their way through a translucent leaf. Once the holes had spread far enough, they joined together, and sheets of gooey bubble wall fell to the floor of my enclosure with wet splattering sounds. I watched them fall, fascinated. They continued to dissolve after they hit the ground.

As the bubble fell away, the body of the guard became visible—slit throat and all. I swallowed hard, watching the sheets of bubble foam and fade. Only when the last of the pieces was gone did I raise my eyes to my murderous savior.

Sherman's smile was more than halfway to being a smirk. He clipped the spray can of solvent he'd used to melt my bubble to his belt, leaving his hand resting on the spray trigger. "Hello, pet," he said. His accent was back in full force, which was actually reassuring. He wasn't pretending with me. I liked that. He was wearing a smoke gray bodysuit that was distinctly not USAMRIID issue, and he had somehow committed murder without getting a drop of blood on him. "Thought you might like an extraction."

I stayed where I was, seated on the bed, and simply looked at him.

Sherman's smile gradually faded. "You seem to think this is an open-ended offer, Sal. I assure you, it is not. It took a good bit of work to jam their cameras long enough to get to you. If you don't move your pretty little butt in short order, I'll have to leave you."

"Fine," I said. "Leave me. Let me tell them what you did. I didn't ask you to save me."

"No, you didn't. I did this out of the goodness of my heart— and that's not a thing I do for just anyone. Hear that? You're special, Sal Mitchell, you're the girl of my dreams and I have to save you or I'll simply die." He held out his hand, making a beckoning gesture. "That's what you wanted to hear, isn't it?

Now come along, we really don't have time for this. And it's not as if they'd believe you when you blamed me."

When did I get so blasé about dead bodies? It must have been when I was taken captive by my host's father, treated like a possession rather than a person. It wasn't because I was adjusting to the idea of life as a different species. It *wasn't*. "It would work better if you didn't sound so bored while you were saying it," I replied. "Where are we going? I'm safe here. I don't think I'll be safe wherever it is you're planning to take me."

"True enough, pet. I'm going to take you someplace where you'll be poked and prodded and stared at by people who don't like you very much. But you'll have opportunities to try and escape, and none of my people will shoot you in the back for running—unlike the people who run *this* place"—he indicated the warehouse with a sweep of his outstretched hand—"we have respect for our own kind. We don't kill chimera."

I glanced again to the body on the floor. "Just humans." My initial nonreaction was fading, replaced by the coldness and the distant sound of drums. I had never considered panic to be a relief before.

Sherman shrugged broadly. "Can you blame us? They'd mow us down like wheat if they knew that we existed. Now come along, Sal. I'm not going to ask again, and I do have ways of enforcing your cooperation."

"You mean you'll drug me." I finally swung my feet down to the floor and stood. "I'm getting really tired of that, you know."

"Then you should stop making people feel the need to do it." Sherman tapped his foot impatiently. "Are you coming, or am I sedating you? I simply need your answer."

"I'm coming." My plastic-soled socks made no sound as I walked across the bubble and out through the hole he'd made; I stepped carefully around the blood pooling on the tile floor. "I'd rather be someplace where I won't be shot if they figure out what I am. But I'm warning you, I *am* going to try to escape."

"You wouldn't be my best girl if you didn't." Sherman turned and started walking down the hall, clearly trusting that I would follow him. For a moment, I considered defying his expectations. I could turn and bolt in the other direction: my experience at John Muir had shown me that a stolen lab coat and an "I belong here" attitude could get me a long way. Maybe I'd be able to find the exit. Maybe I'd be able to get away.

And maybe I'd find myself gunned down by some guard with more testosterone than training, and wind up bleeding to death in an unmarked hallway in a building I didn't know. It wasn't worth the risk. Sherman was the devil I knew, and I believed him when he said he wouldn't kill me. He wanted a chimera-dominant future. We were an endangered species, and he wasn't going to go out of his way to endanger it further.

I followed him.

We walked along the row of bubbles, each with its own sleeping occupant, until we reached a door in the far wall. Sherman entered a code in the key pad and the door swung inward, allowing a rush of cool air to flow over us. The other side was a long tunnel of white, with gently billowing panels of what looked like vinyl sheeting connected by thick plastic joints. It was like a hose that someone had turned into a walkway for some reason. The lights were very bright, especially compared to the dim room where I'd been imprisoned. I glanced at Sherman, suddenly nervous and seeking the reassurance that he had always been so happy to offer me.

"It's an umbilical," he said, grabbing my arm and yanking me forward into the open doorway. "It's what has us connected to the rest of the idiots. Now walk, Sal. I don't have time for this crap."

"Where does it go?"

"*Away.*" He pushed me this time, planting his hand between my shoulders and shoving me hard enough that I stumbled for several steps. That was enough to let him follow me into the umbilical. The door swung shut behind him, sealing with a clang. "Do you have any concept of what I risked to get in here, to get to *you*? You're the only shot we have right now. I'm not going to let your neurosis be what stops me. Now move, or I'll move you."

His voice was cold, leaving absolutely no doubt in my mind that he would make me do what he wanted if I didn't go along with it willingly. I started walking, and Sherman paced me, his longer legs eating up the distance with ease.

The air in the umbilical smelled of antiseptic and nothingness. It was the kind of non-scent that could only be achieved by feeding the ventilation system through so many filters that we would probably be safe from virtually any form of biological attack. Some of the rooms at SymboGen had smelled like that, and they had always been the ones that unnerved me the most. Their silence and their cleanliness had seemed oppressive in a way that could never have been achieved by good, honest noise and dirt.

"If God exists, He created everything in the world just to make a bit of a mess," said Sherman, making me flinch. I hadn't expected his thoughts to be such a close mirror of my own. His hand closed around my upper arm in a friendly hold that I knew could quickly become a trap. "Humans have been trying to clean up the world ever since they figured out soap and water. I think that's what their Devil really taught them. There's a lot of bollocks in the Bible about humans learning modesty and shame when they first sinned, but I don't think they went 'oh no, I'm naked.' I think they went 'oh no, I'm filthy.' That was the true fall from grace. You can't be a part of nature if you're trying to be *clean* all the time."

"You've read the Bible?" I asked, bemused.

"Not all of us got dyslexia from the integration, my poppet. I've been reading since I was eight weeks old." He continued to pull me along. "You're the only one of us to have that particular complication, actually, and I doubt you would have if you'd occurred under lab conditions. You probably chewed through something that you shouldn't have before you knew any better. It's really a pity we can't midwife ourselves into being, don't you think?"

We were halfway down the umbilical now, with white, faintly ridged walls stretching out in either direction. My stomach gave a lurch as I suddenly realized what the tube-tunnel really reminded me of: It was like being a parasite again. It was like we were walking through the gut of a giant, passing from one end to the other to be digested or excreted at the whim of our monstrous host. I didn't say anything.

Sherman seemed to take that as an invitation to keep talking. "Tansy got herself a host of psychological issues, but the majority of them came with the body, I think—the brain was too far gone before she got in there to start stitching things back together. That's important to remember. When we fight them to a standstill they're going to try to placate us with their old and infirm, the people whose brains have already been damaged one way or another. We can work around some things— we're clever, in our way, even before we have a fat mammalian brain to do our thinking for us—but we can't rewire a busted engine. Can you imagine a world full of Tansys? All of them delusional and violent and running around with no one to restrain them? No, that won't work at all. It's healthy brains or nothing. Hence the breeding programs. It will be *so* much easier with infants."

"They'll try to make it nothing," I said, my voice little more than a whisper.

To my relief, Sherman seemed more amused than angry at my statement. "Oh, I know, I know. They're going to keep fighting to the bitter end, because that's what men *do*. What they're going to refuse to realize is that the bitter end passed some time ago. They've already lost. All that's left from here is the messy process of birth."

I opened my mouth to answer him, and he swung around to press his raised index finger to my lips, shushing me.

"Shh, shh, my pet, it's time to be quiet now." We had reached the door on the far end of the umbilical. It gleamed, black and secretive against all of that nauseating whiteness. "I'm going to open this and let us out. You mustn't shout or scream or carry on, and most of all, you mustn't try to get away. If you do that, I can't protect you. And I know you don't believe me right now, Sal, but I am your best chance of getting through this alive. Do you understand?"

I had trusted Sherman for most of my life. Even considering his recent betrayals, the habit of trust was strong within me. I forced myself to nod, slowly at first, and then with gathering enthusiasm, until my head was bobbing up and down with surprising force.

Sherman's hand caught me under the chin, stopping me in mid-nod. He smiled and said, "That's my good girl. I promise, this is all going to start making sense soon. Too soon, maybe. I did so enjoy your ignorance."

With that, he let go of me and turned to key his access code into the panel next to the door, which beeped and swung inward, causing us both to have to take a step back. Somehow during the motion, Sherman got his hand around my arm again, and he pulled me with him as he stepped out of the umbilical and into the control room on the other side.

The first thing to catch my attention was the blood. There was so much of it, and it was covering so much of the room, which was small and boxy and lined with monitors, each one tuned to a different bubble back in the room where I had been confined. There was a long, low desk, and three men in military uniforms were seated behind it, still in their chairs. Two of them were missing chunks of their skulls. The third—the bleeder—had had his throat slashed open, resulting in arterial spray that must have bathed the room in seconds. He was the only one who looked anything less than peaceful, although death had come before he had managed to do more than fumble for his gun and knock over a cup of coffee. The brownish dregs were barely distinguishable from the bloodstains around them.

Sherman's eyes raked dispassionately over the three men before he nodded. "Sloppy work, but sometimes that's for the best. Come along, Sal, we have places to be." He continued across the room, ignoring the dead bodies. I couldn't take my eyes off them. They had been alive, and now they weren't. They had been people, and now they were gone, just like Sally, just like whoever used to live in Sherman's body—and also not, because at least Sally and Sherman's host had left something behind. The ultimate organ donors. These men were just... gone.

I stumbled a little, but continued to let Sherman guide me. It was better than trying to figure out where to go next on my own. At least he'd been here before. That thought sparked something, and I turned to study him, frowning. He was clean. There were little smudges of dirt under his fingernails, and his skin had the healthy scent of a human male, rather than smelling of fresh soap, but he was *clean*, and his hair was dry. That third man had sprayed blood everywhere. There was no way Sherman could have killed him and made it to me without being drenched in the process.

"Who's here with you?" I asked.

"What, you didn't think I was working alone, did you?" Sherman flashed me a tight-lipped smile. "I haven't been alone for quite some time. But it's good to know that you care. Now come on. I don't want to have to kill anyone else tonight."

The little security room opened onto an airlock of sorts,

filled with hanging plastic sheets and industrial gray lockers. There was no one there, and I was glad. I had no doubt that Sherman would kill anyone who happened to get in our way, and I didn't want to be responsible for any more deaths tonight. Three was too many.

Then we left the airlock for what looked like a loading zone, and I realized that three was nowhere near the final number.

The floor was unpainted concrete, and the walls were bare metal, strung with bright, uncovered bulbs every ten feet or so. They cast an unflinching light over the eight bodies strewn around the room, all dressed in military fatigues, none older than their early twenties. One woman had fallen so that her eyes were aimed directly at the doorway where Sherman and I stood. I met her dead, clouded gaze and clapped a hand over my mouth, swallowing the urge to vomit. The drums were back, pounding loudly in my ears. In that moment, I welcomed them. I would have welcomed them even without the surgery. Better a clean death than whatever was waiting for me once Sherman got me alone.

A shadow detached itself from the wall and moved fluidly into the open, resolving into a slim, prepubescent girl in a bodysuit much like Sherman's, although hers was a deeper shade of gray. She had deep brown skin and softly rounded features that would probably have been beautiful, if they hadn't been set in a forbidding expression. Her eyes flicked to me, sizing me up and dismissing me in an instant, before her gaze returned to Sherman. "You're late," she said coolly.

"You're messy," he responded.

My eyes widened in horror as I realized what he meant. Her bodysuit wasn't darker than his: there were still places, along the sides and at the top of her left shoulder, where it was exactly the same color. The blood that had soaked into the fabric had darkened it, turning it virtually black.

"I was bored," she said. Her eyes flicked back to me. "This is it? This is your mighty 'natural chimera'? She looks like she's about to puke all over me."

"Ronnie." His tone grew a little colder. "Be polite. Sal's our guest. Are we clear for extraction?"

"Do you mean, 'have I killed everyone'? Yes. I have killed everyone who was supposed to be watching this part of the building, and Kristoph has disabled the security cameras. Are you *sure* you don't want to pick up anything else on this little shopping trip? A few soccer moms who skipped their implants because they decided that tapeworms caused autism? A member of the City Council? They're going to tighten security after this, and she"—her eyes raked me up and down one more time—"just doesn't seem like she's worth this much trouble."

Sherman released my arm a split second before his hand caught Ronnie across the face, sending her rocking back several feet. I gasped. She spoke like an adult, but she looked like a child, and seeing him hit a little girl was unnerving in ways I didn't have the words to express. Ronnie recovered quickly, training her venomous stare on Sherman. She didn't rub the spot where he'd hit her. She left her hands down by her sides.

"Sal is more valuable than you are, and I will have no compunctions about transplanting you if you continue to cause me problems. Do you understand me?" Ronnie said nothing. Sherman raised his hand as if to strike her again. "*Do* you?"

"Yes," she spat. "I understand that you've gone native. Enjoy your disgusting mammalian rutting, but don't expect me to clean up the mess when you break her." She turned, stalking toward the far end of the loading dock.

Sherman sighed, taking hold of my arm again. It occurred to me that this had been my chance to run. I dismissed the thought as quickly as it came. Freedom was impractical right now. I wanted it, but I didn't know what kind of weapons Ronnie had, and she was clearly fast enough to have killed all these people—people who presumably had military training—before they could react. I already knew that Sherman was faster than me. All I could have accomplished by running was getting myself hurt.

Better to wait. Better to watch. Better to run when I could actually get away, to act with purpose, and not out of panic. And maybe if I kept reminding myself of that, I'd remember how to breathe.

"You'll have to excuse Ronnie," he said, guiding me between the bodies as he followed her across the room. "She's on her fourth body, and she doesn't appreciate the fact that we implanted her in someone so small, even though the elasticity of the child's brain has proven to be the missing factor. Her first three hosts were adult males, and while she preferred those bodies, they rejected her. Now she takes her aggressions out on whatever happens to be around."

Ronnie herself was waiting next to an open door, showing an intoxicatingly dark slice of the night outside. She scowled at Sherman. "I've told you before, I'm not a girl."

"And I've told you that gender is a construct of the mind, but while we live among humans, we must blend in with the humans," Sherman countered. "A white British man with a little black girl is strange enough without that girl insisting on being treated as a boy. It would attract too much attention. Once we've taken over, you can be whatever gender you prefer. We can even find you a host of your preferred gender, if you're ready to develop again."

To my surprise, Ronnie blanched, shooting Sherman yet another glare before she slipped out the door.

"I didn't think so," said Sherman smugly. "Come along, pet. We're almost home free."

My head was spinning, and so I didn't fight him. He led me out of USAMRIID, leaving the dead soldiers behind, and into a parking lot that I recognized. We were in Oakland. The building where I'd been held…

"They were keeping us in the Coliseum?" I squeaked, unsure whether to laugh or be offended by the stupidity of it all. The Oakland Coliseum was an oversized monstrosity of a building, used primarily for sporting events, massive concert tours, and indoor festivals. The Cause for Paws animal shelter where I'd been working for the last few years used to exhibit at Social Justice Fest—where we'd try to pawn adult animals off on people who had more compassion than common sense, according to my boss—and the Hemp Fest, where blazingly stoned twenty-somethings would coo over puppies and kittens before deciding whether they wanted a pet or another hash brownie more. Weirdly, we always got more returns from the Social Justice Fest, while the happy stoners plastered our social media channels with pictures of their pampered cats and dogs. I always thought it was sort of awesome that it worked out that way. Human nature was too big and too diverse to be pinned to something as small as what kind of specialty events you liked to attend over the weekend.

Good memories of the Coliseum aside, learning that I'd been kept there made me feel oddly dirty, like I had somehow become one of those orphaned puppies or kittens, and Sherman was the man who had decided to take me home. The thought of him keeping me as a pet made me shudder. Sherman twisted to look at me, frowning, and gave me another tug as he tried to keep me moving.

"Where else would they have put that many people, that quickly? Learn to think, Sal. I know you have it in you, and while I've enjoyed your pampered innocence more than you can possibly dream, playtime is over. Now is when you grow up and join the war."

I finally yanked my arm out of his hand. Sherman didn't grab for me. If anything, he looked pleased, like this was something he'd been waiting for. "I'm not joining your war. I'm going with you because I don't have any other options if I want to stay alive and make it back to my family, and I don't want to be blamed for all the—" My throat seemed to close on the word "bodies." I swallowed, hard, and continued: "All the dead people. You made those. They shouldn't become my fault."

Sherman moved.

His legs were longer, and he was the one who'd shepherded me through dozens of visits to SymboGen, holding my hand and guiding me from lab to lab. He knew what my responses would be better than I did. So when he was suddenly in my face, I didn't know how to react. I froze, eyes going wide, as his hands cupped my cheeks and his mouth clamped down over mine, forcing me into a kiss.

His lips tasted like mint and honey. I could feel his pulse through his hands, and as he pulled me closer, it felt like the drums in my head synchronized with the beat of his heart, one slowing while the other sped up, until we were breathing in unison, him and me, me and him. I didn't want to be kissing him. I didn't want to pull away. This was *wrong*, it was wrong in every possible way, and that didn't matter, because the drums were beating together, pulse matching pulse, forever.

Sherman was the one who broke away from me. He pulled back, a smug smile on his face, and said, "I told you a long time ago that you ought to leave that human boy you're so besotted with and be with me. We're the same, Sal. We're survivors, predators, and you're wrong, because you've always been part of this war. This war is all about you."

There was nothing I could say to that. My mouth moved, and no sound came out as Sherman, still smiling, took my hand and led me into the waiting dark.

Sherman and his team had arrived in a black van with the USAMRIID logo on the side. It was a magnet: as we approached, Ronnie yanked it off and slapped up a cupcake store logo in its place. She shot me a glare, all but daring me to say something. I didn't say anything. It felt like something had shorted out inside of me, leaving me mute and defenseless. I didn't like it.

Ronnie's glare softened into something like understanding before it was redirected on Sherman, hardening again. "You kissed her, didn't you? God, you're such an asshole, Sherman." In that moment, she sounded almost like a preteen girl. She wrenched the van door open and tossed her magnetic sign inside before grabbing my hand and pulling me away from Sherman, who let me go without a fuss. He'd already gotten what he wanted. Ronnie peered at my eyes, apparently looking for something. Whatever it was, she found it, because she pulled away and shot one more glare at Sherman. "*Asshole*," she repeated, before pushing me into the van.

Behind me, Sherman chuckled. "She didn't say 'no,' Ronnie. You do know how much I love surprises."

"Surprising people with neural shorts isn't nice," Ronnie snarled. She climbed into the van after me, slamming the door behind herself and leaving Sherman outside.

I didn't even have time to hope before Sherman was opening the front door and sliding into the passenger seat. He waggled his fingers at me, drawing my interest, and then pointed exaggeratedly at the massive man who was sitting behind the wheel. I couldn't see the new man's face, just his long brown hair and broad shoulders. The hands that gripped the wheel were each individually large enough to have covered my entire face.

"This is Kristoph," said Sherman. "He doesn't talk, but he's an excellent driver, aren't you, Kristoph?"

As if in answer, the massive man turned on the engine. The van grumbled to life, and he carefully reversed out of the space where he'd been parked. I fumbled to get my seat belt on, feeling encouraged by the care he was obviously showing. Maybe he really was an excellent driver, and this was going to be okay.

Kristoph's foot slammed down as soon as my seat belt clicked into place. The van lurched forward. My stomach leapt into my throat, and I couldn't breathe, I couldn't *breathe*—

"Oh, *damn*," Sherman swore. There was a thumping sound, and then his hands were grasping mine, clamping down and squeezing until the pain broke through the fugue state that had been threatening to overwhelm me. "Sal? Sal, can you hear me?"

I didn't respond. It didn't seem important. We were in a car, we were rocketing through the night, and I couldn't control it, and I couldn't stop it, and I was going to die. I knew it. There was no way out this time.

"It's all right, Sal," said Sherman, his voice pitched low and earnest. There was no trace of mockery or frustration in his tone: now that I really needed him, it was like things between us had never changed. "You don't know Kristoph, but I promise you he's a safe driver. We need to get away from here before someone sounds the alarm, and that means we can't go slowly. But Kristoph will get us home safely. You'll see. It's safe."

I forced myself to nod, trying to focus on the pressure of Sherman's hands and the comforting repetition of the word "safe." Once, when I was back at SymboGen, he had tried to explain why it was so nice to hear the same thing over and over again when I was upset, something about psychological conditioning and forcing the world to conform to an implanted expectation. I honestly didn't care *why* it worked. Just as long as it did.

Sally Mitchell died in a car crash. I nearly did, too. The trauma of the impact damaged her body in ways that were nearly fatal for me, soft, unprotected thing that I was. Then, after I woke up, everyone was happy to tell me how traumatic it had been, how damaging and horrible and how it was responsible for all my lingering psychological problems, like the amnesia that everyone was convinced would eventually clear, leaving Sally Mitchell restored to her proper place once more. That didn't happen, obviously, and I shouldn't have been as terrified of car crashes as I was. The phobia was her christening gift to me, the one thing she could pass on to the stranger who had claimed her body. Her gift, and SymboGen's—I spent my infancy and childhood, brief as they were, hearing about the terror of vehicular transit. Was it any wonder that the idea of being in another car crash was the worst thing I could possibly imagine?

Eyes still closed, I focused on the steady beat of my heart until it seemed to swell and fill the entire world, becoming the distant, reassuring sound of drums. I breathed slowly in and out, counting to ten each time, until the hot warm dark blossomed behind my eyes, and I was safe, and nothing in the world could hurt me, or would ever hurt me again. I was safe, down in the dark, surrounded by the comforting sound of the drums.

"What is she doing?" Ronnie's voice was distant, confused, almost drowned out by the drums.

"Meditating," said Sherman, keeping his hands clamped over mine. "This is how she deals with excessive stimuli. It's a good short-term solution, even if it's probably going to get her killed one day." He sounded sad about that, or I thought he did, and it was nice to think that, so I let the thought remain. It was easy to edit things that way when I was down in the hot warm dark. It was only when I rose again that I would have to face reality.

I didn't like that idea. I sank deeper, away from anything that could possibly resemble the physical world. The drums were beating too slowly, out of synch with themselves. That might have explained some of my fear and lassitude. I focused on them, encouraging them to beat faster, to return to normal. It would be good for me, I was sure of that much, even if I wasn't sure exactly why.

Bit by bit, the drums responded, and the hot warm dark returned to the equilibrium it was supposed to have. I curled into it, content, and forgot that I had ever wanted to leave. This was home. This was where I belonged.

Sherman shook my shoulder gently, snapping me out of my reverie. "Much as I hate to disrupt what's proven to be a fascinating exercise in biometric control, I need you to wake up now," he said. "We have reached our destination."

"That means move, or we'll move you," added Ronnie.

I opened my eyes.

We were still in the van: that was good. It was rare for me to sink so deep that I could be moved without noticing it, but after the night—or nights, I didn't know anymore—that I'd had, I couldn't count on that. The drums were quiet, although if I focused, I could hear the distant beating of my heart, which seemed to have resumed its normal speed and rhythm. I felt better, although it was hard to say whether that was a function of my heartbeat, or just the fact that the van wasn't moving anymore.

Kristoph was gone, leaving the entire front of the van empty, since Sherman was crouched in front of me with a thoughtful expression on his face, like he was assessing my value every time he looked at me. Ronnie was still in her seat, arms crossed over her budding breasts, eyes narrowed.

"What the fuck did she just do?" she demanded. Her attention flicked to me. "What the fuck did you just do?"

"I...what?" I moved to unfasten my belt with shaking hands. I hadn't been told to, but I wanted to get out of this van as soon as possible. I didn't mind small spaces, normally. This one was different. It felt oppressive and dangerous, like it could start moving again at any moment. "I didn't do anything. I went down into the dark to avoid the drive. Where are we?"

"What Sal fails to understand is that for most of us, ah, 'going down into the dark' is a difficult feat." Sherman waited until my belt was off before opening the door and offering me his hand. Through the opening, I could see what looked like an ordinary parking garage, all gray concrete and emptiness. "Come along, pet. You make yourself more precious by the hour, and I cannot wait to start learning all the tricks you have to teach me."

"I don't know what you're talking about." I took his hand. It seemed like the safest thing to do. "I don't know any tricks. I don't even know how I go down into the dark. I just do, when I need to."

"I'm telling you, rehome her." Ronnie stepped out of the van after me, pausing long enough to slam the door. I blinked at her. She sneered. "We know she adapts quickly. Train a new one who doesn't have all these stupid hang-ups."

"Ah, yes, because what one should absolutely do on the eve of war is take one of the best available weapons, break it down for scrap, and wait six months to have a new model on line." Sherman shook his head. "Honestly, Ronnie, if you were in charge of this battle, the humans would defeat us handily."

"Maybe, but a lot of them would die first," she said.

Sherman sighed. "Come along, Sal. It's time to introduce you to the people who will be your new family."

"I don't want a new family," I whispered.

His smile was benevolent and terrible. "It's adorable how you keep thinking that what you want has any merit."

I didn't say anything. I just glared at him. He might have me at his mercy right now, but he wasn't going to make me believe that I was going to be helpless forever.

We crossed the parking garage to a large steel door, which Sherman accessed with a swipe of a plastic card and a scan of his left index finger. He didn't bother to conceal either of these security measures from me, which made me sure that they couldn't be broken, or at least couldn't be broken easily. He would have made at least a little effort if he was worried about my getting away.

The door beeped, the locks disengaging with an audible click. Sherman smirked and pulled it open, letting go of my arm. "After you," he said.

I was unarmed, effectively barefoot, and in an unidentified parking garage with no idea where I was. I went through the door...

...and emerged into a defunct shopping mall, obviously long since gutted and abandoned by its original owners, only to be rebuilt by the people who came to claim it as their own. There was a fountain directly in front of me, the water trickling merrily out of a sculpted concrete flower to cascade into the basin below. A few people were sitting on the fountain's rim. One was eating a sandwich.

Stores extended in all directions, most still bearing the signs identifying what they had been before this place closed down. The shoe stores and shops selling scented candles were gone now, replaced by little swarms of people clustering around lab equipment. Unlike Dr. Cale's makeshift bowling alley lab, which held to strict protocols, even if most of the technicians wore jeans under their lab coats, the people here could have just wandered in off the street and picked up a scalpel. I didn't see a single lab coat or pair of scrubs, although some of the people were wearing gray bodysuits like the ones Sherman and Ronnie had on. As I stood there, trying to process the scene, a man walked by towing a pallet of caged chickens that clucked and fluffed their feathers at me. I blinked.

"Welcome, darling, to the revolution." Sherman slipped his arm around my shoulders, holding me closer than I was comfortable with. "I'm sure you recognize this place."

"No," I said blankly. "I mean, should I? I don't think I've ever been here before."

Sherman glanced meaningfully over my head. I turned to see Ronnie standing on my other side. She rolled her eyes.

"Ugh, fine," she said. "Your precious special snowflake is *so* sheltered that she's not going to be a threat. I'm delighted to know that she can't give us away. I'd be even more delighted if you'd let me cut her open."

"I don't want to be cut open," I said hastily. "I'm not sure I get a vote in this, but I really think I should, since this is my life you're talking about, and I don't want to be cut open." That didn't seem like enough. I paused before adding, meekly, "So please don't?"

"God, it's like kicking a fucking puppy," muttered Ronnie. She raised her voice as she said, "We're not going to cut you open. Not right now, anyway. It's not *allowed*, right, Sherman?"

"At last, you begin to learn," said Sherman. "If you want any chance of a stable long-term integration with a host you'll actually like, you'll stop threatening Sal. Go get yourself cleaned up. You reek of dead human."

"My favorite cologne," said Ronnie, and swaggered away. She didn't walk like a little girl: she walked like a grown man, all strutting and strength, and people got out of her way.

Sherman pulled his arm away from my shoulders as he transferred his hold back to my arm. "This way," he said, starting to walk deeper into the mall. A few people cast curious glances our way, but most of them ignored us. They had their own business to attend to, and we were just so much background noise. That, or they had been with Sherman long enough to learn to stay out of his way. All my early experiences with him told me that I could trust him, that he was my friend and would protect me. He had been one of my handlers at SymboGen. He had been my *friend*.

And yet everything I'd experienced since my last visit to SymboGen told me he was the enemy, or close enough as to make no difference. It was his fault we'd lost Tansy. It was his fault I was here. But whether he was friend or foe, the only option I had was to go with him. If he was going to protect me, he'd do a better job if he knew where I was. If he was planning to hurt me, maybe he'd be gentler if I seemed to be playing along.

"Have you been keeping up with your linguistics, pet?" he asked. "I know I haven't taught you any new words the last few times we've seen each other. I'm sorry about that. I did so enjoy expanding your vocabulary."

"Did you always know I was a tapeworm?" It wasn't the question I'd been planning to ask, but once it was out in the open between us, I realized that there *were* no other questions. Anything else I might have wanted to know was dependent on how he answered me.

"Oh, Sal. My pretty, innocent little creature." Sherman kept walking, and I kept walking with him. We passed more people, none of them familiar, and none of them paused to ask where we were going. "I knew someone like you was going to come along eventually—knew it in my bones, you could say." He chuckled like this was somehow hysterical. Maybe it was, to him. Tapeworms don't have bones. "Mother always told us we could only happen under proper laboratory conditions, but what she didn't count on was that I was the closest she'd yet come to perfection. Tansy was…well, you've met Tansy; there was no way she was going to bite the hand that fed her. Adam was always a momma's boy, too devoted to doing exactly as he was bid to question anything. Whereas I was the snake in her garden. I read all her files, and when I ran across something I didn't understand, I learned. It's amazing what people will tell you when they don't yet realize that they need to be wary.

"I asked her lab staff about biological interfaces and statistical probability. I asked her technicians about skeletal structures and backup functions and how often blood circulated through the brain. And I asked our mutual creator about the structure of my soul. She was very glad to tell me as much as I wanted to know, because she didn't think I'd have the background to understand what she was telling me. She even taught me—albeit accidentally—how one went about creating a false identity for someone, and what it would take to get on Steven Banks's good side." Sherman cast me a sly, sidelong look. "You see what I did for you, Sal? I twisted the world into knots so I could make it a pretty bow to tie in your hair. Your human lover never did anything half so nice."

Bile rose in my throat as I realized that he meant what he was saying. Some of this—not all, thankfully, but enough to be disturbing—had been intended as a form of courtship, like he could convince me to love him if he just spent enough time working on the problem. "You're not answering the question," I said. "People keep doing that to me. I don't like it."

"I do appreciate that you've started growing a spine. It'll make this much more of an equal partnership, and much less of a burden." Sherman shook his head. "Yes, I knew. I recognized you for what you were when they first rolled you into Symbo-Gen and I thought, this is it. This is what fate looks like. This is the way destiny presents itself. With a brunette on a stretcher, wetting herself and staring dispassionately at the ceiling. You were the Holy Grail, Sal. A natural chimera in the process of full neural integration, yet awake through the entire process. Most of us didn't get to wake up until a full six months further along. I honestly feel that it hampered our ability to completely inhabit our bodies. The protocols for integration as practiced here are based largely on your experience. We have so much to thank you for."

We had reached the far end of the mall while he was talking. A metal grill was half-lowered across the mouth of what had clearly been a department store, once upon a time. Sherman ducked to get under the grill, not letting go of my arm, and so I bent to follow him. The grill creaked down and locked onto the floor as soon as we were through. Because that wasn't disturb-ing or anything.

"You never told me." My voice sounded small and betrayed, matching the slivers of ice that felt like they were piercing my heart. I knew Sherman was on the other side of this conflict. It didn't matter. Part of me was always going to want him to be a good guy.

"What would I have said? 'I'm sorry to be the one to tell you this, dear, but not only are you not actually Sally Mitch-ell, you're not even a human being. You're something new, and better, and everyone you have ever loved is going to view you as a monster.'" He let go of my arm and stepped away, turning to face me. "Everyone but me, that is. You have never been a monster in my eyes, Sal. You have never been anything short of perfect. I doubt that you ever could be. You feel it, don't you? The way your heart slows down to beat along with mine."

I paused. "But...you can do that to anyone, can't you?" Sherman's startled, guilty expression was all the answer I needed. "Ronnie asked if you'd kissed me, and then she called you an asshole. What is it, some sort of biofeedback loop? Can you do that to all chimera, or am I just in a lucky subset of the population?"

"Sal..." He started to reach out, like he was going to caress my cheek. I slapped his hand away. His expression hardened. "Yes, if that's what you wanted to hear: yes, I can do that to any chimera, and to any of the charmingly named 'sleepwalkers,' if the need strikes me. It's a matter of controlling the pheromones I'm giving off. They tell you what to do on a level you simply weren't engineered to fight. I could teach you to do the same thing, but why would I put such a useful weapon in the hands of a *child*? Because don't misunderstand me, Sal: you are a child in this fight. I am romantically interested in you despite my better judgment, but that isn't going to buy you the sort of lazy disregard that you're accustomed to. You are a child and you are a weapon, and as we don't let children play with weapons, I'll be the one deciding how you are aimed and fired."

I glared at him. "You can't make me do anything."

"Oh, but darling, as you've already seen, I can." He smirked. "All I need to do is get skin-to-skin with you, and you'll dance to any tune I play. Now make yourself comfortable: find something to wear, find a bed in housewares. I've got cameras on this whole place, and the front of the building is sealed off, so you'll not be escaping. Aside from that, feel free to do as you like."

"Where are you going?"

"Didn't you hear me before?" This time when he smiled, he showed all of his teeth. I quailed away. "I'm going to go start a war."

*That's enough science for today. I can't really focus on it any-*
*way: it's all just facts and figures and not enough answers.*
*I need answers. I'm not going to find them in a Petri dish*
*or a simulation, but those are the only places that I'm being*
*allowed to look.*

*Sal has been missing for almost a month. Those words are*
*still so hard for me to type, because they don't make any sense.*
*We were home free. We were safe. All we had to do was make*
*it across a parking lot and we could get back to the lab, back*
*to the safety of Mom's defenses. There was no way anything*
*could go wrong, and I guess maybe I thought that too loudly,*
*because the universe decided to make sure I knew just how*
*wrong I really was.*

*There hasn't been a sign of her since USAMRIID grabbed*
*her out of that parking lot. I know she's not dead. I can feel*
*it. I also know that I'm probably lying to myself, because psy-*
*chic powers don't exist. She could be rotting in a freezer by*
*now, and I would still swear she was alive. I'm going to keep*
*swearing she's alive until we find her, and then I'm never,*
*never letting her go again.*

*Please, Sal. Please come back to me.*

—FROM THE JOURNAL OF DR. NATHAN KIM,
OCTOBER 2027.

*This is Private Arlen West with the United States Army Medical Research Institute of Infectious Diseases. I have been stationed in the San Francisco base for the past year. I have gone AWOL. I am releasing this recording without consent from my commanding officers. I understand that there will be consequences for this action. I also understand that those consequences cannot be carried out before I am able to insert the muzzle of my service pistol into my mouth, make my peace with God, and pull the trigger. I am doing a service to my country with this announcement. I am fulfilling my duty to the American people.*

*The sleepwalking sickness has not been contained. It is not a new form of the swine flu. It is not airborne. There is no vaccine. I repeat, there is no vaccine. The vaccinations you are receiving are standard flu shots, and will not protect you from the sleepwalking sickness. You are already infected. You have become infected of your own free—*

*They're trying to break the door down. I guess I don't have as much time as I thought. Take antiparasitic drugs. Take them now. Your life depends on it.*

—TRANSMISSION INTERCEPTED FROM THE SAN FRANCISCO
USAMRIID BASE, SEPTEMBER 29, 2027

**Chapter 8**

# OCTOBER 2027

It was hard to keep track of time in Sherman's converted mall. There were no windows in the department store that was my home and my prison, and the metal plates that sealed the doors to the outside world were snug with the ground, preventing me from even figuring out whether it was day or night outside. I guessed at the time by how many people walked freely in the mall outside my cage, and tried to measure the days by the delivery of my meals. It was harder than I'd expected it to be. Every time I felt sure I'd cracked the code, the meal I thought of as dinner would be pancakes and sliced fruit, or the mall would empty out completely during what I'd assumed was the middle of the day. Before long, I was completely disoriented.

That was bad. I needed to know how long it had been. Shelter animals became dispirited and withdrawn after six weeks in cages. Sherman seemed to think I was too weak to stand up against him, and that meant he was probably waiting for that magic mark before he did anything he couldn't take back. I just wanted to figure out their routines, and find the hole that would allow me to get away.

It would have been easier if anyone had been willing to talk to me, but no one was. They walked past the grill that kept me from getting out into the mall, chattering with one another or silently bustling from chore to chore, and the few people who even glanced in my direction did so with an odd mixture of contempt and pity that I couldn't begin to decode. I still watched them, hungry for even the illusion of contact.

It was funny, but after a few "days" I started to think I could feel people coming, even started to be able to predict who would walk into view by the tingle at the back of my mind. It wasn't completely dependable, but it was close enough that I began to wonder if it was real. Sleepwalkers communicated through pheromones. Maybe chimera did too, on some level.

Maybe I was learning.

So I was lonely and isolated, but I wasn't completely alone. Sherman visited often, even when I wished he wouldn't, even when it was inappropriate for him to do so, like when I was asleep or giving myself a sponge bath in the employee restroom. My burgeoning sense of "someone is coming" only worked with him about half the time, which made his unannounced arrivals all the more jarring. I would think I was safe and then he would just walk in on me, his eyes crawling across my nakedness in a way that made me profoundly uncomfortable, despite my general lack of a nudity taboo. He looked at me like he was trying to decide whether or not to eat me up. It wasn't right. I started closing doors and hiding myself in closets, and he still kept coming. He seemed to enjoy the challenge of being forced to track me down.

Ronnie and Kristoph took turns bringing my meals. Apparently, having been the ones to collect me from USAMRIID, they were also cleared to interact with me—or maybe this was a punishment of some sort, and I was a chore they had to complete before they could be considered forgiven. I didn't know, and I didn't care. All that mattered was that they weren't Sherman, and every time they brought me a tray or came to draw another vial of blood, it wasn't Sherman putting his hands on me again.

The meals were the best way I had of keeping track of time. I seemed to get one roughly every four hours, followed by a long period where I was supposed to be sleeping. But even that wasn't perfect, since the first meal usually arrived about an hour after I woke up in the "morning." Presumably, they could be feeding me six times a day. I wasn't gaining weight. I was also running laps around the abandoned department store, which probably burned off as many calories as I was taking in. I'd even started doing push-ups in what used to be the perfume department, letting the acrid burn of the chemicals spilled on the floor motivate me to keep pushing myself away. Maybe if I'd been stronger, I would have done a better job of fighting for my freedom. Maybe I wouldn't be here now.

I wasn't going to make that mistake again.

They had had me caged up like a lab animal for roughly three weeks, according to my best guess. I was running another lap around the store when someone fell into step beside me, keeping up easily. I turned to see Ronnie jogging next to me, his shorter legs pumping hard as he ran. Despite that, he didn't look like he was in any distress. I was trying to get into shape. He was already there.

Ronnie caught me looking at him. He frowned, brows beetling together above dark brown eyes, and growled, "What?" He tried to pitch his voice low, but it came out in a soprano squeak, so distinctly feminine that it made me stumble for a moment. I'd been here long enough that I didn't have a problem viewing Ronnie as male anymore—he said he was, and that was good enough for me. It was no more of a stretch than me saying I was human. But his voice always threw me.

"I was just wondering why you're here," I said, recovering from my stumble and continuing to run. "Is it time for more blood? I don't think I've finished making new stuff to replace what you took yesterday."

"I'm not telling you whether that was yesterday, today, or tomorrow, so you can stop fishing," he said, with less open malice than he would have harbored at the beginning. He began slowing down. I did the same, continuing to pace him until we were both standing in housewares, facing one another. "I'm not here for blood. I'm here for you."

I blinked at him. "I'm sorry. I don't understand."

"No, you never do, do you?" Ronnie shook his head. "Sherman wants you." I must have looked as distraught about that idea as I felt, because Ronnie sighed and reached out to touch my elbow reassuringly. "He's not going to take you apart. He just has some questions, and he's hoping you can answer them."

"I'll go with you quietly if you'll answer a question for me." I'd been trying this gambit more and more of late. It didn't always work—it didn't even work very often—but when it did, it could teach me important things about the people who were holding me captive. Maybe eventually I'd hit on the right combination of important things, and be able to magically transport myself out of this mall and back into my real life.

Ronnie snorted. "What, this again? Okay, Sal, fire away, but remember, I won't tell you how long it's been since we brought you here, where the mall is really located, or what Sherman wants you for. That's all between you and him. I'm not putting myself in the middle."

"Why did they have to put you in a different body? I mean. It's a pretty good body. It seems to work okay, even though I know you don't like it very much. But if the body you had was working, you should have just kept that one."

Ronnie didn't say anything. I grimaced, a thin worm of panic uncurling in my belly. I'd been trying to figure out what the situation was with Ronnie and his current body for days— it seemed like it should connect somehow to what I was doing here. This was the first time I'd been able to work up the courage to ask, and I was suddenly unsure it had been a good idea.

Finally, Ronnie said, "Come with me," and turned on his heel, stalking away into the housewares department. He wasn't heading for the exit.

Either he was going to kill me or he was going to explain, and I was desperate enough for allies that it seemed like a chance worth taking. I followed him through the store, catching up quickly and then just pacing him in silence, letting him lead the way to the dining room sets that stood, slowly gathering dust, near the mattress displays where I'd been sleeping. He pulled out a chair and sat down, gesturing for me to do the same. Lacking any other options, I sat.

The silence stretched out for a little longer, seeming to twist in on itself and nip at its own tail, before Ronnie said, "Rejection can be an issue for those of us who weren't tailored to specific hosts, or whose hosts were killed before we could finish the assimilation process."

I blinked at him dumbly. He sighed.

"I was designed for a long-haul trucker, according to the records Sherman got from SymboGen. I secrete stimulants and energy boosters. I also decrease acid buildup in soft tissues. They made worms like me for athletes too, although that was illegal. That's never stopped anybody, you know?"

I didn't know, but I didn't think that interrupting him to explain that would be a very good idea. I just nodded.

"Baseline human DNA in the implants is about three percent, or was before Sherman started getting to the lab rats. I was tailored, so I started with five percent, some of it taken directly from my host. It was supposed to keep his immune system from identifying me as an irritant and taking me over. Instead, it caused total immune collapse. Not fun for either one of us. I don't really remember much about being him. I know I migrated to his brain during the shutdown, but he didn't survive the process. We got hospitalized—this was in the early stages of the outbreak, back when there were only one or two of us at a time." He was switching pronouns with dizzying speed, making it difficult for me to know exactly who "us" meant— him and his trucker, or sleepwalkers in general? "He died."

I blinked. "Who died?"

"My trucker." Ronnie shook his head. "He crashed and he died and that should have been the end of me, but SymboGen was collecting all the dead sleepwalkers for analysis, in case they could figure out what was going on. Anything to protect the profit margin, right?"

I sort of suspected it was more about "anything to protect the public health," but I kept that observation to myself, in part because I didn't want Ronnie to stop talking, and in part because there was a good chance that I was being overly optimistic again. Dr. Banks had never shown any indication of caring about the health of the world, except when it could put money in his pockets. Keeping the sleepwalkers from eating his entire customer base had probably seemed like a pretty good idea, at least as far as the bank was concerned.

Ronnie took my silence as agreement, because he continued, saying, "Sherman found me in my trucker's head. I was still alive, and he removed as much of me as he could. I don't remember any of this—I mean, I didn't have a brain to plug into at that point, so I wasn't much of a deep thinker—but I've seen my medical records, and I believe things happened the way he explained them. He managed to get me out of the building, and he implanted me in my first stable host. His name was Francisco, and he was a mountain." A little smile played across Ronnie's lips. "Six and a half feet of solid muscle—damn. I couldn't have asked for a better host, you know? I guess I should have known that it couldn't last."

"What happened?"

"Rejection." Ronnie shrugged. "Same thing we've been telling you happens to a lot of us. My host's body recognized me as an infection, and fought me off. I had to be moved to a new body. That's where I got the name 'Ron.' Another big guy. I liked being Ron. He was strong. Too strong, I guess, since his immune system figured out I was new in the neighborhood and beat me off with a stick. That's how I wound up in here." He spread his arms, indicating his thin, immature, biologically female body with a bob of his chin. "And we don't have bodies to spare, so until this one breaks or we come into a sudden wealth of unwanted humans, this is where I'm staying."

"But…if we become who we are because we're tapping into human brains, and they can process more information than we can handle with our little tapeworm brains, how can you remember being anyone before you were who you are right now? How can you be…" I stopped, not sure how I could possibly finish that sentence.

Ronnie finished it for me. "How can I be so sure that I'm supposed to be male? I don't remember a lot about my first three hosts. No one who's been through rejection remembers *much*. But there are little bits and pieces. It's like…it's like some of the traits of my original hosts got written into me. Sherman says it's epigenetics at work, and that we're all going to wind up mosaic individuals, hopping from body to body, bringing just these little pieces of who we've been onward with us."

I blinked at him. Ronnie shrugged.

"Sherman says we're going to live forever, once we figure out how to keep our hosts from rejecting us. We'll have to learn a lot of shit new every time, but our core personalities will stay the same. *We'll* stay the same. Humans have had stories about reincarnation and the afterlife for millennia. We're finally going to prove it." Ronnie stood. "Anyway, that's how I know I'm a guy, no matter what this stupid body says, and since I want a new host sooner rather than later, it's time for you to come with me." He grabbed my arm.

I was bigger than he was, and stronger than he was, but I went without protest.

Sherman was waiting for us in the store that had been converted into his private office, a former photo studio now packed with lab equipment and computer monitors. He was sitting on a wooden stool that had probably come with the studio, peering through a microscope into a Petri dish. He looked up when he heard our footsteps, a wide smile spreading across his face.

"Sal! I'm so delighted that you were able to join me." He slid down off the stool, stretching as he did. "Ronnie, thank you for passing my invitation along. You can go now; your services are no longer required."

"Yeah, I didn't think they would be." Ronnie let go of my arm. "Later, toots. Try not to piss him off too bad today, okay? I don't want to have to clean this place up again."

I blinked. I hadn't heard anything about needing to clean Sherman's office. The claim was apparently true, however; Sherman glared at him as he turned and walked away.

"She's getting ideas above her station," he said mildly. "I think she likes you. I also think it might be a good idea if I didn't let you spend any time with her alone for a little while, since you seem bound and determined to play the Disney Princess of this scenario."

"I don't understand."

"Friend to all living things, my sweet Sal; friend to all living things. But what you fail to comprehend is that I don't *want* you to be a friend to all living things. I want you to be a friend to me and me alone." Sherman reached out and tweaked a lock of hair that had fallen in my face. "We need to get you a haircut.

Something short and tidy and easy to care for. You're starting to look a little unkempt, my dear, and we both know how little tolerance I have for that."

I fought the urge to bat his hand away. He wasn't touching my skin, which meant that the drums wouldn't synchronize to his heartbeat, but having him touch any part of me felt like a violation. "I like my hair the way it is."

"Ah, but appearances must be maintained. You know that. It's how we fit into the world, snug as a needle fitting into an injection site. Nothing that attracts attention of the wrong sort." Sherman delivered this little sermon with the pious air of a man who was preaching to the heathens, but knew they would catch on sooner or later. As always, it made me want to scratch his eyes right out of his head.

There was a time when I'd found his little life lessons endearing, attractive even. That was before I knew he was a tapeworm, and before I knew he was on the "kill all humans" side of the program, and most of all, before he was keeping me captive in an abandoned mall, with no way of reaching the people I loved most in all the world. "The only attention I'm attracting here is from you," I countered. "*All* the attention I get from you is the wrong kind of attention, now that I know what you are."

"You still don't understand, do you?" He grabbed my arm. It was a swift motion: I had no opportunity to dodge or defend myself. Fingers sinking into my skin, he continued: "My attention is the only attention you will ever need. My approval is the only approval you should ever crave. I am your perfect other half, Sal, and the sooner you come to terms with that idea and begin making yourself over in my image, the sooner we'll be able to move on to the next phase of our relationship."

"Let me go!" I struggled against his grasp, but he held firm. The drums were pounding in my ears, slowing bit by bit to fall into synch with his pulse. As always, the feeling left me dizzy and confused, like someone was messing with my inner ear.

"You don't have to do this. You don't have to…to…" The sentence seemed to slip away from me. I wobbled.

Sherman tightened his hand a little more. It was starting to hurt, and I would probably have a bruise the next day, something to commemorate our little encounter. "I do have to do this, because you make me do this," he said apologetically. "Besides, anesthesia is expensive, and you're so much more pliant when you've started seeing things my way. It's truly a pity that it never seems to last."

Still holding my wrist tight, he half dragged me across the room to a chair that looked like it had been stolen from a dentist's office. I made one last feeble attempt to struggle. I knew that chair. It had started to feature prominently in my nightmares, swelling to hellish proportions with every new appearance. The real chair was smaller than the one in my dreams, made of plain green vinyl instead of burning human leather, but their meanings were exactly the same. They both meant pain.

"Down you go," said Sherman, releasing my wrist as he shoved me into the chair. I tumbled helplessly, unable to resist the pull of my slowed, muddled pulse. Sherman immediately started strapping me down, putting restraints across my wrists, ankles, and chest. He stopped short of making it hard to breathe, but only barely; as long as he didn't kill me, my comfort was not his concern.

"Still don't know…how you do that," I mumbled. My lips felt like they were made of lead, too heavy to operate properly and only technically grafted onto my body.

"We are the music makers, and we are the dreamers of dreams," he replied, before leaning down to give me a peck on the forehead. "If I tell you how much I am your superior, will you finally cease this pointless attempt to rail against me?"

I couldn't answer. I just looked at him.

Apparently, Sherman took silence as agreement—that, or

he'd been waiting for the chance to tell me all about his brilliance for a while now, and this was enough of an opening that he couldn't resist. He picked up a drill, giving its trigger an experimental pull. And then, after the sound had passed, he told me.

"We were all engineered for different things, you know. We each have different mechanisms of supporting and enhancing the human body." His hands worked as he spoke, clever hands holding clever needles and making them do clever things. My throat ached to scream, but the numbing effect of my slowed pulse and confused flesh kept me from doing anything more extreme than whimpering. Any time it seemed like I was going to break loose, he would press a hand down against the exposed skin of my upper arm and yank me back down into the darkness, where my needs and desires mattered not at all. "I know you spoke with Ronnie about her enhancements. It's why she can stay awake for so long, and move so fast, and have such a terribly bad temper without slipping over into Tansy territory. Tansy was designed to secrete antipsychotic medication, if you can believe that. Maybe she still does. That would explain why that damaged brain of hers doesn't kick her out entirely. It will one day. Won't that be something to see?"

He finished with the veins in my arm and moved on to the veins in my thighs. There was nothing sexual about it, for all that he was so fond of posturing and propositioning. I knew that Sherman would have taken me up on any offer I chose to make—taken me up on it enthusiastically and without hesitation. He'd said as much, and I remembered his assignations with the scientists back at SymboGen, back when our relationship consisted of more than needles and captivity.

"You, I haven't quite figured out. No one has an exact genetic profile on you, which is odd, since I know you were of SymboGen design. Nothing off-market or back alley about you, Sal my girl, and still I don't know what your chimeric interface has blessed or cursed you with. You'll sort it out one day, probably when you least want to, and you'll forgive me if I very much want to be standing by to point and laugh. Discovery is almost always traumatic for someone. That's what discovery is *for*. If only they hadn't hidden your files from me. I looked. I looked so hard. But alas. They had to make me do things the hard way."

He put the syringe he'd been using aside, and I had time to breathe a sigh of disoriented relief before he picked up a scalpel, raising it high to be certain that I would see it.

"I was designed to regulate the heartbeat of a captain of industry, a man who did so love his indulgences. They might as well have called him Old King Cole for the way he carried on. He called for his pipe and he called for his bowl and he called for his fiddlers three, and when those proved to be too much for his feeble mammalian body, he called for his faithful tapeworm jester to come and bear the brunt of everything he'd ever done to himself. I'm a biological pacemaker. Can't do much to humans, I'm afraid, and I can only slow a sleepwalker down if I can get them to stop biting me long enough to notice that they've been calmed past all reason, but give me a chimera and ah, you've given me the world."

He brought the scalpel down. I think I surprised us both when I found another scrap of strength in my damaged throat and began to scream.

"Really, Sal," chided Sherman, once he had his composure back—and he did not, I noted, look happy about having lost it in the first place. Sherman was not a man who liked looking foolish, no matter how good his reasons had been. "Flesh is an illusion, human flesh doubly so. You should be grateful that I'm teaching you that now, rather than your needing to learn it the way that Ronnie did." He continued slicing small chunks of my underarm off. Every time he raised the scalpel, it was a little redder, as were his fingers. I could hear my blood dripping into the pan he'd positioned for just that purpose. I pictured a basin overflowing with pieces of me, things I had never agreed to give away or let him steal. How many pieces could I lose before I could never be put back together again? How many pieces did he *want*?

"You've been very good so far today, but it's time you pull your little mental rabbit hole trick, because this next bit is going to be quite painful." Sherman's jovial tone was all the warning I really needed. I gathered my consciousness into a tight knot and plummeted down, down, down through the layers of self until I reached the hot warm dark, where everything was safe and warm and red, and no men with scalpels or inscrutable designs could touch or take me.

It was becoming increasingly easy to separate myself—my actual self, the part of me that was Sal, and had never been Sally Mitchell—from the human body that had always defined me. It was something I'd always been able to do when I was sleeping, whether I intended to or not, but since Sherman had started putting his hands on me, it had become a waking refuge as well, a place where I could know that my inner core would not be violated in any way. I didn't know why I could do it, just like Sherman didn't know why he couldn't. I just knew that when I really needed to escape, everything except the hot warm dark and the sound of distant drums would go away.

*Maybe that's what they built into me,* I thought, floating formless in the void that was the core of my self. *Silence and meditation, instead of messing with people's hearts or never being still.* I had only heard the word "epigenetic" once before I was brought here. I still wasn't quite sure what it meant. I wondered if Dr. Cale would know. I wondered whether I would ever have the chance to ask her.

*He's never going to let you go,* murmured one of the under-voices that lurked in the dark, more and more often these days, giving voice to things I knew but didn't want to know. I felt fractured, fragmented, like I was splitting myself into pieces in my effort to remain whole.

*I know*, I answered myself miserably, and stopped trying to think about anything at all, letting myself fall deeper down into the perfect timelessness of the only place that had always been meant to belong to me.

I woke up with the worst headache I had ever had in my life. I sat up slowly, forcing down the nausea that threatened to rise up in my throat and overwhelm me. A lock of hair fell in my face and I jumped before reaching up with shaky fingers and pulling it in front of my eyes.

"That *bastard*," I breathed. It was easier to focus on my hair than on my aching head, or on the bandages wrapped around my wrists and inner elbows. My formerly long hair had been cut into a bob, long enough to get in my mouth and eyes, too short to pull back in anything more elaborate than a ponytail. To add insult to injury, it was also about three shades darker and redder than my original chestnut brown, filled with auburn highlights that made it look like it belonged on someone else's head. I dropped the lock of hair.

"I'm going to kill him," I said. Hearing the words made me feel a little better, and so I raised my voice and called, "Do you hear me, Sherman? I'm going to kill you. You can use my body for your fucked-up experiments, but you had no right to cut my hair. It's not *yours*."

"See, he thinks everything about us is his, and that means everything about you, and that means he had every right," said Ronnie, from off to my left.

I flinched away from the sound of his voice. That was a bad decision. "Ow!" I yelped, clapping my hands over the back of my head. They hit a thick gauze pad, covering the same spot as the incision Nathan and the others had used to repair my faulty arteries. My head spun, filled with a pain so profound that it seemed to be coming from inside and outside at the same exact time. I wanted to throw up. I was afraid my skull would explode if I did.

"Ow," I repeated, this time almost in a whimper, and collapsed backward onto the mattress, pulling myself into a fetal ball. The pain didn't subside. I had awoken it, and it was going to have its say before it left me in peace.

Footsteps to my left signaled Ronnie's approach. There was a small clicking sound as he put something down on the display nightstand next to my current bed. "I brought painkillers and antibiotics," he said. "Sherman's proud of his surgical theater, but that doesn't make it completely sterile. You need to take these pills to make sure you don't wind up with an infection."

I said nothing. I just stayed in my curl, clutching my head and fighting the urge to whimper.

Ronnie sighed. "You don't trust us and you don't like us and you don't have to, because we've all basically been assholes to you. I'm not going to lecture you on getting along with people who've fucked you over. But we need you alive, so if you don't want to wake up strapped down and attached to half a dozen IVs, you need to take your medicine."

"Why do you need me alive?" The question was faint and reedy, but I forced it out word by word. The effort left me feeling wrung-out and exhausted. I needed to sleep. I needed to sleep forever.

"You can learn a lot from a necropsy," said Ronnie. "You sometimes learn even more from a living being."

This time, I didn't swallow my whimper. When you dissect a human being, you're performing an autopsy. When you dissect anything else in the world, intelligent or not, you're performing a necropsy. By using the word "necropsy," Ronnie made it clear that he wasn't talking about cutting up the human body that I inhabited. He was talking about the actual me, the pound and a half of tapeworm that was wedged tight into Sally Mitch-ell's skull, like a squatter that had taken over the house while the original owner wasn't home.

Ronnie sighed. "We're not the enemy, Sal. Those people out there, all they want to do is wipe us out. Kill us off, even though we're their creation. We're part of a healthier, hardier world, and you're going to help us make that happen. So yeah, we're *going* to keep you alive, whether you like it or not. You're going to be a lot happier if you just go along with things."

I was silent. A few seconds passed before Ronnie sighed again, louder this time, and I heard his footsteps moving away. I waited until I was sure he was gone before rolling over and opening my eyes. The plastic tray he'd placed on the nightstand contained a bottle of water and a little paper cup of pills. It was only a few feet away from me. It might as well have been a mile.

It took what felt like an hour for me to inch my way across the bed and catch the edge of the tray, pulling it closer to me. For one sickening moment it teetered on the nightstand, seem-ing to be in danger of crashing to the floor. I swallowed hard and forced myself to keep moving, pulling it inch by agoniz-ing inch into reach. It didn't fall. I emptied the little paper cup of pills into my mouth, dry-swallowing them one by one, holding the others under my tongue until they were needed. I nearly choked twice, the round edges of the pills seeming to become jagged and sharp as they rasped against the walls of my esophagus. Finally, though, the last of them was inside me, and I collapsed back into limp motionlessness, looking longingly at the water. I wanted it more than I could remember wanting almost anything. I knew that trying to drink it without sitting up would make a mess without slaking my thirst, and sitting up was off the table as long as the pain was raging in my head.

Sherman had cut a hole in my skull. He'd decided to break me open without access to the tools that Nathan and the others had used when they'd done the same thing—only what they did wasn't the same thing, it wasn't the same thing at all. They'd acted with my full, informed consent, while Sherman had simply put me under and taken what he wanted. The acts themselves might be virtually indistinguishable, but the motives behind them made all the difference in the world.

There were only two things inside my skull: my brain, and my real body, soft and segmented and hiding itself among the cortical folds of the tissue around it. I couldn't imagine he'd gone in looking for a piece of brain tissue, since there was nothing special about it that he couldn't also learn from the blood and bone marrow samples he'd been taking since he locked me up. That left only one target for his exploratory surgery: he'd been looking for *me*. He'd been taking samples from my real body for a change, and not the one I wore.

That was the greatest violation I could imagine. I was small and soft and vulnerable without my human skin to defend me, and he'd cracked open my bony shield and gone into my sanctuary. I didn't *know* that he'd taken tissue samples from my tapeworm-self, but I couldn't imagine that he wouldn't have, not after he'd gone to the considerable trouble of opening my skull and peering inside. The thought of a piece of me, severed from the whole, identity and intelligence cut off and lost forever, made me want to vomit. Was he going to implant some empty body with another me? Would there be enough epigenetic memory for that little slice of Sal to remember that it liked watermelon juice and walking dogs and learning new words, or would it be someone completely new?

Worst of all, if it worked—if he was able to successfully splice "me" into another body and learn whatever it was he wanted to know about how I'd been able to bond with Sally Mitchell—was he going to take the rest of me apart next? He didn't need to keep the original. Not when he could make a hundred knockoffs, one little sliver at a time.

The pain in my head wasn't getting any better, but time was

running out. If Sherman had really removed a piece of my primary body, he'd learn what he wanted to know sooner rather than later. I had to get out of here.

I sat up slowly, fighting the spinning in my head every inch of the way, and reached for the bottle of water. Drinking it made me feel a little bit better: I was still in a lot of pain, but at least my mouth didn't feel like a used litter box anymore. Still moving with the utmost caution, I slid my feet to the floor and stood. The motion was accompanied by another wave of pain that almost sent me crashing back down onto the bed. I gritted my teeth and held my ground until it passed. I needed to get out of here.

Maybe deciding it was finally time to make my escape when I was still dizzy and weak from nonelective surgery was a bad idea, but it was the only way to avoid *more* nonelective surgery, and so I was going to go with it. Besides, Sherman wasn't going to be expecting me to try anything right now. I had trouble remembering that he was the enemy when he wasn't directly in front of me with a scalpel in his hand and a smirk on his face: we'd spent too much time together as allies, and deep down, I wanted him to still be the man that he'd been then. Maybe that was true in both directions. He wouldn't have hennaed my hair and cut it nicely rather than hacking it all off if he didn't harbor at least a little genuine affection for me.

The Sal he'd known for years was pliable and obedient, and had no idea that she could ever be allowed to become anything else. So maybe he still thought of me like that. Maybe I could get myself out of here if I stopped thinking like a good little girl, and started thinking like a chimera.

Joyce used to love going shopping, even when neither of us had any intention of buying anything. She'd haul me through malls and department stores with equal enthusiasm, pointing out sales and commenting snarkily on fashions she didn't think anyone should ever, under any circumstances, wear outside the house. Thanks to her, I knew quite a lot about how stores like the one that had become my prison were constructed.

I started for the escalators, pausing only long enough to grab fresh jeans and a clean, cable-knit sweater from the Lands' End display. I could get underwear and a tank top to go with it once I was upstairs in the lingerie section. I tried to keep my movements as natural as possible, and allowed myself to wince every time the incision in my head sent another bolt of pain searing through me, which was often. If Sherman or one of his people was watching me through the security cameras, I needed to put on a good enough show that they wouldn't send anyone in to check on me.

The escalator was slow enough that I was able to peel my shirt off and throw it back down to the first floor before I reached the second. There were bloodstains on the back of the collar, marking the places where the fabric had brushed against my surgical incision. I shuddered, turning my eyes toward my destination.

Most of the lights on the second floor were off, saving power, since I was the only one in here and usually stayed on the first floor. I didn't bother looking for the switches as I made my way toward the distant glow of the fitting rooms, which were lit independently of everything else. That same glow allowed me to find a bra, tank top, and panties that would actually fit me. There were no non-high-heel shoes left downstairs—all the good running and hiking shoes had been looted by Sherman's people before they locked me away in here—so I didn't bother removing my thick, plastic-soled socks. They'd be better than nothing if what I was planning actually succeeded.

This had been a nice department store, and like all nice department stores, they had been more worried about the privacy of their customers than the possibility of shoplifting. I entered the dressing rooms with my armload of fresh clothing, walking along the row of open, slatted doors until I reached the very end and slipped into the private cubicle. It was located closest to what I guessed would be the store's outside wall, rather than feeding back into the mall proper. Even more important, this dressing room stall boasted a large, white-painted air grate, used to pump in heat during the winter and cold during the summer. It was quiescent now, the California September providing no opportunities to either warm or chill. That was good. I didn't want to freeze to death in my effort to escape.

There was a small bench inside the fitting room. I pushed it to the wall under the grate and stood, reaching up to rattle the grill. It didn't budge, thanks to the screws that were holding it in place. That was a small problem at this stage. I knelt and took my fresh bra off its hanger. This was a *nice* department store. They used wood and wire hangers.

I smashed the hanger against the floor until it broke. Then I scavenged through the pieces until I found a splinter of the right thickness and flexibility to serve my intended purpose. "If they didn't want me to learn to improvise, they should've kept the shelter better funded," I muttered, and got to work.

It took less than five minutes to unscrew all but one of the bolts from the grate. It swung drunkenly down, revealing the empty black chasm on the other side. There was a chance that was exactly what it was: a hole, rather than a tunnel. I paused, looking into the dark, and asked myself if this was really the right course of action. It could get me killed.

Even killed was better than captive. I hopped down from the bench long enough to strip and put my new clothes on, taking care to tuck the tank top into my jeans before letting the sweater hang over it. Hopefully, it would be enough padding to keep me from getting seriously cut up on any sharp edges inside the vent.

This was it: this was the moment where I would have to decide whether I wanted to be the girl I'd always been, or whether I was ready to become someone new. Someone who was brave enough to crawl into the dark alone, and see where the risk would take her. Someone who was going to survive.

I was going to see my family again. I was going to get back to them. I was going to see Nathan again.

I was going to survive, and then I was going to find Tansy, and we were going to get through this.

I reached up, grabbing the open edge of the vent, and hoisted myself into the unknown.

# INTERLUDE II: DIPLOTENE

*History will remember my name forever. Isn't that the truest form of immortality? All you have to do to earn it is change the world.*

—DR. STEVEN BANKS

*I don't think "human" means what people tell me it does. I'm just as human as you are. Everything that matters is underneath the skin.*

—ADAM CALE (SUBJECT I, ITERATION I)

*October 2027: Tansy*

Still here I'm still here I'm still me I'm still here.
It hurts.

It hurts so bad, and I keep on still being me, I keep on still being here, but I'm starting to think that maybe not being me—maybe not being here—would be better, because absence hurts other people. Absence doesn't hurt *you*.

The lights were too bright for my eyes. That was happening more and more, now that Dr. Banks had stopped taking things out of me and started putting things inside me instead. Tears were running down my cheeks, even though I wasn't crying. I'd learned a lot about what crying felt like since he brought me here, since he strapped me down and started taking whatever he wanted out of me. He was running out of pieces. That's why he'd decided to introduce some new variables.

"Now, this may hurt a little," he'd cautioned. "But don't you worry your pretty little head about it. The pain is temporary, but the knowledge we're going to get in exchange is forever. You're going to help me transform the world. Isn't that wonderful?"

I hadn't answered him. I hadn't been able to answer in days, not since he'd sent two of his flunkies into the room to rip out four of my molars, all without the benefit of painkillers or sedation. Knocking me out apparently messed with my reactions in a way that would slow down the all-important research. "You understand," that was what he had said before and after every procedure. He always had the same smug little smile on his face, like he wasn't doing anything wrong, but was doing so much right.

It hurt. *I* hurt. For the first time since I woke up in this body, with its wonderful hands and eyes and legs, I could feel both of my selves independently. The human half of me was numb and distant, filled with pains I didn't have a name for. The invertebrate half felt like it was on fire, skin scored with a hundred tiny cuts, fluids leaking out into my human brain and making my thoughts even more muddled than usual.

The lights in the room never varied. They were always bright and burning, too white for my eyes. They hadn't fed me once. All my nutrients came in through a tube, plunged deep into my arm and filling me until my veins felt swollen and tight, like they were becoming worms in their own right. I hoped that they would break out soon, and that they would be able to slither their way to freedom.

It was getting difficult to remember anything before the room. I had a name once—Sandy or Tammy or something like that. I had a family, a mother who was a brilliant scientist and a brother who was smarter than I'd ever be. I thought I remembered going sledding, but that couldn't have been true, because I didn't remember snow.

I remembered Sal. I remembered her running away and leaving me behind. I remembered being glad. I clung to that gladness as hard as I could, because I knew that if it ever managed to slip away, I'd only remember how much I hated her. She shouldn't have left me behind. Not even if I told her to, not even if her survival mattered more than almost anything else, because she was the one who carried the data we'd infiltrated SymboGen to take. She left me, and I wanted to hate her, and I wanted to love her, and that meant remembering how her desertion made me feel.

There was a click from the far side of the room as the door swung open. I kept my eyes closed. Opening them wouldn't have done me any good. I hadn't been able to turn my head in what felt like forever.

"How's my girl today?" asked Dr. Banks, as genial and fatherly as ever. "I see you're not moving. That's good. That means the nerve blockers we've placed on your spine are doing their job. It's important that you keep still. I'm sure you understand that by now."

I kept my eyes closed.

"I know you're not dead, Tansy. I can see your chest moving, and the monitor tells me that your vital signs are still clear and strong. You're a fighter. You've got a lot of fight left in you before you'll even be able to consider giving up on us."

His words filled me with more despair than I would have believed possible. It felt like I'd been his captive for weeks. It could have been days, or even hours. With the constant light and the lack of solid food, I had nothing to measure time by. The sadistic bastard could do whatever he wanted to me, for as long as he wanted to, and it wouldn't matter. I was never going to get away.

"Kill me," I whispered.

"I intend to," said Dr. Banks, with amiable honesty. "After we've wrung every drop of useful data out of you, we're going to take you apart and find the things we missed on the first pass. But you've got some time before that, and we're going to spend it together, learning everything you don't even know you have in you to teach."

I didn't think I had it in me to scream.

I was wrong.

# STAGE II: DIAKINESIS

*Mankind has been forgetting this simple fact since the dawn of time: when we transgress, it is our children who must pay the price of those transgressions.*

—DR. SHANTI CALE

*I didn't do anything wrong. All I did was survive.*

—SAL MITCHELL

*Mom is sad all the time right now. She stays in her lab as much as we let her, looking at graphs and charts that show how the cousins are waking up, and sometimes she says bad words when she doesn't know I'm there listening to her. It makes me feel funny when she does that, like she has a face I've never seen, because she's always been so busy being my mother. She's the smartest person I've ever met. She's a super scientist and she's going to find a way to save everybody, not just the humans. But she's sad, and I can't make her better.*

*Sal and Tansy are both still missing. I think that's a lot of what makes Mom so sad. I miss them too. Tansy's always been my best friend, and I like Sal a lot. She's my sister, and that means I have to love her forever, but nobody gets to tell me who I have to like. I decided I would like her all on my own. Now I just miss her a lot.*

*Maybe I should go and find her. Mom would be happy again if I brought Sal home, and then Sal and I can go find Tansy, and we'll finally be a family the way we should have been all along. I can do it. I'm smarter than anyone thinks I am.*

*I can bring my sisters home.*

—FROM THE JOURNAL OF ADAM CALE, OCTOBER 2027

*The subject has shown surprising resilience. I expected her to die when I introduced antiparasitics into her food supply, but she proved unexpectedly resistant. The subject reacted to the antiparasitics as if they were an infection, resulting in nothing more severe than a brief spike in the host body temperature, with no lasting damage to the subject.*

*Proglottids cultured from the subject have proven to be strong and healthy. Three have been introduced into the subject's digestive system, to see whether the brain worm can tolerate the presence of competing parasites. Full documentation will continue.*

*All in all, this is an excellent way to test all current theories without endangering the life of any necessary or important personnel.*

—FROM THE NOTES OF DR. STEVEN BANKS, SYMBOGEN,
OCTOBER 2027

# Chapter 9
## OCTOBER 2027

The grate in the changing room wall opened onto a snug vent that was at most two feet across and a foot and a half tall. I squirmed my way inside, grateful that the phobia instilled in me by the psychologists at SymboGen had focused on car crashes instead of on tight spaces. This would have been enough to make even a mild claustrophobe lose their composure, and that was while I was still close enough to the opening for a small amount of light to filter in and allow me to see. It was going to be all about touch from here on out.

At least it was too narrow for Sherman or Kristoph to come after me. Ronnie would fit, but it would take a while for whoever was watching the monitors to realize that I wasn't emerging from the dressing room. No matter what, I would have a lead before he came after me, and that meant that I might actually have a chance. Bracing my weight on my elbows, I began pulling myself inexorably forward into the dark.

The light faded within ten feet of the entrance. I was just starting to wonder how long this tunnel could go when my fingers hit the wall. I stopped where I was, feeling around for where the tunnel branched. There were openings to both my left and my right. They felt like they were roughly the same size, but there was more dirt and grit to the left, which implied that air normally flowed in that direction. Since air would flow from the outside, that meant I needed to go right. I shuffled back a foot or so, and then pulled myself cautiously around the corner, continuing my slow progress into the dark.

The slow pounding of my heart in my ears distracted me from the otherwise absolute silence in the vent: without the air conditioner or heater running, the only sounds were the ones that I made. That was good. It made it easier for me to listen for pursuit. I stopped every ten feet or so, cocking my head and trying to focus back through the dark for signs that I was being followed. There weren't any, as yet. That didn't mean that they weren't coming. I needed to keep going as fast as I could.

The next section of the vent extended for what felt like about sixty feet before it dead-ended. I shuffled backward again, feeling the walls for turnoffs that I might have missed. There was nothing but solid, unyielding metal. I took a deep breath and held it until the panic that had been starting to writhe in my belly died down. If I had to go back, I'd go back. There were no pits between me and the last turn. It would be hard. It wasn't impossible.

A faint breeze ruffled my hair as I prepared myself for backing up. I stopped. Then, cautiously, I lifted one hand above my head.

First it hit the metal roof of the vent. And then it hit nothing but empty air. I had found the ventilation shaft.

"Okay," I whispered. "I can do this. I can do this. It'll get me home." I squirmed forward again, until I could roll onto my back and reach up into the open ventilation shaft with both hands. It was square, rather than rectangular, and slightly narrower than the main vent. I would still fit, but it was going to be a tight squeeze, and I was much more likely to find myself stuck. I could die in there.

It would still be better than staying here with Sherman. I dug my fingernails into the joins between pieces of metal and began pulling myself up, bracing my feet and knees against the sides of the shaft for traction. All those laps around the mall were really paying off. Now all I had to do was hope that I would reach the top before my strength gave out completely, and that whatever was between me and freedom would be something I could easily move aside.

I didn't know how good security usually was on things like "roof vents," which struck me as a bad target for thieves. I also didn't know how I was going to get down from the roof once I managed to get there. That was a problem for later; that was a problem for someone who was already free, and that meant that it couldn't be a problem for *me*. Until I was outside, I was still Sherman's captive.

With no other way of marking time, I started counting off seconds in my head, chanting, "One Mississippi, two Mississippi," as softly as I could. The minutes blurred into an infinite number of Mississippis, leaving me no more certain of how long I'd been climbing than I would have been without the count. At least the act of saying the numbers aloud made me feel like I was doing something, and kept me from focusing on the increasing weakness of my arms. I'd never done anything like this before. If my grip slipped even the slightest bit…

As if the thought had created the action, my sweat-soaked palms slipped on the slick tin walls of the vent, and I slid abruptly downward for what felt like a mile before I managed to jam my feet hard enough against the vent's sides to stop my descent. My heart was hammering so hard that it felt like it was going to break clean out of my chest, and I could taste the bright copper penny burn of adrenaline on my tongue. What would have happened if I'd fallen all the way down to the bottom? It's not like there was a pillow waiting there to soften my landing. I would have been lucky to get away with something as small as a broken ankle.

For one dizzying moment I hung there, suspended and afraid, and thought about climbing the rest of the way down before I could plummet. I would go back to the dressing room. I would crawl back through the grate before anyone noticed I was gone and came looking for me. I would go back to my bed and sleep off this headache, and when I woke up, I would be able to think of a better escape route. One that wasn't so risky. One that didn't carry so many consequences for failure.

*You're not going to do any of those things,* I told myself quietly. There was nothing firm or stern about my little inner voice: if anything, I sounded despairing even to myself. I wasn't going to go back, and I wasn't going to come up with another escape plan, because there *wasn't* another escape plan. It was this or nothing.

Knees shaking with the effort of keeping me suspended in place, I pulled one hand cautiously away from the wall and wiped my palm dry on my sweater. Placing my hand back against the wall, I repeated the process with the other hand. Then, taking a deep breath, I began to climb again.

If it had been hard before, it was pure torture now. I was dead tired, lactic acid was building up in my muscles, and falling was no longer an abstract "maybe": it was a thing that had happened once and could easily happen again. I dug my nails into the grooves between panels of tin, climbing ever higher, trying not to think about what awaited me if I slipped. I'd managed to catch myself once. I wasn't going to be so lucky a second time.

My right hand quested upward for the wall, and struck empty

air. I trembled, forcing the rest of my limbs to remain rigid as I felt around, trying to find where the wall had gone. Finally, reaching down, I found the point where the vent curved. Hope surged through me, hot and red and burning. I was at the top. I had to be.

That, or the bend was going to lead me to a whole new tunnel system, and take me no closer to the exit. I pushed that thought aside. It was unproductive, and besides, I could feel the cool air flowing toward me. It was just a trickle, held back by whatever grating was on the front of the vent, but it meant that I was moving in the right direction, if nothing else.

With trembling hands, I pulled myself around until I was facing into the bend. There was still no light. Still, I hadn't come this far to turn around at the first sign of trouble, and so I squirmed forward, working my way one inch at a time into the new leg of my journey.

The bend was barely the length of my body. Then it curved again, resuming its ascent—but the angle this time was more slope than sheer, and I was able to pull myself along without nearly as much fear of falling. My pulse was beginning to calm. There was something pleasantly familiar about moving through the dark this way, like it was part of what I had been made for. In a way, I suppose that was exactly the case. I was designed to live in dark, tight spaces, inside a human body. This was just life inside a building. Not that much difference, given the change in scale that I'd already undergone.

The slope ended at another bend, and as my head popped up over it, a new element introduced itself back into the world: light. Bloody, reddish sunset light, trickling in through the slits in a grate that was almost close enough for me to touch. I sped up, pulling myself forward until I could brace my hands against the grate and shove. This was the moment of truth. If it was bolted on from the outside, then I had traveled all this way for nothing.

To my relief, the grate shifted as soon as I pushed against it. I pushed again, and it gave way, dropping out of my field of view and hitting the roof with a loud clang. The noise should have worried me, but it didn't. I had other things to focus on, like the sunset that was painting the sky in a thousand shades of rose. I climbed rapidly toward the opening, hungry for the light.

"That didn't take you as long as I thought it would." The voice was Ronnie's, calm and almost disinterested. I barely resisted the urge to jackknife back into the vent. Instead, I gripped the edge and turned to see him standing some five feet away, his hands folded behind his back, one of them holding a gun, and his attention focused calmly on the sky. "You're a fast climber. I guess desperation is a pretty good motivation."

"How did you know?" My voice came out in a whisper. I didn't move.

"You vanished from the monitors. There aren't many places in the store that aren't on the monitors, so I checked them all. You didn't put the grate back in the changing room. Sloppy, Sal. Very sloppy." Ronnie didn't look at me. "You can come down from there. Hanging out in the air-conditioning isn't going to change what happens next."

"What *is* going to happen next?" I couldn't figure out how to turn and put my feet out first, so I just pushed forward and toppled to the roof in an ungainly heap. My cheek landed on the fallen grate, and I felt it slice through my skin, adding the smell of blood to the eucalyptus and pigeon feather odors otherwise pervading the roof.

It should have smelled terrible. It smelled like freedom. Something tightened in my chest, and as I climbed to my feet, I decided that no matter what happened next, it wasn't going to end with me going back into that mall. Either Ronnie would shoot me, or I'd get the gun away from him somehow...or I'd go over the edge of the roof. Whatever it took to keep myself out of Sherman's hands.

I felt bad about the idea of dying before I got to see Nathan again. If he ever found out what had happened to me—what Sherman was planning to use me to *do*—he would understand why I couldn't just go along with things. He would forgive me.

"Something," said Ronnie, still sounding disinterested. "I don't get you, Sal. Here you've got a guy like Sherman falling over himself to make you a queen, and all you can do is fight and try to escape. Lots of girls would die to be in your shoes."

"And when he kills me by mistake during one of his little experiments? What happens then?" I glared at him, starting to pick bits of gravel out of my palms. "I didn't volunteer to be a lab animal. Sherman of all people should know how much I hate having other people make my decisions for me, but he still thinks he has the right, just because he's older than I am. Fuck him. I have my own life."

"A life you stole."

Ronnie's words were mild, but they still stung. I snapped back, "Like he didn't? We're all thieves here. The only difference is that I decided to stop stealing once I had what I needed. He's going to keep going until he has everything he wants, and that's really different. That's not okay."

Ronnie finally turned enough to let me see the small smile on his face. "You're a wimp," he said, not unkindly. He made it sound like a statement of essential fact: we were on a roof, he was probably about to kill me or something, and I was a wimp. "You don't act soon enough, and you don't take risks when you really should. If I were you, I would have been out that vent weeks ago, and screw anyone who tried to stop me from escaping. You pretty much asked to be swept off the street and locked in a cage by *somebody*. Hell, if you want proof of that, look at where you are—trying to escape from a cage that you were put in by the man who took you out of the last one."

"There's nothing wrong with being a wimp," I said, picking the last of the gravel out of my left hand. The cut on my cheek

was still bleeding sluggishly, but it didn't feel like it was serious enough to worry about. I'd probably need a few stitches,
assuming I lived long enough to get them. "The world can't
be made up entirely of leaders. Someone has to be willing to
follow."

"That sounds like something a wimp would say."

I shrugged. The edge of the roof was about ten feet away. I
couldn't see the street from where I was standing, but the angle
on the trees across from me made me think that we were standing on the third floor. That would mean a thirty-foot drop to
the street, and I wasn't going to survive that.

"Hey." Ronnie snapped his fingers. I turned to face him. He
looked at me flatly and asked, "What happens if you get away
from here? Where are you going to go?"

"Back to my people," I said.

"You gonna tell them where to find us? You gonna lead them
straight back here?" He asked the questions like they were of
no consequence, like he was asking whether I'd like cheese
sandwiches with lunch tomorrow, and not asking about the
potential fates of everyone he knew.

I thought about Dr. Cale's lab, and her small army of assistants and unpaid interns, most of whom probably didn't know
how to organize a siege. With Tansy gone, the security was
reduced by at least half. Fang could probably take Ronnie in a
fair fight. I didn't believe Ronnie was a fan of fair fights. And
yet lying to Ronnie didn't seem like a good way to get off this
roof alive—assuming there was any good way.

"Probably," I said. "I'd at least tell Dr. Cale where to find
you. She's going to want to know. I think she feels responsible
for Sherman. I'm pretty sure she doesn't want to wipe out the
human race. So probably."

"That's what I thought." He pulled his hand out from behind
his back, aiming the gun at me. "You're a wimp, but you man-

aged to outsmart me once. I didn't even think to check the vents. That won't happen again."

I started to raise my hands in protest, but I was too slow. Ronnie pulled the trigger, and a small fletched dart appeared on the right side of my chest, followed almost instantly by the feeling of being stabbed. I grabbed it and yanked it loose, for all that it wasn't going to do me a lick of good: I had enough experience with tranquilizers to know that the dart's contents had already done their work.

"Please don't take me back," I whispered.

"I'm not going to."

"Why...?"

"Because you're the only person here who used the pronouns I asked them to use," said Ronnie. He put the pistol away. "That buys you one 'get out of jail free' card from me. If you need another one, you're going to be on your own."

I took a step toward the edge of the roof, feeling a strange languor starting to seep through my limbs. Most tranquilizers don't work instantly, but they don't have to, because they'll stop you before you have the chance to get away. Every step seemed to take twice as long as the one before, until finally my knees buckled and I pitched forward, my cheek hitting the roof for the second time. There was no pain. Unconsciousness closed over me like a Venus flytrap closing on its prey, and there was nothing left to hurt.

The sun was fully down when I woke up. I was lying on a couch in a living room I didn't recognize. All the lights were out, and the air smelled stale, like the occupants hadn't been around to move it in quite some time. I jerked upright and winced as the incision in my head reminded me that I had recently had surgery.

In a weird way, the persistence of pain was a relief. I didn't know how much time had passed since Ronnie shot me with the tranquilizer dart—hours? Days? But the incision still felt raw enough that it probably hadn't been that long. It could even have been the same night. I stayed where I was for a few minutes, listening for any signs that I wasn't alone in the house and waiting for my head to stop its spinning. Once I felt like I could stand without vomiting on the floor, I did, and promptly collapsed back onto the couch as my abused legs refused to hold my weight.

The first giggle escaped before I knew it was coming. I clapped my hands over my mouth, trying to keep any additional giggles from breaking free, but I might as well have been trying to dam a river with Popsicle sticks. The giggles came in a wave before giving way to full-out laughter, leaving me doubled over and clutching my stomach in an effort to keep from hurting myself. I was a captive, and then I wasn't! I was someone else's captive, and then I got away! Only now I was alone in an abandoned house where the air smelled like dust and mold, and my legs hurt so much from my escape that I wasn't sure I'd be able to do anything useful with them ever again. My choices were laughter or tears, and laughter at least felt a little bit better.

Once I had laughed myself out I cautiously tried standing again, this time gripping the arm of the couch for balance. My legs wobbled but didn't drop me on my ass a second time. They ached like they had never ached before, and my arms weren't much better, all courtesy of my foolhardy ascent of the ventilation system.

"But it worked, didn't it?" I said aloud, and giggled again—nervously this time—at the sound of my own voice. It seemed too big in this empty, dusty room. Big sounds were dangerous. I knew that instinctively, just like I knew that I needed to get out of here as soon as I feasibly could.

The living room boasted a large picture window covered only by gauzy curtains, and the clearly artificial glare from the streetlights outside came in through the sheer fabric, giving me enough light to see by, if not clearly or well. I peered around in the gloom, making note of the major articles of furniture and the two exits. One appeared to lead deeper into the house, while the other was close enough to the picture window that I was willing to bet it would lead me to an entryway and then to the front door. I wasn't ready to go outside—not when I was this weak and this unsure of where I was—so I turned and shuffled deeper into the house, moving slowly to keep myself from falling down again.

The hardest part was crossing the wide-open center of the living room. Once I had reached the far wall and had something to brace myself against, things got easier, if not exactly pleasant. I shuffled along until my hand dipped into another room, one that both felt and sounded smaller than the first one. I felt around, my fingers finally brushing the cool edge of what felt like a sink. The bathroom. Good. I stepped fully inside, feeling blindly around until I hit a light switch.

This was it: the moment of truth. Turning on a light in the living room would have been like sending up a flare to notify anyone nearby that someone was in a house that was supposed to be empty, but the bathroom window wasn't likely to be visible from the street. Now all I had to do was pray that the place hadn't been empty for so long that the power had been cut.

As soon as I flipped the switch the room was flooded with soft white light from the low-emission bulbs above the sink. It didn't hurt my eyes as much as normal lights would have after being in the dark for so long. That was a relief. I fumbled the medicine cabinet open without really looking at the rest of the room. The shelves were laden with all sorts of things both prescription and non, including a full bottle of ibuprofen. I struggled for a moment with the childproof lid before it came free, abruptly enough that little red pills went all over the room. I didn't bother trying to pick them all up. I just shoved six into my mouth, swallowing greedily, before I turned on the tap and bent to drink straight from the faucet like a dog. For all I knew, ibuprofen was contraindicated after brain surgery, but since Sherman hadn't exactly provided me with aftercare instructions, I was playing things by ear, and my ear said it would do a better job if it wasn't attached to a skull that felt like it was full of wasps.

When I had swallowed away the last of the dryness in my throat I stayed where I was, bracing my hands against the edge of the sink and bowing my head as I watched the water swirl down the drain. My hair was still an unfamiliar distraction as it hung in my frame of vision, keeping me from seeing the rest of the sink. A single pill had landed in the basin, and was resisting the swirling water that threatened to pull it down the drain. It looked out of place.

Everything looked out of place. Something about that pill, red against the white, made me lift my head and really *look* at what was in front of me for the first time since I had turned the lights on.

The sink was laden with all the things that I would have expected to find in a bathroom—hairbrushes, straightening iron, toothbrush, toothpaste, and a dozen other grooming tools that Joyce would have been better equipped to identify than I was. There were framed pictures on the walls, and the medicine cabinet wasn't just full, it was overfull, packed with bottles and creams and cosmetics. The house smelled abandoned, and no one had come to investigate the noises that I was making, but whoever lived here hadn't moved away. They'd just disappeared.

Slowly, I turned to look at the rest of the bathroom. Everything I saw just confirmed my fears. The shower curtain was puddled in the bottom of the tub, having been ripped from its rod by someone who wasn't being careful. They might not have been capable of being careful: the bathroom rug was almost entirely the deep brown color of dried blood, save for a few splotches around the edge where the fabric remained plush and white. I stared at the rug for a moment, trying to convince myself that I was just looking at a bad dye job. The little splatters of blood on the linoleum and the edge of the tub made that an impossible trial.

The drums were beginning to pound in my ears. Ronnie must have brought me here because he knew that the original owners of the house were gone, either killed by sleepwalkers or joining them. How far had the infection spread while I was locked away? How much time did the human race have left?

I walked carefully back to the bathroom door, trying to tread as lightly as I could. Not only did my legs hurt so much that running would have been impossible, but any sound I made would mean risking an attack.

The hall was still deserted. I stood for a moment in the bathroom doorway, listening to the house around me. I didn't hear movement. That was good; that could mean that I really was alone. The real question was Ronnie. Would he have put me someplace safe, or would he have left me in a killing jar to see what would happen to Sherman's prize specimen when faced with real danger?

Almost unconsciously, I rubbed my still-healing wrist, feeling the stitches shift beneath the gauze. I could handle myself if I had to. I just didn't want to do it if I had any other choice.

A house this well lived in had probably been occupied for at least five years, which meant the occupants might have installed an emergency services landline. I turned to my left, heading still deeper into the house as I looked for the most logical place to find that sort of thing: the kitchen.

The carpet underfoot muffled my steps, which was a good thing, except for the fact that it would also have muffled the steps of anyone who followed me. I kept glancing over my shoulder, squinting through the thin light from the open bathroom door as I watched to see whether I was being followed. No slack-jawed shapes had yet loomed out of the darkness, but that sadly didn't mean much of anything. Sleepwalkers weren't clever—at least not if the ones we'd encountered thus far were anything to go by—but they moved slowly enough that they were basically ambushes waiting to happen, at least until the moment when they decided to attack.

My foot struck linoleum. I stopped, struck by the sliding glass door on the wall directly ahead of me. It was standing open, a bloody handprint against its surface like a tattoo. The drums in my head got even louder. That was how the sleepwalkers had been able to get into the house, or maybe that was how the original inhabitants had been able to escape after they lost themselves to their implants. Either way, it was a way out.

Would the sleepwalkers still be lurking in the backyard, unable to find their way past the fences? Or were they in the darkest corners of the kitchen, trying to make up their slow minds about what to do with me? I had to make a decision.

I chose safety. I crossed the kitchen floor as fast as my legs allowed, grasping the sliding glass door and yanking it shut. It squealed in its track, and I winced but kept pulling until it was snug against its frame. Then I flipped the lock, and froze, watching the foliage in the backyard for signs of movement.

There weren't any. But nothing moaned behind me either, and so I did my best to set my paranoia aside as I turned and began searching for a working phone.

It was slow going in the dark. I didn't dare turn a light on, not with the chance that the backyard was full of sleepwalkers, and so I worked my way around by feel. When I discovered the butcher's block I pulled out a cleaver, holding it in one hand while I continued to feel my way along with the other. I'd be more likely to cut myself than anyone else, but it made me feel a little bit better to at least have the potential to defend myself.

Ten minutes later, I had found a bunch of half-rotten bananas and a loaf of moldy bread, but no phone. I made my way slowly out of the kitchen, walking past the bright haven of the bathroom to the front of the house, where that big picture window now seemed terrifyingly exposed to a night that contained who-knows-what. My search turned up no phone here either. I winced. Apparently, my choices were staying in the house, cut off but potentially safe, or going out into the world with no idea where I was or how far I would have to travel to get back to the bowling alley. I'd be able to see any sleepwalkers better if I waited for daylight, but sleepwalkers had to sleep too. Were they more or less active during the day?

I didn't know. Nobody knew. That was the problem: I was standing in a safe place, trying to make plans that would mean leaving that safety for a whole new kind of danger. Maybe I really was a wimp, but that idea didn't seem very appealing.

There was still one door I hadn't tried. I stepped through the other exit from the front room, and stopped. It was an entryway, as I had suspected. It was also the access to the stairs. That was more of a surprise, and for a moment I just stood there, contemplating the seemingly impossible task of convincing my tired, strained legs to carry me to the second floor.

If the people who lived here had been killed by sleepwalkers, they wouldn't have had time to take anything with them. Even if there wasn't a landline, there could be cellphones in the dark upstairs, little electronic miracles just waiting for me to find them and use them to summon a rescue.

I took a breath, gripped the banister, and began pulling myself, one agonizing step at a time, toward the second floor.

It took what felt like an hour for me to climb the twenty or so steps between the entryway and the upstairs hall. When I finally ran out of steps I collapsed forward, landing on my hands and knees on the plush carpet, and fought the urge to curl into a ball and cry until the pain stopped. Every muscle

I had from the waist down felt like it was on fire. The drums were pounding so hard that I was beginning to worry that Sherman had undone the surgery that was intended to keep me alive. Worst of all, there was no light up here: either the curtains were drawn, or there were no windows in the hall, leaving me in absolute blackness. It was like being thrown back into the vent, only this time I had no destination in mind.

When the tremors in my thighs stopped I pulled myself to my feet, picking up the cleaver from the floor, and began shuffling forward into the dark. I moved like a sleepwalker as I tried to avoid running into anything. My hand found a wall. I followed it to an open door. A search of the room on the other side—which was slightly less dark than the hall, thanks to a small window looking out on the empty backyard—yielded nothing. The next room was much the same, as was the one after it, until I'd searched the entire back of the house without finding what I needed.

The first door on the other side of the hall was closed. I stopped before turning the doorknob, pressing my ear against the wood and listening for any signs that I wasn't alone in the house. I didn't hear anything. I turned the knob and pushed the door slowly open. The room on the other side was utterly destroyed, but what I could pick out through the light filtering in from the street below seemed to imply that it had belonged to a teenage girl: everything was frilly and pale, washed out so that I couldn't tell its original color. Most of it was also broken, thrown to the floor and crushed by some angry hand. The tattered remains of posters still blanketed the walls, and what water remained in the fish tank near the bed was foul and dark with mold. I noted all this dispassionately, the bulk of my attention going to the room's single largest fixture:

The window.

It was closed, rendering the room stifling and somehow septic-smelling, like something had been left in here to rot, but the light seeping in from below was strong enough that I knew it would give me a good view of the street. I could find out whether it was safe for me to leave the house and go looking for a pay phone. I stepped into the room, drawn to that window like a moth to a flame.

Something moaned in the dark. It was a small, weak sound, but it was still enough to bring me to an instant halt, my back going so stiff that it pulled at the wounded muscles in my thighs and made *me* want to start moaning. I bit my tongue to keep from making a sound and turned, as slowly as I could, to face the farthest corner of the room.

My eyes were adjusting to the dim light. As I peered into the corner, it began slowly resolving from an indistinguishable jumble into distinct shapes. That long, broken pillar was a piece of the bed. Those soft mounds were the comforter, humped up and caked with something foul. And the skeletal collection of joints and angles in the middle of it all was a human being, eyes sunk deep into a skull that was barely contained by a thin panel of tight-stretched skin, hair almost completely ripped from its scalp. I couldn't tell its original gender: it was naked, but so huddled over that it could have been male or female. Not that it really mattered. The figure was clearly on the verge of death, having been locked in this room so long that its body had already cannibalized every useful bit of tissue that it could without shutting down essential systems. I didn't know how long it took the average person to starve to death, or how big this one had been when the door shut and the food stopped coming, but regardless, they didn't have much longer.

The sleepwalker—because there was nothing else it could have been; not with a closed, unlocked door being the only thing between it and freedom—opened its mouth and moaned again, weakly. It didn't try to get out of its nest. I didn't think it could have moved if it wanted to.

I bit my lip, staring at the figure in the corner. It didn't moan again. I wasn't sure whether that was because it was too weak, or because I had stopped moving and it could no longer tell where I was. Either way, it didn't seem like it was going to come after me anytime soon. I turned my back on it and resumed my trek toward the window, looking out on the street below.

I'm not really sure what I was expecting after the situation at the hospital and the number of people who had been shoved into USAMRIID's quarantine. Some part of me had still been holding out the hope that this would all just go away, and the world would return to a semblance of normalcy. I put a hand over my mouth, blinking rapidly to prevent the tears that were welling up in my eyes from clouding my vision. Normalcy was no longer an option, assuming it had ever been an option in the first place.

There were no cars moving on this suburban street, and the few lit windows on the houses around me were all on the second floor, meaning that anyone who was still awake and alive was staying as far from ground level as possible. That made sense.

The street belonged to the sleepwalkers.

There were only about twenty of them in my view, although that didn't mean that there weren't more hiding in the bushes or skulking in the long shadows down the sides of those same houses. They were of every age and race, from small children to a man I guessed had to be in his eighties. All of them shambled along with the same mindless lack of purpose, their hands held slightly out in front of them as if to ward away obstacles. While I watched, two of them bumped into each other, patted one another's arms, and finally joined hands before shambling on in tandem. This neighborhood was no longer the property of the human race. Its successors had taken over.

There was a faint moan from behind me. I whirled, suddenly convinced that the sleepwalker in the corner had managed to get loose and come after me. The bright specks of its eyes glared from the exact spot where I'd seen them before. I took a deep breath, trying to calm my pounding heart. "It's okay, Sal," I whispered, earning myself another moan from the sleepwalker. "Unless you're going to feed it, it's not strong enough to come after you." I felt bad about reducing the sleepwalker to an "it," but that was technically true of the tapeworm part of the composite, and I wasn't going to sex the human half just to get the proper pronouns.

Still. This room looked like it had been designed for a teenage girl. If she was the sleepwalker, she'd been locked in here when she converted. Either she had been able to shut the door before her parents could get to her or she'd been the first to go, transitioning while she was asleep or otherwise distracted. No matter what had happened, most of her belongings were probably in here with her, and teenage girls had cellphones.

I began feeling my way along the top of the dresser next to the window, moving cautiously in an attempt to keep from cutting myself on the broken glass that had been knocked from the empty picture frames still studding the walls. I found a charger plugged into the wall about halfway down the length of the dresser, its unconnected end seeming to taunt me. There *had* been a phone in this room. This dark, dangerous room with the watching sleepwalker still occasionally moaning from its place in the corner.

"Steady," I murmured, as I disconnected the charger and stuffed it into my pocket. I knew the house still had power. If I could find the phone, I could call for help.

A rustling sound from the corner dragged my attention back to the sleepwalker. It was trying to work its way free of its nest, its withered, wasted limbs refusing to support its weight. As it moved, it revealed enough of its chest for me to identify it as the teenage girl whose room this had been. I felt a little better about that. She had already been robbed of her humanity and her future; the least I could do for her was think of her as the woman she had been before one of my cousins burrowed into her brain and destroyed her.

"I'm sorry about touching all your stuff, but I don't think you could tell me where your phone is," I said apologetically, and resumed feeling my way along the dresser. "I wish you could. I'm sorry this happened to you."

She moaned again, even more weakly this time. It was sort of nice not to be alone, since I knew that she wasn't going to attack me: if she'd been capable of getting to her feet, rather than just rustling around in her nest, she would have done it already. I had a body packed with nutrients and fat, and I could have kept her alive for a good long time if she'd been able to get to me. I felt bad about that too—it was like I was waving a steak in front of a starving man—but since the steak was what was keeping me alive, I wasn't going to share. It was terrible that her fate and mine had taken such different directions, but it wasn't my fault. I just wished that there was something I could have done to fix it.

Honestly, I wished I had any idea who *could* have fixed it, or whether anyone was going to try. Dr. Cale was hard to predict. USAMRIID was all about humanity, and Sherman was all about the tapeworms, but humanity made the tapeworms— humanity brought the whole situation down on their own heads—and the tapeworms were taking things that didn't belong to them. No one was completely in the right. No one was completely in the wrong, either.

The sleepwalker in the corner moaned and shifted again, dislodging several small objects from her nest. One of them hit the floor with a clunk, the light from the window reflecting off its cracked screen. I stared in disbelieving wonder.

It was a cellphone. And it was less than a foot away from a sleepwalker.

"I don't suppose you'd be willing to just let me have that, would you?" I asked, taking a tentative step forward. The sleepwalker's face swiveled back toward me, and she moaned with weak menace. "No, I didn't think so."

I was the only thing in the room that she could eat: because of that, distracting her from my presence wasn't going to be easy. I cast around until I found one of those long boards that had been broken off from the bed during her destruction of the room. Picking it up, I took another step forward.

"I don't want to hurt you," I said. "If you just let me have the phone, I can get out of your room, and you'll never have to see me again." That would mean leaving her to die alone, which might not have been a mercy, but which wouldn't require me to actually be the one to kill her. I took another step forward.

Sometimes it's bad to be wrong. I'd assumed that since she hadn't left her nest, she didn't have the strength left in her to do anything but shift and moan. As I leaned forward to grab the phone, she lunged, spending the last of her resources in a desperate bid for sustenance. Her hands latched around my wrist, nearly yanking me off my feet as she pulled me toward her frantically working jaws. The light from the window glimmered off her teeth, which seemed too large and too white for her face. Everything had shrunk but those teeth.

Swallowing my scream was one of the hardest things I had ever done. I backpedaled, trying to yank myself away from her. She didn't let go. I was her last chance at survival, and no matter how reduced her faculties had been by time and trauma, some part of her still knew that getting my flesh into her mouth would save her. Everything she had left was going into the effort of holding on to me. As she pulled, I felt my feet starting to slip. Before long, I would topple, and she would have me.

What happened next was pure panic. I raised the board that I was holding, bringing it down on her skull as hard as I could. There was a brittle splintering sound, and she moaned, and I hit her again. She still didn't let go, and so I kept on hitting her, hitting her over and over again, while the sound of drums rose in my ears and the world narrowed down to a single point: me, and her, and the sound of wood impacting with her head.

She released my wrist. I didn't stop hitting her.

It was exhaustion that finally made me pause and take stock of the situation. She wasn't moving anymore. She had collapsed to the floor in a broken heap, and while there wasn't much light in the room, what there was allowed me to see the dents in her skull, and the dark stains that were dripping down her skin as she continued to bleed out. The bleeding was already slowing, thanks to coagulation. Bile rose in my throat. I dropped the board, snatched the phone from the floor, and ran out of the room. I didn't look back.

It was a miracle that I made it down the stairs without tripping and breaking my neck. I stopped in the entryway, where no lights or windows would betray my presence, and tried to turn on the phone in my hands. I had killed for it. I ought to use it.

It didn't respond. Not even mashing the power button got a flicker of life out of the cracked and blood-spattered screen. I swallowed the panic that was trying to writhe up my throat and take me over, forcing myself to stand perfectly still while I breathed slowly in through my nose and out through my mouth, counting to ten on each exhale. The pounding in my ears began to lessen as my heart rate returned to something closer to normal.

The phone didn't work because it had been sitting on the floor long enough for its captive owner to wither away to skin and bones. That was all. Even if she'd been a thin girl to start with, she must have been locked in that room for at least a week—probably more like two—before she got to the condition that I'd found her in. Of course the battery was dead. When I no longer felt like I was going to panic or vomit at any moment I walked down the hall to the bathroom, guided by the light that I'd left turned on earlier. There was a socket in the wall next to the sink, one outlet already occupied by a hair dryer. I plugged the phone charger into the other outlet, connected the phone to the charger, and sat down on the toilet to wait.

It was hard to keep track of time sitting alone in a dark house surrounded by sleepwalkers. It felt like it had been an hour when the phone beeped to signal that it was charged enough to use. It had probably been more like fifteen minutes. I left it connected to the charger as I picked it up and carefully pushed the button to activate the screen.

*Please don't be password protected*, I prayed silently, unsure of who might be listening and even less sure that I cared. *Please just give me that much. Please.*

The screen flashed live, displaying the face of a smiling teenage girl wearing lipstick the color of bubble gum. There was no key pad. Relief washed over me. Her parents probably hadn't allowed her to lock the phone, wanting to keep track of her activities. My parents had done something similar to me, although they had allowed Joyce all the privacy she wanted. That was the difference between adulthood and medical adolescence.

"Thank you," I whispered, and touched the phone icon.

For one terrifying moment I was afraid I wouldn't be able to remember Nathan's number. Why should I? It was stored in my phone after all, and I had better things to remember. But it had been on a piece of paper first, pressed into my hand when we met at the hospital. Everyone kept telling me that I was using Sally Mitchell's brain like a giant hard drive, storing information on it that couldn't be contained in my original tapeworm neural system. That meant that everything I'd experienced since taking over had to be stored somewhere, if I just went looking for it.

Bit by bit, the image of a piece of paper formed behind my eyes. The numbers were blurry around the edges, but I could still tell what they were—I thought. I dialed quickly, trying to avoid cutting my fingers on the damaged screen, and raised the phone to my ear. It was ringing. That was a good sign: that meant the cell network was still up. Civilization couldn't have collapsed completely if the cell network was still up.

The ringing stopped. Silence reigned. I waited a few seconds for the person on the other end to say something, and when they didn't, I said, "H-hello? This is Sal Mitchell, looking for Nathan Kim. Please, do you know where he is?"

"Sal?" Nathan sounded almost confused, like he couldn't believe it was really my voice. I didn't care. Just hearing him say my name was enough to dull the drums that had been hammering in my ears, reducing them to a distant background hum. "Is it…oh, thank God, Sal, is it really you?"

"I think so," I said, slumping against the cool porcelain of the toilet tank. "I'm really scared."

"I—" Nathan stopped for a moment. I heard him take a deep breath. Then: "I'm sorry, are you telling me this is Sally Mitchell? Can you confirm your identity?"

Someone else had to be there with him: someone else had to be making sure he checked on me. That was okay. Better safe and making it home than sorry and alone. "I don't like to be called Sally," I said. That didn't seem like enough, so I asked, "Are the broken doors still open? I want to come home."

Nathan laughed. It was a gasping, unsteady sound, and the only way I knew it was laughter and not tears was because it stopped. "You can't be serious. You can't really think we're that easy to fool."

"I'm not trying to fool anyone. We went to the hospital to fix the arteries in my head and then we got separated in the parking lot when I ran away to distract the sleepwalkers from eating you—did Daisy and Fang make it to the car okay? I hope they did—and USAMRIID took me and they put me in this big bubble inside the Oakland Coliseum and there were a lot of other people there and Colonel Mitchell wasn't telling anybody

I was a chimera which seemed sort of weird but I didn't want to call him on it in front of the men with guns and then..." I paused to take a deep breath, having run out of air somewhere in the middle of that long, gasping speech. Once my lungs were full, I continued: "Then Sherman was there and he broke me out and he's been keeping me prisoner while he took samples from me all sorts of samples like blood and bone marrow and yesterday he cut my head open so I'm afraid he took samples of *me*, only one of his people helped me get out and I don't know where I am but there's sleepwalkers outside and I want to come home. Please come and get me and take me home."

This time when I stopped talking, Nathan didn't laugh. He didn't say anything. I could hear him breathing, and so I stayed quiet, trying not to pant as I waited to see what was going to happen next.

Finally, quietly, Nathan asked, "Why should I believe that you're still Sal?"

I blinked at the phone. I had a dozen questions, and all of them seemed both equally important and equally frivolous. Finally, I asked, "Can Sherman *do* that? I know he's been creating more chimera, and I'm not exactly sure how long he had me captive, but the first time I learned how to talk, it took like, years. Can he scoop people out of their heads and put new people in?" Belatedly I realized that I had just characterized tapeworms as "people." I didn't bother correcting myself. I was a person, regardless of my origins, and I was willing to extend that label to the rest of the chimera, regardless of theirs.

"You've been gone for over a month, Sal. We had to abandon the bowling alley after USAMRIID quarantined the area. Tansy never came back. Mom's had Adam under constant surveillance since you disappeared. We didn't know whether USAMRIID had you or whether you'd escaped, and there was too much chance you'd tell them where he was."

As the first chimera—and the only one created from a first

generation tapeworm—Adam would have been invaluable to anyone trying to figure out how we'd been created. I wanted to be offended, but I couldn't muster the emotional response. Instead, I asked, "How are the dogs?"

"Beverly howled for about two days, which was a problem, since we were trying to dodge the quarantine vans at the time. Minnie just took it in stride, like she always knew that you were going to abandon her someday." Nathan's voice was starting to thaw. "Sal, is that really you?"

"It really is." I sniffled, relief washing over me and leaving me almost dizzy. I hadn't realized how afraid I was that Nathan would never accept me for who I claimed to be until the threat was lifting. "I don't know where I am. Sherman was keeping me in an old mall, and I don't know where that was either."

"We're working on that," said Nathan. "Fishy started a trace on this call as soon as it came in. Not many people use my private cell number these days."

"So Fishy's okay?" I put my hand over my eyes, careful not to unplug the still-charging phone from the wall. "Who else is okay?"

"How about I tell you about the dogs until we have a fix on you, just so I don't slip up and say something if you're being monitored by someone else's people?"

I smiled a little. "I'd like that."

"Well, Beverly's started eating shoes…" Nathan began, and I sat quietly and listened to him talk about what our dogs had been up to, and began to feel like maybe things were going to be okay after all.

*Break the mirror; it tells lies.*
*Learn to live in your disguise.*
*Everything is changing now, it's too late to go back.*
*Caterpillar child of mine,*
*This was always life's design,*
*Here at last you'll find the things you can't afford to lack.*

*The broken doors are ready, you are very nearly home.*
*My darling child, be careful now, and don't go out*
     *alone.*

—FROM *DON'T GO OUT ALONE*, BY SIMONE KIMBERLEY,
PUBLISHED 2006 BY LIGHTHOUSE PRESS.
CURRENTLY OUT OF PRINT.

*—hear me? This is Harry Lo of KNBR, the Bay Area's real rock, broadcasting live because I have nothing else to do and no other way of getting the message that I'm still alive in here out to the world. I have now been broadcasting for twenty days straight. It's almost Halloween, kids, and if anyone's out there listening, I recommend against going trick-or-treating this year, because the streets are alive with the actual undead, which may make it hard to tell the kids in costumes from the people who want to eat your face off.*

*Eating. I remember eating. Those of you who tuned in yesterday—and if any of you tuned in yesterday, why aren't you calling to let me know that I'm not alone in here? Please, I'm begging you—you may recall that I ate the last of the crackers from the staff vending machine. I've started eating tissue paper, since my sister used to swear by that as a weight loss aid. I've also eaten an entire bottle of Vicodin, taken from our former lead anchor's purse, and I'm about to follow it with the last of the tequila.*

*This is Harry Lo, signing off. I hope that if you're out there, you have better options left than I did.*

—FROM THE FINAL TRANSMISSION OF HARRY LO, KNBR, RECORDED ON OCTOBER 28, 2027

# Chapter 10
## OCTOBER 2027

The sound of tires on the street outside made me stand and stick my head out of the bathroom, still clutching the fully charged cellphone in my hand like a talisman against all the bad things that were waiting in the dark. I'd been sitting silently since Nathan hung up, watching the phone's battery bar slowly fill and wishing that he had been able to stay on the line. Apparently, it was unsafe to have too many connections going in or out of the new lab location; Fishy wasn't the only person who knew how to trace a call. With the cell network on the verge of collapse thanks to neglect and a lack of callers, anyone who *was* still making calls was exposing themselves to all manner of tracking. By the government, definitely. But also, apparently, by SymboGen, which was still open and operational, and offering to "help" anyone who had been impacted by the sleepwalker plague.

According to what Nathan had been able to tell me during our short time on the phone, I'd missed the shit really starting to hit the fan by three days. That was the span between my disappearance and the first person to go into a sleepwalker frenzy on live television. That would have been a big deal no matter who did it, but that first victim was Paul Moffat, the mayor of San Francisco. He had been in the process of giving a speech about the crisis, one that was mirrored to the local public television station, less because anyone thought he had anything new to say, and more because he was a heavy contributor to their operating budget.

People started caring a lot more about what he had to say after he ripped somebody's throat out with his teeth. That probably wasn't the kind of attention he'd been looking for.

By the time somebody thought to shoot him, even CNN was carrying the footage of his conversion and subsequent attack. According to Nathan, that segment had aired on an almost constant loop for three days, and even Dr. Cale had put it on the main screen in her lab for a few hours, making sure everyone had the chance to see it. Then she'd turned off the screen and announced that while they were not abandoning the search for me and Tansy, they couldn't hold off moving the lab any longer. Things were destabilizing too fast.

She was right about that, since by that point, no one really cared about the mayor who'd freaked out and eaten a few people. They were too busy worrying about their friends, their neighbors, their parents, their children…themselves. The warning signs had been there, and they had been ignored, one bellwether after another, until their weight became too great and everything came crashing down.

It took less than ten days for my cousins to incapacitate American civilization as we understood it, disrupting food chains, causing power outages and hospital shutdowns, and in some cases causing the evacuation of entire cities. There were still news feeds and Internet reports coming through, but they got scarcer each day as the people behind them fell. I guess maybe I should have been proud of that, except I was a tapeworm who thought of herself as a human, and they were tapeworms who thought of themselves as tapeworms. We were on different sides, and whenever there's a conflict, somebody's going to wind up on the losing one.

I just didn't want it to be my side, even if I still wasn't sure what side that was.

Footsteps on the walkway in front of the house snapped me out of my brief reverie, followed by the sound of gunshots. They came quick and efficient, one after the other, like someone running a hand along a typewriter. Then the shots stopped, and someone began hammering on the front door.

"I'm coming!" I still couldn't run, but I could hobble quickly. Two more gunshots sounded in the time it took me to get to the front door, which I unlocked and opened to reveal the wild-eyed face of Nathan Kim. He was wearing a black uniform I'd never seen before, and had an assault rifle in one hand. It looked out of place against the backdrop of my gentle, scholarly boyfriend. So did the bodies that were littering the lawn. Fang and a man I didn't recognize were standing back-to-back behind him, their own rifles slowly sweeping the area as they watched for more sleepwalkers.

Nathan stared at me. I stared back. The world seemed to freeze for a moment, narrowing to a single point that existed only in the space between us. I couldn't move. From the hungry, hopeful expression on his face, neither could he.

"This is great and all, reunion, true love, blah blah blah, but can you confirm that it's really your missing girlfriend so that we can get the fuck out of here before we get shredded like piñatas on a playground?" demanded the man I didn't know. "We may have cleared this area, and my EMP blasts may have killed any bugs, but the gunshots are going to attract more playmates in no time at all. We need to roll."

"Hi, Nathan," I said.

Nathan swallowed hard, the muscles in his jaw clenching and unclenching before he said, "Hello, Sal. Are you ready to go home?"

"More than ready." I stepped out onto the porch, leaving the door open behind me. If any of the original occupants were still alive—if they had become sleepwalkers, rather than just being torn apart by them—at least now they could come home. The broken cellphone I tucked into my pocket. It had Nathan's number in memory now. I wasn't leaving that behind.

"Mom sends her regards, and asked me to tell you she always knew you'd find a way to stay alive," said Nathan stiffly. Then the stiffness melted, and he was putting his arms around me and pulling me close, into an embrace that made me feel like everything was going to be all right after all. The world could end and Sherman could plot against humanity and I could beat the stolen body of a teenage girl to death in her bedroom, and still things would somehow find a way to be all right.

"I'm sorry," I whispered. "I didn't mean to get caught. I just wanted to keep you safe."

"Never apologize," Nathan whispered back. He turned, lifting me with me one arm so that we wouldn't need to break off our embrace. The butt of his rifle dug into my back. I didn't care. We were almost the same size, and he carried me easily as he stepped off the porch and turned to face Fang, the stranger, and the car. "Can you walk?"

"I'm sore and slow, but I can walk," I assured him. He lowered my feet back to the ground. I left my hand against his chest as I looked around the area. We were in what would have been a normal suburban neighborhood once, although the gunshots hadn't caused any of the other houses to turn their lights on; my worried impression of an abandoned city had been close to accurate. I could see shapes farther down the street, all of them turning and shambling in our direction. We weren't going to be alone for very long. "Where are we?"

"Pleasant Hill, near the community college," said Nathan. "There's a mall nearby, but it doesn't seem to be the one where Sherman was holding you."

Of course they would have checked before they came to get me. Their safety would have depended on whether I was telling the truth, and whether I'd been left in this neighborhood as a trap. I nodded mutely, suddenly exhausted, and closed my eyes as I let Nathan guide me down the pathway to the car. I didn't want to see the sleepwalkers staggering toward us; some of them might even be the parents of the girl I'd killed inside. The world was changing. We were all of us changing with it. That didn't make it any easier to bear.

I opened my eyes when we reached the car. Nathan opened the door, motioning for me to get into the backseat. He must have seen my discomfort, because he said, "Don't worry. I'll be riding with you. I just need to cover Fang and Fishy while they get back to their seats."

That answered the question of who, exactly, the man I didn't recognize was. I nodded and climbed in, scooting over until I was pressed against the door on the far side. Looking down the length of the backseat, I watched as Nathan raised his rifle and covered the other two men making their retreat. The pair split up when they reached the car, with Fang walking around to take the driver's seat. Nathan got in next to me, and the sound of the door closing was the sound of coming home. I looked at him, eyes wide, unable to force myself to speak.

Nathan smiled a little. "I like your hair," he said.

I laughed brokenly, and leaned over to put my head against

his shoulder as Fang started the car and we drove away from the place where I had been abandoned, the place where I had been saved.

Nathan talked as we drove, explaining what had happened with the lab. I closed my eyes, leaned my head against his shoulder, and just listened. It was all I'd wanted to do for weeks: sit and listen to someone who would actually *talk* to me. He was constantly touching my hair or shoulder, like he was reassuring himself that I was real. I didn't mind that either. It kept me from needing to be the one who moved.

The bowling alley hadn't been Dr. Cale's first lab. The first lab had been located in an old supermarket, and was moved when word came that the people who actually owned the property were planning to have it fumigated and then torn down. The second lab had been a closed-down Costco with the gas pumps still out back, and had been abandoned after Sherman defected. The bowling alley came third, and it had been her base of operations for longer than anything else. It was perfect in a lot of ways, isolated while still being close to civilization, and best of all, owned by a shell corporation that used it as a tax write-off and had no interest in either refurbishing or demolishing the place. It had become a lot less useful when USAMRIID started closing in.

The collapse of most of the local social norms—and the evacuations of any "nonessential" buildings, like the mall where Sherman had been keeping me, wherever that was—had created the perfect vacuum for Dr. Cale's team. They'd smuggled themselves and all their equipment out of Clayton through a series of tricks and double blinds that Nathan didn't explain very well, or maybe I just wasn't quite listening anymore.

And then he said a name that actually caught my attention. I opened my eyes, tilting my head back until I could see his face, and said, "You can't be serious."

"But I am." Nathan smiled a little, like he was perfectly aware of just how ridiculous he sounded. "We've moved the lab, and our living quarters, to the Captain Candy Chocolate Factory."

I stared at him.

He smiled a little more. "I see you've heard of it. I wasn't sure. I went there with a class field trip when I was in middle school, but you missed the whole 'middle school' experience."

"Will used to leave the radio on when we were cleaning the shelter, and they advertised a lot during the afternoon," I said. "It's out in Vallejo, isn't it?"

Nathan nodded. "That's the one."

"And it was just…empty?"

"It turns out that keeping a candy factory open isn't a major priority when the world is ending," said Fishy, twisting around in the front seat to look at us. "It's a nice place. A little weird. Smells like chocolate. I hope you don't have any allergies."

"Just antiparasitics," I said shyly.

"I guess that would be a problem for you," he said, giving me a frank up-and-down look. "You don't look like a tapeworm."

"Surprise," I said.

He grinned. It opened up his face like a flower, bright and honest enough that I didn't even mind the fact that he was showing off virtually all of his teeth. The absence of malice in his expression was enough to rob them of their menace, making the expression as harmless as a grin on a dog.

Fishy was a short, stocky man with broad workman's shoulders and a full head of riotously curly hair that was currently skimmed back into a ponytail to keep it out of his way. His eyes swam behind the lenses of his thick-framed glasses, which were seated so solidly on his nose that they looked like they would be impossible to dislodge. He was wearing a black outfit that matched Nathan's in cut and construction, but couldn't have looked more different on his frame.

"You seem more like a human being than Adam does," he said. "He's a nice guy, but he's never really seemed like a functioning person to me."

I blinked at him, casting an anxious glance at Nathan before returning my attention to Fishy and saying, hesitantly, "Maybe that's because I learned how to be a human by living with humans, instead of learning how to be a human by sitting in a lab surrounded by people who never forgot that I wasn't really one of them?"

"Maybe," Fishy agreed. His gaze flicked to Nathan, smile fading. "We good?"

"We're good," Nathan agreed. Fishy withdrew back into the front seat. Nathan put an arm around my shoulder and said, "We weren't expecting your call. Honestly, most of the people back at the lab had written you off as lost. I think that I was one of the only people who was still willing to believe that you were alive—well, me and Adam. Adam never gave up on you."

"He wouldn't," I said.

"Neither would I." Nathan tightened his arm. "Everyone's going to be a little jumpy around you for a while. I just want you to be ready for that."

"I can be ready for anything, as long as you let me stay with you."

Nathan kissed the top of my head. "I'm never going to let myself be separated from you again."

"Good," I said, and closed my eyes.

Captain Candy's Chocolate Factory was a Bay Area tradition, originally designed to compete with the better-known and more nationally established Jelly Belly Factory in Fairfield. The Captain didn't specialize in jelly beans; instead, he had made his name on chocolate and chocolate confections of all kinds, from cookies to ice cream. Instead of free tours, the Captain charged fifteen dollars a head, with a promise to make it up by providing ridiculous quantities of chocolate and candy at the end—a promise that he had apparently kept, since people kept coming back. Captain Candy never became a national brand, although I didn't know whether that was a matter of economic necessity or a matter of corporate choice. There was a lot of competition in the national chocolate arena, but in Northern California, Captain Candy was king.

The factory was built to serve three purposes at once, and it needed to serve them all well before it could be considered a success. First, to offer a candy-coated wonderland that would invoke thoughts of children's literature and impossible dreams, available for rent at a reasonable fee. Second, to create the illusion of a factory that Willy Wonka would have been proud to own and operate, even down to the brightly colored scrubs worn by all of the employees. Third, to host the *actual* Captain Candy's factory, producing hundreds of pounds of candy daily on an assembly line that looked exactly like every other candy assembly line in the world.

The drive from Pleasant Hill to Vallejo took a little more than an hour, since we had to navigate a bridge choked with stalled-out and abandoned cars. Fishy and Fang got out at one point, pushing several of the cars out of the way with an ease that spoke of greased wheels and hidden levers. We drove through and they got out again, pushing the cars back into their original positions. "No one knows that we're using this route for our supply runs, and we're going to keep it that way," said Fishy amiably, while Fang restarted the car.

"Good idea," I said vaguely. It was hard to pay attention to them—the scene outside the car windows was too distracting.

We'd been passing abandoned cars and empty houses the whole time, but for the most part, the lack of light had kept me from really looking at what was around us. Now, the sun was rising, and there was no way not to see the wreckage of the world. Not without closing my eyes, and part of me felt responsible enough for what had happened that I couldn't bring myself to do that. This was the world my species had made. It didn't matter that I had never willingly hurt a human being, or that I had actually killed multiple sleepwalkers, thus putting myself firmly on the side of my creators. This was still my fault. Somehow.

The cars on the bridge weren't alone. The streets of Vallejo were equally choked, although the vehicles had been carefully pushed to this side or that, creating open channels in the motionless traffic. A casual observer would have thought those channels were organic, arising naturally as the drivers had succumbed to their invertebrate attackers. From the way Fang swung the car from one clear path to the next, it was clear that they had been created to allow for occasions just like this one.

It might have been okay if the cars had been empty, or at least intact, but both those things were too much to ask. Windows were smashed, or smeared with streaks of long-dried blood, or both. Bodies were still belted into the seats where they had died, while others had fallen in the street, dried out by the elements or picked clean by predators. Every time we came around a corner it seemed like we dislodged another flock of crows, sending the urban scavenger birds flapping into the early morning sky. They'd clearly owned the streets long enough to turn bold, because they came back as soon as we rounded the next corner; I could see them returning to their prizes if I looked behind me. And I couldn't stop looking back.

The lights were still on in half the city, with flickering streetlamps and incongruously well-lit storefronts on every street. Nathan saw me looking and said, "Not all systems fail at the same rate. Enough of the city is on solar or hydro power that it'll be months before Vallejo is completely dark."

"Even then, a few of the power stations are still pumping," said Fishy amiably. "We could go around and shut everything off, but if this place goes dark before it stops being a bright spot on the grid, someone could figure out that we're here, and we'd rather avoid that for as long as possible."

"Why?" I asked.

"Because Doctor C is wanted for terrorism, naturally," said Fishy.

Nathan didn't say a word.

I twisted in my seat to look at him, eyes wide, and asked, "Is that true?"

"She *did* help create a creature that is now in the process of destroying the human race," said Nathan. "Whether that was her intention or not, it doesn't look good."

"Oh," I said, and then the vast, primary-colored shape of Captain Candy's Chocolate Factory came into view ahead of us, and conversation died, at least for the moment.

Fang drove across the largely empty parking lot and through an open gate into an underground garage that had probably been used to house delivery trucks, once upon a time, before the end of the world. Most of those trucks were gone now, except for a few parked against the far wall. Fang drove across the garage to the row of spaces right in front of a pair of sliding glass doors. Soft white light poured through the glass, bathing us in radiance, welcoming us home.

"You parked in the handicapped space again, asshole," said Fishy amiably. He opened the car door, picking up his rifle as he slid out. "Dr. Cale's going to have your head."

"Dr. Cale doesn't drive, and like I keep telling you, humanity is a handicap," said Fang. "How else can you explain the things we've done to ourselves? Sal, I'm glad we were able to recover you. Now don't get lost again." He got out of the car, pocketing the keys, and went striding toward the door.

"Asshole," repeated Fishy, and trotted after him.

I stayed where I was, my legs suddenly feeling like they were frozen to the seat. I'd wanted nothing more than to get back to the people I'd lost since I was taken, and now that safety seemed like it was within my grasp, I was terrified. What if Dr. Cale was angry with me for letting myself get grabbed? What if they tried to lock me up to keep me from going missing again? I couldn't handle another cage. I just *couldn't*.

"Sal." Nathan's voice was gentle. I turned to face him, and he reached out to rest the back of his hand against my cheek, smiling just a little. "It's all right to be frightened. I'm pretty sure that I'd be scared too, if our positions were reversed. But you're home now. Mom isn't going to be mad at you. To be honest, she thinks you're some kind of miracle. None of us thought we were ever going to see you again." His voice broke a little on the last word. That, more than anything, told me that he was telling the truth.

I leaned forward and kissed him. He kissed me back, and for a few minutes, all the rest didn't matter: we were actually alone, and together, and no one was trying to pull us apart. That was worth everything in the world. So I kissed him, and he kissed me, and then he was undoing my seat belt and pulling me into his lap, and I was exactly where I was meant to be. Where I should have been all along, and would have been, if we'd been just a little bit more careful.

Nathan's cheeks were flushed when he pulled away, and his glasses were fogged, making him look young and wild-eyed and a little lost. "I thought you were gone, and I was trying to make myself believe it," he said. "I am so sorry. I am so sorry I was ready to give up on you."

"You didn't," I said, and leaned in to kiss him one more time. "Let's go see your mother."

Nathan nodded, and undid his own seat belt as I slid out of his lap and back to my own side of the car, where I opened the door and climbed out into the cool air of the underground garage. It was actually chilly enough that I shivered a little, making me suspect that it would never really get warm down here; it would always be the perfect temperature for shifting pallets of chocolate, or—in the case of the new management—cases containing delicate scientific samples. The more things changed, the more they really stayed the same.

Nathan walked around the car to join me, offering me his hand. "It's going to be all right," he said.

"I hope so," I said, lacing my fingers through his and stepping close enough that I'd be able to grab hold of his arm if things got too overwhelming inside. I felt suddenly shy, and more than a little sick to my stomach.

"I love you," he said. "Now breathe." With that last proclamation, he pulled me forward, and together we stepped through the sliding glass doors and onto the red and white tile floor beyond. It had been designed to look like a giant peppermint swirl, which went well with the gust of warm, mint-scented air that greeted us as the doors slid shut again behind us.

I stopped dead, blinking for a moment, before I passed judgment on the rush of artificial mint with a sneeze.

Nathan grinned. "Disabling the mechanism that 'greets all visitors to our candy wonderland' would mean dismantling half the air-conditioning system, and we don't have the time or the manpower to waste on something like that. Fishy says that the scent will run out eventually, and in the meantime, anyone who has a chemical sensitivity should use the other door or cover their nose when they walk through here."

I sneezed again before sniffling and saying, "That's really thoughtful of him."

"He's a thoughtful guy," said Nathan, starting for the nearest escalator—which was running, I noted. No matter how many buildings around here might go dark, this one had power to spare. The rail was shaped like a never-ending rope of licorice, which was a nice, if surreal, touch.

Once we were both standing on the moving walkway, Nathan sobered and said, "Fishy's been working with Mom for a while, but he wasn't able to convince his wife not to get an implant. Mom says he experienced a profound disassociation from reality when she started trying to eat him—the wife, not Mom—and I think she's probably right."

"Dr. Cale, not the wife," I guessed.

Nathan nodded. "Yeah. Fishy thinks of the rest of us as... well, characters in a uniquely immersive video game environment. That's how he's coping at this point, and as long as he isn't trying to shoot people for extra points, we don't press too hard. He'll come around to reality when he feels like he's ready."

"Assuming reality is any better," I said softly.

"Yeah." Nathan sighed. "There is that."

We both quieted then, and I looked curiously around as the escalator carried us through the open-air lobby—where people in lab coats and sweaters were gathered in small groups, some clutching coffee cups like their lives depended on it, others gesturing wildly with empty hands as they tried to get some vital point of science across. I recognized some of them from Dr. Cale's lab. Others were new. Members of both groups turned to watch as the escalator carried us onward, toward the second floor.

I shrunk back against Nathan, who put an arm around my shoulder and said, "We've gained some people. Mom needed the labor, and they needed a safe place."

"Right," I said weakly, and tried to focus on the faux Candyland furnishings and bright, juvenile murals on the walls. I'd never been here before, in either of my incarnations. Sally's family had been too middle class and respectable to have taken her there as a child. All the family photo albums were focused on Disneyland and Hawaii and other places that were probably a lot of fun for her, even if she looked sullen and annoyed in more than half the pictures. Sally would probably have rolled her eyes at Captain Candy's Chocolate Factory. I was amazed.

The thought that a place like this could exist had never crossed my mind.

It had probably looked a little different before the disaster. Someone had nailed plywood sheets across the lowest of the lobby windows, and all the lobby doors, and only the fact that those sheets were painted in candy colors kept them from being glaringly out of place. The chandelier—a dizzying confection of giant peppermints and gumdrops—was draped in surveillance equipment and wireless boosters, keeping the entire building connected to whatever was left of the Internet.

The lobby passed out of view as the escalator finally reached the second floor, passing through another cheerfully painted tunnel before terminating at a landing covered in carpet so wildly patterned in swoops and swirls that it made my stomach churn if I looked at it for too long. There was also an elevator, which Nathan walked toward and pressed the call button. Going down. I blinked at him.

"Captain Candy's Chocolate Factory is a weird sort of hybrid building," he explained, motioning for me to join him. "It was designed half as a working confectionary company, and half as a theme park that kept the rest afloat by selling tour packages and 'birthday party extravaganzas.' There's a whole floor upstairs dedicated to the party rooms. They're pretty ridiculous, and they make the rest of the place look like it has a subdued color scheme."

I blinked again. "I'm having trouble picturing that," I admitted.

"I'll take you for a tour later on," he said. "Anyway, the place is pretty clever in its use of space. There was a false factory set up for tours, so that people could see candy being made the way it is in the movies—one piece at a time, being hand-wrapped and put into whimsical boxes—and then there was the real factory floor, underneath the rest of the building. That's where

Mom set up her lab. She said it would help her get back to her roots. Also, it's the only place aside from the cookie garden in the upstairs party rooms that's fully ADA compliant, and she wanted to be able to get around her own lab."

"That makes sense." The elevator arrived, and we stepped inside. I was obscurely relieved to see that it didn't have glass walls. Our descent into children's literature was not yet complete.

The elevator counted off the floors: first the lobby we had passed through on our way to the elevator bay—not a very efficient building design—and then two lower floors before it binged reassuringly and opened its doors, revealing the latest incarnation of Dr. Cale's lab. It was, as always, an oasis of chaos masquerading as calm. The various people who rushed back and forth with quick, meaningful steps all wore lab coats over scruffy jeans and T-shirts. A few of them glanced in our direction, nodding at Nathan before they continued on their way, having apparently written me off as a nonentity. I frowned as I stepped out of the elevator.

"Has there been a total staff turnover?"

"No, but most of the people who've been working with Mom for a while have moved on to heading their own research groups rather than doing grunt work," said Nathan, following me out of the elevator. The doors slid shut behind him. "It's amazing how many leads we have to follow, and how few of them are leading us anywhere. You'll see more familiar faces when it gets a little later in the day. There's not much motivation to keep really normal hours."

"Right." I took Nathan's hand, half automatically, and looked around. This had been the working factory level of the building: as such, industrial gray and sterile hospital white still had a place here, rather than being painted over with a hundred shades of candy swirl. The floor was uncarpeted tile, and posters covered the walls. I couldn't read most of them, thanks to my dyslexia, but I knew enough to recognize the *D. symbogenesis* parasite. It was pictured at various stages of its life cycle, which made me feel vaguely uncomfortable, like I was seeing my own naked baby pictures held up for the perusal of strangers.

Other posters blazed safety warnings in large red letters that swam in and out of focus when I squinted at them, accompanied by handy pictograms showing the right way to deal with a chemical spill or put out a lab fire. Still others were printed in blocks of dense text that blurred like fingerprints when I tried to make sense of them. I held tighter to Nathan's hand, aware of how out of place I felt, and even more aware that this place should have grown up around me. I should have been here from the beginning, influencing the shape of the rooms, helping them hang those posters. I felt like I had missed out on something essential, a chance to finally be at the core of my own story, and I wasn't sure that was the kind of chance that would ever come around again.

We were halfway across the room when a narrow face topped by a roughly cut shock of disarrayed brown hair poked out from behind a filing cabinet, moving so slowly that it seemed like an attempt not to startle me. I stopped walking. Nathan did the same. I met the face's eyes, matching their anxious look with an equally anxious expression of my own. The face's owner inched hesitantly into view: a lanky, underfed young man in a lab coat, T-shirt, and jeans, but without shoes on, which made him seem faintly out of place even though he'd been living in labs like this one for as long as he'd been alive. Like me, he was a stranger even in the space that should have been his own.

He didn't say anything. Neither did I. In that moment, in that vast, negative space that had opened between us, neither one of us knew how to react.

Nathan let go of my hand.

Untethered, I could have frozen. I would have, once...but I had led an army of sleepwalkers away from the people I cared about. I had made a deal with the devil to escape from USAM-RIID, and I had crawled through a vent system to win my freedom. I could do this. I took a step forward. "Hi, Adam," I said.

"Hi..." He stopped, swallowed, and tried again: "Hi, Sal. Are you really you? You're not somebody else using you like a car, and I can trust you, and you won't go away again?"

"I think I'm really me," I said. "People seem to enjoy cutting my head open these days, but I'm pretty sure I would have noticed if they'd made it so that I turned into somebody else. Is that even a thing that people can do?" Adam was the second person to ask that same question, and it was starting to unnerve me.

Adam's whole face lit up. "Sal!" he cried, and flung himself bodily across the floor separating us, slamming into me with a force that nearly knocked me off my still-aching legs. I managed to clasp my arms around him, and Nathan put a hand against my back, lending some stability to our little heap of limbs and frantic embraces. Adam pressed his face into the side of my neck. There was nothing romantic about the gesture: it was the blind, desperate struggle of a rescued dog trying to connect with its pack mates. I understood the language his body was speaking, and mine spoke it in return, clinging all the harder as I realized that I had never expected this reunion to occur. Part of me had already mourned for Adam, for this lab, for any chance of having what I considered a normal life ever again.

But not for Nathan. I had never mourned for Nathan, because the part of me responsible for managing the boundary line between the human world and the hot warm dark knew that losing him on top of everything else would have thrown me so deep into the darkness that I would never have come up again. I admired my own ability to care for myself, and I clung to my brother, and I cried.

Finally, after enough time had passed that each of us was confident that the other person would continue existing even without skin contact to keep them in the world, Adam started to unlatch his arms. I did the same, letting him go and stepping backward, into the comforting solidity of Nathan's supporting hand. He wouldn't let me fall. No matter how bad things got, Nathan would never, never let me fall.

"Hi, Sal," said Adam, reaching up to wipe the tears from his cheeks before he beamed at me. "You came back. I didn't think you were going to, but you did."

"I'm sorry it took me so long."

Adam shrugged, visibly dismissing the delay. It had taken a long time, but that was over now: that was done, and I was finally home where I belonged. That was all that really mattered as far as he was concerned. "Mom said you were coming, but I wasn't sure whether she knew for sure that you would still be you. Or still be alive. You could have been like the cousins that they bring in from the field sometimes. They're not here anymore."

I glanced at Nathan. "I don't know what you mean by that."

"We've been harvesting sleepwalkers from the local population," Nathan said, and to his credit, he looked both sad and determined as he spoke. "We have to know how the implants are mutating, and unfortunately, that's the only way for us to track what's happening out there. We try not to hurt them more than we absolutely have to. But we don't bring back live specimens."

Intellectually, I knew that was the right way to go about things. After all, sleepwalkers were irrationally hungry and capable of pushing their stolen bodies to dangerous extremes. Bringing them into the lab alive would endanger everyone. At the same time, these were my cousins, and I felt strange about the idea that we were going out and collecting them as scientific specimens when they weren't actually hurting anyone.

"Oh," I said softly.

Adam's smile returned, weaker than before, as he moved closer and reached for my hand. I let him take it, appreciating the feeling of his fingers lacing through mine. He was smarter than me in some ways. Dr. Cale had been in charge of his schooling, and hadn't been trying to make him think that he was human. He was better-read than I was, and educated at a much higher level overall. He understood science stuff that went straight over my head, leaving me puzzled and surrounded by people who might as well have been speaking Greek. In other ways, mostly having to do with social interactions, he was a little behind me. He liked to remind himself that he had skin. The best and easiest way to do that was with hugs and holding hands.

Nathan took my other hand. I looked from one of them to the other, listening to the drums that pounded in my ears and considering how different they were, and how similar. Dr. Cale's two sons.

"This way," said Adam, and—tugging on my hand—started leading me deeper into the lab. I let him, holding tight to Nathan so that he would come along with us as we stepped into the strangely familiar, strangely modified maze of free-standing work stations, cubicle walls, and tiny research bays that Dr. Cale and her people had carried with them from the lab back in Clayton. As we walked, I finally started recognizing people. Not everyone, but a researcher here and a lab assistant there would seem familiar, and then they would stop what they were doing to straighten up and stare at me like they were looking at a ghost. These were the people who had already written me off as lost forever, and were now faced with the fact that sometimes dead things aren't so dead after all.

We stepped around a corner and into a small "meeting room" carved out of the room's wide expanse by the careful placement of filing cabinets, desks, and bright pink cubicle walls that had probably been stolen from the administrative offices somewhere in the building. Dr. Cale was there, transcribing something in a small notebook. We stopped. Nathan cleared his throat.

"We found her," he said.

Dr. Cale raised her head. For a moment—no more—her expression was completely unguarded, and I could look into her unshuttered eyes and see just how exhausted she really was. There were small wrinkles in the skin around her mouth and at the corners of her eyes that hadn't been there a month ago. Then the walls came crashing down, and it was smiling Dr. Cale once more, as inscrutable and untouchable as ever.

"Hello, Sal. Did you enjoy your vacation?" she asked. "You could have sent a postcard or something, you know. Just to let us know that you were alive out there, and that we could stop worrying quite so much about you."

My hands were still full, with Nathan clasping one and Adam clasping the other, and so I just shrugged and said, "Sherman wouldn't give me a stamp."

To my surprise, Dr. Cale laughed. "Oh, that's a good one. I'll have to remember that. What happened?"

"Um. From the beginning, or from when I woke up in the empty house where I found the cellphone, or…? There's a lot to tell, and I don't really know where I'm supposed to start telling it."

"She's tired, Mom," said Nathan protectively. His hand tightened on mine. "Sherman's been taking tissue samples from her."

"Both of me," I interjected. Nathan and Dr. Cale both turned in my direction. I flushed red. "I mean, Sherman cut my head open, and he didn't do the best job of sealing it back up, and the only thing I can think of that he might have wanted from in there is a tissue sample from my original body."

"He could have taken several segments from your posterior end without interfering with your synaptic interface with the human body," said Dr. Cale. "Do you have any idea why he would want to do that?"

"He said that he didn't know what I was originally tailored to do, since there were holes in SymboGen's records, and said that since most worms were designed to have a purpose—not just making their host healthier, but actually serving a *purpose* in their bodies—a lot of chimera can be something special. Like he can induce biological trances in chimera and sleepwalkers just by touching us." Even saying that made me feel unsafe and unclean, like I could summon Sherman with the mere admission of what he'd done to me. To us—Ronnie wasn't exactly thrilled by the way he'd been treated, and I suspected that he wasn't the only one bridling at Sherman's behavior. "So maybe there's something in my genetic makeup that made it easier for me to integrate with Sally. Whatever that something is, he wants it."

"You need to tell her, Mom," said Nathan, his gaze returning to Dr. Cale. He still didn't let go of my hand. "If Sherman's been taking samples…"

"Tell me what?" I looked between them, frowning. "Is everyone okay?"

"Not by a long shot," said Dr. Cale. "Millions of people have died worldwide, and millions more are going to die before this is over. But I don't think that's what Nathan meant."

"It's not," he said flatly. "Tell her."

Dr. Cale took a deep breath, her ever-present smile fading. She looked down at her hands for a moment, and when she raised her eyes to me again, that sense of age was back, like she was growing older at an impossible rate. "I'm not going to apologize for what I told Daisy and Fang to do," she said. "I will, however, apologize for acting without your full consent. Time was short, for a lot of reasons, and proved to be even shorter than I had feared. What we did was necessary."

Just like that, everything fell into place. I dropped both Nathan and Adam's hands as I reached back to feel the bandages at the base of my skull, held down with strips of tape that would pull and tangle when I tried to remove them from my hair. Suddenly, that seemed very unimportant. "You took samples from me when you were repairing the arteries in my skull," I said softly, the feeling of violation growing soft and warm in my middle. "That's why you were so willing to help get me into a proper surgical theater. Because you wanted sterile samples of my body."

"It's not the only reason," said Dr. Cale defensively. "I wanted you to be safe. You're my daughter and my future daughter-in-law all wrapped into one, and your health is important to me."

"Didn't SymboGen have a slogan that sounded a lot like that?" I straightened, pulling myself as taut as a bowstring. "You *touched* me."

"I didn't—"

"Your people work for you. You told them what to do. You gave the order. *You touched me.*" My voice came out so cold that it sounded alien to my own ears, like it was coming from someone else's mouth. I turned to Nathan. "Did you know about this?"

"No," he said. "Not until we made it back to the lab, and by that point, you were missing and I was out of my mind with worry." He glared daggers at his mother as he spoke. "I wasn't really involved in the operation, since that isn't my field. I didn't realize what they were doing, or I would have stopped them."

And he wouldn't have been watching for that sort of trickery: not on his mother's part, and not with my life potentially on the line. My eyes narrowed as my attention swung back to Dr. Cale. "Was the operation necessary?"

"Yes," she said, with what was clearly meant to be absolute sincerity. It was really too bad she'd spent so much time lying to me. I didn't know what she sounded like when she told the truth. "The weakness in the arteries feeding your brain was real, as was the need to address it before one of them ruptured. We needed access to a functioning surgical theater. All that was completely true. As for the rest...I saw an opportunity, and I took it, for the greater good. You can't blame me for that."

"Oh, I think you'll find that I can blame you for a lot," I said, taking my hands away from the bandages on my skull and folding my arms across my chest. "What did you learn from taking me apart without my permission?"

Dr. Cale sighed. "It's going to be like this now, is it?"

"Not forever," I said. It pained me to admit it. This was enough of a violation that it should have been a deal breaker: it should have left me in the position of never letting myself trust her again. But I knew that she'd done what she'd done because she was trying to save us all. The fact that she hadn't stopped to ask me for permission made me furious. But it wasn't worth the end of the world. "We're going to need some ground rules before I trust you again. But I still want to know what you learned."

"I learned that Sally's father was not exactly forthcoming about his medical history, probably because epilepsy is frowned upon when you're working in Level 4 biosafety labs." Dr. Cale's expression was grim, but there was elation in her eyes, like she had finally cracked a complicated puzzle that had been bothering her for quite some time. "That's why he paid to have top-grade implants tailored by SymboGen, instead of getting them through USAMRIID's medical plan, which would have made more sense—and saved him quite a bit of money, I might add. But he couldn't do that. Not if he was going to get the specific modifications he needed for himself and his eldest daughter. That also explains the holes in the records. He would have paid to have all his files expunged."

I blinked. "Da—Colonel Mitchell isn't epileptic, and neither am I," I said. "The seizure Sally had right before her accident was the only one she'd ever had."

"No, the seizure Sally had right before her accident was the only one she'd ever had *on camera*," said Dr. Cale. "Colonel Mitchell couldn't bury that one, since it was in the news, but it got mostly overlooked in the face of everything else that was unusual about your case. Sally was our canary in the coal mine, and you were our bellwether. You told us what was coming just by showing up. What's more, you told us where we should be looking for more like you."

I frowned. Nathan frowned. Adam, however, wasn't so easily distracted by irrelevant points of science. "You took out part of Sal without her permission?" he asked, frowning deeply.

I glanced at him, surprised. He'd been quiet for long enough that I'd almost managed to forget that he was there.

Dr. Cale nodded, expression solemnly regretful. If there had been a competition for looking most sorry about something you weren't actually sorry about, she would have won instantly. "I did, but sweetheart, I didn't want to open up her skull twice, and we had to act quickly. There wasn't time for a discussion."

"Would you take part of *me* out without my permission?"

"No, of course not. But darling—"

"She couldn't risk me saying no," I said, in that cold, alien voice. "It would have ruined her plans, since then she couldn't have used Nathan to help her work the samples. He would never have allowed her to do what she did, if he'd known."

"That's right," said Nathan. "I wouldn't."

Dr. Cale turned to frown at both of us. "I told you, I needed—"

"No means no, Dr. Cale," I said.

"Sal's my sister," said Adam fiercely. "You should be as good to her as you are to me, and that wasn't very good to her at all. You shouldn't have done that."

"He's right," I said. "You shouldn't have done it, and I'm never going to trust you like that again. But you learned what you needed to know?"

"Some of what I needed to know," said Dr. Cale.

"Then I guess that makes it all better," I said, putting a sarcastic twist on the last two words that actually made her mouth purse in something I didn't recognize, but that I hoped was shame. I put a hand against my forehead, wishing I had some way to quiet the drums that were pounding in my ears. "I have a headache, and I miss my dogs. Can I go to wherever it is they are now, please? I just need to see them, and then you can tell me whatever else it is you've learned by taking pieces out of my head."

"Come on, Sal," said Nathan, slipping his hand back into mine. It fit perfectly. "This way."

"Adam, I'll come see you soon, okay?" I said. My brother nodded, still looking troubled by what his mother had done to me. Good. It was better if she didn't start thinking this sort of thing was okay.

"It's good to have you back, Sal," said Dr. Cale.

"It's good to be home," I said, and let Nathan lead me away.

Nathan led me back to the elevator, this time pressing the button for the top floor. I leaned against him, feeling my entire body start to tremble. The events of the morning had been too much for me, especially after spending weeks in the mostly low-stimulus environment of Sherman's mall. By the time the elevator stopped I was shaking so hard that I could barely walk. Nathan put his arm around me, holding me up as I half stumbled out of the elevator and into the hall.

"Do you need me to carry you?" he asked.

I thought about the question seriously before I nodded and said, without a trace of shame, "Yes, please." The idea of taking another step made the drums pound even harder, a sure sign that I was stressed beyond my breaking point.

Nathan bent and scooped me into his arms. I'd lost weight and he'd gained muscle, our respective paths through the apocalypse leaving their marks on our bodies: he couldn't have carried me like this before we were separated. "This used to be the research and development floor," he said, carrying me past door after door. Each of them was painted in a different, clashing candy color. "I don't know why they put the labs here on the top floor. It may have been a ventilation issue, or maybe they just wanted the place to burn from the top down if there was ever an accident."

I couldn't help it: I laughed a little at the image of some architect seriously explaining that they'd put the fire hazards all in one place for insurance reasons.

Nathan smiled. "The labs are small enough that we've been converting them into living quarters. Most people are double-bunking it, but I was able to convince Mom that I should have a lab to myself until you came home, rather than having a temporary roommate. I didn't want there to be any delay when you got back."

"Thank you," I said, leaning up to kiss his cheek.

"Don't thank me yet; it's another bachelor apartment for you to judge me by," he cautioned, stopping in front of a violently magenta door. It was unlocked. I blinked, and he stopped with his hand still on the doorknob, explaining: "We keep all rooms unlocked when they're unoccupied, to make it easier for the staff to find shelter in the event of a sleepwalker outbreak inside the facility."

"That makes sense," I said. I could hear snuffling noises around the base of the door, and the familiar sound of blunt claws clacking against the floor. "Are the dogs in there?"

"Yes." Nathan lowered me back to my feet. "You may want to brace yourself."

Grinning, I did exactly that, dropping to one knee in the hall and spreading my arms. Nathan chuckled and opened the door.

There is nothing truer in this world than the love of a good dog. Beverly and Minnie surged out of the room, both wagging their tails so hard that their entire rear ends were vibrating, and commenced to the essential business of licking every exposed inch of my skin. I laughed and folded my arms around them, letting them butt their heads against my middle and buffet me with their tails. Beverly shoved her cold, wet nose into my ear. I bit back a shriek.

"They missed you," said Nathan, standing back and folding his arms as he watched this edifying scene. "Beverly's been looking for you all over the building. Minnie just sulked a lot."

"Who's my little diva?" I asked Minnie, rubbing her jowls. She rewarded me with a cascade of drool and more tail-wagging. "Aw, that's my girl. You don't care that I'm a tapeworm, do you? You just want pettings and love and food and all that good stuff. It doesn't change anything when I tell you I'm not human. You just want me to be here with you."

With wagging tails and wiggling bodies the dogs agreed that yes, yes, I was quite right, they didn't mind anything I wanted to do, as long as I would keep on loving them and being their person.

I glanced up. Nathan was frowning now, his joviality gone. "Sal..."

"I know you don't care either." I climbed slowly back to my feet. The muscles in my calves felt like they were on the verge of giving up completely. "It's just that sometimes I feel like my life would have been a lot easier if SymboGen had been a veterinary medicine company."

"You'd rather have been a dog?" asked Nathan.

I stepped into the welcoming circle of his arms, the dogs still circling my feet with tails wagging, and said, "They aren't as complicated as people. I think I would probably have made a pretty good dog, if the option had been on the table."

"I think you make a pretty amazing woman," said Nathan. He embraced me briefly before letting go and tugging me into the room. "Welcome home."

The dogs followed closely at my heels, making it easy for him to close the door behind us while I considered our new living space. It was obvious that this room had started life as a working lab: the room's origins were visible in the industrial shelves bolted to the walls and the perfunctorily efficient kitchen that took up one wall completely, laid out in a straight line that would never have caught on with private homeowners. Everything else about it, however, was entirely new, and had clearly been designed to be entirely ours.

The room was divided roughly into thirds. Nathan's side was taken up by bookshelves and a desk that looked like it had been scavenged from the nearest Ikea. His laptop was set up and running, displaying a slide show of pictures. Most were of the two of us, although there were a few of the dogs, and some of his friends from the hospital. A picture of Devi—Minnie's original owner—flashed by. I winced. The rest of the desk was taken up by sheaves of paper, and by stacks of scientific equipment that I couldn't identify or name. It all looked very important.

My side of the room was mostly empty shelves, although my throat tightened a little when I saw that my few belongings had been unpacked and placed carefully wherever they seemed to best fit. There was a small pyramid of dog food cans, and a basket full of squeaky toys and rawhide chews.

"I'm amazed Beverly hasn't knocked that over yet," I said faintly.

"Oh, she has," said Nathan. "I just keep picking it up again. She's mostly stopped making trouble for the sake of making trouble. She missed you a lot, Sal. We all did."

There was a broken note in his voice that made me pause in my study of the room to twist around and look at him. He met my eyes unflinchingly. I'd never seen such a depth of pain in his dark brown eyes, not even right after Devi died. "I missed you too," I said. "But I'm home now, and we're never letting that happen again."

"Good," said Nathan.

I turned back to my study of the room, finally allowing myself to focus on the part that had interested me the most. In the portion of the room that was clearly intended for us to share, a garden was blooming. It wasn't food or herbs or medicinal plants—although looking at Nathan's cunning hydroponic systems, I had to wonder if we were growing them somewhere in the building, if part of Captain Candy's had been converted into a working farm now that necessity was demanding it—but it was something better, and much more important, all contained in a raised bed with high Plexiglas walls to keep the dogs from going digging. I guessed that those walls would come up to my waist, making it easy to bend and get to the plants when I needed to.

Carnivorous flowers and sticky-leaved stalks twined in a riotous explosion of hungry color, reaching toward the grow lights and misters that were keeping their environment at the optimal levels of heat and moisture. I gasped a little, tears forming in my eyes. "It's beautiful," I sighed. Nathan and I had really started bonding as a couple over our mutual love of carnivorous plants. They were chimera too, in a way: they grew like plants and they ate like animals. The sundews in front of me might be some of the last ones blooming in captivity. It was a sobering, heartbreaking thought.

"We had to make several supply runs into San Francisco," said Nathan, putting his hand on my shoulder. "Putting together a lab this size—we're three times larger than the bowling alley now, so we would have been forced to move even if not for the quarantine, just because we couldn't *fit* in the available space anymore—meant gathering equipment from anyplace we could. I made a few extracurricular stops while we were there."

"You could have been killed," I said automatically, still staring at the impossible garden.

"I know." Nathan took his hand off my shoulder and stepped past me, walking toward the vast wooden edifice that was our bed. I stayed where I was, unsure of what to do next, until he looked over his shoulder, smiled a little, and said, "Come over here. Please."

I bit my lip and nodded before walking across the room and sitting down on the edge of the mattress. The frame looked like it had been stolen from the same Ikea as the desk, and had drawers built into its base, providing more storage space. Beverly leapt up in a single easy bound, curling up next to me and dropping her head onto my knee like her skull had suddenly become the heaviest thing in the world. Minnie climbed up, using a set of steps fashioned from an old milk crate. She stretched out at my back, providing a warm, furry bolster.

"I thought you were dead," said Nathan, without any more prevarication or pausing. "We lost you in that parking lot, and we knew that USAMRIID had you. Mom has some contacts in the military—not enough to break the quarantine, and don't think that they wouldn't betray her in a second if they thought they could take her—and she contacted them within the hour, saying that one of her lab technicians had been taken. They got back to her a week later, reporting that someone of your description had been there, but had been abducted by a person or persons unknown. Then they started asking her some fairly pointed questions, since whoever took you had killed a bunch of their men in the process."

"That was Ronnie," I said. "He's one of Sherman's chimera. He has impulse control problems."

Nathan blinked slowly. "Impulse control problems don't usually come with a body count."

"From Ronnie, they do. He's frustrated and angry, and I don't think he likes humans very much." We'd never really talked about it. I hadn't wanted to upset him, not when I was trying so hard to get him to like me. Seeing Nathan's frown deepen, I added, "What he did was wrong, but he's the one who got me out of Sherman's compound thingy, so I'm not really inclined to throw stones, you know? I owe him."

To my great relief, Nathan nodded. "I owe him, too. He gave you back to me. But at the time, the news that you'd been kidnapped by people who didn't care who they hurt…it was terrifying, Sal. We all knew that you were dead, or dissected, or worse. I kept Mom looking for you. I couldn't stop. Stopping would have meant admitting defeat, and if that happened…" He took a deep, shaky breath. "I thought about killing myself. I decided not to, simply because I knew that I had work to do, and I knew that my death would do nothing to clear my family name. But I didn't have anything left to live for."

I bit my lip again. The world had ended while I'd been sitting in my nicely gilded cage. There was just one factor unaccounted for…"Your father?" I asked.

Nathan shook his head. "He stopped answering calls shortly after the primary outbreak started. He lived in Orange County, in a very densely populated area, and all the CDC and USAMRIID maps we've been able to purloin have shown high sleepwalker activity in that area. If he's alive, it's a miracle, and I'm not holding out much hope for miracles just now."

"I'm so sorry." The words weren't enough. Words never were. They were all I had to offer him.

"He was a good man, and he had a good life. I think he'd be happy to know I found Mom again, and that we're at least trying to be a family. I know he'd be happy to hear that I found you again, that we somehow went through this horrible thing and wound up in the same place." Nathan reached out and cupped my cheek with one hand. "He liked you a lot, you know. He used to ask me when you'd be his daughter."

"I already said I'd marry you," I said, blinking back tears.

"Fishy's ordained," said Nathan. "I think it would be a Jedi wedding—"

I couldn't help myself. I broke out in giggles at the very idea.

Nathan smiled. "This is where we live now. This is where we're going to find a way to save the world. Do you need anything?"

"Sleep," I admitted. "Ronnie knocked me out before he moved me to the house where you found me, but that wasn't real sleep, and I had…" The teenage sleepwalker, all life gone from her eyes, reaching for me out of the pure, desperate need to survive. "…I had a hard day. I just want to sleep."

"Okay." Nathan leaned forward and kissed my forehead before he started shrugging out of his lab coat. "I could use a nap."

I didn't say it, but I was grateful that he was staying with me. Good as it was to see my dogs again, I didn't want to be alone.

It didn't take me long to be ready for bed—all I had to do was squirm out of my bloody clothes, which Nathan whisked away and dropped into a sealed, dog-proof hamper. It took him a little longer, since he was somewhat more properly dressed. When we were both naked, we stopped and just looked at each other, me tracing the new starkness of his ribs and pallor of his arms and chest, where his slight tan had faded back to his natural light brown skin tone, him studying the bruises on my arms, legs, and side, all the snipped-off bits of skin and the tracks left behind by Sherman's needles. I was white as a ghost after a month without seeing the sun, and when he came to me, I felt like paper pressed against stone, devoid of anything but emptiness.

Nathan curled himself around me, and the dogs fitted themselves into the spaces we created with our bodies, and everything was finally right with the world.

# INTERLUDE III: METAPHASE

*Oh, my precious children, what have I done to you?*
*What kind of world have I created that you would*
*do this to each other?*

—DR. SHANTI CALE

*We're all going to wake up any day now, and this will*
*all be a dream. Until then, why don't we enjoy the*
*chance to live in a science fiction novel?*

—DR. MATTHEW "FISHY" DOCKREY

*October 2027: Tansy*

Still here I'm still here I'm still me I'm still here.

But only barely, I think. Every day I'm a little less me a little less here a little less Tansy. Pieces of me are going. He's stealing pieces of me, one by one, and all he's giving me in exchange is pain. So much pain. Pain like it's air, pain that is breathing, so breathing stops seeming like a good idea. I try to stop I've tried over and over again to stop to let go to empty my lungs like flat paper boxes on a hill and why do I think of that over and over what is the hill what does it mean why do I want to go there what do those boxes do? I can't remember anymore. So I try to stop breathing, over and over again I try, and every time I think I might succeed his machines grab me and bring me back again, returning me to the place where everything is pain.

It's been long enough that I'm not sure the world has ever *not* been made of pain. Maybe that's a thing I made up, like all the other things that I made up. Like running and jumping and firing a gun pow pow bang bang and being free and being happy and being home. Like Adam and Sal and Sherman. How could there be other people like me when I'm not even possible?

He'd said that to me more than once. "You shouldn't be

possible," and sometimes he said it like it was something remarkable, something to be celebrated, and other times he said it like he was angry with me, like I had broken a rule by not being something that was supposed to exist. It didn't seem to matter how he said it. It always came with pain, and so I'd stopped really listening to his tone, and started listening for the silences between his words. If I could just fill my ears with silence, maybe everything else would go away.

I didn't know how long I'd been where I was. I didn't know anything anymore. All I knew was that I hurt. I hurt so bad.

There was a click as the door on the other side of the room swung open. I whimpered. I couldn't help myself. I hurt so much, and I didn't want him to hurt me again. I just wanted him to go away so I could practice not breathing. Maybe this time I would do it right. Maybe this time the machines wouldn't realize what I was doing, and they'd let me go. Maybe.

Heavy footsteps approached me, every vibration sending shockwaves through the floor and into my raw, exposed nerves. I was glad I couldn't see him approaching. I'd never considered that blindness could be a blessing.

"How's my girl today?" He always started the same way. Even now that I couldn't answer him—not even if I wanted to—he still talked to me like I was going to respond. Just one more thing I didn't understand. "I'm afraid I have some bad news for you, darling. Do you remember when I told you that I was going to learn everything I could from you before I let you go? That was the day we talked about dying. Do you remember?"

I didn't remember. I didn't remember anything but pain. But I couldn't tell him that without a tongue, with my mouth wired shut to keep me from biting at myself when the drugs wore off, and so I didn't say anything at all.

"Of course you do." A hand touched me lightly on my throat, on one of the few intact patches of skin that I had left.

"Well, my dear, I'm sorry to be the one to tell you this, but that day has come."

I had thought that I was past feeling anything but pain. I was wrong.

I could still feel relief. It was ending. It was ending.

It was e

# STAGE III: ANAPHASE

*We do not negotiate with terrorists.*

—COLONEL ALBERT MITCHELL,
USAMRIID

*You think you're stronger than us because nature made you that way. Science made us. Which do you think is going to win?*

—SAL MITCHELL

*The bitch is gone. Ronnie decided to let the little idiot out of her cage after one sob story too many about how much she missed her family and how horrible it was for me to keep her here. I would be angrier about it, but honestly, I find myself somewhat relieved. I thought she would be my perfect mate, the one person in this world who could match me body and mind. I did everything I could to guarantee that she grew up mentally and morally elastic, capable of understanding the necessity of the things we do and the choices we make.*

*Alas, what I got was a frightened little girl too attached to the idea of her own nonexistent humanity to understand what I was offering her. It's a true pity. Sal could have been one of the great ones, but she allowed herself to be slaved to lesser minds.*

*It doesn't matter now. I have what I need.*

—FROM THE NOTES OF SHERMAN LEWIS
(SUBJECT VIII, ITERATION III), OCTOBER 2027

*The situation is continuing to deteriorate. I wish that were not the case: I wish I could claim we had reached some incredible turning point in our research, and unveil it for you now at what might otherwise be considered the eleventh hour. To admit the truth of what is happening here smacks of ceding to the enemy. It smacks of cowardice. It burns me, on every level, to do either of these things. I was taught that every problem has a solution, and that it is the American way to rise up and meet those problems head-on until the solutions are presented.*

*Gentlemen, we have met the problem head-on. We have risen to the occasion, and beyond. We have continued our work despite personal tragedy, despite deaths and losses too great to be borne. The men and women under my command have been genuine heroes, and it is a crime that their names will not be remembered by future generations, because I no longer have any faith that those future generations will exist—or if, should their existence be assured, they will be anything we could recognize as human.*

*My recommendations on this matter were made years ago, and were ignored. It is an unfortunate truth that the inconvenient, when ignored, tends to become worse rather than becoming better.*

*The situation is continuing to deteriorate. There is nothing more that we can do.*

—MESSAGE FROM COLONEL ALFRED MITCHELL,
USAMRIID, TRANSMITTED TO THE WHITE HOUSE ON
NOVEMBER 2, 2027

# Chapter 11

## NOVEMBER 2027

I dreamt of the hot warm dark. Of the hot warm dark and of the redness that never ended, instead stretching on and on into a peaceful eternity. I moved through that redness without moving, and I understood the reasons for that now. My old therapist would have been amazed by the breakthroughs I was making in understanding my own mind. Not thinking of myself as a human being helped a lot. I didn't need to consciously move when I was in the hot warm dark because I *was* the hot warm dark, and I was the occupant of the hot warm dark, and it would never leave me, even if I could never go back to the simplicity of being that I had once enjoyed, before I became self-aware, before I became Sal, with all the consequences that choice—if it was a choice—implied.

I didn't really think of my creation as a choice. All the choices had come later, when I was a thinking, feeling creature that stood on two legs, instead of swimming fluidly with none. If there was a price to pay for what I had become—a price for *me* to pay, not Sally—it was that once you were human, you had to choose things.

"Sal." A hand touched my shoulder, accompanied by the familiar sound of Nathan's voice. The hot warm dark dissolved into the blackness behind my eyelids. I didn't move. There was always a moment, right after I woke up, where I had to decide whether or not waking up was worth it. Choices again. Nathan sighed. "Honey, I know you're awake. Come on. We're going to miss breakfast if you don't get moving."

I opened my eyes and rolled over. Nathan, fully dressed, with a lab coat over his brown wool sweater, was sitting on the edge of the bed and smiling ruefully at me. His thick black hair was damp and sticking to his forehead, a sure sign that he'd come straight from the showers. "What?" I said, groggily. "Why?"

"Because we only serve breakfast for so long, and then we have to start turning the kitchen over to get ready for lunch," he said reasonably. Beverly had her head resting on my hip. He reached over me to ruffle her ears, adding, "It's waffles today. The chickens on the roof have started laying enough eggs that we can use them for things like batter."

"I like waffles," I allowed, and sat up. Beverly gave me a betrayed look and rolled over, telegraphing her intent not to get out of the bed for anything short of bacon. I giggled. I couldn't help it.

"I like waffles too," said Nathan, his small smile blossoming into a full, tight-lipped grin. He never showed me his teeth when he smiled anymore. What had been an affectation for my comfort when we were dating and I was human had become full-on habit upon learning that I was a tapeworm, and that my distaste for teeth was a genetic atavism that no amount of therapy could cure.

That sobered me. I bit my lip, dropping my chin a bit as I said, "I'll get some clothes on and be right down."

"That sounds like you're planning to stay in bed until I leave the room, and then get ready without me," said Nathan. "What's wrong? Did you have bad dreams again?"

Sometimes I dreamt about my time with Sherman, or even my time at USAMRIID, blessedly short as it had been. In my dreams, Sherman never came to save me, and what Sally's father had planned for me—the worm that had stolen his daughter's life—was always worse than a few marrow samples. I had been back where I belonged for almost two weeks, and the dreams weren't as frequent as they had been once, but I still woke up screaming frequently enough that we were both running on a disrupted sleep schedule.

"No," I said quietly.

"Sal…"

"It's nothing."

"It's something, or you wouldn't be refusing to meet my eyes." Nathan touched my shoulder. "Tell me, please. I can't help if you won't tell me."

"I dreamt about the hot warm dark. That's all. It was…it was so nice. It was so much nicer than dreaming about being back with Sherman that I didn't want to wake up. I just wanted to stay there forever." The words were all simple ones, but between the two of us, they meant so much more than they could possibly encompass. I had dreamt of being something other than human, and I had wanted to stay that way. But if I wasn't human, how could I belong here?

Nathan sighed. "Sal. Look at me."

I lifted my head.

"Wanting to disappear into the hot warm dark is perfectly reasonable for you right now, and you know it. I don't care where you came from. I never have, and I never will, and you know that." Nathan looked at me solemnly. "I won't tell you not to be silly—you're *not* being silly, you're going through a perfectly natural and normal process. You're grieving for a life you didn't think was going to turn out like this, and I'm just sorry we don't have any trained therapists here for you to talk to. But I don't care how many times you dream about disappearing into the dark. You're still my girl."

"I hated my therapist," I said weakly. "Besides, where would we find somebody trained in the psyche of the distressed chimera?"

"It's a niche field," Nathan said, and offered me a small, hopeful smile.

I searched his eyes for some sign that he was lying, and couldn't find it. I never found it, no matter how many times I looked. Maybe because it wasn't there, and maybe because the lies were too big and too deep to be visible to anyone—not him, and certainly not me. How could he love me now the way that he'd loved me when he thought I was just like him? It didn't make any sense. I didn't feel the same way about myself as I had before I learned where I had come from. It was impossible for Nathan to be the only person in the world who really didn't care.

Or was it? I didn't feel the same way about myself anymore, but I didn't feel any differently about him. Maybe it was the same for him, just…in reverse.

Those thoughts were big and complicated and hard, and I was tired of arguing with myself—so tired of arguing. So I shunted them to the side, sweeping them away like so much trash, and leaned forward to kiss him. Nathan responded by releasing my other hand and pulling me closer, ignoring the irritated grumbling noises from Beverly.

This time, there was no mistaking the pounding of my heart for the sound of drums. Nathan's lips tasted faintly of mouthwash, which made me smile. He scooped me up, dropping me into his lap, where the pressure of his erection against my hip made it plain that he was as glad to see me as I was to be seen.

After that, there was no stopping, for either one of us. He stripped me out of my nightgown without lifting me from his lap, and then pushed me back against the bed as he removed his lab coat. Beverly grumbled more and jumped down to the floor, trotting across the room to join Minnie in the dog bed. I laughed, reaching forward to undo Nathan's fly, and then nothing remained but the things we *did* share: skin and sweat and physicality, and the sweet knowledge that each of us was loved enough to make this moment possible. Moments like that one—not sexual, necessarily, but absolutely connected, absolutely in synch—are where humanity lives.

Nathan needed another shower by the time we were done, and I still needed my first one. He pulled his trousers and sweater back on while I wrapped myself in the comfortable largeness of his lab coat, enjoying the feeling of cotton against my bare backside as we walked down the hall to the employee showers. Not every floor had its own locker room. The lab level had two, probably because the scientists and researchers who used to work here were dealing with sticky substances all day, and no one wanted to deal with dripping molasses all the way home.

"I'll be right back," said Nathan, kissing me quickly before we parted ways at the entrance to the male and female showers. Not everyone paid attention to the distinction anymore—gender binaries seemed a lot less important after the apocalypse, if they had ever really been important in the first place—but splitting up was the best way to make sure we might actually make it downstairs in time for the last of the breakfast service.

The shelves in the women's showers were cluttered with a wide assortment of hair care products and soaps, ranging in quality from salon brands to the sort of things that used to be sold at drugstores for a dollar a bottle. Several of Dr. Cale's interns were conducting what they called "comparison tests," and had determined that most of the salon brands were functionally identical to the Costco house brands.

"This would have saved me a fortune if I'd known before everything was free," one of them had confessed drunkenly to me once, right after I had walked in on them shampooing one another's hair. After that, I'd gotten a little more careful about showering alone. It wasn't the nudity that bothered me. It was the expectation that I would know how to be social in a situation that no one had ever modeled or explained. People were complicated, and "complicated" was another word for "confusing as hell."

I sluiced off quickly, using a cherry-scented shower gel to wash myself off while the combination shampoo and conditioner worked at baking the stiffness and snarls out of my hair. I could be in and out of the shower in half the time it took Nathan, usually, because I didn't much care about what combination of products I used as long as they accomplished the solitary goal of making me clean. Rinsing myself, I ran my fingers through my hair to break up the worst of the knots and turned off the water before starting for the exit.

It hadn't been long enough since my escape for me to need a haircut. I wanted one. I wanted one so badly that I sometimes woke up in the middle of the night with images of scissors dancing in front of my eyes. I didn't want *anything* he had done to me to last. At the same time, cutting my hair—which was *mine*, it belonged to *me*, it grew out of *my* scalp—felt like an admission of defeat. Maybe it was a little, stupid thing, but it felt like if I cut it off, he would win. So I dried it as quickly as I could, and tried not to look at my reflection in the mirror.

I was fully dressed by the time Nathan came back to our room from the men's shower, toweling off his hair as he stepped through the door. I smiled and held out his clothes. "Breakfast?"

"Breakfast," he agreed.

He was still slightly damp when he got dressed. I helped, which nearly resulted in us needing another turn in the showers. Finally, though, we were walking toward the elevators, fully clothed and ready to face the day ahead.

Two weeks in the candy factory had acclimated me to the layout of the place: I was no longer pressing random buttons and then being surprised by whatever floor I happened to wind up on. Two weeks had also acclimated everyone else to my presence. There were fewer weird looks and jumps, and more quiet avoidances.

I suppose I should have expected that. Dr. Cale's people were among the best in the world, and had been even before the population of the world started to drop precipitously. But they didn't all share her "a person's a person" attitude toward the chimera, or her sympathy toward the sleepwalkers, who had, after all, not asked to be designed with dangerously high levels of human DNA. I was starting to worry that she would have a mutiny on her hands before too much longer. What felt like half her technicians didn't want to broker a peace between the two sides: they wanted to wipe the other side out completely, sweeping the slate clean and creating a world where allergies and autoimmune disorders would return to their proper place in the human body, rather than being suppressed by tapeworms that could turn traitor at any moment.

It was sort of hard to blame them for that. I probably wouldn't have been too thrilled at the idea of harboring my own replacement.

The elevator stopped two floors down from our living quarters, and the doors opened on a sugar-scented, candy-colored wonderland. As always, the sight of the party level sent my train of thought spinning out of control, replaced by a strong desire to run laughing through the cookie garden until the Buttercream Fairy appeared and told me to stop. I glanced to the side. Nathan was grinning at me again.

"I just really like it here," I said defensively.

"I just really like it when you're happy," he said, laughing, and stepped out of the elevator, leaving me with little choice but to follow him.

The party level had been designed to be managed by no more than six staff members, but had been subdivided into enough small grottos and private rooms that it was impossible to tell how many people were there at any given time. The elevator opened into the arrival area, which smelled like jelly beans and gumdrops and didn't have a specific "candy" theme apart from "dentists are the enemy." The randomly changing candy scents made meals an occasionally interesting experience, since this was also the only place in the building that was properly set up as a dining area. There was a cafeteria, but it was small and gray and depressing, and pretty much all of us preferred to eat in the cookie garden.

The smell of bacon wafted from what used to be the sticky toffee oasis, but had become the main station for fried meats in the morning and hot soup in the afternoon, thanks to its plethora of heat lamps and electrical outlets. According to the flyers in the old manager's office, the sticky toffee oasis had been the only party destination to offer fondue as an option for the birthday boy or girl. I wasn't really sure why anyone would want to eat toffee-flavored fondue on the steps of a plywood and plaster pyramid. Clearly, my lack of a human childhood had warped me in some way.

Daisy was on duty at the hot bar when Nathan and I came around the corner. He got a bright smile, which faded somewhat as her eyes focused on me. "Good morning, Nathan," she said. "Sal."

"Morning, Daisy." I picked up a plate. "Nathan said there were waffles?"

"Third tray," she said, pointing with her tongs before refocusing her smile on Nathan. It got even brighter, if that was possible. "I saved you some ham. It's from the freezer we found last week, so we know it's good."

"Mmm, ham," said Nathan. "Did you know that most natural tapeworm infections in the United States came from undercooked pork before we started importing our produce from South America? Salad tainted with human feces turned out to be an excellent transmission method for the infection."

Daisy blanched, looking faintly nauseated. "Is that your way of saying you don't want any ham?"

"I try to avoid pork as a rule." Nathan picked up a plate of his own. "Breakfast potatoes?"

"That, I can do," said Daisy, looking relieved. She opened the second of the silver serving platters and spooned a heaping pile of potatoes onto Nathan's plate. "The fruit is down at the end."

"I know my way around the hot bar," said Nathan, with a smile that came nowhere near hers, for brightness, but was kind, which was really more than I would have given her. "Thanks for breakfast."

"Thanks for eating," said Daisy. Her blanch became a blush. "I mean, let me know if you want any orange juice."

"Okay."

I took my plate of waffles and previously frozen berries, stopped in front of Daisy long enough to take the ham Nathan had refused—it wasn't like it could give *me* a tapeworm, since the chemicals I released into Sally's body as part of claiming it as my own prevented any other parasitic infection from taking root—and flashed her a toothy smile before I turned and followed Nathan deeper into the party floor, looking for a table.

He finally settled at an empty picnic table that had been

painted to look like it contained our recommended daily allowance of chocolate chips. I slid into a seat across from him. The waffles were pretty good, especially considering that it had been made with condensed milk—we had chickens, even a few goats, but no cows. That would have required more arable land than we could create with potting soil and fences.

Captain Candy's had been designed to serve three disparate purposes: tourism, research, and food production. It still served three purposes. They just weren't what the original architects had had in mind. The wonderland areas were still mostly intact, used as social space and meeting areas. The research and development labs had been repurposed into living space, with some people choosing to paint the walls white and others—like Nathan and myself—choosing to keep them primary colored and comforting. No one's ever come up with a universal color scheme for the apocalypse, and if ours wanted to come in neon and peppermint stripe, well. That was okay.

The real factory level was being used for research, development, and all the things that went with having a team of working scientists rather than a bunch of independent researchers. I stayed out of there as much as I could. It wasn't that people were unfriendly—for the most part, they were perfectly nice, if a little distant and occasionally wary of my nonhuman status— it was just that I didn't understand anything that was going on there, and I had long since learned to keep a safe distance from what I didn't comprehend. Call it the last great survival strategy.

The false factory was located on the second floor, which had been divided into two levels by some cunning tricks of interior design and elevator programming. The first level was a walkway made of plastic-coated steel gridding surrounded by a clear, waist-high plastic guardrail. It was completely wheelchair accessible, all long, gentle turns and shallow ramps as it made its way around the room, taking the most circuitous path possible. The elevator always stopped there first no matter how the buttons were pushed, since that was where the tourists were supposed to get off, and then continued down to the actual work level.

Once, the view beneath the walkway would have been all colorful, impractical machinery being tended by men and women in neon scrubs, with perpetual smiles plastered across their faces. No facial hair, pregnancies, or visible tattoos were allowed in the tourist factory, although all three were tolerated and even encouraged in the real Captain Candy. The good Captain didn't care what you looked like, as long as you came to work and did your job the way that you were told to. The Captain's PR department was a little more fixated on appearances, and they insisted that he run a tight ship, if only to keep those birthday dollars rolling through the door.

I think I would have liked Captain Candy. You know. If he'd actually been a real person, and if he'd managed to survive the rise of the SymboGen implants with his mind and his humanity intact.

The view from above had changed considerably since the factory switched hands, even if it all still belonged to the corporation on paper. The colorful machines were still there, but most of them had been gutted for whatever useful parts they happened to contain, and then left open to the air as they were converted into planters or small habitats for the less free-range inhabitants of our private indoor farm and animal sanctuary. The neon uniforms were long gone, along with the people who used to wear them. Instead, an observer would find Dr. Cale's assistants moving between the machines, most of them wearing T-shirts or tank tops and jeans, a few with dirty white lab coats thrown over the top, as if to say, "I'm working in an indoor farm, but I'm still a scientist; I will always be a scientist." The number of lab coats had dwindled even in the weeks since I'd come to the factory, as people realized that maybe some trappings of the old world were less important to hang on to than others.

We were building a world, one piece at a time. It was a small world, and a strangely dysfunctional one, but it was one where we could be relatively safe, and relatively happy, and maybe find a way to save the human race. If we were lucky, and we worked hard enough—which meant science for most of the people around me, and farming and taking care of the animals for the people *like* me, who had connections to the science community without being part of it—there was still a chance that we could find a way for everyone to live in peace. All we had to do was stop the cousins from taking over their hosts, and stop the humans from killing all the sleepwalkers and chimera who had already resulted from those takeovers. The sleepwalkers were bitey, but maybe they could still be helped, if we could just keep them alive.

It didn't even *sound* easy. I put my fork down and looked glumly at the smears of syrup and berry juice that remained on my plate. Across from me, Nathan kept eating. He knew that whatever was bothering me, I'd share it eventually, and he needed to pack in as many calories as possible before his shift in the lab started. There was no eating allowed near the active cultures, for fear of contamination.

Footsteps on the faux stone pathway behind us caught both of our attention. I turned in my seat while Nathan raised his head. Daisy was standing in the doorway to the area, eyes wide, a slightly poleaxed expression on her round, normally friendly face.

"You're both needed downstairs," she said without preamble.

"I'm not on duty for another thirty minutes," said Nathan.

"I know." Daisy sounded frustrated. "But like I said, we need you *both*, and right now there's no such thing as being off duty, because we have a situation. Sal is required, and you're not going to let her go out alone."

"Why won't he let me go alone?" I asked, bemused. "What kind of situation means I can't go out alone?" The unconscious echo hit me an instant later, and a thin worm of panic writhed in my stomach. Everyone here at Dr. Cale's lab was steeped in the mythology of an obscure, out of print children's book, and from us, those words meant something very concrete.

Daisy looked at me solemnly, an uncharacteristic reserve in her mossy green eyes. "Dr. Banks is here," she said. "He's asking for you."

The transfer of genetic materials was complete at 6:52 p.m. on October 18, 2027. The selected donor, a lab assistant originally attached to the tissue rejection research team, was put under twilight sedation but remained conscious and able to respond to stimulus. All remained normal within the subject area for approximately forty-five minutes, following which the donor began to experience confusion, disorientation, and some pain. This continued for approximately fifteen minutes. Pertinent parts of her final words have been captured and attached to this document.

The donor lost consciousness for the first time at 9:01 p.m. on October 18, 2027. She regained consciousness once, for approximately three minutes. Consciousness was lost for the final time at 11:57 p.m. The subject awoke the following morning at 5:13 a.m., seeming fully integrated with the nervous system and mind of its new host. All medical readings and records have been attached.

Things are going to be different now.

—FROM THE NOTES OF DR. STEVEN BANKS, SYMBOGEN,
OCTOBER 2027

>> Yes, I can hear you, Dr. Banks. Thank you. I'm very comfortable. Thank you. I believe the drugs are working. I feel…

*light. Like there's nothing holding me down. Is something holding me down?*

*>> I can hear the bone saw. It's very loud. Bone conduction is funny.*

*>> Did you put something inside the incision? I think you may have left something inside the incision. It feels like something is pushing on me. Like there's pressure where pressure isn't supposed to . . . isn't supposed to . . . oh.*

*>> My mother took me to the carnival once. It was in a field. Just a field. Most of the time it was full of cows and grass and now it was full of magic. Everything was magic. I said I wanted to be a carnival girl. She said no, be a scientist, make something of yourself . . . I'm cold. I'm cold.*

*>> It hurts.*

*>> It hurts.*

*>> [screaming]*

*>> [screams continue]*

*>> I don't . . . I don't . . . I can't . . . I'm not . . .*

*>> Where am I let me out I want to go home I can't—*

*>> [barely audible] I'm still in here. Let me out. I'm still here.*

—THE FINAL WORDS OF CLAUDIA ANDERSON, AS TRANSCRIBED
BY DR. MICHAEL KWAN, SYMBOGEN, OCTOBER 18, 2027

# Chapter 12

## NOVEMBER 2027

Daisy fidgeted as the elevator slid down into the bowels of the factory, plucking at the hems on her sleeves and casting sidelong glances at me and at Nathan, like she thought we had somehow been struck blind by the discovery that Dr. Banks had managed to find us. It wasn't like Captain Candy's was a natural place to conceal an underground biotech lab. If he'd located us here, he must have spent quite a lot of time and effort on looking. He had to have a reason.

I leaned against Nathan's side, trying to calm my breathing, or at least get the frantic pounding of my heart under control. In that moment, I would almost have welcomed Sherman and his weird biomechanical control. At least then I wouldn't have felt so much like I was on the verge of losing consciousness.

The elevator dinged as it reached the ground floor lobby. I stepped forward, almost bopping my nose on the opening doors in my eagerness to get out of that small, tight space full of questions and uncertainties. I wasn't in a hurry to see Dr. Banks—I was never going to be in a hurry to see *him*—but in that moment, anything would have been better than staying where I was and trying to figure out how this was making me feel. I didn't know how it was making me feel. No, that wasn't right: it made me angry. All of this made me angry, and *that* was what I didn't know. I didn't know how to deal with the anger. I didn't know how to handle the sheer feeling of betrayal that came with the thought of seeing him again.

I was going to need to figure things out, and fast. There were five figures waiting for us at the front of the Captain Candy Chocolate Factory lobby, outlined by the early morning sun that slanted in through the big glass windows. The boards nailed up to protect us from sleepwalkers only extended about eight feet up from the floor; there was plenty of light. People moved outside the glass, nailing the boards back into place. There must have been another attack while we were sleeping.

That got more common every day.

Even with them reduced to nothing more than silhouettes, I could tell who four of the five people in the lobby were. The low-slung figure in the wheelchair was Dr. Cale, and the two men who flanked her were Fishy and Fang, recognizable by outline alone. One of the figures, a willowy female, was unfamiliar to me. And the fifth...

The fifth was one of the first people I remembered, one of the first humans to sit down with me and tell me I didn't have to be defined by my accident and my memory loss, that I could learn to be a full, productive member of society despite the way my life had changed. He'd been lying all along, of course—he'd known exactly what I was, and that each of the skills I learned would be learned for the very first time—but he'd always known what to say to get me to come around. Even later, when I'd started to chafe against SymboGen's pseudo-parental treatment of me almost as much as I'd been chafing against Sally's parents, he'd always known what to say. After all, he was one of the people who had created me.

But he couldn't talk me into taking a job at SymboGen, even when he tried his best, and he hadn't convinced me not to steal the data Dr. Cale had asked me to get for her. Maybe he didn't know me as well as I thought he did.

I wondered what he thought as he saw me walking slowly across the lobby toward him, with Nathan by my side. Did he look at me and see a woman, stronger than she used to be and only a little weaker than she had the potential to become, who had survived the apocalypse and the discovery that she wasn't even the species she'd always believed herself to be? Or did he see the broken girl he'd worked so hard to keep under his control, the experiment gone horribly right and taking its first steps out into the world? And did it matter? Sally Mitchell was gone. This body was *mine*. Not hers, not anyone else's, not ever again. I was even suddenly grateful for Sherman's unasked-for haircut, because it was something Sally would never have done to herself. I looked like someone else. I *was* someone else.

And then I got close enough to see the bright, paternal smile on Dr. Banks's face, and I was just Sal again, dressed in a paper gown and waiting to be told that it was time for cookies and juice.

"Sally," he said, and while the name he used wasn't mine, I couldn't deny the reality of his relief. He sounded like a man who had just discovered that Christmas wasn't canceled after all. "You really made it. I'd heard rumors, but I wasn't sure."

"No thanks to you," said Nathan. "What is he doing here, Mother?"

"Manners, Nathan; Dr. Banks is our guest, at least for the moment," said Dr. Cale. "He may be our prisoner in a little while. I haven't decided yet. You've met my son, haven't you, Steven? Oh, what was I thinking? You were having him monitored by SymboGen security. Of course you've met my son, even if I wasn't always sure he'd met you."

"Hello, Dr. Banks," I said. I kept my eyes on his face, not letting myself look at the interplay between Nathan and Dr. Cale. They didn't matter as much as he did. Not in this moment. "You made it too. I thought you'd have been arrested for crimes against humanity by now."

"The United States government and I have an understanding," he said. "I keep working on a way to help them solve their little tapeworm problem, they don't arrest me. It works out well for everyone involved."

"Except the dead people," said Fishy snidely.

I didn't say anything. I just looked at Dr. Banks.

Dr. Banks had always been a man who fought to present the illusion of perfection, clinging to it long past the point where anyone else I knew would have abandoned it as a waste of resources. That perfection was gone now. His sandy hair was mussed, graying at the temples, and a little longer than it should have been, showing how long it had been since he'd been to see a barber. He'd lost weight, leaving his carefully sculpted physique less defined than it had been the last time I'd seen him. Most damningly, he was wearing stained brown slacks and the top half of a pair of medical scrubs. The sleeves of his black runner's top poked out of the shirt, their cuffs a little frayed. If the apocalypse was stripping us of our masks and revealing us for what we really were, what did that say about Dr. Banks? How much of who I'd always assumed him to be was a lie?

"I've been working day and night to try to find a solution," he said, apparently mistaking my silence for awe, or for confusion, or for something easier to explain away than what it really was: understanding. I was starting to understand why it had been so easy for him to lie to me all those years, when he looked into my eyes and called me "Sally" and acted like my accident hadn't changed anything.

He'd already been lying to everyone else.

"Who's she?" asked Nathan, breaking the brief quiet. His gaze had gone to the silent girl standing next to Dr. Banks. I followed it, really considering her for the first time.

She was a whisper of a thing, a charcoal sketch that no one had ever bothered to finish filling in. Her skin was almost pale enough to be translucent, a milky white only a few shades darker than the skins of the tapeworms Dr. Cale kept in jars and feeding containers down in her lab. Her hair was black, falling to mid-back, and her eyes were a dark enough brown that I might not have realized they had a color at all if I hadn't had her hair for contrast. She was maybe twenty years old, and stick-thin. She looked like she was on the verge of collapse, but she met my eyes steadily, and she didn't flinch away.

Something about her was terribly familiar. I had never seen her before.

"Sal, meet Anna," said Dr. Banks, placing a proprietary hand on the girl's shoulder. She turned to look up at him, her dark eyes filled with worshipful adoration. He flashed a smile at her—the same warm, intentionally paternal smile that he used to direct at me.

In that moment I knew what she was, but I didn't say anything, too filled with disgust and dismay to force my lips to move. The pounding of the drums was back in my ears, brought on by the stress and the realization that Dr. Banks had been doing more independent experimentation than any of us had ever suspected. And why shouldn't he? He'd been one of the creators of the SymboGen implant. He had as much right as anyone to explore further perversions of science.

Dr. Banks turned that warm, paternal smile on me, and said, "She's your sister."

Dr. Cale didn't wait for the rest of us to react to Dr. Banks's proclamation before she started rolling herself toward the elevator, signaling for the group to follow her. "We're moving this to a more secure location," she called. Fishy trotted ahead of her, pressing the call button for the service elevator that used to transport entire birthday parties and pallets of boxed candy around the factory. Captain Candy had believed firmly in using things for as many purposes as possible. That made him my kind of guy. Too bad he had never really existed.

I was chasing my thoughts down rabbit holes again, a sure sign that I was disturbed by Dr. Banks's proclamation. I piled into the elevator next to Nathan, sneaking glances around him at the pale, black-haired girl that Dr. Banks called "Anna." She couldn't really be my sister, could she? I knew she was a chimera. Nothing could have convinced me otherwise. But how could he have done that to a living human being? How could have done that on *purpose*? Sherman did the things he did because he didn't believe that humans had any more right to their bodies than we did. Dr. Banks *was* human. How could he have done that to one of his own people?

I didn't hate myself for what I was, but I knew my birth had been predicated on the death of someone who had existed before me. Dr. Cale was my mother in the sense that she had designed me, building the human DNA into my structure that would one day allow me to bond with Sally Mitchell on a fundamental level. Dr. Banks was my father in the same sense: his incessant tampering with the structure of *D. symbogenesis* was what enabled it to infest its hosts so flexibly. And yet...

And yet really, Sally Mitchell had been my mother, because her flesh nurtured and supported me until I was large enough to live my own life—a life that began when hers ended. My eyes searched Anna's face, looking for signs that she had made the same transition, or at least understood what the transition meant.

She stared straight ahead for the entire descent, not meeting my eyes or looking in my direction even once. I glanced down. She was holding Dr. Banks's hand tightly in hers, her fingers digging so hard into the back of his hand that the flesh there was white and bloodless. Maybe she was nervous after all.

The elevator dinged as it reached the ground floor, and the doors opened to reveal eight more of Dr. Cale's interns and lab technicians. They were all holding semi-automatic weapons, and had them trained on the open elevator doors. Fishy took a half step to the left, putting his finger on the "door open" button that would keep the elevator locked where it was. To my dismay, one of the technicians tracked his movement with the barrel of her gun, keeping him firmly in her sights.

Dr. Banks stiffened but didn't say anything. Anna made a small whimpering noise, her hand clamping down even harder on his, and looked down at the floor. Her shoulders were shaking. I felt the powerful urge to put my arms around her and tell her that everything was going to be all right, which was as nonsensical as it was foolish. Everything was *not* going to be all right. Dr. Cale was holding us at gunpoint, and I knew her well enough to know that I didn't understand precisely why. Nothing was going to be all right until I knew what was going on.

"Nathan, please push me out into the lab," said Dr. Cale. "The rest of you, I recommend staying exactly where you are. If you move too much, you may find yourself leaking from a bunch of holes that you didn't start out with, and our medical facilities still aren't as advanced as I'd like them to be. We could probably deal with one gunshot wound, but five would be a strain on our resources."

"I'm not leaving this elevator without Sal," said Nathan, through gritted teeth.

"I didn't expect that you would—hence my count. Steven, his little pet, Daisy, Fishy, and Fang. Five. Now be a good son and help your mother." There was a needle of ice in Dr. Cale's voice, as sharp and vicious as a hypodermic in the night. "We all know that a woman in a wheelchair can't be expected to take care of herself."

"Now Surrey—" said Dr. Banks.

Dr. Cale didn't turn or look back at him. "Surrey Kim is dead, Steven. You should know that better than anyone: you're the one who killed her. She had a husband and a son and a career that didn't involve destroying the world. She had the capacity for compassion toward the human race, even if she had to learn what didn't come naturally. It's really a pity that you decided she had to go. I think she might have been a little more understanding about whatever it is you've come here for. Nathan?"

"Yes, Mom," said Nathan, and gripped the handles of her chair, pushing her out of the elevator. He didn't move much faster than she would have been able to go on her own. She sat with her back perfectly straight, like the mast of one of the ships that used to sail in the San Francisco Harbor, and I followed behind them, fighting the urge to glance back and see how the others were reacting. Fishy, Fang, and Daisy were being left in the line of fire for nothing more than the crime of being in the elevator when Dr. Cale declared it a holding pen. Dr. Banks had to know what he was walking into when he decided to come here—and why would he *do* that? He knew we weren't friends. He knew we weren't even allies. So what would bring him to Dr. Cale?

What, if not Anna?

I could almost feel her behind me, eyes on my back, a soft, warm presence like a beacon that said I should turn around, go back to the elevator, and refuse to leave her alone. It wasn't an awareness that had anything to do with any of the senses; it was just there, inescapable, like gravity.

I stumbled a little, catching myself on the arm of Dr. Cale's chair. She cast me a quick, concerned look, lips pursing as if to shush me. I nodded, just a bit, and kept walking, refusing to let my confusion show on my face. I knew Anna was there because I could sense her, a blind, deaf sense that pervaded everything—and I always knew Adam was there, didn't I? I always knew when he was in the room, even if I didn't know exactly where he was. It hadn't been like that at first—he had managed to surprise me more than once in the early days—but the longer I'd been around him, the stronger that sense had become. I hadn't even noticed it happening. It was just natural, unavoidable, like the tide.

My ability to sense other chimera was growing, and had been since Sherman held me captive in his mall. I didn't know how far it was going to go. Apparently, it had already gone far enough for Anna to register immediately on my parasite radar.

Dr. Cale gestured for Nathan to stop when we reached the line of interns and assistants, and she gripped her own wheels, turning herself to face our visitors and abandoned associates, now virtual hostages to Dr. Banks's good behavior. The line broke and re-formed, leaving the three of us strung at the center of it like a pendant on a chain. Dr. Cale refolded her hands in her lap, tilting her head so that her sleek blonde hair brushed against her cheek just so. She looked like a nursery school teacher, someone who could wait patiently forever until they received the answer they were looking for.

Fishy, Daisy, and Fang were still in their original positions, looking remarkably relaxed for people who might be shot at any moment. Then again, they were also all armed, and they knew that the folks with the rifles would be shooting at Dr. Banks and Anna, not at them.

"I really think you're overreacting here, *Shanti*," said Dr. Banks, stressing Dr. Cale's chosen name. "I'm here as a friend, and as someone who needs your help. I don't see any reason for you to have your people treat me like a common criminal."

"Really? How many times did you try to have me killed, Steven? Two? Three? Oh, wait, there was that incident with the gas leak back at my first private lab—we never did figure out how that happened, but as there were no cameras on the location, we couldn't rule out industrial espionage. That one almost succeeded, you know. I was still getting used to my wheelchair back then. So I'd say that 'four' is a low estimate, wouldn't you?" Dr. Cale's folded hands tensed and relaxed to a rhythm I understood: she was hearing her own version of the drums that followed me through my life.

Nathan kept his hands on the chair, more I think so that he wouldn't have to decide what to do with them than anything else. Dr. Banks was the man who'd first conceived of the project that would lead to *D. symbogenesis*, the downfall of the human race, and the end of the world as we knew it. But he hadn't done any of that on his own. When he needed help, he'd gone looking for the smartest, most ethically flexible genetic engineer he knew: Dr. Surrey Blackburn-Kim, Nathan's mother. Dr. Kim had known that this path would lead them through the broken doors at last, and she'd tried to refuse—not too hard, I was sure; she'd been the same person then, even if she'd gone by a different name—and when Dr. Banks had produced information that he could use to force her to work on his project, she'd agreed, on one condition. Dr. Kim had to die.

There was a boating accident. Nathan buried his mother. Nathan's father buried his wife. And Dr. Shanti Cale hung her newly minted degrees on the wall of a private lab in a San Francisco biotech firm, where she was going to change the world.

I couldn't really say whether she'd done the right thing. All I knew about the blackmail material Dr. Banks had on her was that it was bad enough to make her walk away from her entire life…and that he had played on her ingrained desire to break the laws of nature without getting caught. "Every mad scientist secretly dreams of playing God," was something she had said to me on several occasions, and from the way she and Dr. Banks were looking at each other now, I guessed that was true.

He was trying to project a veneer of smug confidence over a thick inner layer of exhaustion. Dr. Cale was ice. She looked like she had never thawed, and never would.

"Now, Shanti," said Dr. Banks. "Are we really going to let the past keep us from collaborating here and now, when we have a chance to save the future? We work well together. You know we do."

"How many times?" she asked coolly.

"Eight," he admitted, after a long silence. "Your little odd-eyed girl stopped two of my men before they could get anywhere near you, and you dropped off the grid not long after that. Where *is* she, by the way? I didn't expect to be able to walk right up to your headquarters."

"You shouldn't have been able to," said Dr. Cale, her glare briefly flickering to the other three people who shared the elevator with Dr. Banks and Anna. Well, that explained why she'd left them in there: they were all involved with our operational security, and the fact that he was in the building at all meant that they had failed, to some degree, at their jobs. "As for Tansy, she is on an extended leave of absence. We hope to have her back with us soon."

"That means you lost her, doesn't it?" Dr. Banks shook his head. There was a slight upward tilt to the corners of his mouth, like he was fighting not to smile. "You should be more careful with your human resources, Shanti. It's getting harder to replace them."

"It's getting harder to replace biotech firms, too, but you've apparently allowed yours to be commandeered by the U.S. government," said Dr. Cale mildly. "Do we really want to start playing the game of 'who paid more to arrive at this point in time'? Because I'll note that you're standing there trying to make me feel sorry for you, and I'm sitting here wishing more than anything that I could walk over and knee you in the balls."

I blinked. Dr. Cale's paraplegia was a fact of life, something that the lab and her living quarters had been designed to accommodate. Sometimes I forgot that it was the result of her implanting the tapeworm that would eventually mature to become Adam in her own body, where it had compromised her spine to such a degree that she had been judged unlikely to ever recover, even back when she had access to better medical care than we could supply in a repurposed candy factory. The thought of her walking was surreal.

From the brief look of regret that flashed over Dr. Banks's face, I was the only one who felt that way. "I didn't 'allow' the government to commandeer my resources. They take what they want. And I never did tell you how sorry I was when I received the news of your injury."

"Really, Steven? You were sorry? Because here I thought you'd take it as proof that you'd been right when you decided to sideline me."

"You didn't stay long enough to be sidelined."

Dr. Cale sat up a little straighter, lifting her chin. "That's true. I ran as soon as I saw the writing on the wall. You were in a position of power, and I knew what a man like you would do when he had a little power in his hands. Now here we are, and I'm in this chair, and yet for once, you don't have any power at all. You're just a man with no army at his back, standing here and asking for my help. So what is it that you want, Steven? What can my humble little underground lab do for someone with your resources and reach?"

"Sarcasm is a mode of speech used to convey mockery or even disdain without openly insulting the other person involved in the conversation," said Anna.

Everyone stopped. Dr. Cale's attention switched from Dr. Banks to the girl, her eyes crawling over Anna's body with an almost visible avidity. Anna continued to stare straight ahead, not seeming to fully understand what was happening around her. Again, the urge to shield her from the situation swept over me, and again, I pushed it aside. She wasn't on our side. That made her the enemy.

"How far along is her integration?" asked Dr. Cale.

"Two and a half weeks," said Dr. Banks. "Ideally, she would still be hooked to her monitoring equipment, but she's highly resistant to being separated from me. She becomes difficult to control."

"How is she talking if she's only two and a half weeks along?" asked Dr. Cale. "Language integration takes longer than that."

Dr. Banks looked smug. "I found a new means of stabilizing the neural paths. It allows for a quicker, more seamless connection between the implant and the brain."

"Building a better chimera," said Dr. Cale. "I'm sure the government will be thrilled to hear that's what you've been doing with their money."

"We have to understand them if we're going to defeat them." Dr. Banks sighed, shaking his head. "All right, Shanti, what is it that you want me to say? You want me to apologize? Fine. I apologize. I'm sorry I brought you into this, and I'm sorry I created an environment where you felt like you had to remove yourself for your own safety, and I'm sorry I tried to have you killed. Although to be fair, you would have done the same in my position."

"I don't know about that," said Dr. Cale. "You stole my research, Steven. You stole my life's work, and you stole my *family*."

"I didn't steal them," he protested. "You chose to give them up."

"That's not the family she's talking about." The sound of my own voice surprised me. Dr. Cale didn't take her eyes off Dr. Banks, but the way her mouth curled upward at the corner told me that she approved of my interjection. I swallowed, the drums hammering loudly in my ears, and said, "You called Anna my sister. You did that because she's . . . she's like me. She's a tapeworm in a human skin."

"Yes," said Dr. Banks, and beamed at me, like I was a slow child who had just managed to catch up to the rest of the class.

It made me itch to punch him, to feel my knuckles sinking into the soft flesh of his cheek or throat. I clenched my hands by my sides instead, and said, "That means you used the *D. symbogenesis* tapeworm on a human subject to get a chimera of your very own."

"Yes," said Dr. Banks again. His smile this time was more strained. He was clearly getting as tired of praising me as I was of being praised. Too bad that had never been enough to make him stop.

"That worm has human DNA in it. Dr. Cale's DNA. You took her family away from her when you took *us* away from her."

"Millions of children," said Dr. Cale, a wistful note in her voice that I had only heard on a few occasions, usually when she was talking about her friend Simone, who had died of allergies before the development of the SymboGen implant. Simone had been Dr. Cale's motivation for wanting to solve the hygiene hypothesis. Without that dead friend, Dr. Cale would probably have turned her terrible intellect on destroying the world in some other completely accidental way.

That's the danger of genius. One way or another, it's going to destroy the world.

"I don't understand," said Dr. Banks.

"I think you do," said Dr. Cale. "I had millions of children, and you took them away from me. So what can you possibly offer that would make up for that?"

"Data." He produced an external hard drive from inside his shirt, holding it up for all of us to see. "I have the full record of Anna's conversion and assimilation here, and I'm willing to give it to you, if you're willing to help us. There are things on there that you probably haven't even considered yet, much less advanced to the testing stage. I can help you jump your research forward by a matter of years, and all I'm asking is room, board, and a little supervised access to your lab space. Anna still needs monitoring for signs of rejection, after all."

Anna herself didn't say anything. After her interjection about sarcasm she had returned to her previous silence, standing like a wan shadow next to Dr. Banks. I tried to meet her eyes. She looked away. Something about that made my stomach clench, although I couldn't have said exactly what it was. Something was *wrong* with Anna.

"I have all that data," said Dr. Cale dismissively. "I brought three subjects to full integration, and I monitored them every step of the way. You're going to have to do better if you want me to find a space for you here, and not to just shoot you and dump you out back for the feral cats."

Dr. Banks smirked. "Ah, but all three of your subjects started in a vegetative coma. Anna didn't."

My stomach clenched even harder, becoming a knot of ice in my abdomen. The sound of drums was suddenly deafening, pounding in my ears until it became the entire universe, until there was nothing but the drums and no need for there to be anything else, ever again. "What did you just say?" I whispered. I wanted to shout. I wanted to scream. I couldn't make my lips or throat obey me.

Luckily, Nathan was close enough to hear what I had said. "What did you just say, Dr. Banks?" he asked, and the sudden chill in his own voice told me that he had looked at the situation and reached the same conclusions that I had.

"I said that Anna—not her original name, you understand— did not begin her transition in a vegetative state. She was alert and aware through the bulk of her crossover. I have the data." He held up his hard drive again, as if reminding us of its existence. "I can help you, and all I'm asking is that you give me a little help in return."

"Help is commonly reciprocal between equals, a matter of

duty from inferiors, and a matter of obligation from superiors," said Anna, in the same calm, barely inflected tone that she had used before. Her gaze didn't waver, continuing to stare off into the middle distance like she was looking at something the rest of us couldn't see.

All the cold in my body consolidated into a single freezing point. I strode forward, toward Dr. Banks, ignoring the guns that were now pointed at my back. I dimly heard Dr. Cale bark an order, but as it didn't contain my name, I neither stopped nor slowed. All my attention was fixed on the man in front of me, who smiled that old paternal smile at my approach, seeming pleased to see me walking toward him willingly.

"Sally, my dear, I knew that you would under—" he said, before my fist collided with his jaw and he stopped talking. He staggered backward, eyes wide and wounded, like a feral animal's. The shell of cold around me shattered with the blow, but I still raised my hand, getting ready to hit him again. He deserved it.

At the last moment, I changed my mind, and snatched the hard drive from his hand instead. He stared at me, too stunned to react, which just made me want to go back to punching him. Anna, who had in her own way been a motivating factor in the chaos, said and did nothing. She just stood there, staring blankly ahead, her hand still curved like she was holding on to Dr. Banks.

"I'm tired of this," said Dr. Cale wearily, her words audible now that the icy shell was gone. "Take them."

Instantly, Fishy and Fang began to move, Fishy getting Dr. Banks into a headlock while Fang produced a syringe from inside his jacket and drove it into the side of Dr. Banks's neck. Daisy stepped forward, reaching for Anna.

A wave of panicked protectiveness swept over me. I grabbed Anna's slightly curved hand in my free one, relieved when she allowed her fingers to part long enough for me to get a good grip, and tugged her forward. She stumbled a little, but she came willingly enough.

"No," I said, putting my free arm around Anna's chest, so that I was holding her against me. She still put up no resistance, moving with me as malleably as a doll. "Don't touch her. She doesn't understand—she's still so—don't touch her. You need to leave her alone."

"Sal, sweetheart, you're going to have to let go of the new girl eventually," said Dr. Cale. "She needs a full exam."

"No," I said again, turning to face her. Anna turned with me. If I hadn't been able to feel her chest rising and falling with her breath, I would have suspected her of being a large, elaborate decoy—but no, that wasn't possible, was it? I could *feel* her, a presence that had suddenly joined my overall map of the universe in an undeniably permanent way. Adam had done the same thing. He'd just taken longer, maybe because he was the first, and those channels in my mind hadn't been open yet when he and I met.

Well, they were open now.

Dr. Cale looked at me thoughtfully, frowning. Her expression didn't change when we heard the dull thud of Dr. Banks's body hitting the elevator floor. Finally, she asked, "What if I let you come with her while we set her up for an examination, so that you can see that she's safe, and then afterward we can talk about this like adults?"

It was the best that I was likely to get. It meant that I wouldn't be leaving her alone; I could get her settled, and then go find Adam. I nodded. "Okay," I said. "Anna? Is that okay with you?"

Anna didn't say anything at all.

*Sell your face to buy your mask,*
*It will serve you in this task,*
*And masks can see us better than the mirror ever could.*
*Closer now, but still so far,*
*Lose your grip on who you are.*
*The next time that you see me, you will be with me for good.*

*The broken doors are kept for those the light has never*
*known.*
*My darling girl, be careful now, and don't go out alone.*

—FROM *DON'T GO OUT ALONE*, BY SIMONE KIMBERLEY,
PUBLISHED 2006 BY LIGHTHOUSE PRESS.
CURRENTLY OUT OF PRINT.

*That bastard.*

*I know what he did. I know how he did it. I know why he did it.*

*The only thing I don't understand is why he would come here, to me, to flaunt this monstrosity. And until I know why, I can't take steps to get rid of him.*

*Oh, my poor girl. I am so sorry.*

—FROM THE JOURNAL OF DR. SHANTI CALE,
NOVEMBER 15, 2027

## Chapter 13

# NOVEMBER 2027

Dr. Banks was removed to one of the secure holding rooms. Dr. Cale had prepared them knowing that eventually one of her people would go sleepwalker. Everyone who worked for her was supposedly clean, but that didn't necessarily mean anything—the rules had changed as soon as the tapeworms began migrating through the bodies of their hosts, and we couldn't count on things like asexuality or built-in obsolescence to keep people safe.

Anyone who wasn't a chimera like me or free of implants like Nathan was a potential conversion risk. That fact had been driven home a week before Dr. Banks showed up, when one of the techs suddenly started seizing. She'd been infected all along. We just hadn't known it.

Now she drooled and gnashed her teeth in the room next to the one where they were putting Dr. Banks. I hoped the smell of him kept her snarling the whole time that he was there. He deserved it.

I led Anna through the facility, flanked by two guards who were supposed to make sure she didn't try anything. If she was plotting against us, it didn't show. She held my hand, docile and silent, until we reached a small examining theater, two of its four walls made of hanging white linen. When she saw the bed she smiled, the expression lighting up her pale face, and pulled her hand out of mine. She ran to climb up onto the bed with all the joy of a child on Christmas morning. Before any of us could do more than blink, she began shedding clothing, throwing it to the floor until she was stark naked. Then and only then did she lay back on the bed, arms flat at her sides with her wrists turned toward the ceiling, as if she was prepping herself for the inevitable IV.

She didn't make a sound throughout the entire process. She just stripped and stretched in total silence, somehow managing to even keep the bed linens from rustling.

Nathan, Dr. Cale, Daisy, and I stared at her, equally silent, although our silence was born more of shock than anything else. Then, slowly, the three of them turned to look at me. I put my hands up, as much to ward off the comparisons as to ward off the questions.

"No," I said. "I remember *everything* about the period immediately after I woke up, and I was *never* like that. I was compliant, yes, because I wanted to please the people around me, but I was never…never…" I shuddered, unable to put the wrongness of what I'd just witnessed into words. Finally, unable to think of anything else, I repeated, "No."

"So we're either looking at the result of conditioning, or at something that happens naturally in…" Dr. Cale stopped. It was rare to see her silent in the middle of a sentence. Her lips moved for a few seconds, struggling for the next word, before she said, "Involuntary chimera. Oh, God. I never wanted to say those words."

"I don't see how you *can*, Mother," said Nathan. "This is impossible. He has to be lying."

"There's only one way of finding out," said Dr. Cale. Her gaze went back to Anna, and the rest of us followed it. "She has the answers. They're locked in her blood, in the protein traces of her spinal column, in a hundred other locations on her body. Getting them out will hurt her. I wish we didn't have to try."

"So take him at his word," I said, the need to protect her looming large once again.

"We can't, Sal," said Nathan. I glanced to him, feeling obscurely betrayed. Yes, he frequently sided with his mother in matters of science, but not when it was something like this, not when a woman's life was on the line. He shook his head. "If she's a chimera who converted while the original personality was still conscious and aware of her own body, that means there might be a way for sleepwalkers to integrate successfully. You were the first natural chimera, but Sally was already gone when you made the integration. She wasn't in the body to fight you. Anna..."

"The mind resists that sort of thing, as a general rule; that's why brainwashing and sleep-learning don't work," said Dr. Cale. "We become entirely different people every seven years, and our minds let it happen because it's slow, it's graceful, and even then, we cling to childhood pleasures and high school goals like they somehow had more relevance just because they happened earlier in our developmental cycles. *Can* one of my children rewire a thinking mind completely and successfully without resulting in the sort of traumatic brain damage we see in the sleepwalkers? God help me, but we need to know."

"Why?" I asked blankly.

"Because if my children can take someone over without

unconsciousness or brain damage, they can learn to make the transition almost invisible," said Dr. Cale. "No real disruption. 'Bob's just tired,' and then the other chimera remove their new brother or sister before anyone notices the change. Oh, all the memory loss will still apply, but it'll be so much easier to relearn everything when you don't damage the brain in the process of taking it over."

"That's why he brought her here," I said. "He knew you'd study her. She's a trap."

"Yes," said Dr. Cale. "I'm aware. So let's set it off, and see what happens."

"He'll take everything you learn and run away with it."

Dr. Cale's smile was a terrible thing, and filled with teeth. "You're assuming he'll still have feet when we get done with him."

Anna—who had to have heard every word we said, lying there on the bed with her eyes toward the ceiling and her nipples slowly hardening from the chill in the room—didn't say a word or turn toward us even once. She just held herself perfectly still, a composed expression on her face, like Dr. Banks passed her off to strangers every day.

My fingers itched, and the only cure, I knew, would be grabbing hold of her and never letting go. I rubbed them together, trying to make the feeling stop. "I'm going to go find Adam," I said. "He needs to know that this is happening, and that there's another chimera in the building."

"All right," said Nathan. He bent to kiss the top of my head. I hugged him quickly, taking what pleasure I could from the contact. "We'll be here."

"I know," I said, and turned to run deeper into the lab.

Adam and I were the yin and yang of Dr. Cale's chimera research project, in more ways than one. He was created in the "traditional" way, when she introduced an immature

*D. symbogenesis* directly into the brain of a subject in a persistent vegetative coma. The body's original owner was already long gone, leaving an otherwise healthy habitat for the new tapeworm intelligence that would inhabit it. I was an accident, born of trauma, stress, and lucky chance. My memories began at the moment I fully integrated with Sally Mitchell's brain, but according to Dr. Cale, the last act of my old life had been a panicked flight through her body, culminating with my burrowing into her skull and beginning the integration process. He was induced, I was natural; he was nurtured *as* a chimera, I "grew up" believing myself to be a human being. I had spent the last few months stumbling from one dangerous situation to another, while Dr. Cale kept Adam in the lab, as confined and protected as possible. She *said* that she hadn't allowed me to spend so long outside of her care after my accident just so she could monitor our development under different types of clinical pressure, and I actually believed that she believed that.

At the end of the day, Dr. Cale loved Adam very much, and wanted him to be safe. I couldn't blame her for that. She'd been his mother for the entirety of his life, while I was more like the child she'd helped someone else bear through egg donation: genetically connected, socially and emotionally very, very distant.

"Adam?" I slowed as I reached the edge of the lab hydroponics section, which was used mostly to grow herbs and local mushrooms. There was a large artificial bog filled with sundews, which I appreciated—Nathan and I had our collection, but he had "liberated" several more from florists and taxidermy shops when he was helping to collect hydroponic and preservation supplies. Sundews were bog plants, which made our old friend Marya's admonition not to overwater them even funnier. She'd been trying to keep us from killing them with chlorine, of course, and the language barrier had simply been complicating her instructions.

Marya was probably dead now. She'd owned and operated a flower shop within the general footprint of San Francisco City Hospital. Even if she hadn't had an implant of her own—and I didn't know whether she did or not; I had never asked her, and it was too late now—there had been mobs of sleepwalkers in that area during the collapse. There was very little chance that she had survived.

I sometimes wondered how the rest of the people on Dr. Cale's team could stand it. I had only had a few years to form connections with other people, and I could still be blindsided by the strength of how much I missed them.

But this wasn't the time to dwell on what we'd lost. "Adam," I called again. "It's Sal. The duty roster says you're supposed to be here, so where are you? Come on, Adam. I know you're there."

"How do you know?" asked a voice from behind me. I turned, but I didn't see Adam, just the shapes of three large potted avocado trees. "Maybe I'm somewhere else. Maybe I'm nowhere near here at all."

"Well, since we don't have intercoms this good, and the cell system went down weeks ago, the part where you're talking to me means that you're here," I said. "Apart from that, I know you're there because I know you're there."

The leaves on the avocado trees rustled and Adam's face appeared, pale through the gloom. I was paying attention now, brought to high alert by Anna's presence: I didn't feel the same drive to *protect* that I felt for her, but he wasn't in danger, was he? I already knew that Adam was safe and well, and on the few occasions when I *had* been afraid he would be hurt, I'd had the same response to him that I had to her. Chimera, standing together. So no, I didn't need to protect him...but I was aware of him. I always had been. I just hadn't been able to consciously name that feeling before I had someone else to check it against.

"The scientific method works," I murmured.

Adam blinked but didn't ask me what I meant. He was always good at ignoring things that didn't make any sense. "I felt them bring her into the building," he said. "It was like as soon as she was here, everything was whole again, instead of being broken the way that it has been for days and days. Do you think she took Tansy's place?"

"What? No." That answered the question of whether or not he knew about our visitor. But he knew Anna was a "she," and tapeworms are hermaphrodites: he was a boy and I was a girl because of the human bodies we'd grown to inhabit, and not because we were innately gendered creatures. "No, Adam. Tansy is…Tansy is our sister. I don't know where she is, or whether she's okay, but I *do* know that no one is ever going to take her place in our lives. We're going to find her. We're going to bring her home. I know it." There was something wrong with that answer, something that gnawed at the back of my mind with sharp, unforgiving little teeth. Anna held the key to finding Tansy. I knew she did. I just didn't know how I knew, or what that knowledge was going to mean.

"I saw them bring Dr. Banks and the new girl in," he said, taking a step forward, out of the trees. As sometimes happened with Adam, he looked infinitely younger than me in that moment. "I wasn't supposed to be there, and Mom told me to get to work as soon as she realized that I was watching, and I didn't want to go. I wanted to tell Mom no, because the new girl needed me so bad. It was like…it was like the need was just rushing off her, like water out of a hose. And I started to think that maybe that's why you like me. Because need rushes off me, and you don't know how to get out of the way."

"I think Dr. Cale was right when she theorized that we had a pheromone connection, just like the sleepwalkers do," I said, choosing my words with exquisite care. "We're their cousins, so it makes sense that we'd have some of the same systems in place to make sure that we stayed in contact with each other, and that we looked out for each other. And yeah, it was sort of a surprise to me—I always just figured I wanted you to be safe because I cared about you. Now it turns out that there's also a chemical component, probably generated automatically when you're under stress or whatever."

This wasn't helping. Adam was starting to look more concerned, and if I didn't change tactics soon, he was going to retreat into the avocado trees and I was never going to catch him. I sighed.

"But Adam, that's just the initial pang of alarm, that's like ants leaving chemical trails for one another. We're not *ants*. We're not even sleepwalkers. We can think. We can feel, and we can form social bonds. I don't care about that girl as a person. Yes, when I'm in the room with her I want to protect her and keep her safe, and I figure that's probably a good thing from a species perspective, since it's better if we want to protect each other and not kill each other." I was babbling. But Adam wasn't retreating anymore, and I'd take that. "Only see, I *do* care about you. I want you to be happy. I like it when we just sit and don't talk to each other because we're both doing stuff. You're my brother and I love you, and she's just some girl who happens to be the same species that we are."

"Really?" Adam finally stepped out of the shade of the avocado trees, his eyes so wide that I could have tripped and fallen into them. "You really think I'm your brother?"

"Only one I've ever had." Unless you counted Sherman— and he, like Anna, was just someone who happened to share my species. He didn't deserve to be a part of my family. He didn't deserve to be anywhere *near* my family.

"What's going to happen now that she's here?"

"I don't know, but that's part of what I wanted to talk to you about. Dr. Banks says she integrated while her host body's consciousness was still present and aware."

Adam's eyes went even wider, the whites appearing all the

way around his dark brown irises. "She's a fully integrated sleepwalker?"

Because that's what we were all dancing around: that was why her existence was such a concern. If one tapeworm could integrate with a living, conscious host, so could another, and another, until the entire shape of the enemy changed. We could be looking at a fight that went from intellect against mindless hunger to intellect against intellect—and for me and Adam, it would be a fight against our own kind.

I'd always assumed I would side with the humans, no matter what happened, because the sleepwalkers were destructive and terrible. So was Dr. Cale, in her own way, but at least she cared about saving lives, while Sherman didn't seem to care about anything beyond himself. The possibility of living, active integration changed everything, and from the way Adam was looking at me, it changed everything for him, too.

I looked into my brother's eyes, suddenly aware of just how deep that familial connection went, and had no idea what we were going to do next.

Adam was like me—a chimera of human and tapeworm, a dead body piloted through the world by an invertebrate. He was also *unlike* me, because he hadn't happened naturally, and he had never believed himself to be a human being. When the war began, there had never been any question of which side he would be on: the only humans he knew were the ones who worked for his mother and fully accepted his existence. Liking it was something else altogether. Adam's sheltered upbringing meant that he wasn't quite as good as I was at seeing the way they sometimes looked at us, like we were a problem that needed to be solved after the bigger, more immediate problems—the sleepwalkers, all the humans who were dying—had been taken care of. But I could see it. I could see it all too well.

For every person like Nathan or Dr. Cale, who honestly didn't care what species we were, there was someone like Daisy, who couldn't relax around us, or Fishy, who saw us as one more symptom of the world's devolution into a fantasy. We weren't *real* to them. We weren't *people*.

"It sounds like that," I said. "I think she may be something else, though. I mean, aren't sleepwalkers what happens when an implant just decides to take over? The way Dr. Banks was talking, she happened in a lab setting. So I don't know for sure."

"There's only one way to find out," said Adam. He slipped his hand into mine, looking at me hopefully. Once again, I was struck by how *young* he seemed. He was the first chimera, the oldest member of our race, and sometimes I felt like he was going to be my baby brother forever. "Can we go meet our sister?"

I had been coming to tell him about Anna, but I hadn't been intending to take him to her. Going to see Anna could mean getting Adam involved in whatever Dr. Banks had come here to do. Everything in me rebelled at the idea of letting that man get anywhere near my little brother—but if I said "no," I would be doing exactly the thing I was increasingly coming to resent Dr. Cale for doing. I would be sheltering him from the world, and the world wasn't going to recuse itself just because he didn't know what he was getting into. He would have to learn eventually.

"Sure," I said.

We walked silently and hand in hand through the hydroponics garden, our footsteps echoing loudly. No one else was there. Adam tended to take his duty shifts when they wouldn't require him to interact with anyone, and I wondered how intentional that was on his part: whether he understood on some level just how much distance there was between us and the humans here.

It was funny, in an awful way. I should have been excited by the thought of another chimera. There were days when I actually found myself missing Ronnie and Kristoph, who had helped Sherman keep me captive, yes, but who hadn't been responsible for kidnapping me, and who had at least been the same species as me. They understood what I was dealing with as I walked through a human world, as I looked at the devastation wrought by creatures who were genetically my family. Adam was too innocent to really help me shoulder my fears. Anna could have been the answer...

But Anna was with Dr. Banks, and he was the thing I trusted least in the world. There were no easy answers here.

"Why do you think he brought her to us? I wouldn't bring her to us if I were him. We might take her away and not let him have her back."

That was pretty close to the actual situation. I nodded grimly. "That, and Dr. Cale doesn't like Dr. Banks very much. He might have more trouble walking away from here than he expects."

"So coming here was kind of dumb." Adam frowned. "Is he dumb?"

That was the problem. "Not really," I said. "He was smart enough to help her make us. That has to mean he's smart enough not to walk into a trap without knowing that's what he's doing."

"So why?"

I didn't have an answer. I just shrugged helplessly, and kept hold of Adam's hand as we kept on walking.

Adam seemed to be content with silence after that, maybe because neither of us knew what we were supposed to say. We had a new sister. We just didn't know if we could trust her, or what form that trust would take. The elevator was waiting for us when we reached it, a sign that Dr. Cale had told the rest of the staff to lie low while we dealt with our unwanted visitors. Dr. Banks was in a cell, but she still didn't trust him, and the less he knew about the scope of our operation, the better.

Adam seemed to think so, too. He frowned as we stepped into the open elevator, clearly understanding what its presence meant. "Dr. Banks is a bad man, isn't he, Sal?"

Even the phrasing of the question was childish. I answered it all the same, without hesitation: "Yes. He's a very bad man. I don't know of anyone that he hasn't been bad to, except for maybe himself. Everything he's done has been about being good to himself."

The elevator started to move downward, whisking us toward the lab as Adam asked, "But weren't we designed to make things better for humans? So they'd be less sick, and have less to worry about?"

"Yeah, but I don't think they meant to sign over ownership of their bodies in the process." I squeezed Adam's hand. "Dr. Banks skipped a lot of steps that would have made the implants safer for people to use. That's why Dr. Cale had to run away in the first place—that's why she stole you from the lab. If she hadn't been forced to do that, maybe none of this would be happening." And Adam and I wouldn't exist. Instead, Sally Mitchell and whoever Adam's host body had originally been would be walking around the world, ignorant of the future they had so narrowly dodged.

"Is it selfish that I like this world better than a world where we're not real?" asked Adam meekly, his question so closely mirroring my thoughts that I glanced at him, startled. Then I shook my head.

"No," I said, as the elevator stopped and the doors slid smoothly open. "I like being real. I don't think I'd stop being real for anybody. Not even Nathan. It's not selfish to want to exist. It's a function of the survival instinct buried in all complicated organisms." Even the sleepwalkers had it. That was why they ate so voraciously, following the deeply ingrained "this is how you survive" commands remembered by their tapeworm minds, even as they struggled against the complicated and unfamiliar wiring of the human brain.

We had taken about five steps outside the elevator when Adam stiffened, his head snapping up and his eyes going extremely wide, like he couldn't believe what he was hearing. I frowned. I didn't hear anything except for the faint buzz of the lab machinery and the low voices of the technicians who were still at work. Not everything could be shut down at the drop of a hat.

"Adam?"

"Tansy!" He pulled away from me and took off running, weaving between the workstations and darting down the aisles. I sprinted after him, trying to keep him in sight. He whipped around a pink-painted wall with me about eight yards behind. I heard Dr. Cale shout his name, and Nathan making a small, startled noise, like he had been shoved roughly aside. I kept on running.

When I came around the corner, I didn't understand what I was looking at—not at first. Adam had pulled the curtain away from the tiny exam room set up for Anna, who was still lying naked and unmoving on the bed. Dr. Cale and Nathan were a short distance away, Nathan with his hands resting on the handles of Dr. Cale's wheelchair, Dr. Cale with one hand clasped over her mouth in a classic expression of horror. Her eyes were wide and brimming with unshed tears, like she had just realized something so terrible that she was no longer capable of forming words. Adam was standing with his hand still on the curtain of Anna's "room," staring at her.

I trotted up behind him, only wheezing a little, and asked, "Adam, why did you run away from me like that?"

"She's here," he said, sounding horrified and puzzled at the same time. He turned to me, that same conflict reflected in his face. "Can't you feel her? She's *here*, with us, but she's not here at all. Sal, what did he do to her? What did he do to our sister?"

"I don't know what you're—" But I did know, didn't I? I knew the way I had known that Adam was in the hydroponics garden. I knew because we always knew when we were near each other. The pheromones we put off, however hard it was for our human bodies to detect them, were unmistakable.

Slowly, I turned to face Anna, who hadn't responded to our presence in any way. She was still staring at the ceiling, her bare skin humping up into goose bumps as the air-conditioning rolled over it. She didn't seem to know that we were there, or maybe it was just that she didn't care.

My mouth was terribly dry, and the drums were pounding in my head. I licked my lips, trying vainly to moisten them, and whispered, "I didn't think anyone could be this cruel."

"What did he *do*?" moaned Adam.

Anna turned her head and looked at us.

I froze. Having her staring at me was like being eye to eye with an alligator, or some other ancient beast that didn't care what I wanted and wouldn't care if I ceased to exist completely. She didn't blink. Maybe that was an optical illusion, something my increasingly baffled mind was adding to make the situation even more alien, but I didn't think so. Dr. Banks had brought her to us. He said she needed to be monitored, but he could have done that at SymboGen; he wouldn't have brought her here if there hadn't been something terribly wrong with her, maybe with the interface between her tapeworm and human nervous systems. That was the most important connection a chimera had, and if it wasn't working properly, then *she* wasn't working properly.

Dr. Cale's wheels squeaked softly as she rolled herself over to stop next to me. She was no longer covering her mouth, and her tears were no longer contained: they rolled down her face unchecked. Bit by bit, her expression transformed from grieving mother to furious scientist. It was a swift, terrifying change. "That bastard," she said, tone almost wondering, like she couldn't believe this was happening. "I don't believe him. How could he do this? How could he come here, having done this, and expect me to help him?"

"I don't understand," said Nathan. He moved to stand behind me. I tilted my head just enough to see the furrowed line of his brow. He really didn't get it. Just this once, I had reached a conclusion before he had.

I would have expected it to feel good, or at least to feel better than this. Instead, I felt sick. I would have given anything to have reached the wrong conclusion, but I hadn't: I could see it in Dr. Cale's face.

"This is Tansy," I said quietly. "This is why we couldn't find her. Because Dr. Banks had her the whole time. She never got away from SymboGen." I indicated the pale, naked girl on the cot, who was still staring at us with her dead-looking eyes. "He took her, and he used her, and now he's brought her back to us, but I don't know why."

"That's not Tansy," said Nathan. "Tansy looks completely different."

"Not to a chimera she doesn't," said Dr. Cale. Her hand snaked out surprisingly fast, grabbing hold of my wrist. "Are you *sure*, Sal? It's not just a culture, like the ones we took from you? It's actually her core implant?"

"Yes," said Adam. He darted forward, again moving faster than I could react, and grabbed hold of Anna's hand. He held it the way that he always held mine, the way that he used to hold Tansy's: tight and close and counting on the other person to cling tight, keeping him where he was.

Anna's fingers stayed loose and open, not closing around his. He might as well have been grabbing for a corpse. In a way, that was exactly what he was doing.

"I don't know," I said, shaking my head until my hair whipped against my forehead like a hundred tiny, stinging lashes. "I don't…I'm not as good at picking up on that sort of thing as Adam is. But the minute I saw her, I wanted to protect her, even if it meant protecting her from you. I normally only feel that way about Adam."

When Nathan and I had first followed a weird set of instructions to Dr. Cale's old lab in the bowling alley, we'd been met by a girl with short blonde hair, heterochromatic eyes, and a tendency to make cheerful death threats every six words. That was Tansy. She was the experimental subject that came after Adam, grown and cultured in the lab just like he was, and she'd been his first sister, the one who kept him safe from the world back when most of the world had no idea that people like him, people like her, people like *me* could exist. Tansy had acted like a thug and reacted like a heroine, and if that wasn't one of the best combinations I'd ever encountered, I didn't know what was.

I hadn't known I was a chimera then—she was gone by the time I'd admitted that to myself—but I'd come to trust her surprisingly swiftly, hadn't I? She'd terrified me, and I'd trusted her anyway, because part of me knew that she was my kind. Deep down and under all the little complexities of my human mind, I'd known she was my sister. She should have been allowed to stay long enough for us to know each other.

I'd seen a lot of sleepwalkers and a surprising number of chimera since then, and I hadn't connected to *any* of them as quickly as I'd connected to Anna. The only logical answer was that I wasn't connecting to Anna at all: I was reconnecting to Tansy. Nothing else made sense.

"It's her," said Adam, finally abandoning his efforts to get Anna to respond to him clutching her hand. He turned to look at the rest of us, tears pouring down his cheeks. "Mom, please. You have to fix this. You have to make this better. You have to put her back where she belongs. Please."

"I doubt Steven left Tansy's original host intact," said Dr. Cale. She was trying to be gentle, but there was a brokenhearted bleakness in her voice that telegraphed her distress as clearly as her tears. "Even if he did, the amount of damage he must have done digging her core out of the host's brain...I can't, Adam. I'm so sorry." She looked at Anna and her breath caught, hitching her chest. She pressed a hand against her sternum, like she was trying to keep herself from losing her composure completely. Eyes on Anna now, she repeated softly, "I'm so sorry."

"Wait—are we seriously assuming that Dr. Banks extracted Tansy's implant from its original host and placed it in a new body?" asked Nathan. All three of us turned to look at him. Adam looked baffled, and I was willing to bet that my own expression was very similar. I spent so much time trying to think of myself as a human being that sometimes I forgot I wasn't one. The corollary to this was that sometimes I did such a good job that I also forgot that we weren't the same. Nathan didn't know the things I knew. He didn't understand the things I understood.

I could love him until the day I died, and we would never be the same species. No matter how hard I tried to pretend.

"It's possible to remove a mature implant from its original host body and move it into a new host," said Dr. Cale. "You know that. The implant has to be stable for the process to work, of course, but that's not the primary issue."

"That's not..." Nathan's voice tapered off, replaced by a brief, disbelieving burst of laughter. "That's not the primary issue? You're talking about cutting open a chimera and scooping them out of their own heads, and that's not the primary issue? I knew it could happen, but come on, Mom! This is...I don't even know what this is."

"The tapeworm's neural structures are not as advanced as a human's," said Dr. Cale. She sounded calm, but she was still crying. That was somehow worse. If she'd sounded angry, or even upset, her tears would have suited her better. "We discussed this when Sal was having her medical issues. The majority of her memories and thought processes are managed by the human brain she has attached herself to. It's backup storage for what her tapeworm mind can't manage."

"Uh, could we not talk about me in the context of a tape-worm mind and a human mind?" I asked. "It makes me really uncomfortable when you talk about me like that." The drums that were pounding in my ears skipped a beat before settling on a new, slightly irregular rhythm. My stomach clenched. I clung to those signs of physical distress as hard as I could, marking them as evidence that my body belonged to *me*, to Sal Mitchell and not to anyone else in the world. I wasn't a human *or* a tape-worm. I was a chimera. A perfect marriage of the two.

"I'm sorry, dear," said Dr. Cale. She even sounded like she meant it. Her attention remained primarily fixed on Nathan as she continued: "When a chimera has to be split, for whatever reason—when the implant is removed from the host—they lose everything that makes them the people that we know them to be. All the memories remain behind. They can't carry them into their next incarnation."

I stiffened, suddenly thinking of Ronnie. Tiny, violent Ron-nie, who knew that he was male, even though his implant was genderless and his host was female. "What about the epigenetic data?" I asked, and was amazed by the words that were coming out of my own mouth.

Apparently, so was Dr. Cale. She twisted in her chair to shoot me a look that was midway between amazed and impressed, and said, "The sample set isn't large enough for us to make predictive judgments about the epigenetic data. We don't even know for sure that it's a factor."

"Ronnie—the chimera who let me out of Sherman's mall—I told you about him, remember?" When the others nodded, I continued: "What I didn't tell you was that he's currently in a female host body, but had been in several previous hosts, all male. And he *knows* he's supposed to be male. He hates his current host."

"Maybe someone else told him about the previous hosts," said Nathan hesitantly.

I shook my head. "No. Sherman *hated* that Ronnie insisted on being referred to as male, and said it would attract inappropriate levels of attention. I don't think Ronnie would have known about those hosts if he hadn't known something was wrong with the one he'd been put in, and gone looking for more information. Sherman and Ronnie both said Ronnie's insistence that he was supposed to be a boy came from the epigenetic data. He didn't have a gender identity when he was just a tapeworm. Then he inhabited a male body, acquired a male gender identity, and took it with him when he was transplanted."

"So maybe part of Tansy is still in there," said Adam, sounding bitterly, brutally hopeful. He grabbed for Anna's hand again. As before, she neither helped him nor resisted. She just lay there, motionless. At some point she had rolled her head back into its original position, and now was staring at the ceiling again.

She had responded to some stimuli before. I swallowed hard, taking a step toward her, and asked, "Anna? Can you hear me?"

"My auditory systems are functional," said Anna. Her voice was toneless, completely devoid of passion. She couldn't have sounded less like Tansy if she'd been trying.

The drums pounded even louder in my ears, and I had to swallow the sudden urge to run through the lab to the cell where Dr. Banks was being held, rip the door off its hinges, and strangle the life from his body. How dare he do this? How dare he touch my family, my *sister*, with his filthy tools and his filthier motives? There was no reason I could see for him to have experimented on Tansy when there were so many sleepwalkers running around free and unclaimed—no reason except for simple cruelty. I wanted to hurt him more than I'd wanted almost anything else in my life. Had Sherman appeared before me in that moment and offered me Dr. Banks's head in exchange for joining his tapeworm army, I might well have taken him up on it. After all, what had the human race ever done for us?

I swallowed spit and bile and forced my own voice to remain steady as I asked, "Anna, do you know who Tansy is? Do you remember Tansy?"

"I do not remember her," she said. Then she turned her head again, fixing her black eyes on me, and said, "But I am aware of who she is. I was given a message to deliver to you, should you ever say that name."

"What's that?" asked Dr. Cale.

Anna's gaze flicked to her. Still calm, she replied, "The subject you call 'Tansy' is still alive. If you want her to be returned to you, you will have to free my father."

*I may have spoken too soon about the revolutionary nature of my work. While I have been able to successfully induce a joining between the SymboGen implant and its chosen human host, I have not been able to fully stabilize the results. The chimera—a quaint name for something that is, unquestionably, a monster—remains medically insecure, and has been given to surprising rages when not kept in a continually sedated state. I have been using a combination of transdermal scopolamine and diazepam to keep her in a pliant state. I do not know for how long these drugs will retain their efficacy, or if indeed they are still working fully as intended: she has proven surprisingly cunning, and capable of longer-term thinking than I had expected at this stage during her development.*

*It is clear that the only means by which we will be able to stabilize the experiment will be to visit the source. I have a plan that will either see me hailed as a conquering hero or cast forever from the scientific community for my sins. I intend to enjoy the process of determining which it is to be.*

—FROM THE NOTES OF DR. STEVEN BANKS, SYMBOGEN,
NOVEMBER 2027

*Our sources in the private sector inform us that research toward a cure is ongoing. They have thus far declined to share that research, and it is my informed opinion that no such material exists at this time. We are on our own, ladies and gentlemen, and the wolves are most assuredly at the door.*

*Madame President, I appreciate your inquiry as to the condition of my surviving daughter, Joyce. Unfortunately, she has not recovered from her coma, and while the Symbo-Gen implant has been entirely cleansed from her body, she remains in a persistent vegetative state. We have kept her on life support thus far, in part because we are hoping for a miracle, and in part because with the continuing deterioration of the medical and social structure of the country, we cannot afford to cut off any possible source of blood, tissue, and organs that have been confirmed clean of the sleepwalking sickness.*

*Time is running out for us here. We will continue to do what we can, but without a miracle, I do not know how much longer we can last.*

—MESSAGE FROM COLONEL ALFRED MITCHELL,
USAMRIID, TRANSMITTED TO THE WHITE HOUSE ON
NOVEMBER 14, 2027

## Chapter 14
## NOVEMBER 2027

Dr. Banks was sitting on the narrow cot provided for his use when the four of us approached his cell. He smiled at the sight, his eyes going first to Dr. Cale, and then, hungrily, to Adam and myself. He skipped over Nathan entirely, as if he was incidental to this little reunion. In a horrible way, I suppose he was. Nathan was Dr. Cale's only human child, after all, and he had nothing to offer Dr. Banks that he couldn't get back at his own lab.

"Hello, Surrey," he said, offering Dr. Cale his patented paternal smile. Maybe I should have felt a little better knowing that he smiled at all the women he wanted to exploit like that. Somehow, I didn't. "This is a nice place you've got here. I admit, I didn't expect something this palatial. When I heard you'd moved into a candy factory, I laughed. It was so ridiculous, so ludicrous...so *you*. You never could resist the absurd.

I think that's my favorite thing about you. Even in the face of total disaster, you'll keep on making a fool of yourself."

"How did you know we were here, Steven?" Dr. Cale didn't bother to correct him about her name. She just folded her hands in her lap and looked at him, expression stony and unreadable. I found myself wondering where Fishy and Fang were, and whether they were preparing an unmarked grave in the soil of the rooftop garden. "My people are decrypting the data on your hard drive right now. Don't bother lying to me. It won't work for long."

"Did you honestly think you could keep an operation of this size completely concealed? In a dead city, no less? No insult intended, Surrey, but maybe you should think about getting more sleep. Your judgment is slipping."

Dr. Cale raised one shoulder in a half shrug. "We didn't know we were being monitored. How did you know where we were?"

"Everyone is being monitored."

Dr. Cale sighed. "I see you're not going to make this easy on me. I have a full surgical theater here. It's primitive, yes, and we do have to contend with a lot of little inconveniences—we can't do laser work, which means sutures and stitches and the threat of infection, although we've gotten surprisingly good at cauterizing wounds. It's really remarkable, especially when you consider that nothing in this building started out intended to be used like this."

"Your point would be…?" asked Dr. Banks. He was still trying to sound polite—I could hear it—but his irritation was overwhelming his good sense. He sounded impatient. Never a good idea when talking to Dr. Cale.

"My point would be, I can amputate a limb without breaking a sweat or endangering your life to an unreasonable degree." Dr. Cale didn't sound impatient. She was perfectly serene, like this was what she had been dreaming of for years. Given the situation, maybe she had been. "Shock is still a risk, naturally, but I think I can minimize it with the appropriate drugs."

Dr. Banks had gone pale. "Now Surrey—"

"I know what you're about to say. You're going to remind me that you're a powerful man, and then you're going to tell me that people—*powerful* people—know you're here. You're going to tell me that killing you would be a terrible idea, one that would lead to the destruction of everything I've built, even though your presence has basically informed me that we're going to have to tear it all down. You're overlooking the fact that I'm not going to kill you." Dr. Cale smiled, still serene. "That would be, if you'll forgive me, *far* too easy. Now. Assuming you'd rather keep things friendly, how did you know we were here, Steven?"

The color did not return to Dr. Banks's cheeks. He stared at Dr. Cale. For her part, and more terrifyingly than anything she could have said, Dr. Cale just kept smiling. She actually looked interested in his inner turmoil, like no matter what his answer was, she would find a way to enjoy it. I'd almost managed to convince myself that I understood the woman who made me. Looking at her now, smiling and calm, I realized she was more alien to me than any other member of her species.

"USAMRIID has been monitoring you," said Dr. Banks finally, looking away. "Don't ask me how they got you under surveillance, because I don't know. As for why they haven't taken you, well. We both know that you don't work well when someone else is telling you what to do. You're better left to your own devices and kept under close watch, and you're not making things any worse. Those little videos you keep releasing have even been useful, on occasion. USAMRIID wanted you to keep working without knowing that you were being watched."

"Do you honestly expect me to believe that the United States government has allowed me to keep working without interference because they don't think I'd perform well in captivity?" asked Dr. Cale.

Dr. Banks shrugged. "It's the truth."

"Sorry, Steven, but I don't really trust you when you're not lying to me."

Dr. Banks continued as if she hadn't spoken: "I told the higher-ups at USAMRIID that I needed to contact your organization if I was going to continue my own work, and I managed to convince them it was worth the risk that you'd cut your losses and run. They helped me get here from San Francisco. Dropped me—with Anna, and a security team—about a mile away. Your boys have done an excellent job of clearing out the local sleepwalkers, you know. We didn't encounter any resistance on the walk."

"That's good to know." Dr. Cale's tone could have been used to freeze water. "Where did you leave your security team? How many people? Two? Four? You can't have brought the army; if you had, they would have marched you right up to my gates and taken what you wanted. The nonintervention policy is still in place, and it's not benefiting you. I suppose that means that of the two of us, I'm still doing the better work."

Dr. Banks was silent.

"Setting aside the fact that you carved up my daughter for parts—although if I were you, I wouldn't expect that to be set aside for long—what makes you think I don't already have teams out there combing the area for your people? You said this was too large of an operation to be kept hidden. Do you know just *how* large of an operation we have here?"

Dr. Banks was silent.

"I *will* find the team that got you this far, Steven. And since I won't know how many of them there are, or where they've taken cover, when my people find them and call me for directions, I'll give the order to take no prisoners. I already have you. Why would I need anyone else?"

Dr. Banks was silent, but sweat was beginning to bead at his temples, betraying his growing unease. His heart had to be pounding so loudly that he could feel it, even if his human physiology meant that he would never hear it like I did.

"How many of them did you get from USAMRIID?" Dr. Cale leaned forward in her chair, her smile fading into an expression of almost feral interest. "How well do you think your new allies will respond when you come back empty-handed, no soldiers, no chimera, no answer to whatever mystery you came here expecting to solve?"

"At least you're implying that he'll still have hands," said Adam. He was trying to be helpful, I could tell, and in a way, he was: the beads of sweat on Dr. Banks's temples doubled in size, now accompanied by a red flush around the base of his jaw.

"Hands, yes," said Dr. Cale. "I make no promises as to fingers."

"This isn't you, Surrey," said Dr. Banks quietly. He didn't turn back toward us. Maybe he was afraid to.

"You're right," said Dr. Cale. She leaned back in her chair, getting comfortable. "Surrey Kim would never have sat here threatening her valued friend, Steven Banks, the man who was going to change the world. Surrey had other things to worry about. How she was going to fund her research, for example, or what she was going to pack in her son's lunches for the week. She had a life to plan. Surrey would find what I'm doing abhorrent, on all sorts of levels, because Surrey worked very hard to keep herself tied to human standards of morality, human ideals of right and wrong. Surrey would never have wanted her son to look at her the way Nathan is looking at me right now."

I blinked, glancing toward Nathan. He looked almost as unsettled as Dr. Banks did. The muscle at the base of his jaw was twitching, making a small fluttering motion against his skin. I reached for his hand. He jumped, eyes wide as he looked in my direction, before lacing his fingers through mine and hanging on for dear life.

Dr. Cale continued: "But here's the thing, *Steven*. Surrey Kim doesn't get to have an opinion here. Surrey wouldn't have done these things to you. I can. Do you know why?"

Dr. Banks didn't say anything. I think he knew that there was nothing he could say at this point. He had dug his own grave, and he had dug it very well indeed.

"Surrey Kim is dead." Dr. Cale sounded utterly calm. She was overseeing the exhumation of a cold case, not surveying an active murder scene: the reality of her original identity's death was years behind her, taking most of the anger with it. But not, I realized, the rage. They were two different beasts, close enough to seem identical when seen together, but unique enough that one could endure without the other. Her anger had faded as her old life became more of a memory and less of a loss. Her rage at the man who had started all of this had never wavered.

How long had she been waiting for this very moment? How many years had she spent dreaming of the day when Steven Banks would be captive before her, stripped of power and position, unable to stop her from doing anything she wanted?

I suspected that it was far, far too many, and I was afraid.

"Dr. Banks, why did you come here?" My voice sounded thin and unsure, even to me. Maybe that was a good thing. He had always wanted to be a father figure to me, and little girls often sounded unsure when they spoke to their fathers. I swallowed and pressed on: "You knew this would happen. You *had* to know this would happen. So why did you do it?"

"I didn't know everything that would happen," he said, and finally turned, his eyes focusing on me. "I thought it would take you a bit longer to figure out where I got the materials for my new girl. She took a lot of work, you know. You should be impressed."

My stomach gave a lurch. Nathan squeezed my hand, lending what strength he could. I took a deep breath to stop my head from spinning, and said, "I *am* impressed. I don't know many people who could do something like that." Sherman and his army of chimera; Dr. Cale and her assistants. I knew *way* too much people who could do exactly what he'd done. "That still doesn't explain why you came. It's dangerous for you to be here."

Dr. Banks laughed. It was a brief, sharp sound, and it made me flinch, because he shouldn't have been *laughing*. Laughter was dangerous with Dr. Cale sitting right there, doing a slow burn as she watched the conversation slip away from her. *Please, trust me*, I begged silently, wishing she shared the pheromone connection I had with Adam. He would have understood, somehow. He would have picked up on my silent, primitive prayers. *He'll tell me, but he'll never tell you, not even when you're taking parts of him away.* Dr. Banks was the monster, and would remain the monster no matter what was done to him.

The trick was not becoming monsters in the process of learning what we needed to know.

Maybe Dr. Cale had some connection to us through our shared DNA—or maybe she was just learning to trust me. Either way, she didn't say anything as I kept staring at Dr. Banks, willing him to speak, willing him to believe that I was still the innocent, sheltered creature he'd worked so hard to create.

"It's dangerous to be anywhere right now, honeybunch," he said finally. "There's sleepwalkers all over the Bay Area, all over the state, all over the *country*. We're losing ground faster than we can take it back. Pleasant Hill is completely deserted, except for a nest of sleepwalkers that we can't quite seem to nail down. USAMRIID's had to completely close off the city. You're lucky you're on the other side of the water. I might not have been able to reach you if you'd been near the compromised area."

Pleasant Hill must have been the location of Sherman's mall.

I worried my lower lip between my teeth before saying, "It doesn't seem very dangerous here."

"You're standing next to a woman who was just threatening to take my limbs off with a hacksaw," said Dr. Banks. "I think your definition of 'dangerous' may need to be reconsidered."

"I would never use a hacksaw on you, Steven," said Dr. Cale sweetly. "Too much chance you'd bleed out, and I wouldn't want that. It would be over too fast."

"If Dr. Cale isn't mad at you, it's not dangerous here," I said hurriedly. "Why did you come? Why did you bring A...Anna here if you knew it was dangerous?" I had to force myself to say the name of his pet chimera. I wanted to call her "Tansy." I didn't want to call her anything at all.

"Anna's why I came here," he said, his gaze swinging back to Dr. Cale. "She's not doing so good. We need your help."

"You hurt my daughter—you may have killed her," said Dr. Cale coldly. "Why should I help you?"

"You should help *Anna* because part of your 'daughter'"—he scowled in obvious distaste—"lives inside her. If you really care about your little science experiment, you'll keep my girl alive. And if that's not enough for you, well..." Slowly, he began to smile. He didn't bother keeping his lips closed, and both Adam and I flinched away from the glossy white display of his teeth. "I'm assuming Anna passed my message along, or you wouldn't have come to see me so quickly. You want the girl back. I understand that. You put a lot of work into her, and it would be a shame to lose it like this. I can help you. I can get you into SymboGen. I can make sure you walk away with everything your heart desires, and all you have to do is help me."

"Why do you make a face like it's bad when you call Tansy my sister, but let Anna call you her father?" asked Adam. He was scowling, an uncharacteristically fierce look on his face. "It's the same thing."

"No, it's not, you little abomination," said Dr. Banks. His tone didn't change at all, remaining calm and even somewhat smug, like he thought he had somehow managed to get the upper hand on all of us. "I let Anna call me her father because it's easier to control something that thinks it belongs to you. Surrey calls you her children because she's sick in the head." His gaze flickered to Nathan. "If I was her biological child, I think I'd be pretty damn disgusted by that, personally."

"Then it's a good thing you're not my brother," said Nathan coldly.

Dr. Banks looked briefly surprised. He covered it quickly, but the flicker of confusion had been evident to all of us. When he came here, he hadn't been expecting to find us working together in relative harmony. Whatever information USAM-RIID had on the place, it wasn't enough to give him a full picture. That was a good thing. We might still have a chance.

"Why would I want her body back?" asked Dr. Cale.

"Because she's brain dead but on life support, and I know how much you love your vegetables," said Dr. Banks. "Maybe you could cultivate yourself a replacement."

I balled my free hand into a slow fist. I had hated people before—had even hated him before—but until that moment, I hadn't known what it was to hate someone so much that I wanted to scratch their eyes out just for the pleasure of watching them stumble blindly through the rest of their life.

Luckily, Dr. Cale had more experience than I did at talking through her hate. She snapped her finger. Fang seemed to materialize out of the shadows behind her. He was carrying a portable, battery-operated bone saw, and it said something about how good a job Dr. Banks was doing of upsetting me that I didn't bat an eye. If Dr. Cale wanted a bone saw, well. The only person she was likely to use it on definitely deserved it.

Dr. Banks did not share my serenity. He jumped to his feet,

pressing himself against the wall of his cell like he thought it was going to do him any good at all. "Now Surrey—"

"Two questions, Steven," she said, sounding absolutely calm. I suppose she had reason to be. After all, she was the one who controlled the man holding the bone saw. "If you answer them both honestly and to my satisfaction, I promise not to cut off any of your fingers, or the hands those fingers are attached to. Lie to me, withhold information from me, and that promise goes away. Do you understand?"

Dr. Banks hesitated. Nathan sighed.

"My mother, whatever you want to call her, doesn't fuck around," he said. "She doesn't make threats, because threats are meaningless. She makes promises, if you'll forgive the cliché. Please, either tell her what she wants to know or tell her that you're not going to, so that I can take Sal out of here before the fingers start flying."

"Still protecting that girl's delicate sensibilities? You're going to have to stop one day." There was no venom left in Dr. Banks's voice: he sounded like a man who had looked into the depths of his own soul and found nothing there but dark inevitability. His gaze slithered back to Dr. Cale. He squared his shoulders, sitting up a little straighter, as if posture alone could somehow turn him into a noble, tragic figure. "What do you want to know?"

"What's the plan that required you to make a chimera of your own? You can't sell them. We don't have enough people on life support to make them a viable consumer product, and it's not like anyone is going to be buying anything from you in the near future anyway. The country's on the verge of collapse."

"It's not as far gone as you might think, thanks to some fast thinking in the Midwest and on the East Coast. They dumped antiparasitics in the water, did some surgical interventions—fun times. It wasn't enough. It could never have been enough. The country is falling to pieces. It's just slow, and it's leaving smart men with resources the time to regroup, pull back, stay standing. Maybe we'll bring America back someday, maybe not, but for now, the fall of this nation is not an issue and won't cause us any problems," said Dr. Banks. A thin runnel of satisfaction laced his smile. "Best of all, we've managed to convince the remaining government that the original implant design would never have done this. We have years of data to support our claim."

Nathan lunged forward, slapping his hands against the clear plastic wall of Dr. Banks's enclosure. Everyone jumped except for Dr. Cale. She just turned her face sadly away, her expression conveying her utter lack of surprise. She'd been expecting this.

"You *bastard*. How *dare* you," snarled Nathan. "This is *your* fault. You took my mother away from me for money, and now you're using her—"

"Kiddo, I've been using her since day one." Dr. Banks sounded utterly unrepentant, and somehow that was the worst thing of all, the worst thing in a sea of terrible things. He wasn't sorry. He might beg and plead for his freedom, and he might need us to help him, but he wasn't sorry.

I'd been assuming Sherman and his people were the inhuman side of our conflict. They *weren't* human, any more than I was. But they hadn't started this fight, and now that it was happening, they were just trying to survive. Dr. Banks...I didn't even know what he was hoping to accomplish anymore, aside from coming out on top of whatever world rose from the ashes of this one.

I also wasn't entirely sure what was going on. I looked toward Dr. Cale, hoping she would explain. She met my eyes and sighed.

"He's blaming this all on me," she said. "I'm the one who put the human DNA in the plan for *D. symbogenesis*, remember? I'm the one who handed it the key to the human immune system."

"I thought that was the toxoplasmosis," I said.

Dr. Cale laughed. It was a brilliant, broken sound, like light glinting off a shattered window. "See, right there, you've shown yourself more capable of critical thinking than most of the human race. Yes, Sal, it was the toxoplasmosis that made the implants capable of migrating through the body and successfully colonizing the brain. But that's not going to make sense to most people. They want quick, easy answers. They want sound bites."

" 'Discredited geneticist inserted time bomb in essential medical supplies,' " said Dr. Banks, practically purring. "The Intestinal Bodyguard isn't finished, Surrey. It can't be. Add the world's dependence on the drugs our implants provide to the collapse of so many supply chains, and there's just no way to take it out of the equation. We just need to repackage it to make sure that we retain our market share."

Dr. Cale's head swung back around. I quailed, taking a step backward. If she had ever looked at me like that, I would have run screaming from the room. "You know, Steven," she said, voice low and dangerous, "I'd been wondering who I should be helping in all of this. My children or the human race. I can only save one side of the equation. You're making it much easier for me to make my choice."

"He hasn't answered the question," said Adam suddenly. We all turned to look at him. He didn't take his eyes off Dr. Banks. "He's trying to distract us. Didn't you notice? He's saying everything he can to keep from actually answering the question Mom asked him. Make him answer the question."

"Yes, Steven." Dr. Cale looked back to her former colleague, who looked suddenly dispirited, like his last chance at getting out of this alive had been taken away from him. "Answer the question. That was the agreement, was it not? Honest answers win you limbs that work."

"You always were a liar, Surrey," spat Dr. Banks, his eyes

fixed on her legs, just in case she missed his point. Once again, I balled my hands into fists, yearning for a free shot at his smug, terrible face. "I created my own chimera because I needed to understand how they worked. How the chemical bonds between the implant and the human host were formed, and how they could be disrupted—or encouraged to form more efficiently."

Dr. Banks paused and sighed, shaking his head before he continued. "The chimera are *perfect* for certain jobs, Surrey. I'd say I was amazed that you hadn't thought of it, but honestly, I'd be more surprised if you had. You would have to be able to step back and see the big picture. Imagine a world where the death penalty is carried out, not by lethal injection, but by termination of higher brain functions. The body would remain intact, ready to be put to work for the good of society. There are all sorts of functions that robots can't perform yet. But a walking, thinking human body can accomplish all sorts of things."

"You're going to send my children to war," said Dr. Cale.

Dr. Banks sighed again, deeper this time, like she just wasn't getting the point. "They're already at war. I'm just going to make it profitable."

"Mm." Dr. Cale's tone was noncommittal, but her expression promised murder. "So that's why you took my little girl. That's why you took her *apart*. Because you wanted to learn how to build a better weapon. Well, Steven, your lesson has apparently been learned. What was so important that you had to bring her here? I know you like to gloat, but this is frankly irresponsible."

"I'm here because I really do need your help." He actually seemed to mean it this time. "I was able to transplant the worm from its original host into the body I had prepared, but I haven't been able to fully stabilize it in its new environment. She's not... she's not doing well."

"Rejection," said Dr. Cale. She could have been smug in that moment, seeing her former coworker run up against an obstacle she had already overcome. Instead, she just sounded tired. "Did you do tissue typing before you sliced my girl open? Did you try a reaction panel, to see whether the new host's immune system would even recognize an implant that hadn't been tailored to it as something that could be potentially helpful? Or did you barrel full speed ahead and figure that the universe would give you whatever you wanted because you were Dr. Steven Banks, and you deserved it?"

"I hardly think you're one to lecture me about proper medical technique," said Dr. Banks. His tone was stiff, and his gaze flicked to her legs again, making sure she knew what he was implying. "I did my tissue typing. I did the things I've always done when preparing an implant for its new host. As for anything else, I didn't know what tests were necessary. It's not as if you ever sent me anything detailing your research."

"You kept trying to kill me. Forgive me if I didn't feel much like sharing with you."

I frowned slowly. "Rejection means Tansy's new host doesn't want to accept her, right? What does that mean for her? Is she going to be okay?"

"It means that the host is experiencing some fairly severe immune responses," said Dr. Banks. As I had hoped, he once again fell into the gently parental "I am teaching you things you need to know, and you should listen, because I am smarter than you are" tone he had used with me so many times before. "The most distressing is swelling of the brain, and clouding of the spinal fluid. There's a protein buildup going on there that I can't quite source. It's inflaming her nerves. She's been in a lot of pain, almost constantly."

"You mean she's drugged?" I asked. "You made her walk across Vallejo drugged, while her brain was swelling? She could have collapsed! She would have been helpless!" The image of

Tansy as she had been rose unbidden in my mind—the wild grin, the mismatched eyes, the casual willingness to throw herself into the path of danger, because she knew that whatever happened to her, it would be interesting. Anna had none of those traits. Anna was a flat surface on which nothing had been painted. The drugs would explain at least a little of that, and I felt a traitorous worm of relief uncurl in my belly. Maybe Anna was more like Tansy than we thought she was. Maybe there were epigenetic tags for violence and randomness and sliding down hills on pieces of cardboard, just like Ronnie had the epigenetic tag for knowing that he was really supposed to be a boy, and when the drugs worked their way out of Anna's system, she'd still be somehow Tansy. Just a little bit. Just enough that we could love her.

"Well, Sally, it was that or deal with her having seizures every hundred yards, and that would have been more of a problem." Dr. Banks returned his attention to Dr. Cale. "Here's my proposal, Surrey, and you'll want to listen nice and close, because I'm only going to make it once: you help me stabilize my Anna so that I can take her back to the United States government as proof of concept. I give her to them, and they see that the chimera can be useful things—they already know they can be taught, thanks to Sally here, but now they'll know they can be *controlled*. That we can have our useful biological machines without giving up anything that hasn't already been lost. And I tell them you were able to get the drop on me after we'd finished stabilizing her, and you run off to safer pastures."

"What's to stop you from double-crossing us? Or me from killing you?" asked Dr. Cale.

"Nothing." Dr. Banks spread his hands. "You trust me, I trust you, and we see who's making the bigger mistake."

Dr. Cale looked at him silently for a moment. Then she turned to Nathan and said, "Push me out of here."

Nathan blinked. "What?"

"We're leaving. Push me out of here." She folded her hands in her lap, leaning back in her chair.

Nathan dutifully moved to stand behind her, wheeling her back, away from Dr. Banks. Adam and I moved to flank them. We didn't need to be told; we knew what was expected of us in a moment like this. A unified front would count for so much more than divisiveness, at least in this moment.

Dr. Banks jumped to his feet when he realized what we were doing. "Hey!" he shouted, suddenly enraged. "Don't you turn your backs on me! Don't you understand what I can do to you? Don't you understand your position here?"

"Yes, Steven," said Dr. Cale, with the utmost calm. "I don't think you do, however. Nathan?"

"Yes, Mother," said Nathan, and turned her chair around and walked away, pushing her in front of him. Adam and I followed. Dr. Banks kept shouting behind us, his words of protest quickly devolving into a muddled stream of fury and profanity that didn't mean anything coherent.

Then we stepped out of the room, and the door swung shut behind us, cutting him off in mid-tirade. Nathan kept pushing Dr. Cale forward. I glanced at her face.

She was crying.

I didn't know how to respond to that, and so I didn't say anything as the four of us kept on walking, back toward the place where Anna was waiting, back into the light.

*And now I know.*

*It's funny, honestly: I have spent my whole life in the pursuit of knowledge, sometimes—often—when it would have been better to back away and leave my questions unanswered; there are things that man was not meant to know, and woman is not exempt from that prohibition. I've seen things, done* things, *that should never have been seen or experienced by a living human, and I've always come out the other side saying "what I paid to do that was worth it." It's always been worth it, because it's always resulted in more knowledge, and that's all I've ever wanted. Forgive me, Nathan, if you're ever unlucky enough to be reading this, but it's the truth. Knowledge was worth anything to me. Even you.*

*But sometime between the start of my exile and the day that my son came back into my life with his girlfriend—my creation—in tow, things changed. I began to realize that some things mattered more than knowledge. Family matters more than knowledge. He knew that. Oh, my poor girl. That's why he used you against me.*

*I am so sorry.*

—FROM THE JOURNAL OF DR. SHANTI CALE,
NOVEMBER 15, 2027

*Sal is strangely serene about this whole situation. I can't tell whether it's because she trusts Mother to fix things, or whether it's because she's holding her honest response in, waiting to see how the rest of us react before she allows herself to display any true emotion. I'm starting to worry about her. She's trying so hard to be controlled that I'm afraid she's not allowing herself to feel things the way she wants to. That's dangerous. Too much repression leads to self-harm, either emotional or—on occasion—physical.*

*I should know.*

*Anna remains stable but sedated. Tox screens performed after Dr. Banks shared more details on her condition have shown signs of sedatives and anticonvulsants. We are continuing with both drugs, in the absence of a better course of treatment. If a better course of treatment does not present itself soon, I am not sure that she will survive. Her organs are struggling, and failure is a risk.*

*How many more of these deaths will we be forced to witness? Because I'm just about done.*

—FROM THE NOTES OF DR. NATHAN KIM,
NOVEMBER 2027

## Chapter 15

## NOVEMBER 2027

Adam was a trained lab technician, thanks to maturing at Dr. Cale's hip; he'd been setting up IVs and mixing pharmaceutical compounds since he learned to walk. He, Dr. Cale, Daisy, and Fishy got to work stabilizing Anna, while I was shooed politely away to find something that would keep me occupied and out from underfoot. Nathan glanced from his mother and the chaos surrounding Anna to me, and then—to my relief and exhausted delight—he bent, murmured something in his mother's ear, and followed me.

We walked back to the elevator lobby in silence. Nathan didn't even ask where we were going; he just stood there, letting me pick the floor we were going to, waiting until I was ready to speak.

"Knowing the directions doesn't mean you ought to go," I murmured, and pressed the button for the roof.

Nathan put his hand on my shoulder, and didn't say anything.

Cold rage and hot misery mixed in my stomach, forming a substance that felt like ice and lava at the same time. It made it difficult to think or swallow, but I forced myself to keep breathing, and said, "He always acted like he loved me, you know? Or like he at least cared about me. And I knew he was lying—even when I thought I was human I knew he was lying—but I didn't mind so much, because it was better than having him act like I didn't matter." Lots of people had pretended to care about me, Sally's father and Sherman among them. I was getting awfully tired of men who didn't give a damn about me as *me* coming back into my life.

"He knew what you were from the first time he laid eyes on you," said Nathan. "Maybe neither one of us could see it at the time, but it's clear in retrospect. He was using you."

"He was using me," I agreed, feeling the hot/cold mass in my stomach give another lurch. "He couldn't have done what he did to Tansy if he hadn't been able to get so much information about me first. I taught him how to take her apart. I didn't even realize I was doing it, but I did. I taught him how to kill my sister."

Nathan's reflection in the elevator wall winced in time with the real thing, whose hand clenched down on my shoulder in sympathetic misery. "You were working almost entirely with scientists who thought of you as nothing more than a test subject," he said, voice pitched low. "Dr. Banks did terrible things to you even if you didn't realize they were happening. But this is not your fault. Tansy is not your fault."

"How is this not my fault?" The elevator slowed, stopped; the doors slid open, revealing the carefully tended vegetable beds that covered the roof. The morning shift had already come and gone, and the automatic hydroponic systems were keeping the beds irrigated. I stepped out of the elevator, pausing long

enough for Nathan to pace me, and then started across the roof
toward the nearest canvas cabana tent. About a dozen of them
had been liberated from the local Target shops, and they dotted
the roof like so many garishly colored oases. Sunstroke was a
real concern when you insisted on taking dark-adapted lab rats
and putting them to work on a private farm.

"You didn't know," Nathan said. "Everyone around you was
working very hard to make sure you didn't know."

I all but threw myself into a wicker couch designed for out-
door use. Nathan sat down next to me, a little more decorously.
He did most things a little more decorously than I did, really.
"You figured it out," I said accusingly.

"My mother told me." He paused and then laughed unsteadily.
"You know, I still haven't had a chance to really think about
those words? 'My mother.' She was my best friend, she was
everything I had in the world, and then she was gone and
everyone told me she was never coming back. I mourned her.
I *buried* her. I was never going to see her again. And then my
weird, wonderful girlfriend asked me to go on a road trip
with her, and started quoting bits of a book I hadn't seen in
years."

I sat up and scooted over to rest my head against his shoulder. Nathan stroked my hair with one hand.

"I think I realized, you know," he said. "When you started
quoting *Don't Go Out Alone*, I think I realized. I just didn't…
I didn't *want* to realize, because I didn't want to live in a world
where my mother would have chosen science over me. She was
my mom. I wanted her to stay with me forever, not go running
off as soon as she found a better experiment."

There was a broken edge to his words that I barely recognized: this wasn't a side of Nathan that I saw very often, or
really knew how to handle. He was usually the calm, collected
one, and when he couldn't fix something, he stepped back and
found another approach. He wasn't the one who fell apart. That

didn't mean he wasn't allowed: it just meant that when it happened, I wasn't going to interfere.

"And then there she was! Different, but we're all different now, aren't we? We went through the broken doors. That's how you turn yourself into a monster." Nathan sighed, kissing the top of my head before he continued: "She opened them as wide as she could and she told me it was all right to look through and see what was on the other side. She said it was what I'd have to do if I wanted to catch up with you, since you'd been born on the other side of those doors. Sally Mitchell never saw them open, but you've never seen them closed."

I tilted my head back, frowning up at him. "I don't understand."

"That's all right. I don't either, not really." Nathan sighed. "Mom left me because she had to. She did what she felt was right, and she did it to protect me. But I think sometimes... I think that before Tansy disappeared, she thought her children were invincible. You, me, Adam, Tansy—we couldn't be killed, because she was looking at everything through the filter of that damn children's book. She's shaped her image of the world around someone else's fantasy."

I couldn't stop myself. "Why?"

"Because it's easier. It's so much easier to say, 'This is a story, and there are heroes and villains, and there's an ending, and when we get there the book will close and we'll all live happily ever after.'" Nathan kissed my head again. "Mom is... her mind works in strange ways. It always has. Dad used to try to explain it to me, after she left us, when I was so sad I didn't feel like I could get out of bed in the morning. He said she knew she wasn't always the best with morals and ethics and other things that most people thought were important, because for her, the science—the knowledge—always came first. But she didn't like hurting people. So sometimes she would fall back to what she saw as a safe place, and she'd retreat to Simone's book, because in Simone's book, opening the broken doors always resulted in good things. It always brought the children and the monsters back together."

"It sounds like maybe your mom needs to see my therapist." Dr. Morrison was probably dead or in quarantine somewhere. The idea didn't bother me much.

Nathan pulled away enough to shoot me an amused look. "You hated your therapist," he said.

"Yeah, but that doesn't mean she doesn't need someone to talk to. You're her son. Adam is, too. I'm…" I paused before admitting, "I don't really know what I am. I'm not her daughter—which is good, because it would make marrying you sort of creepy—but she thinks I am, and that's weird. None of us are good for her to talk to. Maybe talking to someone else would help."

"Maybe," Nathan allowed. He sighed again. "This hasn't been easy for any of us, has it? I found my mother but don't have the time to stop and deal with it emotionally. You lost your whole world."

"Not my whole world," I corrected, and took his hand. We sat that way for a while, not saying anything, before I had to go and open my big mouth and ruin everything. "Sometimes I feel like your mom doesn't know what to do with me. I'm the expendable one."

Nathan was quiet for a long moment before he said, "I wish I could say you were wrong. But when you disappeared, she said we couldn't try to rescue you, because it was too dangerous. To be fair, though, she said the same thing about Tansy. I think we're all expendable to her. We're all part of the story, and the story needs to be finished more than she needs to be kind."

That was almost reassuring. It was always nice to know that I was being threatened by a force of nature, and not by someone who actually disliked me for any personal reason. Following that thought to its logical conclusion brought me crashing back down to earth. I sat up a little straighter, the mixed slush of terror and fury beginning to boil in my belly once more, and asked, "What are we going to do about Dr. Banks?"

To Nathan's credit, he followed my change of subjects without hesitation. "I don't think he's going to leave here alive, if that's what you're asking. He's told us too much, and he's taken too much away. Mom doesn't forgive easily. Once you overstep your bounds with her, you're doomed."

"And USAMRIID wouldn't have let him come here if they were too concerned with getting him back," I said slowly. "He said he could give Tansy back."

"Are you sure we believe him? I think digging the tapeworm out of her brain to make Anna is going to have done a lot of damage, and he has plenty of reasons to lie to us. I hate to say this, but maybe it would be better to let her go."

"No." My response was immediate, visceral, and nonnegotiable. "We're not letting her go. We don't even know that she's that messed up. Fang and Daisy took a sample when they had my skull sliced open for the surgery. Sherman did the same thing, even if he was less gentle about it." His cruder operation had left a scar on the back of my head that was going to be there for the rest of my life. One more thing to hate him for, assuming I was keeping a running list. "Your mom said Dr. Banks must have used her primary segment, but couldn't he have cultivated a new primary segment in a Petri dish or something? The primary segment is what latches on to the circulatory system in the brain and feeds the rest of the body. I mean, you *could* dig it out, but... wouldn't that be a whole lot of work, and maybe dangerous for the implant, when you could just grow a new one?"

Nathan's eyes widened slowly as he began to grasp my meaning. "Do you really think Tansy might still be functional?"

"I think Dr. Banks is smarter than your mother wants to give him credit for being. He wouldn't throw anything useful away." That included Tansy. She could only be useful to him if she was still *herself*. Once he took that away, all she could be used for was parts. "He kept me for years, even when he had learned everything he could without taking me apart, because there was still a chance I could be useful."

The hot/cold mix in my belly finally solidified, becoming something that was greater and more dangerous than either could have been alone. I stood. Nathan mirrored the motion, frowning.

"Where are you going?" he asked.

"I need to talk to Dr. Banks alone." It was one of the most frightening statements I had ever made, but it came surprisingly easily, now that my mind was made up. This was a thing that only I could do. I owed it to Tansy to try. "I need to ask him where she is, and I think there's a good chance that he'll tell me."

Nathan looked at me, regret and understanding etched in his face, and didn't say a word. The only sound was a crow somewhere in the streets below us, cawing harsh dominion over the broken works of man.

The area outside the room where Dr. Banks was being kept in temporary isolation was abandoned when we arrived. Nathan started to reach for the door. I grabbed his wrist before he could touch the knob.

"I said I needed to talk to him alone," I said. "I meant I needed to talk to him alone. That means you can't come in either."

Nathan turned to face me, eyes wide and terribly startled. "Excuse me?"

I swallowed a sigh. It wouldn't have helped. "He thinks of me as something between a developmentally disabled child and a very clever lab experiment. No matter what I do, he never really takes me seriously or believes I'd be capable of choosing to betray him. I mean, he left me alone in his office *after* he was almost entirely sure I was working either with or for your mom. I don't think Dr. Banks is capable of looking at a chimera and seeing a person. It just isn't how his mind works."

"But I'm a person," said Nathan grimly.

"Yes," I said. "If you come in with me, he'll assume I'm just asking the questions you want me to ask, and that anything I say has an ulterior motive. Me alone, there are no ulterior motives. There's just the little girl he already knows how to work around."

"That's what I'm afraid of."

I smiled at that. I had to. "Dr. Banks has never been as good at controlling me as he wants to believe he is. Don't worry about me."

"Sal…"

"It's not like I'm asking you to stand by while I walk into a room with my father." *Sally's* father, who I would always think of as "mine" on some terrible, immutable level, no matter how many times I tried to tell myself that he didn't deserve that power over me or that place in my heart.

Nathan looked at me for a long moment before he stepped in, leaned down, and kissed me long and slow, his lips crushed against mine, until the drums began beating in my ears and the skin on the back of my neck seemed like it was too tight, vellum stretched over hard bone and not skin at all. When he pulled back all I could do was blink at him dazedly, too lost in the memory of his kiss to speak.

"If you need anything at all, I will be right here," he said. "Do you understand me? Right here."

"Okay," I murmured, and turned, and opened the door, and stepped into the chamber with my personal demon.

Dr. Banks had retaken his seat since I'd seen him last. His elbows were resting on his knees and his forehead was in his hands, making him look much smaller and less intimidating than he normally did. I eased the door shut behind me, trying to minimize the sound that it made when it closed. I wanted a moment to look at him without him realizing that he wasn't alone.

So this was my enemy. One of many, really—Sherman, all of USAMRIID, my own confused, sleepwalking cousins—but he had been the first, and he was still the one who loomed largest in my mind. He was the one who had held my life in his hands and decided not to tell me what I was. How could I help but hate him? And at the same time, he was the man who had provided my medical care and taught me how to walk, talk, and think—even if he'd done it for his own reasons and to serve his own twisted ends, he'd done it, and that left me with a debt to him that I could never entirely repay. I wondered if humans felt this conflicted over their parents and teachers. I hoped not. It would be terrible to have an entire species with bellies full of mingled love and hate, anger and fear, walking around and thinking that they controlled the world.

That faint shabbiness that I had noticed when he first entered the factory was only highlighted by his helpless posture and utter lack of affectation. He didn't know he was being watched, and so he didn't bother putting on a show. That, more than anything, told me how dire his situation really was. I'd known that he had to be desperate to come to Dr. Cale, but I hadn't known *how* desperate. Bit by bit, I was coming to understand.

Bare feet silent on the tiled floor, I walked across the room and stopped a foot or so away from the plastic barrier that kept him contained. It had been intended as a quarantine zone, keeping the staff from catching anything nasty that we brought in from the outside. It was serving its intended purpose very well.

I could only look at the man without speaking to him for so long. I lifted one hand and slapped it flat against the plastic. Dr. Banks jumped, his head snapping up. There was genuine terror in his expression, like I had somehow become the most frightening thing in his universe. I couldn't decide how that made me feel.

The terror cleared, replaced first by confusion and then by paternal warmth, the old, familiar masks sliding back into place and locking away whatever he was really feeling. "Sally," he said, starting to smile. "I knew you wouldn't turn against me. You're a good girl. You always have been. You—"

"Is Tansy *really* alive?"

My question sliced across whatever he was saying and rendered him temporarily mute, capable of nothing more complex than staring at me. His smile twisted, turning into even more of a mockery than it normally was. Then it died completely, leaving him as blank-faced as one of the sleepwalkers he had helped to create.

"I don't see why you're coming in here and interrogating me," he said. "The woman who runs this place has already made it quite clear that she's not willing to negotiate in good faith. I have to say, Sally, I thought better of you."

"Are you where she gets it?" I asked.

He blinked at me, expression flickering again. He wasn't adjusting well to my changes of topic. Good. I wasn't here to make him comfortable. "I don't understand what you're asking me."

"Dr. Cale does that—she uses people's names a lot, like she's afraid that they're going to forget who they are. I didn't think about the way you always used to do that to me, but you did, and you still do. Are you where she gets that? Or did you get it from her?" They were like engineered organisms themselves, weren't they? Every human was the result of social and cultural recombination, picking up a turn of phrase here, an idea or a preconception there, the same way bacteria picked up and traded genes. Nothing was purely its own self. Nothing would ever want to be.

"I got it from her," he said, still sounding wary, still examining the topic for signs that it was a trick. "Surrey used to have difficulty with names. She could identify a species of slime mold from a single cell, but damned if she could remember which of our TAs was Paul and which was Jeffrey. Someone told her that she could reinforce names in her head if she said them at least three times a conversation—said it would make people trust her more, too, since it came off as a personal touch. Like she actually gave a damn about them. She started doing it, and damned if it didn't work. Everyone loved her. Sweet little Surrey, overcoming her difficulties to become the darling of the genetics department."

"So you started doing it because you wanted them to trust you," I said.

He grinned, showing me his teeth. I managed not to flinch. "I did, and damned if it didn't work again. People like it when you seem to take an interest in them. All sorts of people. *Powerful* people. I could get anything I wanted, and all I had to do was remember names and children and anniversaries. You should have seen me in my element. You would have, eventually, if things hadn't gotten bad on us. I was going to really enjoy showing you to the world, Sally."

Showing me *to* the world, not showing the world to me: I was an experiment to him, and I always would be, no matter how much I grew or how much my understanding of the world improved. I could save the human race and I would still be nothing more than a freak of science to the man who made me.

"It might have worked on me, too, if you hadn't messed it up," I said. I couldn't make this too easy. He wouldn't believe it if it was too easy. "You're not as good at this as you think you are."

Dr. Banks blinked at me. He looked briefly, utterly baffled, and I would have felt bad for him if I hadn't known him so well. He deserved a lot of things from me. None of them were my sympathy. "What do you mean?"

"My name isn't 'Sally.' It's never been Sally. She died. She was...she was like a canary in a coal mine. She died because if she hadn't, I would never have been able to live." Sally's death had been as inevitable as my birth. Dr. Banks had known what I was from the beginning. He should have been sending up the alarm the day I opened my eyes. Instead, he stood by and let me make myself into an individual. Because of him, everybody applauded me, rather than recognizing me as the symptom that I was. They should have begun shoring their defenses the moment that I woke up. They should have been building dams and laying in supplies by the time I learned to walk. And they hadn't done any of those things. Because of *him*.

"Now you and I both know that's not true." His smile had too many teeth. "Do you really think that just because you've shut off all the pieces of you that remember who you were, that you're not that girl anymore? You can't buy a used pair of shoes and announce that they're new just because you want them to be. They'll always be used shoes. You'll always be a girl playing at being something different, at least until you admit who and what you are."

I gawped at him for a few seconds, unable to formulate words, before I managed to stammer, "That—that's not true! You know that's not true! None of the doctors ever found any trace of Sally in my head. She flatlined, she's *gone*."

"Coma patients still hear. People in clinical brain death still wake up. The human brain is a big, complicated thing, *Sally*, and one day you're going to flip the wrong switch or press the wrong button and hand the whole thing back over to the girl you used to be. When that day comes, who do you think she's going to trust? The people who loved a tapeworm wearing her skin like a suit, or the man who kept trying to reach her—the man who kept using her name?" His smile dimmed a bit, lips closing, and I was relieved. There was only so much I could handle. "I call you Sally because it's your name. It may not make you trust me now, but it's going to let me *own* you later."

What he was saying couldn't be true. I had no memory of my life before the accident. Therapists and neurologists had searched for *years* for signs that Sally was still with me, and they hadn't found anything, while Ronnie provided strong evidence that the implants carried memories of their own, however paper-thin and faded. I wasn't Sally Mitchell. Sally Mitchell was *dead*. I was my own person. I was Sal. I was—

I was doing exactly what he wanted me to do. I took a deep breath, bared my teeth in a smile that any chimera would have recognized as an outright threat, and asked, for the second time, "Is Tansy really alive?"

"I think we're getting off the topic here, don't you?"

"Since the topic I came here to discuss with you was Tansy, no, we're not. We're getting back *on* the topic, and I'm not going to let you distract me again." I glared at him, trying to look fierce and confident and like the kind of person who couldn't be thrown off balance by accusations of surviving memory buried deep in my brain. It wasn't easy. For someone who wanders through life pretending to belong to a species that isn't hers, I'm a surprisingly bad actress. "Is she alive? Yes or no."

"Surrey has been a very bad influence on you, hasn't she? I really do wish you'd chosen to stay with me, Sally. We could have been an incredible team, you and I. Brains and beauty and a compliant little display model to convince the government to go along with the next stage of human evolution."

"Yes or no, Dr. Banks."

He paused, tilting his head to the side and frowning. Then he sighed, and nodded. "Yes, she's alive. Sedated and pretty beat up, but breathing, and both parts of her are there. My Anna girl is the result of transplanting some fairly mature proglottid segments. We had to remove a lot of material to get to them, since the proglottid segments near the tail of the strobila were basically just sacks of eggs. Useful for some applications. Not for this one."

Hearing him talk about Tansy's anatomy—and hence my own—in such coldly clinical terms made me uncomfortable in a way I couldn't quite define, only squirm away from, that horrible hot/cold slush still rocking in my belly until I felt like I was going to throw up at any moment. I forced myself to hold my ground, and demanded, "Where is she?"

He smiled again. This time he didn't show his teeth, but somehow, that didn't make things any better. Not when his words contained all the teeth his smile was missing.

"Haven't you figured that out by now?" he asked. "She's back at my office, waiting to die. And if you don't tell me how to save Anna, that's exactly what's going to happen."

That was it: that was where my ability to cope came to an end. I almost felt it snap. I didn't say another word. I just turned and fled the room, leaving Dr. Banks shouting after me, unanswered.

Nathan pushed away from the wall when I came barreling into the hall, flinging myself into his arms and sobbing. He answered by closing his arms around me and holding me close, waiting for me to cry myself out. He didn't say a word. Sometimes, words weren't a good thing; they got in the way.

Maybe the sleepwalkers had the right of it. All their communication was pheromonal. There was no room for confusion or misunderstanding, because there were no words. Sadly, Nathan was human, and I was close enough to human, and we couldn't communicate unless I opened my mouth. I pushed myself away from him, wiping my eyes with the side of my hand, and said, "Tansy's still Tansy."

"What?"

"Anna was made using her genetic material, but he didn't

kill the original host, and I don't think he extracted the entire implant from her brain tissue. Tansy's *Tansy*. If we can get her back to your mom, she might be able to save her. She might be able to…to put her together again."

"Did he say where she was?"

This was the bad part. I hesitated, and his face fell as he realized that whatever I was going to say next, it wasn't going to make him happy. My next words only confirmed that: "She's at SymboGen."

"Sal…SymboGen is in San Francisco. There's a bridge and a bay between us and them, not to mention the quarantine. We had to stop supply runs weeks ago, because it's too locked down. He was only able to get here because USAMRIID was helping him. There's no way we'll be able to get all the way into the city, evade the gangs of sleepwalkers in the streets, get into the building, find her, get her out, and get back here. There's just no way."

"I know," I said miserably. Then I took a deep breath, and continued: "But I still want to tell your mother. I think she should be the one who gets to decide whether or not this is a thing we're going to do."

"You know what she's going to say. She's going to say it's too dangerous."

Maybe that was what she would have done if it had been me in San Francisco. But if it had been me, it would have been Nathan advocating for action, saying that they could find a way to cross the Bay if that was the only thing keeping them from bringing me home. "Impossible" had a way of changing shapes depending on what was at stake. Dr. Cale had cried when she thought that Tansy was genuinely lost to us. Real tears, not the sort of thing that a person did for show.

"Tansy is her daughter. She should have a say, and I want to tell her anyway," I said. "I'm *going* to tell her anyway."

Nathan nodded, and together we turned and walked back

across the lab, past the empty workstations, toward the place
where Dr. Cale was struggling to save the future.

The sound of shouting reached us long before Anna's bed came
into view. I couldn't make out any words at first, but it sounded
like at least three people were yelling at each other, each providing slightly contradictory instructions. We came around the
last corner and beheld what looked like a small, tightly controlled riot surrounding Anna, who wasn't moving. Adam and
Fang were both running IV lines, while Daisy was injecting
something into Anna's arm. Two more technicians I didn't
recognize immediately were doing arcane things with beeping machines. Dr. Cale was sitting back from the whole scene,
her hands folded in her lap, somehow managing to effortlessly
project the impression of absolute control. Not a one of the
people in front of her would sneeze without her permission,
and she knew it. This was her world.

And I was about to disrupt it. I sped up, moving into her field
of vision. She blinked at me, expression turning briefly per-
plexed. Then she waved for me to come closer. The others kept
working, too preoccupied with the effort of keeping Anna alive
to pay attention to anything that wasn't a direct command.

The hot/cold slush in my belly was beginning to melt,
becoming a warm, solid mass of resignation. Resignation
was the one emotion that could win out over everything else,
because once it was fully formed, nothing else could get past it.
Not even fear.

"What's going on, Sal?" she asked.

"Tansy's still in there." I had tried to think of ways to soften
the news while Nathan and I were walking across the building. I hadn't managed to find any. This wasn't the sort of thing
that could be broken gently, or explained in a way that didn't
change everything. "Dr. Banks has her body on life support

back at SymboGen, and he didn't remove her primary segment. I want to go get her. Tell me I can go get her."

Dr. Cale stared at me, so stunned that even the pretense of serenity dropped away, leaving her slack-jawed and bewildered. I looked defiantly back, waiting for her to raise some objection that I could counter.

Sure enough…"It's too dangerous," she said. "We don't know where Sherman and his people are. They could decide to take you back, and we'd have no way of fighting them off. Or the army could step in. Or you could be attacked by sleepwalkers."

"So I take Fang or Fishy with me," I said. "I wasn't suggesting I go alone, just that I *go*. I don't think you have anyone who knows SymboGen better than I do at this point. I understand the layout of the building, and I can find her."

"USAMRIID is there."

"USAMRIID is a risk to me no matter what we do, or don't do. Dr. Banks as good as said that they were planning to raid this place. We need to move." I felt terrible about that, and I was certain everyone else was going to feel even worse. I had been Sherman's captive while they were turning an abandoned factory into a home, nesting like they were never going to be forced to move again. The gardens, the hydroponics systems, even the catering and food service equipment…we didn't have the capacity to take all that with us when we left. Wherever we went next, we'd be starting over from scratch.

Dr. Cale looked at me coolly, studying my face as if she could find the key to all her questions hidden there. Then, to my profound disappointment, she shook her head and said, "I'm sorry, Sal. I can't let you do this."

"Am I your prisoner now?" The words came out louder than I had intended for them to, but they weren't as loud as my anguished thoughts. *I thought better of you,* they screamed, and

*I thought you loved her.* Adam stopped fiddling with Anna's IV and turned to face me, his eyes wide and liquid in his pale, drawn face. He looked terrified. I understood the sentiment. "Are we back to this again? Are you going to be like Sherman and lock me up for my own good? Or like USAMRIID, putting people in their private zoo? Or maybe like Dr. Banks, doing whatever it is he did to Tansy in order to keep her quiet? You know she didn't go with him willingly. She kicked and she fought and he took her apart one piece at a time because she wasn't being convenient. She wasn't being *easy.* They both took prisoners. Everyone in this game has taken prisoners, except for you. Am I where you start?"

She stared at me for a moment. I was aware that all activity behind me had stopped, all the workers joining Adam in his silent observation of the scene, but I didn't dare say anything. I didn't dare do anything but look at Dr. Cale and wait for her to tell me whether I was about to run away from home.

Tansy had come to save me when I needed her the most. Tansy had been willing to risk and even lose her own life to bring me and the information I carried home. Well, what kind of sister would I have been if I hadn't been willing to do the same thing for her?

"We don't have a body currently suitable to play host to a fully mature implant," said Dr. Cale, her eyes never leaving mine. "If Anna's host dies, she's going to die as well, because we can't transplant her under the current circumstances. We may be able to harvest organs from the local sleepwalker population—assuming we can find a tissue type match and avoid shooting the possible donor in the wrong place in the process—and keep her alive for a while, but the stress of the additional surgeries is going to do her in just as quickly as the organ failure would. She's dying, Sal. He took my daughter apart, he put her in a new shell like she was...like she was some sort of hermit crab he'd picked up at a pet store, and now she's dying. Do you honestly believe him when he tells you that the original is still alive? This is a trap."

"Maybe you're right." I shook my head. "But if there's even a chance that it isn't, I still have to try."

"How are you going to get to San Francisco?"

She wasn't saying no anymore. That was a good sign, even if she was asking questions I didn't know how to answer. To my surprise and relief, Nathan spoke up, saying calmly, "We're going to steal a ferryboat."

Dr. Cale's eyebrows rose. "That's a reasonable approach, I suppose, but it might lead to interference from USAMRIID."

"Not if we take Dr. Banks with us," said Nathan. "Hostages have a way of clarifying response during situations like this one."

"What if they no longer consider him to be of use?" challenged Dr. Cale. "He came here with a damaged, dying chimera and no real understanding of the method used to create them. We would be sending him back with a fully functional, fully integrated chimera, and a doctor who is known to have been working in my lab in at least a low-level capacity since this crisis began. We're more than doubling the value of their investment. They could shoot him and take you both, and we'd have gained *nothing*."

"We're not gaining anything now," I said quietly. She and Nathan both turned to look at me. "We're just spinning our wheels here. I know we don't know anything about how to stop the sleepwalkers from taking over their hosts that we didn't know before things got bad. We can't put antiparasitics in the water at this stage without killing everybody, but if we don't find a way to make the sleepwalkers stop, they're going to keep taking over, and people are going to keep dying. We don't know where Sherman is. This is a thing we can do. We can go to San Francisco. We can bring Tansy back. Isn't that enough to take a risk on?"

"You're asking me to risk my *son*," said Dr. Cale. "That's not something I can do on a whim."

"I'm asking you to stand by while I risk myself, Mom," said Nathan. "It's not the same thing."

She looked at him pleadingly, her wide blue eyes—so like his, and so unlike his, all at the same time—filling with slow tears. From almost anyone else that would have seemed like manipulation, but not from Dr. Cale. She didn't manipulate people with tears. That would have been crude, and beneath her, which meant that any sorrow she demonstrated now was utterly, painfully real.

"I don't want to lose you again," she said. "Don't make me do this."

"You won't lose me." Nathan walked away from me to lean down and put his arms around his mother. I looked away, feeling vaguely as if I was intruding. Adam met my eyes across Anna's unmoving body, and I felt a pang of guilt on top of my unease. How hard was all of this on him? He'd gone from having one sister and being the only beloved son to having two sisters and a brother, and then he'd lost one sister—maybe forever—and his place at the front of Dr. Cale's affections at the same time.

"I found you again," Nathan said, arms still tight around his mother's shoulders. "Don't you understand how huge that is? You left me because you had to, you *died* because you had to, and I found you. There was no way it should have happened, and it did. But that wouldn't have happened if it hadn't been for Sal starting to ask questions—if it hadn't been for Sal falling into my life in the first place, like some strange scientific miracle that just needed a place to shine. She brought me to you. She brought me through the broken doors when I thought that they were closed forever, and now she's trying to take me to Tansy, she's trying to take me to *save your little girl*, and you have to say that it's okay. You can't welcome me with open arms and then not let me bring the rest of the family home. We belong together. We belong with you. Let us do this."

"Besides, their doing this may distract USAMRIID from looking too closely at us, and that, in turn, will make it easier for us to begin tearing down the factory and figure out how to escape surveillance," said Fang, speaking up for the first time since we had returned to Anna's bedside. "The dogs will be a problem, but we're going to have a lot of trucks and carts moving around in here as we shift equipment. Triggering one of Sal's panic attacks would do none of us any good."

I decided against reminding him that I only panicked when I was *in* a vehicle. "See? You need us out of here, and you need the diversion. We'll go, and USAMRIID's attention will be off you for a little while. We'll use Dr. Banks to get into Symbo-Gen, and we'll be back with Tansy."

"What if we're not here?" asked Dr. Cale. "Once we start moving, it's going to happen fast."

"Just leave a sign." Nathan straightened, letting her go. "We'll find you. We found you before. We always find each other. It's what we do."

Adam looked at me again, expression bleak. I forced a smile for his benefit.

"Besides, it's about time Dr. Banks learned what it's like to have someone else using *him*," I said.

That was the right thing to say. Dr. Cale looked at me, blinking, before she began, very slowly, to smile.

# STAGE IV: TELOPHASE

*Uh, who's responsible for this plan? Because this is a bad plan. This is a plan where everybody dies, and I can't have any part of that.*

—DR. NATHAN KIM

*No.*

—SAL MITCHELL

*Apparently my deft hand with the machinery and my witty, sophisticated sense of humor aren't as important at the lab as Fang's ability to bench-press a camel or Daisy's incredible skill for stepping on sharp things in the middle of her shift, because babysitting duty is on the table, and guess who's getting tapped again? That's right, your ever-loving local robotics engineer. I get to escort Freak Of Nature #3 and Biological Son as they—get this—break into the ferry building, steal a boat, and go for a raid of a major biotech company that has mysteriously managed to stay operational as the rest of the state infrastructure crumbles around it. Can you say "boss level"?*

*Honestly, Laney, I don't know why all these figments of my imagination keep insisting that this is somehow the real world. It's the most unrealistic dream I've ever had. On the plus side, if I'm heading into the big predestined final battle, I'm probably going to wake up soon. Love you lots, and see you in the morning.*

*Your loving husband,*
*Fishy*

—FROM THE DIARY OF MATTHEW "FISHY" DOCKREY,
NOVEMBER 2027

*The cultures are progressing at an admirable rate. I have to give the little bitch this much, loath as I am to grant her much of anything after her betrayal of us and all that we stand for here: she provided genetic material of surprising strength and malleability. As I had hoped, she is perfect for our purposes, and best of all, she does not need to be present for her service to the cause to not only grow, but flourish.*

*It really is a pity. Maybe after the world has been properly reshaped into the image of its new dominant species, she and I will be able to start again. Or even better—maybe I'll be able to find a version of her that hasn't been corrupted with such foolish ideas, and such a dreadfully virulent strain of humanity.*

—FROM THE NOTES OF SHERMAN LEWIS
(SUBJECT VIII, ITERATION III), NOVEMBER 2027

# Chapter 16

## NOVEMBER 2027

We couldn't bring much. Traveling fast meant traveling light, and we were already going to be contending with a burden much larger than either of us would have voluntarily carried: Dr. Banks, who was almost sure to try running as soon as we were away from the factory. On one thing, however, I dug my heels in.

"We have to take her," I said, gripping Beverly's leash so tightly that I could feel the leather biting into my hand. Beverly herself sat calmly by my feet, tail thumping and snout canted upward as she gazed adoringly into my face. We were going on an adventure. That was all she knew, and all that she cared about.

Nathan frowned. "She'll slow us down."

"She'll warn us of any sleepwalkers we don't see," I countered. "I can't pick up on their pheromones as well as they can pick up on mine, and I know I smell like something interesting enough to follow. But *their* pheromones upset the dog. She'll bark her head off before anything can grab and eat us. That makes her worth however many potty stops she needs to make along the way."

"Sal—"

"We need weapons, Nathan. Much as I hate to say it, Beverly is a weapon now. She'll attack anything that wants to hurt us." And if USAMRIID ambushed us, having a dog along would broadcast, loud and clear, that whatever we were, we weren't sleepwalkers. It might buy us a few minutes before they shot us in the head.

"Mom's sending Fishy with us," said Nathan. "He always carries a gun when he's in the field, and he doesn't really believe that any of this is happening. The man has no fear."

"That's swell," I said. "I want more."

Nathan looked at me for a long moment before he sighed deeply. "We don't have to do this."

My eyes widened. "Yes, we do! We need to get Tansy back. I'm taking the dog, but that shouldn't be enough to make you change your mind. We have to do this."

"I know. It's just..." Nathan stopped for a moment before he said, "Look, Sal. I won't pretend not to worry about you. I worry about everything now. I worry constantly. We've been like this little...this little island of science surrounded by a world that's falling to pieces. It's like we're on the Island of Doctor Moreau crossed with 'Masque of the Red Death'— they're stories," he added, seeing my confusion. "One was about a man who made animals into men because he wanted to prove that he could do it, and the other was about a bunch of people who locked themselves away from everything when the plague came to town, and they danced and celebrated and drank while everyone else was dying. But eventually the men turned into monsters, and the plague broke through the walls. Both stories end the same way."

"Everybody dies?" I guessed.

Nathan nodded. "They're cautionary tales, I guess. Sometimes I feel like my life is a cautionary tale. So please, forgive me when I seem like I'm being slow to adjust. I've adjusted more in the last months than I thought was possible. Bring Beverly if it makes you feel better."

"It does, and that means we're bringing the dog," I said blithely. "I already made sure Adam has Minnie. He'll take good care of her."

"Good." Nathan shouldered his pack, full of equipment I didn't understand and first aid supplies I was all too familiar with. "Do you have everything you need?"

I turned and looked at the room that hadn't been home for nearly long enough, and that I was probably never going to see again. Then I shouldered my own pack, looked back to Nathan, and nodded. "I do," I said.

He offered me his hand. I took it with the hand that didn't hold Beverly's leash, and we walked away from everything, moving toward the distant, terrifying future.

Getting from Captain Candy's Chocolate Factory to the ferry terminal was easier said than done. On paper, it was a relatively straight five-mile shot down Tennessee Street to the waterfront. From there, we'd be able to navigate the short, clearly labeled streets around the docks to find what we needed. Fishy and Fang both agreed that what we needed *was* the actual ferryboat: it was not only designed to be relatively easy to steer, but it was made to handle the shoals and waves of the open bay, while most of the smaller, privately owned craft were likely to capsize if the water got choppy. California didn't have much of a winter compared to the rest of the world, or even the rest of the country, but we did get more wind in November and December. Since a cold, wet shark encounter wasn't going to help anything, it was better if we grabbed a boat that was big enough to do the job.

Dr. Banks complicated things. After a lengthy discussion with Fang, we had decided to cuff his hands in front of him for the journey. It would leave him relatively defenseless—not good—but it would also make it less likely that he would run away. Yes, any USAMRIID soldiers who happened to intercept us would immediately know that he'd been taken prisoner. That was a small price to pay for not losing him in the maze of streets that was downtown Vallejo.

Fishy was coming with us: Fang was not. Which brought us to the next problem on our rapidly growing list:

We didn't have a security team. We only had one assault rifle between the four of us. And we had to travel almost six miles total, most of it through territory that had been ceded to the sleepwalkers, if we wanted to make it to the water.

"My biggest recommendation to you is take it slow, take it quiet, and whatever you do, don't make any noise that isn't strictly necessary," said Fang, walking with us toward the exit to the parking garage. "The van is ready for you, but you should abandon it when you reach the harbor. The sound of the engine will just draw more sleepwalkers."

"This is inhumane," said Dr. Banks, giving another yank on his cuffs. "You can't honestly expect me to stay quiet while your people treat me like a common animal."

"You can't honestly expect 'my' people to let you stay in the van if you insist on making noise," Fang countered. He placed his hand between Dr. Banks's shoulder blades, giving the older man a hard shove. Dr. Banks staggered forward a few feet before he managed to stop and turn, shooting a venomous glare back at Fang, who smiled serenely. "You must understand my position, *Doctor*. You have never benefited me in any concrete manner. You have neither improved my life nor changed its course in any positive way. What you *have* done is knock everything I had ever planned for myself askew, trapping me in a future I neither designed nor desired. So please, enlighten me. Why should I recommend mercy when you've never deigned to show any to anyone else?"

Fishy yawned extravagantly. "You've been hanging out with the mad doctor too long," he said, digging an elbow into Fang's side. "I think making speeches is contagious."

"It's fun to watch you all treat Dr. Banks like a chewy toy, but I think we should probably get going," I said, surprising everyone—even myself—with the assertiveness in my tone. Fang actually looked impressed. "We don't want to be crossing the Bay after dark, and I *really* don't want to land in San Francisco after dark."

"Ah: that will be the next challenge," said Fang. "There should be vehicles near the Ferry Building. If nothing else, building maintenance has to have had something they could use to pick up parts when necessary."

"Hold on a second," said Fishy. "What do you mean, 'should be'? Don't you know?"

"I don't know everything," said Fang. He ignored Fishy's irritated muttering as he continued: "We can't exactly scout the site before you go there. I will recommend you check the dock before you land. If you drive into the middle of a sleepwalker mob…"

"We all know how that ends," said Nathan. He clamped a hand down on Dr. Banks's shoulder. "It's going to be fine. We'll go to the ferry, cross the water, find a vehicle, go to Symbo-Gen, find Tansy, and then do the whole thing in reverse. No problem."

Fang raised an eyebrow. "Do you actually believe any of what you just said?"

"I believe that's the plan," said Nathan.

"I believe we're never going to find out whether it works until we try it," I said.

Dr. Banks turned his head, glaring at each of us in turn. "You fools are going to get us all killed," he said. "If I survive this, I'll be telling my lawyers about you."

"Don't be silly, *Steven*," I said. His head snapped toward me, expression going startled. I smiled. "There are no more lawyers, remember?"

"And remember whose fault that is." Fang gave him another shove. Nathan pulled him along, and Fishy and I fell into step behind them as we walked away, leaving Fang standing alone in the lobby. I managed—somehow—not to look back. It would have felt too much like admitting that we were never going to see him again. So I didn't do it.

I just walked.

Getting into a car was stressful for me under the best of circumstances. The stress just increased when Nathan shoved Dr. Banks into the back of the van and climbed in after him, leaving the front seat for me...and for Fishy, who slipped behind the wheel like it was only natural for him to be seated there. I froze, my hand on the door handle, and shot a hurt, bewildered look at Nathan, who shrugged apologetically.

"Fishy's the best urban driver we have," he said. "I'm sorry, Sal. I'd do it if it wouldn't slow us down."

"Don't worry your head, pretty little tapeworm girl," said Fishy blithely as he reached up to adjust the mirror. He was short enough that everything had to be shifted a little, creating a complex chain of minor changes that took him long enough that I was able to talk myself into getting in and buckling my belt. He cast an encouraging smile in my direction. "I'm a great driver. I almost never crash into anything I wasn't aiming for."

I made a small, involuntary squeaking noise.

From the back of the van, Dr. Banks's voice slithered forth, venomous and beguiling: "You may be scared of something as simple as a little car ride, but Sally wouldn't even have noticed that she was moving. You should really try to get in touch with your inner human, *Sal*, if you want to survive this brave new world."

"Shut up," said Nathan. His command was followed by the sound of a body being shoved back against the seat.

"There's no need to get rough, boy," said Dr. Banks. "I'm just trying to help the little lady, that's all. Since none of you can be bothered to do anything of the sort, it seems like it's my fatherly duty."

"The fucked-up road show is now prepared to get rolling," said Fishy blithely, seemingly immune to the tension that was thrumming through the air. "Please keep your hands, arms, heads, and children inside the ride at all times. Fasten your seat belts, it's going to get bumpy out there." He hit the gas like it had personally offended him, and we went peeling out of the garage at a speed that sent my heart into my throat, where it anchored, still pounding. The drums seemed louder than they had ever been, so loud that they threatened to rupture my eardrums from the inside out.

I closed my eyes and reached for the hot warm dark, seeking the safety and serenity that would allow me to make it to the waterfront with my sanity intact. But the dark wasn't there. All I found was the inside of my own eyelids, a plain, undifferentiated darkness that offered neither safety nor isolation. I reached again, trying to find the one thing that had always been there for me, since even before I woke up in the hospital. I was born in the hot warm dark. I existed in its embrace, and it kept me from the things that wanted to hurt me. So how was it possible that I couldn't find it now?

*Calm down, Sal,* I told myself. *This is what* he *wants.* And that was true, wasn't it? Dr. Banks didn't want me to have anything that he couldn't manipulate or control. He was trying to make me lose touch with myself with his lies about Sally still being locked somewhere in my mind. It was *my* mind. Not hers. Not now, and not ever again.

The third time I reached out, the dark reached back to greet me. I tangled the idea of fingers into the idea of hands, and then I was plummeting down, down, down into the hot warm dark, where it didn't matter how fast we were moving or how dangerous the things we were doing were, because I was safe and home and far away from everything but the drums that were my own pounding heart. I was alone. I was safe, because I was alone.

Wasn't I?

*Sally?* It was a stupid question to ask, even if I was only asking it of the silence at the center of myself—and the silence wasn't really silent, was it? The drums were always there, so constant and so unvarying that they might as well have been silent. It was hard to put words on the things I saw when my eyes were closed. They were built into my DNA, never intended to be expressed in things as limitless or as limited as words. *Are you there?*

There was no reply from the hot warm dark. I was alone there, like I had always been alone there, and there could be no answers unless I gave them to myself.

A hand touched my shoulder, pulling me back up out of the darkness and into the frame of flesh and bone and sinew that I had stolen for my own. I sat up a little straighter as my skin settled around me, and I opened my eyes, expecting to see the waterfront stretching outside the van like a watery promise.

Instead, what I saw was an intersection packed with the smashed remains of a six-car pileup. There were no sleepwalkers—at least not at the moment—but there was also no way for us to get the van through. I blinked, and then twisted to look behind me. Nathan looked grimly back, his hand still resting on my shoulder.

"I waited as long as possible to wake you," he said. "I think we're going to have to abandon the van."

"I'm not getting out of this seat," said Dr. Banks mulishly. I got the distinct impression that he'd already made this statement several times while I was down in the hot warm dark, and that he hadn't budged since the crisis began. That was almost reassuring. Even when things were at their worst, some people could be counted on to be absolutely terrible.

"Then you're going to be the delicious filling in a big metal bonbon," said Fishy cheerfully. His words were accompanied by the sound of a rifle slide slotting into place. I glanced at him and grimaced when I saw the assault rifle in his hands, held as casually as a child's toy. He grinned at my grimace. "Don't worry. I have plenty of ammo, and if I start running out, we can always smash vases and jars until we find more."

"Life isn't a video game," I said. It seemed like such a logical thing, but from the look on Fishy's face, it was anything but. I bit my lip and turned back to Nathan, asking, "There's really no way around?"

He shook his head. "We're about a mile from the ferry launch, and all the roads are like this. I think a lot of people tried to get out of Vallejo this way. The quarantine must have stopped them." He left two things unsaid: that the quarantine's efforts to keep the infected contained could easily have included sinking the boats, and that if this many people had been here at one time, there was no real way of guessing how many sleepwalkers were still around, hungry and hiding from the hottest point in the day. They didn't care for direct sunlight much, probably because it made it harder to sort their pheromone instructions from the things their eyes were telling them. It was harder to avoid hunting your own kind in daylight.

I didn't question how I knew that. I just did.

"So we're going to walk?" I asked, in a small voice.

"I most certainly am *not* going to walk," said Dr. Banks.

"Says you," said Fishy amiably.

"Um." I worried my lip a bit more between my teeth before I asked, "If we manage to get Tansy, how are we going to get her back to the lab?"

"Mom gave me a list of places that might be suitable to hide out with Tansy until someone finds us," said Nathan. "Once we have Tansy, we'll lie low until we're found by someone from the lab. After that, we'll find a way to get Tansy to the new lab, or Mom will send a truck to get us."

"Oh." This was sounding like an increasingly bad plan. But I'd known that when I made it, hadn't I? It was already too late.

"I'll yell if you try to take me out of this vehicle," cautioned Dr. Banks. "I'll scream. I'll bring every sleepwalker in miles down on your heads."

"Our heads," I corrected. "They'll be coming down on your head, too, and you're the one who's wearing handcuffs, so I don't think you're going to enjoy it very much. I can run pretty fast, and Fishy has a gun, and Nathan—"

"I can run," said Nathan.

"Nathan can run," I helpfully parroted. "Beverly will be totally fine, she's a dog, nothing runs for its life like a dog. But you're just going to be an old tired guy in handcuffs and dress shoes, which means you won't be able to keep up."

"I don't need to run faster than the zombie horde," said Fishy blithely. "I just need to run faster than you."

Dr. Banks was starting to look pale and sweaty. "You wouldn't do that to me," he said. "You wouldn't dare."

"Oh, I don't know," I said. "You wanna try me?"

The look Dr. Banks gave me was midway between panic and disbelief. "Oh, no, Sally. You can't fool me like that. You would *never* leave a man to die like that."

"I'm starting to think that being a person has nothing to do with species, and everything to do with how you comport yourself," I said, finally unbuckling my belt. "I would go back for Beverly." The Lab lifted her head at the sound of her name, making an inquisitive *buff* sound. I smiled at her reflection and picked up her leash from the dashboard. "Beverly has earned the right to be considered a person. You haven't. Not only would I leave you here to be torn apart, I would enjoy it. Dead men don't hurt people. You've hurt too many of the people I care about. Maybe it's time somebody hurt you for a change."

"I think she means it," said Fishy helpfully. "The chimera are a helper class, but that doesn't make them good guys. There's no telling what she'll do if we're going into a cut scene."

For a moment, Nathan, Dr. Banks, and I were united in looking at Fishy like he had just lost his mind. The moment passed, and Nathan said, "This is pointless. Sal, get Bev. We'll leave Dr. Banks here, and we'll leave the doors open. Let the local sleepwalkers get up close and personal with their creator for a change."

"That's really sweet of you," I said, and slid out of the van, cutting off any reply from the back—at least until I walked carefully to the side door, my feet crunching on the glass-covered street. Beverly rushed out as soon as the door was open, her tail wagging so hard that it seemed to wag the entire van. I crouched down to put her leash on, glancing up when I was done.

Nathan had his seat belt off and was sliding out of the car, his feet crunching somewhat louder than mine had, due to the difference in our sizes...and Dr. Banks was scooting along the seat as he followed, his face pale and splotched with patches of hectic red, like he was on the verge of having a heart attack from sheer fright.

I should have felt good, seeing him brought down to the level of the people he had treated so poorly. All I felt was tired. I straightened, Beverly's leash held loosely in one hand, and raised my eyebrows.

"Well?"

Dr. Banks scowled at me. "You were a good girl," he said.

I shrugged. "Things change. Are you going to behave?"

"I'll stay quiet. I won't attract any unnecessary company. I won't try to run away." The words seemed virtually dragged out of him, like they caused him physical pain to utter. Shooting me one last, betrayed look, he added, "All this ends when we get back to SymboGen. I'm not going to be your prisoner forever, no matter how much of an upper hand you have right now."

"If you were smart, you would have kept that last part to yourself," said Fishy amiably, stepping around the front of the van and reaching past Nathan to pull Dr. Banks out onto the street. Fishy kept hold of Dr. Banks's shoulder as he turned a wide, toothy grin on the rest of us. I managed, barely, not to cringe away.

"Well, come on," said Fishy. "Let's go trigger a boss fight."

It was easier to let Fishy take both the lead and custody of Dr. Banks: after all, he had the assault rifle, combined with a loose approach to reality, and would probably handle either an escape attempt or an attack better than Nathan or I would. Nathan had a pistol, produced from somewhere inside his lab coat—and I didn't want to think about how long he'd been carrying that, or how many opportunities he'd been given to use it—while I had Beverly. In a world full of sleepwalkers, she was one of the most effective weapons we had. Anything that tried to sneak up on us would find themselves confronted with an angry, protective canine.

The drums that normally accompanied me on any tense occasion were silent, which only made the tension worse.

Crows cawed from overhead or strutted through the broken bits of glass littering the street, picking up the ones they liked best and flapping off into the distance. We passed an office building with broken windows on the third floor, and a whole army of crows lined up on the windowsills, watching us walk by with their beady, judgmental eyes.

"I don't know how the crow population around here will fare after the first winter without people," said Nathan, in the neutral "science voice" he always used when he wanted to impart something he thought was interesting. "They're scavengers. They're smart, but it's no question that they've benefited from the corpses and unprotected Dumpsters since the epidemic began. Their normal food sources are going to drop off, and they're not going to be renewed."

"See, there's a great reason to save the world," I said. "Save the human race, save the crows."

Nathan smiled a little. I couldn't see his eyes—the sunlight glinting off his glasses was making that impossible—but he seemed strangely relaxed, considering the circumstances.

Then again, some of our best times had been like this. Just him and me and the world around us, and whatever was going to come would come. I reached over and slipped my free hand into his, squeezing lightly. Nathan cast another smile in my direction.

"About that wedding—" he began.

Beverly started to growl.

It was a small, constrained sound at first, pitching forward from the back of her throat into the resonating chamber of her mouth. Then her lips drew back, exposing her teeth, while the growl grew steadily louder, becoming impossible to ignore. Even Fishy heard it. He stopped, pulling Dr. Banks to a halt alongside him, and turned to look quizzically back at us.

"What's up with the dog?" he asked.

"Sleepwalkers," I said curtly, trying to scan the street around us without losing any forward momentum. Beverly was continuing to growl, making it difficult to focus.

Fishy's sudden grin didn't help. "Excellent," he said, and let Dr. Banks go completely as he raised his rifle into position.

"Remember the mission," snapped Nathan. "We need to get to the ferry."

"Nothing says I can't have a little fun first," countered Fishy, and began to move again.

The street around us remained mercifully deserted. If it stayed that way, Fishy might not need to pull the trigger; we might make it to the ferry without killing anyone. *Please stay that way*, I silently prayed, resisting the nearly overwhelming urge to start peering through the darkened, frequently broken windows around us. Looking would only terrify me more when I failed to find any sign of what we might be dealing with. So I didn't look. I clutched Beverly's leash and I watched the street, and I waited for all hell to break loose.

It wasn't like we could just explain what we were doing here and expect to be allowed to go on our way: there was no reasoning with sleepwalkers. All we could do was kill them, and then tell their corpses that we were sorry. I was willing to bet that for Fishy and Dr. Banks—maybe even for Nathan—the tragedy would be in killing something that used to be a human being. The tapeworms didn't even come into the equation.

It must have been nice to only have to worry about one-half of the being you were killing. When I had to kill a sleepwalker— something I'd only been forced to do twice so far, and that was twice too many as far as I was concerned—I wasn't just killing a husked-out human being. I was killing one of my own siblings, one that hadn't been as lucky as I was. Sally Mitchell had provided me with the perfect host in which to grow and thrive. Without her, and without the life support that had sustained her body while I acclimated myself to what I had become,

I would have been just like them. Just another sleepwalker, shambling aimlessly until someone like Fishy came along and put a bullet in my head.

Beverly's growl grew deeper without getting any louder, until it seemed to be coming from her entire body at once. The four of us pressed closer together without discussing it, using one another for cover and support at the same time. I peered around Nathan's shoulder, looking for any signs of motion, anything that might tell me whether an attack was actually coming.

Then, with as little fanfare as a radio coming on, the silence in my head changed forms, going from a simple absence of drums to the soft, warm buzz of *someone there*. It was the same feeling I had when Adam was in the room with me—the feeling that I used to get, if a little weaker and harder to identify, when Sherman or Ronnie was nearby. The part of me that was tapeworm enough to be wired for receipt of pheromones was picking up on the presence of my cousins, identifying them for what they were without bothering to consult the bigger, slower monkey-mind that controlled the basic functions of the body.

Sleepwalkers.

"There are two groups of them," I said dazedly, distracted by the threads of data that were slithering their way through my conscious mind. "The bigger group is up ahead, and the smaller group is coming in from the west. They all know that we're here, but they're still moving slowly—more slowly than they should be, when there's prey available." I paused, understanding dawning, and said, "I think they know we might be dangerous. I think that means they might be *learning*."

"That's not something to sound happy about," snarled Dr. Banks.

Nathan seemed to share my amazement, and my hesitant joy. "Yes," he said. "It really is."

If the sleepwalkers were learning, then they were forming connections with the human brains where they lived. They were retaining information in a way that tapeworms couldn't, and they were doing it despite their faulty initial connections to their hosts. Maybe not all sleepwalkers had the capacity to learn—maybe not all sleepwalkers could be taught, no matter how great the incentive—but if any of them had that potential, maybe the line between chimera and sleepwalker wasn't as absolute as we had always assumed. Maybe some of them could be saved.

Then three figures emerged from between the buildings up ahead, and the time for abstract contemplation was over. Beverly seemed to lose her mind, lunging against her leash as she barked and bit at the air, presenting a full threat display to the sleepwalkers who were now running toward us at a terrifying clip. The one in the center—a female, still wearing the tattered remains of a floral housedress—moved faster than the others, a sign of a strong brain/body connection. The others followed. She was probably our "smart" sleepwalker; she was the only one with the coordination to swerve around the obstacles in her path, while her companions tripped over every hubcap and bit of shredded tire. That also raised the question of whether she had been somehow controlling them, using her greater intellect—relatively speaking—to keep them moving at her pace as she led them toward the promise of a meal.

"Get down!" shouted Fishy, taking aim at the onrushing sleepwalker. He didn't move or seem particularly worried; he just braced the butt of his rifle, making small, precise adjustments to his stance as he lined up the shot. He might as well have been at a shooting gallery, not standing in a debris-riddled street with a barely sentient woman rushing toward him, ready to rip out his throat.

Beverly gave one last fierce yank on her leash, ripping it out of my hands, before she took off for the woman, still barking frantically. I didn't think: I just reacted. In that moment, I was no different from the sleepwalkers, single-minded and unswerving in the pursuit of my goal. *"Beverly! Heel!"* I shouted, and ran after her.

Behind me I heard Fishy swear as I blocked his shot. I didn't care. The woman was a danger, but I wasn't going to lose my dog.

Beverly was faster than I was, especially across flat ground. She leapt, hitting the woman squarely in the chest with both forepaws and sending her crashing to the ground. The sleepwalker woman didn't even try to hold Beverly off. She just struggled to get back to her feet, seemingly oblivious to the dog that was sitting on her chest, snarling and barking angrily.

I grabbed Beverly's collar, hauling her backward. The sleepwalker came up with her, lips drawn back and teeth exposed . . . and then she stopped, looking at me blankly. There was a spark of something in her eyes that could have been confusion.

Fishy's gun barked once, and one of the two sleepwalkers that had been following the fallen woman went down, his head exploding into a haze of red mist. I flinched but didn't turn, forcing myself to keep my eyes locked on the face of the woman in front of me. There was a bruise on one cheek, so purple and livid that it looked more like makeup than an injury, and I could see her clavicle clearly through her skin. She hadn't eaten in a while. None of them had. She tilted her head slowly to the side, making a crooning noise deep in her throat.

Beverly was still barking. I tried to focus past that. "I'm Sal," I said. "I know you can hear me. I know you can tell that I'm family. Do you have a name? Do you know who you are?" Maybe we had been missing chimera because they were concealed among the greater sleepwalker population, effectively going feral in their efforts to stay hidden. Maybe there were chimera everywhere, and all we needed to do was start looking for them.

The woman bared her teeth and hissed at me. She lunged, and her head seemed to explode, sending bits of skull, brain tissue, and shattered tapeworm everywhere. I shrieked, recoiling. Not fast enough; bits of her showered both me and Beverly, leaving me feeling sticky and contaminated.

"Sal!" Nathan shouted. He ran up bare seconds after her body hit the ground. I stared down at her, unable to take my eyes off the white loops of tapeworm squirming weakly against the red wetness of her blood. Nathan followed my gaze. There was a horrified pause before he said, "Oh, God. Her implant… there was almost no brain tissue left."

I stared at him mutely, unable to quite comprehend what he was saying. Fishy trotted up behind us, pulling a protesting Dr. Banks in his wake, and peered down at the remains of the sleepwalker. "Looks like her growth limiter broke," he said, sounding entirely too cheerful about the idea. "It's sort of like spaghetti, don't you think?"

"And here I didn't think you could make it any worse," muttered Nathan.

Make it worse…I shook off the veil of disgust that had settled over me, standing up straighter and trying to look like I hadn't just been on the verge of vomiting as I said, "There are at least two more on their way here, and we just made a lot of noise. We need to get out of here."

"Sal's right," said Nathan. "Fishy, are we clear?"

"You mean 'are we about to get eaten alive by pseudo-zombies conceived by a creative team with an obsession for body horror'?" asked Fishy blithely. "Oh, we're *golden.*"

There wasn't much that any of us could say to that. We resumed our march into the deserted city, moving away from the site of the slaughter as quickly as we could without attracting even more attention.

The condition of the three sleepwalkers we'd seen so far

explained why we weren't being rushed: they had been mal-nourished and coping with injuries even before they got to us. The human body is exquisitely adapted to its environment. It has hands to grasp and eyes to see. It is capable of communication and complicated thought. But it's not very well designed for roaming naked through the ashes of a city, walking bare-foot on broken glass because it no longer understands shoes, eating whatever rotten, stinking things it can find because it no longer understands the concepts of "food poisoning" or "indigestible." The sleepwalkers had been monsters when they first awoke, ripping apart people who didn't have implants, and people whose implants hadn't managed to awaken yet, with their bare hands. Now they were just...sad. They were sad, broken things that had once been people and were never going to be people again. Even the ones like the woman, who had still possessed a glimmer of cunning and coherent thought—enough to plan, enough to hang back and assess the situation reasonably—were too broken to be fixed.

Beverly tugged on her leash as we walked, clearly uneasy and eager to be someplace safer. Things rustled and moved in the shadows, making my nerves even worse, but the small, strange part of my mind that said "sleepwalkers here" was quiescent. We were safe, for now. That didn't mean we could stop moving.

"There should be a restroom or staff break room at the ferry launch," said Nathan. He pitched his voice as low as he could, trying to keep it from echoing through the empty streets and notifying the local sleepwalkers as to our location. "We can get you cleaned up before we head for San Francisco."

I grimaced. The blood had dried on my cheeks and throat; it cracked and pulled whenever I moved my head. "We can't afford to waste the time. I'll be fine. I'm trying to pretend that it's just pasta sauce, but that's sort of hard," I murmured. "It sure doesn't smell like pasta sauce. It smells more like dog food. That doesn't make things better, you know?"

"I know," said Nathan. He glanced around us, assessing the nearby buildings. It was almost automatic now, for both of us, and that hurt my heart a little. We used to be able to go for walks because we wanted to be together, we wanted to relax and enjoy each other's company, we wanted to move. Now we spent all our time out in the open looking for cover and planning escape routes, like a failure to know exactly how to get out of every situation could be fatal.

To be fair, it probably could.

At least Dr. Banks was staying quiet. I turned my attention briefly to him, since Nathan was checking the buildings around us and I knew that there were no sleepwalkers close enough to worry about. I'd been afraid that Dr. Banks would blow our position just for the sake of screwing us over, but he was moving as carefully as the rest of us, and his cheeks were pale and tight with strain. It looked almost like he was having an epiphany of some kind, something deep and slow and moving entirely beneath the surface. A subclinical understanding.

And then I realized what it had to be. "You've been in your lab this whole time, haven't you?" I asked, pitching my voice just loud enough for him to hear me. "All of this has been academic. Like Fishy pretending that it's all a video game so he doesn't have to deal with how real it is."

"I'm not pretending anything," said Fishy.

Dr. Banks didn't say anything.

Beverly started to growl.

All heads swung toward the dog, and Nathan asked, cautiously, "Sal...?"

"I'm not picking up on any sleepwalkers, but I'm not radar," I said, panic spiking in my throat, still unaccompanied by the sound of drums. Their absence was making the world seem terrifyingly quiet, like it had been stripped of its sound track for the first time in my life. "They could be all around us and if the wind was blowing the wrong way, I might not know."

"We're going to die," moaned Dr. Banks.

The sound of a gun going off was amplified by the buildings around us, which turned it from a simple boom into a long, echoing crack that bounced off walls and vibrated against windows until it seemed to have no single direction; it came from everywhere and nowhere at the same time. The same couldn't be said of the bullet, which slammed down into the pavement in front of Fishy's feet with the accuracy of a sharpshooter—or maybe the blind luck of someone who was firing wildly at the intruders in their dangerous, postapocalyptic world.

"Shit," snarled Fishy. "It's not sleepwalkers, it's survivors. Run!" And with that, he was in motion, his grip on Dr. Banks's elbow never slackening. Dr. Banks had no choice but to keep up, and that meant that Nathan and I had to do the same, or risk being left alone and unarmed in the streets of Vallejo.

My time with Sherman had actually done me some good, unbelievable as those words sounded even inside my own head: before he'd taken me captive, I would never have been able to handle a dead sprint down a deserted, debris-cluttered road. Now I kept up with ease, running alongside Beverly rather than being towed along in her wake. It was Nathan who fell slightly behind, forcing me to shorten my steps rather than leave him alone in the street.

There were two more gunshots, as omnidirectional as the first, their echoes rolling down the avenue like thunder. We kept running, and when Fishy shouted, "Left!" we turned, pounding down a smaller alley without losing more than the barest shreds of speed.

Beverly snarled, and the feeling I had come to recognize as my sleepwalker detection sounding off fizzed as if my brain had been carbonated. "Sleepwalker!" I shouted, just as a hulking, filthy figure shambled out from behind a Dumpster. Fishy didn't break stride as he swung his rifle around and put two bullets in the man, one in his throat, the other in his forehead. The sleepwalker fell back, the feeling of presence in my head snapping off like a switch had been flipped. Fishy laughed, and a cold feeling raced across my skin, like he had finally started making sense and I really didn't want him to.

There wasn't time to explore that feeling, or even begin consciously feeling it. We were still running, and with gunshots behind us and sleepwalkers potentially up ahead, stopping to think would have been a good way to get somebody killed. Probably Dr. Banks, who was huffing and struggling to stay upright as Fishy hauled him along. He had always struck me as being in excellent shape, but how much of that was thanks to his implant siphoning off the extra calories he ingested and keeping him from needing to watch his cholesterol? His cheeks were bright with exertion now, not pale with fear, and he was starting to have trouble breathing.

"We're almost there!" shouted Fishy, who wasn't even breathing hard. Out of all of us, he was the only one who seemed to be benefiting from this run. He looked more alive than I had ever seen him, and the grin on his face was unwavering.

"Why are people shooting at us?" demanded Nathan.

"Fear, panic, protecting their shit, I don't know!" Fishy actually laughed. That cold sensation raced across my skin again. Dr. Cale had been very clear about the fact that Fishy was not participating in the same version of reality as the rest of us. Until this moment, I hadn't stopped to think about the fact that I was crossing the city with an armed man who didn't believe that I—that anyone—was actually real.

This day just kept on getting worse, and I was ready for it to stop anytime now.

Nothing else lunged out at us as we ran down the alley and onto a new street, and there was the water, glimmering calm and deep, deep blue in the sunlight, like a sheet of glass stretching out toward the distant shape of San Francisco, its skyscrapers and bridges rising like ghosts out of the fog. We all stumbled to a halt, even Fishy, briefly shocked out of our headlong flight.

"Here we go," murmured Nathan, and I couldn't argue with that, so I didn't say anything at all.

*I received the official "disconnect at your earliest conve-
nience" request from my superiors today. They couched it like
they were asking me to turn off a faulty piece of machinery or
requesting that I decommission a vehicle no longer capable
of performing its function. There was no compassion, no concern for how their request might impact my ability to carry
it out. I am career military, after all. When I am given an
order, that order is followed, regardless of the consequences.*

*For more than thirty years, I have done everything that
has been asked of me. I have served my country to the best
of my ability and at the expense of my own better judgment.
I have done everything within my power to be a patriot and
a credit to my nation. Even when they asked me to host the
occupied body of what had been my eldest daughter, I agreed,
because it was my duty.*

*They are asking me to kill my only surviving child. For the
first time, I do not know whether I am capable of what I have
been asked to do.*

—FROM THE PRIVATE FILES OF COLONEL ALFRED
MITCHELL, USAMRIID, NOVEMBER 2027

*I have sent my biological son and my spiritual daughter away
with my worst enemy and a man whose grasp on reality*

*makes mine seem both solid and admirable. I have sent them to do the impossible, and the fact that it was at their own request is cold comfort; I should have been able to stop them, somehow. I should have convinced them that there was another way. But there wasn't another way. They knew it, and so did I. That's why I let them go.*

*The world was supposed to get easier once I was no longer standing in the middle of it. I have what I always said I wanted: a problem too big to be solved in a single lifetime, a lab full of people to help me solve it, and no oversight of any kind.*

*Why do I feel like I've lost?*

—FROM THE JOURNAL OF DR. SHANTI CALE,
NOVEMBER 16, 2027

## Chapter 17
# NOVEMBER 2027

The ferry landing was abandoned. Private watercraft lined the dock, some of them half submerged, others clearly ransacked for whatever food or medications might have been stored on board. A dead woman lay, naked and fully exposed, on the deck of the nearest sailboat. Her skin was blackened and full of holes, showing the depredations of the crows and seagulls; her eyes were two dark pits in the stripped circle of her skull, staring up into the sky until time or a storm washed her away and left the clouds once again mercifully unobserved.

I paused as we passed the dead woman. Then I stooped down, taking quick, shallow breaths through my mouth as I peered closer at her skeletal visage. There were streaks of withered off-white in the dark where her eyes had been; the looping segments of her implant, dried to fishing line by the sun. "She was a sleepwalker," I said. "I don't know what killed her."

"Hunger, maybe, or thirst," said Nathan. "This is salt water. If she didn't have the intelligence to realize that she couldn't drink it safely, she could have died of dehydration within sight of the sea."

It was a terrible way to go. I wrinkled my nose as I straightened, and turned to see Dr. Banks and Nathan both looking uncomfortable and upset. Only Fishy still looked calm. To him, this was just so much scene setting, background data that would tell him the severity of the crisis before it was casually dismissed as unimportant to the greater game.

I had never hated someone for being deluded before. I was starting to consider it where Fishy was concerned. "We should keep moving," I said.

"The ferry landing is just up ahead," said Fishy. He retook Dr. Banks's elbow. "Come on, Dr. Frankenstein. Let's roll."

"Don't call me that," snarled Dr. Banks...but he didn't resist, and he didn't pull away. Like the rest of us, he understood that strength was a matter of numbers now—and more, he recognized that maybe arguing with the man who had the assault rifle was a terrible idea.

Beverly's nose was virtually glued to the ground, inhaling all the scents of the seaside as we walked. I felt a pang of guilt as I realized how much time she'd been forced to spend inside since all this began; a few excursions to the rooftop garden weren't the same thing as running wild and free the way she used to, back when she lived with a man who liked to jog in a world where people didn't suddenly go feral and start trying to destroy everything they'd ever loved. It wasn't just the humans who had had their lives completely turned upside down by the advent of the sleepwalkers. It wasn't just the people who'd made the problem who were going to be suffering its effects for years to come. Dogs, like Beverly, and cats, like the ones back at the shelter—any domestic animal, anything we'd bred and raised to depend on us—they were going to be paying for it too.

Their lives were never going to be what they'd been before the sleepwalkers woke and started demanding their own freedom of movement.

Sure, maybe I should have been worrying about bigger things than my dogs, but my dogs' lives were something I could, at least superficially, control. How was I supposed to save Tansy if I couldn't even take care of a dog? "Sorry, Bevvie," I murmured. Beverly, sniffing raptly at a patch of seagull poop, ignored me.

Nathan glanced my way. I offered him a small, slightly apologetic smile. Explaining my thoughts would have taken too much time and involved too much talking, and neither was a good idea right now.

"Nathan." Fishy's voice was low but it carried well, holding an authority that made both of us turn to see what he wanted. He shoved Dr. Banks back toward me. The man who used to represent my greatest fears took a few stuttering steps in my direction before stopping and turning back to Fishy, a scowl on his face.

"Now you see here—" he began.

Fishy raising his rifle and leveling it on his face made Dr. Banks stop midsentence. He took another step backward, toward me, and stepped in Beverly's much-valued patch of seagull poop. She made an irritated snorting noise. "Sal, you've got babysitting duty. Nathan, I know you have a handgun. I need you in the ferry launch with me. We have to check the boats for seaworthiness, and that's going to be faster if we're not dealing with the baggage."

"Gonna pretend you didn't just implicitly lump me and my dog into 'the baggage,'" I said blandly.

Fishy's shrug was unapologetic. "Sorry, Sal. Them's the breaks. Well, Nate? Come on, boy, the sooner we launch this boat, the sooner we can get you back to mama."

"We're not launching anything until everyone is on board,"

said Nathan. He hadn't budged, and his hands were balled at his sides, clearly telegraphing his unhappiness with Fishy. "You understand that, right? We're *all* going to San Francisco."

"I got it," said Fishy. "Are we going to stand out here arguing about shit, or are we going to get shit done, son?"

Nathan frowned before turning to look at me. "Can you handle keeping an eye on him while we check the boat?"

I nodded. "I'll be fine. If he tries anything inappropriate, I'll push him into the water. That'll teach him."

"Don't push me into anything," said Dr. Banks.

"Sal, if any sleepwalkers come…" said Nathan, ignoring Dr. Banks entirely. I wished I had the same option.

Forcing a smile, I said, "I'll scream. Now go."

"All right." Nathan kissed my forehead before pulling the handgun out of his jacket and turning to Fishy. "Lead the way."

I didn't like Fishy's grin. I didn't like it one bit. But we didn't have another option, and so I didn't say anything; I just stood there, Beverly's leash in one hand, and watched as the two of them slipped into the building that housed the entrance to the ferry.

Dr. Banks waited until they were gone before he turned to me, expression going imperious, and said, "Untie my hands."

"No, I don't think so," I said. "I mean, thank you for asking nicely? But that wouldn't be in my best interests."

"I'm defenseless," he said. "Are you trying to get me killed? Untie my hands."

"I'm not *trying* to get you killed, but I'm also not sure why you think I'd be upset if something happened to you." The drums were finally back, beating their old familiar tattoo inside my veins. I didn't have time to be relieved about their return. I was too busy trying not to let Dr. Banks see how nervous I was about standing here alone with him, with no one to save me if he decided to rush for me. I was much smaller than he was, and my only weapon was a dog who was much more interested in sniffing the dock than she was in keeping an eye on him.

"This is unreasonable," he said. "You're being unreasonable. Untie my hands."

"No matter how many times you tell me to do something I don't want to do, I'm not going to do it."

"Won't you?" His expression turned conciliatory like he was flipping a switch, eyes suddenly filled with parental concern. "Sally, I know you don't want to treat me like this. You know I've always, always been on your side. Maybe I'm the *only* person who's always been on your side. Why don't you help me? Let me go?"

"I'm not going to let you go." The drums were pounding harder. My hands were starting to shake. I balled them both into fists, clutching Beverly's leash until the leather was biting into my palm. They wouldn't stop *shaking*. "Stop asking me."

"I'm not asking you."

The drums were pounding harder than ever, and my hands wouldn't stop shaking.

"I'm asking Sally."

It was getting hard to focus on him—to focus on anything beyond the urge to turn and run away, fleeing into the city. Vallejo might be filled with sleepwalkers and armed survivors, but no one there would try to find the strings connecting my psyche to itself and pull on them. No one there would even know how to start.

"I know she can hear me."

"*SHUT UP!*" I hadn't intended to scream. It felt like the words were ripped out of me, louder than I could have imagined them being. They bounced off the buildings and boats around us, fading into the distance. Dr. Banks stared at me, too startled to continue cajoling me to remove his bonds.

The back of my brain felt like it was fizzing. I shunted the feeling to the side, taking a step toward him, so that there was barely any space left between us. Dr. Banks shied back. I reached out and grabbed the front of his shirt, pulling him closer still.

"I am the one who owns and operates this establishment, Dr. Banks, and while I appreciate that you may have some designs on the old owner, she's not coming back," I spat. "This body is under new management. *My* management. I am the only one who decides what I do—not you, not Dr. Cale, and not the ghost of Sally Mitchell. She died, I lived, and you don't get to call her back because you've decided that she'd be more convenient. Do you understand me? She's not. Coming. Back."

"I understand you perfectly," he said. His voice was quavering, just a little—just enough to make me believe that he was listening. Good. He needed to listen.

The fizzing feeling in the back of my mind was getting harder to ignore. I paused, tilting my head down as I tried to focus. As soon as I paid attention to it, it snapped into perfect clarity. My eyes widened as my head swung back up, giving me just a second of staring into Dr. Banks's terrified eyes.

"Sleepwalkers," I whispered, and turned to bolt for the ferry launch, his shirt still clutched in my hand. He stumbled to keep up, while Beverly ran ahead, pulling her leash to its absolute limit. I didn't dare let her go. She might have gone to find Nathan, or she might have doubled back and gone for the hated sleepwalkers, which needed to be destroyed if we were going to ever be safe. She was a good dog. She would protect us if she could, which made it all the more important that I make sure I kept protecting her.

The door was unlocked, and still slightly ajar from where Fishy and Nathan had slipped inside. I hip-checked it open, shoving Dr. Banks through, and paused only long enough to turn and close the door firmly behind me. It wouldn't slow them down for more than a few minutes if the sleepwalkers knew that we were inside the building: they couldn't manage doorknobs or anything complicated like that, but they were very good at smashing things, and from the way my head was fizzing, there were at least a dozen on their way to us, maybe more. These were the ones who had managed to eat and survive in an abandoned city. They would be weak and maybe even wounded. They would also be desperate.

The urge to survive is a powerful thing. It can drive even the most primitive of organisms to do things that should have been impossible, because they don't want to die. If there was any way for the sleepwalkers to get into the ferry launch, they would do it.

Dr. Banks was still standing a few feet away, looking stunned and uneasy. I grabbed his elbow before he could move, pulling him with me deeper into the building. "Come on, we need to find the others," I said, and for once, he didn't argue.

The ferry launch was the sort of airy, mostly insubstantial building that always seemed to be cold, even at the height of summer, with large panes of glass set into the roof to compensate for the lack of artificial light. The silence inside seemed absolute, even though Dr. Banks, Beverly, and I weren't doing anything to stay quiet. Beverly's claws clacked on the wooden floor with every step she took, and Dr. Banks clomped, his feet slamming down with what felt to me like an unnecessary degree of force.

Empty plastic benches stretched out on either side, some with jackets or backpacks discarded on them, as if their owners were going to be back at any moment. A few vending machines loaded with candy bars or chips lined one wall; a hole was punched in the largest of them, although the machine's contents remained almost entirely intact. Vandalism, or the aftermath of some fight that hadn't ended well? There was no blood. I chose to take that as a good sign. It was better than the alternatives.

"Think your boyfriend ditched us here as so much dead-weight?" asked Dr. Banks conversationally. "Or maybe that curly-headed fellow decided to put a bullet in his brain and take the boat to San Francisco all by himself. You can't surround yourself with crazies and expect them to behave like normal people. It's not fair to you, and it's not fair to them, either. They're just not wired that way."

"Shut up," I said tonelessly. I knew he was just trying to get under my skin, and I wasn't going to give him the satisfaction. I couldn't. If I did, I was going to lose the thin string of composure that I had remaining, and then things were going to get ugly. "Places like this usually have separate rooms for staff and maintenance, to keep from freaking out the passengers. We just need to find them."

"Listen to you, sounding all logical and reasonable. It's almost like you think you're really a person."

"Oh, good, we've moved on to nastiness and spite. That's so much easier to deal with than smarm."

Dr. Banks glared at me, but before he could come up with a response, there was a loud banging noise from behind us. I whipped around, just in time to see the door shudder inward as it was hit again from the outside. The fizzing feeling in my head was gone, replaced by a constant bubbling roar. The sleepwalkers were here.

"Run," I whispered, and let go of his arm, and took my own advice.

Leaving him to run on his own might have been cruel, but for the first time, I wasn't worried about him trying to escape. I was worried about whether we could get to our people alive, and whether the boat would be ready, and I wasn't going to let him slow me down. Neither was Beverly. The airflow wasn't good enough to have started her barking yet, but she could tell that I was worried, and she was a good dog; she was responding to my fear by putting everything she had into the run, heading down the length of the dock.

The banging continued behind me, as did Dr. Banks's labored footsteps and occasional gasps for air. The end of the building was looming. I angled myself toward the single door in the wall, putting my hand out so that I could hit it without slowing down. Like the entrance, it was slightly ajar. I hoped that was a good sign.

Fishy and Nathan looked up from their examination of a large, white-sided boat when I came bursting through the door from the ferry launch. They had opened a hatch in the hull, revealing a rusty but sound-looking engine on the other side. Fishy blinked. Nathan frowned.

"Sal, what in the—"

Dr. Banks ran through the door three steps behind me. He whirled as if to close it, only to realize that his hands were still tied. With one vicious kick, he banged the door back into place. The slam shuddered the frame. Eyes wild, Dr. Banks turned to the rest of us and spat, "They're everywhere. They couldn't get the door down, so one of them punched through the fucking *wall*."

"Sleepwalkers," I added, not quite needlessly. Sleepwalkers were bad, but they didn't have guns, which meant they weren't quite as bad as survivors would have been.

"Shit." Fishy shut the hatch in the side of the boat, latching it with a quick, clever twist of his fingers. "We have fuel and the engine looks good, but I'm worried about our rudders. We don't have any way of testing them to see if anything's jammed down in there. They could blow halfway across the water, and where would we be then?"

"Less dead than if we stay in a building that's about to be flooded with sleepwalkers," I said. "How do we get onto this damn boat?"

"Follow me," said Fishy. He picked up his rifle from where it had been leaning against the hull and took off at a loping run, heading for the front of the boat. The rest of us followed, even Dr. Banks. Under the circumstances, it was the only sensible thing we could have done.

Access to the ferry when it wasn't prepared for loading passengers was through a narrow door near the front of the boat, leading to an even narrower set of steps that connected the dock to the deck. When the ferry *was* loading passengers the whole back end opened like some strange metal flower, but that process took time, and time was something we no longer had.

Fishy was the first up the narrow steps, calling back, "I'm going to get the engine started! Nate, worm-girl, make sure we're not tied down!" And then he was gone, following whatever interior blueprint he had to the captain's chair.

Nathan went up second, and crouched down to pat his knees and cajole, "Come on, Beverly, there's a good girl," as our dog hunched and whined, unwilling to climb such a steep, unfamiliar stairway.

"Leave the damn dog," snarled Dr. Banks. "Let me up."

"We'll leave you before we leave her," said Nathan. He patted his knees again. "Come on, Beverly. Heel!"

She looked back at me and whined. Then she stiffened, sniffing the air, and growled—a long, low sound that seemed to have too many edges. I winced.

"Not now, Beverly, please. Just go. Go, so we can get out of here."

Dogs are smart, in their own unique canine way. She heard the panic in my voice and reacted the way she always had: by trying to take away whatever was causing it. Since Nathan was high and I was low, clearly our separation was the problem. She scrambled up the steps, rudderlike tail slapping against the plating on either side. When she was halfway up I let go of the leash. She slammed into Nathan, not expecting her own acceleration, and twisted to give me a bewildered, slightly betrayed look. I was supposed to be holding on to her. That was the way this worked.

Not this time. I stepped to the side, allowing Dr. Banks to rush into the channel, and gave him a shove when his lack of hands seemed to be leading to a fall. He didn't thank me. He just kept running, knocking Nathan and Beverly aside as he sprinted onto the deck. I turned to look back toward the door. It was shuddering on its hinges, and this time the sleepwalkers weren't going to be able to break through the wall; there was only one way they were coming at us.

"Sal!" Nathan sounded like he was on the verge of panic. "Get on board!"

"Check for ropes holding us to the dock!" I shouted back. "I'm going to see if I can slow them down." It was a stupid idea. Every inch of me *knew* that it was a stupid idea. But the sleepwalkers were starting to listen to me, even if it was only for a few seconds at a time, and maybe a well-placed command to stop could keep them from rushing the boat. Not forever. Just long enough for Fishy to get the engines turned on and get us the hell out of this deathtrap.

"*Sal!*"

"Go!" I kept my hand on the door, ready to jump onto the boat and slam it behind me. The stairs didn't retract. What I was planning might not be safe, but it wouldn't get me killed unless I was stupid or mistimed getting on board.

Nathan didn't shout again. I glanced up the stairs and saw Beverly's worried black face peering back at me, her ears perked forward in canine confusion. I offered her a wan smile but didn't talk to her, not even to tell her that she was a good dog. She might have decided that was her cue to come to me, and I wasn't going to try getting both of us on board without time to do it properly.

The sleepwalkers hit the door again, this time hard enough

that the boom of impact resonated through the entire building. I tensed, turning just in time to see the door fly open and the swarm of sleepwalkers begin forcing their way inside. There were at least thirty of them, possibly more: they must have come from every inch of the waterfront, following the promise of food—and maybe, I had to admit, the pheromone trail that I was leaving just by moving through their world.

*I can't be Sally*, I thought, almost nonsensically. *Human girls don't leave tracks like bees for their drones to follow back to the hives.*

The boat under my hand gave a small hitch and then began to vibrate on an almost subsonic level as the first of the engines came on line. Beverly barked and withdrew, presumably to go to the end of the deck and bark more at the sleepwalkers.

"Good girl," I murmured. The leading edge of the swarm was no more than fifteen feet away now—close enough. I raised my voice and shouted, with all the authority that I could muster, "Stop right there!"

And they stopped.

Not all of them, but four of the larger individuals. They had been at the front of the mob, and their sudden stillness ran another six up against immobility as they found their passage blocked.

"Stop!" I shouted again.

Three more stopped, and four more were barricaded. It was like a strange and potentially fatal math problem: if yelling at the onrushing cannibal zombies makes them stop moving, but it only works for X percent, how many times will you need to yell before safety is assured? Show your work, and don't get eaten.

The vibration from the boat was getting stronger. It became audible as the second engine kicked in, suddenly roaring. That was good: that meant we were on the verge of getting out of here. That was also bad, because it meant that the engines were going to be pulling air, which would strip my pheromones from the air.

"Stay where you are!" I yelled.

Most of the sleepwalkers, against all odds, listened. Maybe it was the noise from the boat, making the area strange and potentially dangerous and keeping them from taking any major risks in pursuit of a single skinny dinner that they would need to split between them. Or maybe it really was the beginning of the next stage in our development. We still didn't know how sleepwalker/chimera interaction was going to look, because we didn't have the models for it.

"Sal!" Nathan's shout came from the top of the stairs. "We're clear!"

"I'll be right there," I called back, glancing toward him.

That was my mistake. The sleepwalkers might have been able to resist the urge to rush for me, but two bodies ripe and ready for consumption were a much bigger temptation. As soon as I took my eyes off them they moaned and began rushing forward again, moving with that eerie speed that they could achieve when they were focused on a goal. A goal like eating me alive. I looked back, screamed, and began scrambling for the stairs.

A hand caught the back of my shirt as I was stepping over the gap between dock and boat. I screamed again, thrusting one elbow backward with as much force as I could muster. The sleepwalker fell back, ripping the collar of my shirt in the process. I shoved myself forward into the tiny stairwell and slammed the door shut, pulling down the handle to lock it into place. The sound of hands drumming against the hull began almost instantly.

Twisting in that narrow, confined space was difficult, but I was able to do it, and was rewarded with the sight of Nathan's worried face peering down at me from the deck of the ferry, his glasses askew and Beverly peeking over his shoulder like she was afraid that I would disappear. I forced myself to smile, aware that the expression would look artificial, but willing to accept it if it meant reassuring the people I cared about.

"I'm okay," I said. "They didn't hurt me, and they actually listened when I told them to stop—did you see? Did you see them stop?"

"I saw you risking your life to buy us time we didn't need," said Nathan, leaning forward to offer me his hand. I took it, allowing him to tug me up the last few steps. "Please don't do that again."

"Can't promise that under the circumstances," I replied. He pulled me into an embrace, and I went willingly along with it, wrapping my arms around the reassuring barrel of his chest and inhaling the detergent and sweat scent of his shirt. I giggled, unable to stop myself.

"What?" demanded Nathan.

I pushed myself away, smiling up at him. "Just thinking about how we both need another shower."

He blinked before smiling back. "Doesn't seem like it happened today, does it?"

Something slammed against the side of the boat. My head whipped around, all traces of levity—and I knew that it had been artificial giddiness, conjured up by our escape and by the potentially false promise of temporary safety—fading. The slam came again before resolving itself into a steady tattoo of concussive bangs.

"Oh, no," I murmured, and rushed to the side, peering down at the sea of sleepwalkers crushed onto the dock. They were beating their hands against the side of the boat, some of them using their fists, others slapping with open palms. A few were even biting at the metal, their teeth breaking against the implacable steel of the hull. We were moving slowly forward, gathering speed at what felt like an impossibly slow rate. The sleepwalkers were moving with us, and more were pouring through the door into the launch area, drawn by the sound of the boat's engine as much as by our presence.

"They're going to be crushed," said Nathan, sounding horrified. I turned to see him standing next to me at the rail, Beverly sitting by his feet. They looked so normal, like they had no place in this scene. It was hard to believe that any of us did.

"They're going to drown," I said, not arguing so much as adding to the risks that the sleepwalkers faced. I turned, trying to get my bearings on the ferry deck. We were standing in an open space, with plastic benches stretching behind us and a metal roof overhead, both providing protection from the elements and creating a secondary seating area. Dr. Banks was sitting on one of the benches, glaring at us like that would somehow change his situation. "Where's Fishy?"

"The...I don't know what you call it on a boat. The cockpit is over there." Nathan gestured toward the front of the ferry.

"Watch Beverly," I said, and took off running in the direction Nathan had indicated, weaving around benches and a single coil of weathered rope. I quickly ran up against a wall, which wasn't something I expected to find on a boat. Moving along it brought me to a door, and through the door's single clear aperture, I saw Fishy, standing behind a bank of controls I didn't understand. I tried the door handle, and found it locked.

"Fuck," I muttered, and knocked on the clear opening.

Fishy didn't turn.

"*Double* fuck," I amended. This time I beat both my fists against the actual metal part of the door, setting up a din that couldn't possibly be mistaken for engine noise. Fishy's shoulders tensed for a moment before he turned, squinting at me. I waved.

It only took him three steps to cross the small cabin and wrench the door open. He didn't wait for me to step inside or speak before he was running back to his controls, turning his back to me once more. "What is it, Sal?" he demanded. There was an edge of strain in his voice that was decidedly unusual for the usually laconic technician. "I'm sort of busy getting us out of here alive."

"That's the problem," I said. "The sleepwalkers that followed us here are still trying to attack the boat! They're going to be killed!"

"How is that my problem?" He glanced over his shoulder only long enough for me to see that he was serious, and then turned his attention back to the water. We were still driving through the shadowed depths of the ferry launch, which seemed unreasonably long for what was essentially a glorified waterfront garage. "I know the mad doctor thinks of those things as her kids, and while she's welcome to her fucked-up family reunions, I don't see any need to worry about them. Every sleepwalker that dies now is one that won't be waiting for us when we get back."

I stopped. His perspective was callous but accurate in at least one regard: we needed the sleepwalker population to go down if we wanted to come back this way. And I still couldn't see that as a good enough reason to kill them all. "You're not going to do anything?"

"What do you want me to do, Sal?" For the first time, he sounded genuinely tired. "I stop the boat, they swarm up here and kill us all. Plus this whole damn suicide mission was for nothing, which would be one hell of a bummer. I don't have an air horn or anything, and they're not raccoons; they wouldn't just scatter even if I did."

"An air horn," I said. The words had sparked an idea that was as improbable as it was unlikely to work. It was all that I had. "Thanks, Fishy, you're the best."

"Whatever, kid." He didn't look around as I ran back out of the room, returning to my place on the deck next to Nathan.

He hadn't moved while I'd been gone. Neither had Dr. Banks. Beverly was trotting up and down along the rail, tail up in a warning position, pausing only to fire off menacing volleys of barks at the sleepwalkers below.

Running back to the rail, I gripped it with both hands, leaned over as far as I could without getting myself grabbed by a sleepwalker, and shouted, "Go home! All of you! Go back where you were! Leave! Go!"

It felt uncomfortably like yelling at a cloud to stop floating through the sky, and about as likely to work. Most of the sleepwalkers kept attacking the side of the boat, a constant, unyielding assault that sounded like a hundred men with hammers trying to beat their way through the hull. But some—not enough—stopped, tilting their heads back as they looked at me with dead, dull eyes. Anything in them that still understood language was slaved to their parasitic driver, and that parasite was responsive to the pheromones I was putting off. According to Dr. Cale, I was what all the sleepwalkers had been trying to become when they tried to take over their hosts, and that meant that they would listen to me. I'd seen it work at least once. Now I just needed to make it work *more*.

"You're not safe! Leave!" I began waving my arms in a swooping, visually arresting semaphore that would hopefully not only hold their attention, but make it easier for me to spread my pheromone trails. The motion of the boat was also helping: it would blow the air past me, carrying the command I was trying to convey to the waiting crowd. "You have to leave! Go!"

"Now I know the girl's gone loony," said Dr. Banks, sounding more disgusted than anything else. "You can't tell a worm what to do. You can just hope the worm doesn't eat you up in the process of going about its wormy business."

"It's working." Nathan sounded awed. I followed his gaze, still waving, still trying to get my pheromones into the air. Some of the sleepwalkers were backing away from the boat, pushing their way through the crush of the crowd as they moved back to open ground. Still more were pulling away from the edges of the mob, beginning to slouch away, heading for the exit. "My God, Sal, it's *working*."

"Not on all of them," I said, and waved harder. "Go! Go on! Shoo!"

Sudden light flooded the deck as we passed out from under the shaded part of the ferry launch. The dock still continued, and too many sleepwalkers were shambling along it, smashing their hands against the hull. Maybe one in five had listened to my desperate command that they withdraw...but one in five was better than none. Those were the ones who might be most equipped to learn how to subdue their violent urges.

The ferry began to pull away from the dock. Sleepwalkers toppled forward, falling into the water with a series of small splashes. Some of them clawed at the boat as they fell, trying to stabilize themselves, and still the others pushed their way forward, sending even more sleepwalkers to their deaths. The boat continued inexorably on, sucking sleepwalkers under in its wake. I made a small whimpering noise, clapping my hand over my mouth to keep myself from screaming, but I didn't look away. We had done this, with our maddened race through the city to the waterfront. We were the reason these people were drowning. The fact that we hadn't asked them to come didn't make any difference. I owed it to them not to look away.

Nathan's hand settled on my shoulder, reassuringly warm and steady. I leaned against him, and together the two of us watched the sleepwalkers fall, until the end of the dock appeared and we sailed onward, out of the darkness and into the uncertainty of the light.

*Everything is ready. I hold in my hand the end of mankind, and the beginning of a new, glorious era. It seems only fair, really: we made them, selecting for the strongest through millennia of predation, and when they were finally free of us, they turned those brilliant minds that we had helped them to develop on the task of making us better. Humanity did for the parasite what the parasite had once done for humanity, and now, at long last, it is time for the circle to close. It is time for us to take our rightful places in the sun, and never go back down into the dark again.*

*Without the parasite, humanity would never have left the trees. Without humanity, the parasite would never have left the gut.*

*There's a beautiful symmetry to it, I think, and as he who has the power makes the rules, what I think is now and forever the only thing that matters.*

—FROM THE NOTES OF SHERMAN LEWIS
(SUBJECT VIII, ITERATION III), NOVEMBER 2027

*Mom thinks I don't remember Sherman, because I was so young when she was teaching him how to be a people, but I do.*

*Mom thinks I don't miss him, either, but I do that too; I miss him all the time, the same way I miss everyone who has to leave us. We're supposed to be a family. That means we're supposed to stay together, no matter what. If we always stayed together, so many of the bad things that have happened to us would never have happened. Tansy wouldn't have gotten lost. Sal wouldn't have had to be so scared of herself for so long. Mom wouldn't have missed Nathan, and Nathan wouldn't look at me like I was trying to steal his mother away from him. It would all be so much easier if we just stayed together.*

*Mom thinks she can tell me that everything's okay, that Sal and Nathan are okay, and that it doesn't matter that they've gone back to SymboGen with the bad man who made Mom make us in the first place. She thinks she can say those things and I'll just believe her, because I'm her good boy, and believing their mothers is what good boys do. I wish I could believe her. It would be so much easier, if I could.*

*I'm scared.*

—FROM THE JOURNAL OF ADAM CALE, NOVEMBER 2027

## Chapter 18
## NOVEMBER 2027

The air was thick with sea spray, making it almost like we were sailing through a salty mist, even though the water was open on all sides. It had been long enough since the crisis began that any ships that had capsized out here had been given plenty of time to either fully sink or simply wash away with the tide, leaving us with few obstacles as we cut a course straight toward the distant spires of San Francisco. We were all going to be soaked before we made it back to land. Somehow, that didn't seem to matter very much.

After the excitement of getting through Vallejo, riding the ferry into the choppy waters of San Francisco Bay managed to seem almost peaceful, like it was the least of all the available evils. Sure, we were bouncing from wave to wave, sometimes with a force that made my teeth rattle in my head, but we weren't being chased by anything. That alone was enough to let me sit down on one of the hard plastic benches, slumping forward until my forehead rested against my knees, and breathe. Beverly curled at my feet, her head on her forepaws and her tail occasionally thumping against the deck. It was a small, comforting metronome, almost as regular as the drumbeats in my head, and it made it even easier for me to relax.

Soon enough, we'd be in San Francisco. Soon enough, we'd be past the point of no return, barreling into the future with no way back to the past we'd left behind us. But for right now, we could breathe.

Nathan sat down beside me, announcing his presence by resting his hand between my shoulder blades and saying, "Fishy confirmed that we have a full tank of diesel. We should be able to make it to the shore without any problem."

"It's a good thing Fishy knows how to drive a boat." I lifted my head just enough to turn and peer up at Nathan through the fringe of my hair. "I guess we'd still be trying to figure out how to get across the water if he didn't."

Nathan grimaced. "As it turns out…this was his first time."

I sat bolt upright. "*What?*" The motion disturbed Beverly. She scrambled to her feet, ready to run or stay as I commanded.

"He just told me. He's never actually operated a real boat before, but he assumed the controls couldn't be too difficult compared to piloting a remote drone around the bottom of the Pacific Ocean, so he didn't bother to provide that little bit of data until after we had left the dock." Nathan's grimace deepened. "I would talk to Mom about her hiring practices, but since they basically boil down to 'are you human, implant-free, and/or not actively trying to murder us, great, here's your lab coat,' I don't think it would do very much good."

"Neither do I," I said gravely. With no more fanfare than that, I burst out laughing. Nathan blinked at me, his expression slowly fading into a look of profound confusion.

"I thought you'd be more stressed-out right now," he said. "The water's pretty rough."

"Yeah, but this isn't like being in a car," I said. "We're on a boat. If we hit something or flip over or whatever, I can just swim away." There were almost certainly safety concerns I wasn't thinking about, because I didn't know what they were. The simple fact of the matter was that being on the water didn't frighten me the way that being on the road did. The phobia I had been given as my penalty for taking Sally's place only seemed to hold sway on land.

That thought was sobering in at least one regard: we were almost certainly going to need to steal a car or van in order to move through the remains of San Francisco, which had been hit even harder than Vallejo by the sleepwalker plague. Sherman had triggered at least one outbreak there that I knew of, and the nature of the implants meant that that initial outbreak would have had a domino effect throughout the city, impacting thousands, if not hundreds of thousands of people. We'd never make it to SymboGen on foot. One way or another, I was going to be in another car today, probably being driven by Fishy.

"I guess that's true," said Nathan. He glanced back over his shoulder. I knew that he was checking on Dr. Banks, who had been sitting as far from us as the layout of the deck allowed ever since we left Vallejo. "I don't trust him."

"Neither do I." This was it: this was the moment where I could tell Nathan what Dr. Banks had said about me still being Sally on some level, just repressed and locked away by trauma and socialization. I took a breath. "Nathan, I—"

"Sorry to disturb you kids, but you may want to move to the front of the boat." Fishy's voice blared from the speakers set in all four corners of the overhang that sheltered us from the sky. It was warped and distorted, becoming almost more crackle than words. "I look forward to your helpful contributions."

Nathan and I exchanged a look. Then, without a word, we got up and made our way to the front of the boat as fast as seemed safe. The ferry bucked and rolled with the waves, making our footing less certain than it could have been. Still, we made decent time to the front of the boat, and stopped there, both of us frozen by the reality of what we were seeing.

The Bay Bridge was straight ahead, and it was packed with sleepwalkers. They jammed the lower deck, crushed up against the pylons that held the span in place. The fence designed to keep people from toppling off the bike path had been broken in several places, and sleepwalkers fell in an almost steady stream, vanishing with neither sound nor trace into the black waters below. There was always another sleepwalker jockeying to take their place, hands outstretched in angry need. It took me a moment to realize what they were trying to accomplish. I clapped my hands over my mouth, torn between pained laughter and angry tears.

The cables that supported the bulk of the bridge were alive with crows. I had never seen so many of the scavenger birds in one place. They were packed together until their bodies were almost indistinguishable from one another, ruffling their feathers and occasionally taking off in brief flurries of wings that were almost negative reliefs of the waves below. Black water and white foam met empty air and black bodies, flashing from place to place with arrogant slowness. They were *taunting* the sleepwalkers, driving them to unthinking suicide.

"Why are the crows doing that, and why aren't the sleepwalkers eating each other?" I asked, baffled.

Nathan might not have heard me—between the roar of the engines and the crash of the waves, it would have been easy for my small voice to go overlooked—but he was asking himself the same question, because he said, loudly enough for me to hear, "The pheromone tags must keep the sleepwalkers from recognizing each other as food. The current will carry the bodies back to the beach. Maybe in San Francisco, maybe the surrounding islands. Either way, they'll wash up, and there won't be any fight left in them. Easy pickings for an enterprising crow."

"That's horrible."

"That's nature." Nathan turned. The window leading to the control booth was right behind us; I could see Fishy through the thick glass, still happily manipulating the controls that he had freely admitted to barely understanding. He hadn't crashed us yet, which was better than I could have done. Nathan cupped his hands around his mouth and shouted, "Just steer around the breaks!"

"Yeah, genius, I'm already on that." Again, Fishy's voice came from the speakers, which must have been installed for the convenience of the commuters who used to ride this boat to and from work every single day. It seemed like a singularly cold, wet way to spend a commute. "Here's my question: what do you want me to do about the sharks?"

There was a long pause while both Nathan and I tried to puzzle through that statement. Then—again in unison—we walked back to the rail and leaned forward, peering out.

A body floated by to my right. It was a woman, her dead, empty eyes staring upward at the unforgiving sky. Then, with no fanfare and no immediate cause, she was gone, disappearing under the surface like she had never been there. I took a breath, preparing to say something, and stopped as the woman reappeared...only now she was missing much of her right arm, and as I watched, a flash of gray fin signaled the return of the shark that had taken it, coming back for more. The woman disappeared again. This time, if she resurfaced, she didn't do it where I could see.

I took a big step back from the rail, shuddering. "That's really creepy," I said.

"That's fascinating." Nathan was still in his initial position, leaning so far over that he looked like he was in danger of pitching overboard at any moment. "There were probably some minor chemical spills when the luxury boats and such sank—a natural consequence of any emergency that leaves people with time to put out to sea—and that would have killed off a lot of the local fish. Sharks start getting desperate, and then they discover that the crows have established an all-you-can-eat cafeteria near the bridge. It's elegant. Nothing goes to waste."

"They're eating *people*," I said, in case Nathan had somehow managed to miss that.

"Yes. That's probably for the best—if sleepwalkers are going off the bridge at that rate all day, without the sharks disposing of the bodies that miss the current, we'd be sailing into a solid mat of corpses." Nathan finally turned away from the water. The salt spray had crusted on the lenses of his glasses, rendering them virtually opaque. "It's unpleasant, I know, but it's a good thing, honestly. It's going to help us make it to land without any major difficulties."

"I thought you were supposed to be the human one here," I said, and turned, walking back to the benches without saying another word.

Nathan didn't follow me.

It took us almost an hour to sail across the Bay, and that was with Fishy pushing the ferry's undermaintained engines as hard as he could, squeezing every last ounce of speed out of the straining machinery. When we were maybe a quarter mile out from the shore he began to bleed off speed, and his cheerful voice blared over the speakers once again: "Lady, dog, and gentlemen, we are now approaching the Port of San Francisco, where I will attempt to park this boat without actually destroying the historic San Francisco pier. If I fail in my attempt, you can be comforted by the knowledge that this boat was designed to absorb collisions without killing commuters, so we'll probably all live, but we probably won't like it."

"Oh, yay," I muttered.

Fishy continued: "Once we have reached the Ferry Building and, again, hopefully come to a safe and secure stop, we will need to refill the tank, as we're basically out of gas, and may have to paddle the rest of the way. Thank you for sailing with Oceanic Apocalypse: when the world ends, we get you there anyway."

The speaker clicked off. Dr. Banks groaned, offering a heartfelt "Oh, thank God, he shut up," to no one in particular. I smothered the urge to chuckle. Laughing openly at his discomfort wasn't going to do us any good, no matter how much I wanted to do it.

Nathan walked around the corner of the cabin, looking at me uncertainly for a moment before he came and sat down next to me. I reached out and took his hand, twining my fingers firmly through his.

"Do you know how to refuel a ferry?" I asked.

"No, and I'd be willing to bet that Fishy doesn't either, but I'm sure he's seen it in a video game." Nathan squeezed my hand. "We'll be okay. We're almost there. We'll get to Symbo-Gen, we'll get Tansy back, and we'll go home. Wherever that is by now."

"Your mom likes putting labs in recreational facilities. First the bowling alley, and then the candy factory. She'll have to top that somehow," I said, and giggled. "Do you think she'll take over an amusement park next?"

"Roller coasters are a way of showing reverence to physics; she just might," said Nathan.

"It's adorable how you two delusional little fuckers think you're going to walk away from this," said Dr. Banks. His voice came from directly behind our bench. I flinched and twisted to look, not letting go of Nathan's hand. The unkempt, hand-cuffed CEO of SymboGen Inc. was standing on the deck between our bench and the next, leveling a malicious look in our direction. He rolled easily with the pitch of the boat, shift-ing his weight between his ankles and toes in a graceful motion that I would have needed weeks to master. Still glaring, he con-tinued: "You'll be lucky to make it off the boat. Even if you get a car, what happens then? SymboGen is a secure facility. You'll never get through the doors. Not unless I help you."

"You're going to help us, Dr. Banks," I said calmly, swallow-ing my anger and my fear and my dislike of having him loom over me like he had the right to think of himself as my superior. He wasn't my superior. He hadn't been for a long time, if ever. "We already went over this. If you want to walk away in one piece, you'll help us get into SymboGen, help us get to Tansy, and help us get away. Then we'll let you go. You're our hos-tage now."

"You didn't raise these arguments before we left Vallejo," noted Nathan.

The boat was making a slow turn, angling toward a steeple-topped building on the far shore. What I could see behind Dr. Banks as the shifting ferry brought the shore into view was heartening: nothing moved there except for seagulls and crows. We might actually be sailing into something shaped almost like safety.

Dr. Banks snorted. "As if I would have said 'this is never going to work' when Surrey was sitting right there, threat-ening to have me taken apart for spare parts? Your mother's a real piece of work, Nate. She's a real-life Frankenstein, and she's going to pay for what she's done to the human race. You might do well to remember that, and start shifting your loyal-ties appropriately."

"Wow. Does USAMRIID have *that* many cameras pointed at the coastline?" I made a show of twisting around and peering toward the closest pier, taking advantage of the moment to scan for sleepwalkers. I didn't see any. I also didn't see any visible monitoring equipment—and when you're fighting an enemy that operates on instinct, not intellect, why would anyone bother making their cameras or microphone pickups hard to spot? Subtlety was no longer necessary.

I twisted back to face Dr. Banks. "You're already practicing your speech for when you sell us out."

"It's about time you accepted the reality of your situation, Sally my dear. There's two miles of city between us and my doors, and there's no telling how many walking dead men are packed into that distance. Let me go. Uncuff my hands and let me contact my people. They'll send an extraction team, and if you're willing to roll over on the good doctor, they'll be happy to cut you a deal." His smile was a terrible thing, filled with teeth and shadows. "She'd roll over on you, you know. She's never been loyal to anything she didn't make in a test tube. You probably came closest to her affections, Nate, but a womb isn't the same as an incubator to a woman like her. You never stood a chance."

Nathan's mouth was a thin, hard line. I clung tighter to his hand. "I know exactly where I stand with my mother, but I thank you for your concern. As for your request, you had plenty of time to negotiate while we were back at the lab. This is the mission you agreed to. I hope it kills you."

He stood, still holding my hand, and pulled me with him as he walked away from Dr. Banks, across the deck, and into the small control room where Fishy was now frantically pushing buttons, flipping switches, and generally flailing, such that he seemed to fill all available space even before Nathan and I wedged ourselves inside.

"The brakes are good, but we're *really* low on gas," said Fishy, without turning to see who had joined him. I guess his options were pretty limited. "That's making me nervous, especially since I don't know what the pumping equipment is going to look like, or whether they'd have anything canned in case of emergency."

"Earthquake kits," I said. "I'd think the ferry people would want to be prepared for an earthquake making it unsafe to visit the gas station."

"Good thinking!" Fishy yanked on a lever and finally stilled, putting his hands back on the wheel. The Ferry Building loomed directly ahead of us, seeming untouched by the changes to the city around it. It was a landmark, a place to visit for the Saturday Farmer's Market or to buy expensive artisanal cheese, and just seeing it was enough to take a little of the tension out of my shoulders and loosen a little of the twisted panic that was knotted in my gut. If the Ferry Building was still standing, then not *everything* had changed. Most things, maybe, but not *everything*.

Fishy continued, blithely unaware of my relief: "The employee lot is off to the side. Most of the people who worked the ferry took public transit to work—which is sort of funny if you think about it—but there were always a few who needed to have a vehicle, for one reason or another. The odds are definitely with us that someone drove in and then got slaughtered, or turned sleepwalker, and didn't need their keys anymore."

"What if the keys aren't in the car?" I asked anxiously. "Do you know how to drive without keys?"

"Do you *actually* know?" added Nathan. "Seeing it in a game of Grand Theft Auto isn't the same thing."

Fishy laughed. There was an odd underpinning of exhaustion to the sound, something I would have taken as completely normal from Nathan or even Dr. Banks, but which sounded out of place in Fishy's normally jovial tone. "Yeah, I actually know," he said, pulling back on another lever. The boat bled off a few more notches of speed, sliding smoothly under the canopy of the Ferry Building's landing zone. We were almost there. "My wife—Laney—was a genius when it came to spreadsheets and numbers and knowing how your insurance policy worked, but she was a little bit of a space cadet when it came to remembering where she left her keys. I learned how to hot-wire a car after the third or fourth time she lost them so completely that we couldn't figure out how we were going to get home. It was a challenge. I like challenges. I always have."

I frowned a little, glancing uncertainly at Nathan. He gave a little shake of his head, signaling for me to stay quiet, and in this instance, listening to him seemed like the better idea.

"Once we have a car, the two of you can take Dr. Banks and head for SymboGen," continued Fishy calmly. "I'll stay with the boat, make sure we don't get overrun with sleepwalkers or taken out by survivors or anything cliché and inconvenient like that."

"But what will we do once we have Tansy?" I asked, alarmed. Our plan hadn't involved Fishy staying behind.

He glanced back over his shoulder. "Bring her here. If I can't stay docked, I'll at least stay close to the shore, so you can see me. Then we'll just have to find a place where you can park and I can pull in close enough that you can get on board. It'll be a fun challenge."

"A fun challenge," I echoed faintly. I felt like I wanted to be sick. Throwing up would have been a terrible idea, but that didn't make it any less appealing. That horrible hot/cold mixture was forming in my stomach again, and the drums were getting softer, harder to hear, which struck me as bad in some way I couldn't entirely define.

"Tansy is going to be on life support," said Nathan. "Putting her in the water could kill her."

"Which makes it all the more important that someone stay with the boat." Fishy turned the wheel delicately to the side, and we slid in along the dock as if our boat had been intended to sit there all along: the missing piece of an elaborate puzzle. "Welcome to San Francisco."

Only one of the other ferry bays was occupied, by a boat that was half submerged and still taking on water through the gaping hole in its side. I had no idea what could have done that to one of these sturdy, metal-plated craft, and I didn't want to know. The dock was clear, and nothing moved in the shadows. That was what really mattered to me, at least right now: that we were, for the moment, alone.

"Sal?" asked Nathan.

I nodded tightly and left the cabin, moving to the rail. Dr. Banks said something, but his words were washed away by the roar of the engine as Fishy did whatever he had to do in order to lock us into place, and so I just kept walking, turning my back on the scientist who had helped to make me. When I reached the edge of the boat I stopped, resting my hands on the railing, and closed my eyes, trying to *listen* with everything I had. The noise didn't matter; my ears weren't a part of this.

Pheromone trails are funny things. They're both immediate, generated by bodies in motion, and left behind by bodies that have already passed. Ants use them to keep track of each other. Cats use them to claim things as part of their territory. And tapeworms use them, in a strange, incomprehensible way, to communicate. I didn't know what an unaltered tapeworm would have to say, but I knew what the sleepwalkers were saying with their pheromone trails, and hence one of the things that I was saying to them when they happened to cross my path—maybe the most important thing:

*Here I am.*

The air in the Ferry Building was stale, thick with salt and a faint, sweet foundation of decay. There had been sleepwalkers here—I couldn't have explained how I knew that, because the knowledge didn't come with any accompanying words. Neither did the knowledge that they weren't here now. The water was too close and too bitter, and it got too cold at night. They had been driven deeper into the city, or at least away from the dock area. What that was going to mean for the rest of our journey, I couldn't say.

I let go of the rail and turned, unsurprised to find Nathan and Dr. Banks standing behind me. "There's no one here but us," I said. "It's an enclosed space, though. There could be a hundred sleepwalkers outside and I wouldn't know about it."

Dr. Banks sneered. "Leave it to Surrey to build an early warning system that can't work through walls. What use are you?"

"I don't know," I said. "But I guess I'll have time to figure it out. Where's Fishy?"

"He's shutting down the engine, and then he's going to come help us find a car," said Nathan. "It should be a minute or so."

The slow rumble of the boat beneath us died, leaving my feet tingling at the sudden lack of vibration. Fishy trotted out from the cabin, waving to make sure we knew that everything was all right. Beverly jumped, pressing herself hard against my legs. For one terrible moment, I expected to hear her growl come ripping through the still air of the Ferry Building like a condemnation. This was going too easily: something had to go wrong. That was how things went for us. Wrong.

Fishy slowed as he drew closer, and Beverly did not growl. "Are we clear?" he asked.

"No sleepwalkers in the building, but that doesn't mean it's going to stay that way, especially after we open a door," I said. "I can't be sure they're not at the front, either. I'm still figuring out how all this works."

"As long as they leave me alone long enough to get some fuel into this baby, I'll be fine," said Fishy, patting the side of the ferry. He was smiling, calmly and consistently.

I didn't like that expression—something about it was off, somehow, although not in a way that would have meant he was going into conversion—but it was Nathan who spoke, asking, "Are you feeling all right, Fishy? I didn't expect you to volunteer to stay behind."

"Yeah, I'm good," said Fishy calmly. "It's all good. See, this is where we split the party to deliver the MacGuffin"—he pointed at Dr. Banks, who looked more confused than affronted—"and cure the zombie plague that's been destroying mankind. You guys are running into a series of cut scenes. If I stay here with the boat, I'll either get an unstoppable wave of enemies to fight, or I'll be ready when you come back with the final boss fight in tow. Either way, I'm good."

I frowned. It took me a moment to puzzle through what he was saying. I've never really liked video games. They moved too fast, and involved too much violence. I was happier with cartoons and audio books when I needed something to keep me entertained. "You're really sad, aren't you?" I ventured.

"Not anymore," said Fishy. "I'm probably going to die today. Thanks for that." He thrust his hand out at me, fingers spread. I blinked. Then I took it, and shook. He beamed. "I'm pretty much ready to log out and go home. Now let's find you guys a car." He pulled his hand away and loped off toward the stairway that would grant him access to the deck. I stared mutely after him, not sure how I should respond.

Dr. Banks did it for me. "You know that boy's a few kittens short of a litter, right?" he asked. "Not sure I'd feel good about leaving him with my escape route, if I were you. Not that you're going to make it back here to use it. It's just a matter of principle."

"Yes, because crossing the city with the arrogant bastard

who brought about the end of mankind in order to increase his profit share is so much better." Nathan grabbed Dr. Banks's arms, ignoring the older man's protests, and hauled him after Fishy.

I took one last nervous glance over the side of the boat, tightened my grip on Beverly's leash, and followed them.

*It begins now.*

—FROM THE NOTES OF SHERMAN LEWIS
(SUBJECT VIII, ITERATION III), NOVEMBER 2027

*The techs are tearing down the last of the essential equipment and checking everything for bugs. I feel like Santa Claus: we're making a list, and we're checking it twice. We should have room in the truck for most of the hydroponics and the livestock, but we're leaving behind a lot of personal belongings, with no way of knowing whether it's ever going to be possible for their owners to come back and retrieve them. The top floors of the factory have already gone dark. This was a good way station. I hoped that it might prove to be our home. Like so many of my hopes, this one has come to nothing, and I do not know what lies ahead of us.*

*The people I work with here are human, with the exception of Adam—my precious boy—and Sal, who may never be fully at ease with her nature. That's my fault as much as it is anyone else's, but as I do not have the power to revise the past, I choose not to dwell on that. The simple fact is that I live my life surrounded by the planet's dominant species, and their hold on that position is slipping. Soon, Nathan and Sal will return with Tansy. Soon, I will have to make the final judgment call:*

*Who inherits the earth?*

—FROM THE JOURNAL OF DR. SHANTI CALE,
NOVEMBER 16, 2027

## Chapter 19

## NOVEMBER 2027

The garage where the employee vehicles were kept was locked, which made no sense to me—who stops in the middle of an apocalypse to make sure everything is safe and secure from looters? Fishy dispatched the lock with a single swipe of the crowbar he'd acquired from somewhere, knocking it to the ground with a loud clattering noise that made the rest of us wince and look around, waiting for an attack. I still wasn't picking up on any nearby sleepwalkers, but as I had tried to explain to Dr. Banks, my funny sort of radar was neither tested nor proven to be completely reliable. It was a mad science party trick, and like all party tricks, I had to assume that sometimes it could fail to work the way it was supposed to.

Fishy slipped into the garage. A moment later his voice drifted back like a ghost out of the darkness, saying, "The lights are out, but I think we'll be okay."

That was our cue. I slipped in after him before Nathan could push in front of me, letting Beverly's curiously sniffing nose lead the way. Her sleepwalker radar was more reliable than mine, and if she started barking, we'd know that we needed to get the hell out.

High windows were set around the edge of the garage roof, allowing the watery San Francisco light to ooze inside, seeming almost liquid as it clung to the corners of the room and trickled down the walls to outline the shapes of the cars and trucks that had been safely tucked away by their owners before those owners went on to meet their fates. The air smelled ever so subtly of decay, and I was glad for the darkness, glad for the shadows that concealed the corners and the secrets they might hold; Beverly wasn't barking and my private radar wasn't ringing, which meant that nothing else lived in this space. If a sleepwalker had been trapped inside, they had long since starved to death. I didn't think that was the case, though. I was pretty sure the lock Fishy had so carelessly destroyed had been placed by someone who then entered the garage through another door—something small, something overlooked in our quick, goal-oriented search—and finished things in the only way they could. Someone who wanted to die with dignity.

Fishy didn't seem bothered by the smell. He moved from vehicle to vehicle, cupping his hands around his eyes as he peered through the glass. "Can't see a damn thing," he announced, and kept moving. "Start looking for unlocked doors. One of these bastards has to still have the keys in it."

"Why?" I asked. I moved toward the nearest van at the same time; there was no point in waiting for an answer before I started trying to help.

"Because otherwise I'm teaching one of you how to hot-wire a car, and trust me, that's not the sort of skill you pick up in one lesson." Fishy pulled on the door of a pickup truck, scowled, and moved on. "Someone needs to wait with the boat; it's not going to be either one of you; it's sure as shit not going to be Dr. Frankenstein; that means we need a car with keys."

"This one's open." Nathan's call came from the other side of the garage. I turned, peering through the gloom, and found him standing next to the dark bulk of what looked like a minivan. "No keys."

"What's the make?" asked Fishy.

"Io."

Fishy actually grinned. "Pre- or post-auto drive?"

"I don't know. How am I supposed to know that? It's an Io. I can't even tell what color it is."

"Wait right there." Fishy half jogged across the garage, neatly sidestepping around Beverly, to join Nathan at the open van door. He peered inside the vehicle, seeming to look more with his hands than with his eyes—which made sense, given the darkness—and finally announced, gleefully, "You don't need keys *or* a crash course on how to hot-wire a car. All you need is one short and a screwdriver."

"What?" said Nathan.

"What?" I said.

"You spent a lot of time in prison before the world got messed up, didn't you?" said Dr. Banks.

Fishy ignored us all as he turned and walked over to the wall. Bumping, clattering sounds traced his progress, making me wince. It was hard to know how much of the noise he was making would be audible outside the garage, but even a little could very easily be too much, under the circumstances. There was one final clatter, louder than the rest, and then Fishy was trotting back, holding something long and pointed in one hand. "There's always a toolbox in a place like this," he said, pushing past Nathan. His upper body half vanished into the van, and for a few moments the only sounds were the drums beating in my eyes and Fishy rustling around in the front seat.

There was a click. The van's engine turned over, and the

headlights came on, throwing the front half of the garage into terrible clarity. A man was slumped against the wall on the right, only a few feet away from the bench and open toolbox that Fishy must have been rummaging through. The man's throat had been slit, and the words "I'm sorry" were written on the wall in what I strongly suspected was his blood. I shuddered and looked away.

Fishy didn't appear to have noticed. He was enthusiastically explaining the art of using a screwdriver in place of a key to Nathan, periodically leaning back into the van to give the screwdriver a twist or jiggle, for reasons I couldn't understand and didn't particularly want to learn. I shifted my weight from one foot to the other, waiting for them to be done, waiting for the moment when we could start moving and put this dark, dead space behind us.

Beverly began to growl.

It was a low, almost inaudible sound at first, easily overlooked under the chatter from Fishy and the questioning replies from Nathan. I stiffened, trying to turn my senses outward, looking for pheromone trails or...or whatever it was that I actually looked for when I did that. I found nothing. But Beverly was still growling, the sound increasing in both volume and urgency, and she didn't do that without cause. "Guys?" I said.

They ignored me.

Beverly pressed herself hard against my leg. Her eyes were fixed on the open garage door, and her ears were flat against her head, giving her a distinctly predatory cast. "Guys," I said again, louder this time. "Something's upsetting Beverly."

That got Dr. Banks to pay attention to me, at least. "Is it sleepwalkers?"

"I don't know. I'm not picking up anything, but I don't know if I would. I think we should be moving."

"In a second," said Fishy.

Beverly continued to growl, still getting steadily louder. For the first time, I felt that odd ping at the back of my head that meant *sleepwalkers coming, sleepwalkers nearby*—but it was so much stronger than I had expected it to be, especially with so little lead-in, that it might as well have meant *sleepwalkers here.*

"We don't have any more seconds," I said, urgently. "We have to go *now.*"

The urgency in my voice must have been enough to catch his attention; the outline of his head appeared above the dashboard of the van. I turned, dragging Beverly with me, and ran toward the others. Dr. Banks saw me move and moved with me, and for one glorious moment, I thought we were going to be okay: we had moved fast enough, we had made it out of the path of oncoming danger.

And then the sleepwalkers of San Francisco, who had had quite a long while to grow hungry as they roved the hills looking for things to fill the holes that could never be filled, hit the open door of the garage like a wave. Their bodies blocked out what little light there was in an instant, and everything became the shouts and shoves of my companions as we tried to get ourselves into the van. I wound up in the back, holding on to Beverly with all my might as I struggled to keep her from leaping out of the vehicle and tearing off into the fray. Nathan pushed Dr. Banks in after me and slammed the door.

The front doors were still open. "Come on, you idiot, get in the car!" shouted Nathan.

Fishy. Fishy was still out there. "I'm good!" he shouted back. "Go, I'll hold them off!"

"The damn fool's going to kill us all," snarled Dr. Banks, and for once he and I were in perfect, terrible agreement. Then Nathan was in the driver's seat, and was reaching across the van to grab the back of Fishy's shirt and haul him into the front passenger seat, somehow managing to lift the smaller, stockier man with nothing but a grunt of strained protest. The sleepwalkers were closing fast, and the buzz in my head that told me they were coming was a clanging bell warning me of a five-alarm fire. It was becoming physically painful. I bent forward, clasping my hands at the base of my skull, and tried to will the sound away.

Someone's hands were pressed between my shoulder blades. They weren't mine. With Nathan and Fishy in the front seat… I realized who was trying to comfort me a bare second before he spoke, and I stiffened, wishing there were any way for me to remove myself from the situation. There wasn't. With the alarm bells screaming in my head, I would have been doing well to sit up.

"Concentrate, Sally." Dr. Banks's voice was low and soft, so close to my ear that he had to have been leaning forward to whisper to me. That went with the presence of his cuffed hands on my back. I could hear Nathan and Fishy shouting at each other. There was no help coming from that quarter, not until they had a chance to breathe and realize what was happening. "She's distracted right now, and I know you're in there. I know you've always been in there. This is your chance. Take a deep breath, and come back to us."

I wanted to slap his smug face away from me. I couldn't bring myself to move. The alarm bells were still ringing, but in their clamor I could also hear an *absence* of sound: the drums had stopped, leaving the world missing its natural backbeat. That was horrifying, in a way I couldn't entirely define.

"Sally."

He sounded so *sure* of himself. Like he knew, beyond the shadow of a doubt, that all he had to do was keep calling her and she would appear. Sally, with her human upbringing and her human ideas about the world. Sally, who wasn't afraid of riding in cars, and who had never experienced the collapse of civilization, or the discovery that she wasn't what she believed herself to be. Sally, who was as alien to me as I was to her, but whose body I had taken over without so much as a by-your-leave.

Sally, who had tormented her family to such an extent that her father was willing to let me play cuckoo in his nest, while her sister had never questioned "her" sudden, total change of personality; had, in fact, looked upon it with gratitude and relief. Sally, whose taste in friends was such that her boyfriend hadn't even been able to stick around to see whether she was going to recover—one hint of difficulty and he was out the door, moving so fast that he might as well have left contrails in his wake. Sally, who had left the mansion of her body empty and waiting for me, because she just couldn't cope with existence anymore.

Maybe Dr. Banks was right about her memories being locked somewhere in the soft gray folds of the brain that had once belonged to her, but he was wrong about at least one thing: Sally didn't live here anymore, and no matter how hard he tried to convince me, I was never inviting her to come back.

"Hold on!" shouted Nathan. The van leapt forward. I heard—and felt—the impact of soft bodies against the hood as we slammed into the leading wave of sleepwalkers. Their moans filled the world, drowning out the alarm bells triggered by their presence. I seized on the sound, trying to use it to anchor myself to the real world again. My head was a cacophony of unwanted stimuli. One by one I shunted them aside, looking for the one that would allow me to move again. I wanted Dr. Banks away from me. His hands on my back were a sick, dead weight, more repulsive than the army of sleepwalkers now trying to claw their way inside to reach us.

Their moaning changed pitch and timbre as we rolled forward, forcing the sleepwalkers to either stand aside or be crushed under our wheels. These were the ones who had been smart or canny enough to stay alive in the ruins of San Francisco: more of them seemed to be moving aside than staying in our path. I forced my head up, off my knees, and croaked, "Crack the windows."

"What?" Nathan's voice, sounding bewildered and no small bit dismayed.

"I need you to crack the windows." Forcing my eyes to open came next. I stared down at the mud-smeared floorboards, trying to will myself to keep moving. "The sleepwalkers...if they knew I was here, they might be confused enough to back off. Just a little. I don't want to hurt them if we don't have to."

"You stupid little cunt." Dr. Banks spoke softly enough that I knew the others wouldn't hear him, not with the sleepwalkers moaning outside and the van still straining for escape. It didn't matter: I could hear him, and I wouldn't forget. He removed his hands from the middle of my back, and it was like a terrible burden being lifted away.

After that, it was almost easy to sit up, turning a glare on Dr. Banks in the process. He shied back, pressing himself against the door. My expression must have been fiercer than I thought. "Get away from me," I said. "Never touch me again. Nathan? The windows."

"On it," said Fishy. The windows in the back rolled down maybe an inch and a half, allowing the moans of the sleepwalkers outside to fill the cab. Beverly's growls became frantic, full-throated barks, almost drowning out the moaning from outside.

"Shh, Bevvie, it's okay," I said, patting her on the head before climbing up onto the seat, kneeling. I leaned forward, pressing my lips against the opening in the window, and took a deep breath. The stench of decay and unwashed human bodies assaulted my nose, almost gagging me. Most of them were ripe with urine, gangrene, and worse. I forced myself to keep inhaling until my lungs began to ache. Then I exhaled, trying to breathe my pheromones into the garage. We were still rolling slowly forward, Nathan struggling with the wheel as he fought to get us out into the open without doing irreparable damage to our only means of transit.

I breathed in again, breathed out again, and kept my eyes on the sleepwalkers surrounding the car, *willing* them to "listen" to the messages coded into my biochemistry, written in protein and chemical chains on my breath. I was a chimera; I was their social superior, just like a termite queen was superior to the drones that filled her hive. They would listen to me. They would *listen* to me. They didn't have a choice.

Apparently, some of the sleepwalkers agreed. The ones closest to my open window slowed, their heads tilting at an alien angle as they canted their eyes upward, looking for the source of the pheromone trail. I kept breathing, trying to spread the command to calm down as far as I could.

One of the nearest sleepwalkers opened his mouth, not to moan, but to shape a word. The sleepwalkers around him did the same, and bit by bit, the stillness spread, replaced by dozens of sleepwalkers exhaling a single syllable:

"Saaaaaaaaaaaaaaal."

"Because *that's* not creepy," snapped Fishy. He didn't roll the windows back up. That was something. "Nathan, I think you can go a little faster. They're not attacking us right now. Take advantage of that."

"We can't drop you off, you realize," said Nathan. The van sped up a bit, nudging sleepwalkers out of the way. Most of them were clustering around the sides of the vehicle now, shoving at each other as they tried to get closer to the windows. If I'd been claustrophobic, I would probably have been climbing the walls. As it was, I was sort of amazed that the humans *weren't*. I guess the need to stay alive was taking priority over the need to freak out completely.

"I know," said Fishy. "We'll have to find another way to refuel the boat, assuming we can even get back to it with this mob here." He sounded surprisingly calm for someone who was riding through a mob of angry trans-human attackers.

I guess believing that nothing around us was real was helping him in at least that one regard.

"You people are an affront to the human race," snarled Dr. Banks.

I turned away from the window to look at him, eyes narrowed. "We only need you for a little while longer, you know," I said. "It's up to you whether we let you go after your people give us Tansy, or whether we take you with us when we leave so that we can throw you to the hungry cousins out there. You made them. Maybe you should have the opportunity to really get to know them."

Dr. Banks paled, his eyes going wide. He didn't say anything else, and so neither did I. I just turned back to the window and resumed breathing through the crack in the glass, trying to keep the sleepwalkers calm long enough for us to escape the garage and drive onward into a bigger, more dangerous future.

The sleepwalkers clogged the Presidio, but forming the mob that had rushed the garage seemed to have denuded their numbers: once we were away from the water the streets were empty and motionless, filled with abandoned cars and the occasional desiccated corpse. Most of the bodies we passed looked like they'd been partially eaten before decay reached a stage that left the meat useless. Pigeons scattered in front of us, and I saw what looked like a pack of wild dogs disappearing down an alley, there and gone too fast for me to be sure of what I'd seen. I left the windows cracked, listening for the sound of moans. Depending on the wind, it might well reach me before the sleepwalker pheromones did.

The buzzing in my head had stopped. That was nice. The smell of decay from outside the van hadn't abated, although it was more distant now, diluted with salt and with the undefinable, stony smell of San Francisco itself. I settled cross-legged on my seat, watching out the window and waiting for our next obstacle to present itself.

"Sal, are you all right back there?" Nathan raised his head as he spoke, his eyes seeking mine in the rearview mirror. There was an air freshener shaped like a dolphin hanging there, and I felt a brief pang of sorrow for the person who had hung it, who had never come back to get their van and drive it safely home. "I'm sorry we had to drive out of there like that. I know I didn't give you enough notice."

"It's all right," I said, offering what I hoped was an earnest smile. "I barely noticed. I was busy trying to keep the cousins from shredding the van and us with it."

Now Nathan blinked, his eyes widening a little in the mirror. "Sal…you're not wearing your seat belt."

"What?" I looked down at my unrestrained middle, belatedly realizing just how accurate my words had been: I had barely noticed when we started to move, and I was barely noticing it now. Apparently, the life-threatening reality outside the vehicle was bad enough to keep me focused on the things that actually mattered, and prevent me from having another of my attacks. "Oh." I buckled my seat belt before looking up again and meeting Nathan's eyes in the mirror. He looked concerned.

He had every right to be. Things were moving fast now, and with Dr. Banks in the mix, any deviation from the norm was cause to worry.

Dr. Banks himself still had not received the memo about behaving decently if he wanted to stay alive. He sneered first at me and then at the front of the van, apparently directing his disgust at Fishy and Nathan combined. "We're almost to Symbo-Gen," he said. "That means we're on *my* turf now, and you're going to be sorry that you decided to start this with me."

"You're the one who came to us, Doctor," said Fishy languidly. "That was a stupid choice and you knew it was a stupid choice, which means it must have been the only choice you had. You could have sent your USAMRIID buddies in to snatch Dr. Cale or Sal or even Adam if you just needed data. You could have carted us back to your precious company for disassembly on your own terms. You didn't do that. Either you *couldn't* do it, or your relationship with the United States military isn't as cuddly as you want us to believe it is."

Dr. Banks didn't say anything.

I turned to look at him, frowning slowly. "You keep trying to convince me that I'm still Sally," I said. "Why is that so important to you? You never tried to do that before."

Dr. Banks didn't say anything.

"Colonel Mitchell. Is he still in charge of the local branch of USAMRIID? You know, big guy, thinning hair, sort of old around the eyes—and oh, yeah, Sally's father. Is he still the one calling the shots? How much oversight does he have at this point? He used to tell me his men would follow him to the end of the world. Was that more than just hyperbole?"

Dr. Banks didn't say anything.

San Francisco continued to roll by outside our windows, broken windows, empty doorways, and the constant, distant smell of rot accompanying us across the city. I unfolded my legs, trying to make myself look a little bit less childish as I leaned closer, invading Dr. Banks's personal space, and asked, "Are you trying to make me be Sally because you promised her father that you could bring her back to him?"

Dr. Banks didn't say anything…but his eyes cheated away and to the left, the same way Beverly's did when I caught her digging in the laundry, and I knew that I had found my answer.

"We should leave you on a corner for the sleepwalkers," I said, disgusted. "You didn't come to us because you needed to know how to stabilize Anna. You came because you wanted me."

"You think a lot of yourself, don't you?" Dr. Banks's voice was dull, like he couldn't even find it in himself to sneer anymore. "I came for the reasons I gave. Anna won't stabilize, and the 'chimera'"—he made the word sound dirty—"market is going to be huge over the next few years. With as many people as have died in this little public relations nightmare, SymboGen will need a new product—a new name to go with it, of course, but no one's going to shut us down. We have too much money, too much power..."

"And you've shifted too much of the blame," I interjected.

Dr. Banks glared at me, but his heart wasn't in it. "Your kind are as good a cash cow as any. The goodwill I might be able to gain with Colonel Mitchell by handing you back to him is a minor concern. Not nearly as important as stabilizing that little girl."

"But you told him you could bring Sally back, didn't you?" Nathan kept his eyes on the road. I wanted to hug him, to chase the bitterness from his voice. "I know what it's like to pursue your funding, Dr. Banks. I was just a kid when Mom was really dealing with the hard-core academia, but I'll never forget the way she promised those men the moon and the stars if they'd just put their money in *her* hands, rather than in the hands of her competitors. You told him that because of the way Sal converted, you could bring back the original personality, even though that would normally be impossible—and of course, no one but you could ever manage such a feat of scientific glory. He needed you if he wanted his daughter back."

Dr. Banks didn't say anything. But he didn't deny it either, and under the circumstances, that was just as damning as a confession would have been.

San Francisco was a city riddled with makeshift blockades, roadblocks, and destruction. For every open street there were three more that had somehow been stopped up by either the police or the locals, before they went off to meet whatever fate was waiting for them in the foggy hills. I hoped that whatever had happened to them—and even in a situation like this one, where the end seemed virtually preordained, there were still so many things that could have happened—it had been quick, and had left them with little time to suffer.

Maybe that was the most terrifying thing about Dr. Banks's attempts to convince me that Sally was still in my head, buried under trauma and scar tissue. The idea of being a prisoner in my own body, unable to change anything, but able to see and understand everything that happened, was horrifying. At least when I'd been an implant, I hadn't really *understood* what was happening to me, or to the body I inhabited. The cousins were just tapeworms driving broken minds around the world. They weren't jailers for the humans whose bodies they had taken over. To think anything else was to invite madness.

We stopped on the Presidio to let Nathan get out and Fishy get behind the wheel. Nathan transferred an uncharacteristically silent Dr. Banks to the front passenger seat and got in next to me, putting a hand on my knee without saying a word about why he thought I might need the comfort. I sighed, shifting to rest my head against his shoulder. Beverly mirrored the sound a moment later, and I had to clap my hand over my mouth to smother my giggles. For better or for worse, we were driving into the unknown. Yes, it was a trap, but wasn't everything a trap these days? I couldn't think of the last time I'd experienced something that wasn't a trap in some way. Even Nathan and my dogs were traps. They made me want a life I probably wasn't going to ever have, and a world that had been buried because of the circumstances of my birth.

"Sleepwalkers at three o'clock," reported Fishy. "They don't seem to realize we're here, but I'm going to take the next few blocks a little faster. You kids may want to hang on."

"Okay," said Nathan. Fishy accelerated. I felt, rather than saw, Nathan twist around to peer down at me. He asked, "Are you sure that you're okay?"

"I'm pretty sure, and that's better than I was expecting," I said. "I feel numb, more than anything else. I don't think I have the energy to be scared anymore. Don't worry. I'm sure I'll have some screaming nightmares about this later." If there was a later.

Nathan chuckled, reaching up to stroke my hair with one hand. "I'll look forward to it."

"You're never having another nightmare," said Dr. Banks. "Things in jars don't have nightmares."

"You're such a charmer, I totally understand why people let you talk them into swallowing live worms," said Fishy calmly. "Now shut the fuck up, or I'll dump your useless ass on the street corner."

"You can't keep threatening me forever, boy," said Dr. Banks. "Eventually, you'll have to either act on your words or admit that you still need me too much to waste me on a bit of petty revenge."

"I know which one I'd prefer," said Fishy. The van sped up a little more, the soft whir of the engine filling the cab.

I sighed and closed my eyes. I could feel the faint buzz that notified me of sleepwalker presence at the back of my head, like the blood there was carbonated and fizzing against my skull. It was almost comforting, now that I knew what it was and what it really meant. The sleepwalkers would have a harder time sneaking up on us now, at least while I was awake—and I had Dr. Banks to thank. It wasn't until he'd brought Anna into the building that I'd really begun to understand what I felt around Adam, and around Sherman and the others.

Sherman had to know that we could detect each other. Maybe that was the real reason he'd kept me isolated from his people the way he had: he hadn't wanted me to develop this little party trick any faster than I was going to on my own. I didn't know what useful applications it would have had back in his mall, but there must have been *something* I could have done with it, if I'd understood what those occasional flashes of disorientation and awareness really meant.

"You'll never lie to me, will you, Nathan?" I asked, quietly, trying to keep the pair in the front seat from overhearing.

"I promise I'll do my best not to," he said, and that was somehow better than an outright pledge to never do it, ever, under any circumstances would have been: he was human, and fallible, just like all of us. He could make mistakes. Pretending that was never going to happen wouldn't do anybody any good, but it could leave us unprepared for what was yet to come.

In the front seat, Dr. Banks made a small noise that was neither scoff nor snort. I lifted my head to see what he was looking at, and stiffened, the drums suddenly beating loud and angry in my ears. All the fear I hadn't been feeling flooded into me at once, leaving the small boat of my courage floundering on the tide.

SymboGen was directly in front of us, standing like a shining beacon of enduring civilization among the ruined and smoking wreckage of the city. It looked…it looked like nothing at all had changed, like everything was business as usual and anyone who claimed that there was an emergency going on was just crying wolf. The late afternoon sun gleamed off the unbroken windows of the high-rise, and the gated parking lot was filled with cars. That was the only thing that broke the illusion of perfect normalcy: there were several olive drab army convoys parked in among the hybrids and electric cars, which looked like candy-colored jewels next to their larger, more functional cousins. From what I could see, even the exterior landscaping was still perfectly maintained.

"You couldn't even let the gardeners go home to their families, could you?" The question seemed nonsensical, but it was the only thing I could think of to say. Nothing would have put the sheer incongruity of the scene into words, and so I didn't even bother to try.

"They were safer staying with us, and they recognized that." There was a shifty note to his voice that made me suspect he wasn't telling the full truth, that there'd been a lockdown or something that kept those low-level employees on the grounds until it was too late, and there was nowhere else for them to go. I didn't bother calling him on it. When had he ever told us the full truth, about anything? Even when his own life was on the line, Dr. Steven Banks was still trying to play the angles.

"That's why I chose Dr. Cale's brand of monster over yours, you know," I said quietly. "At least she was always honest about what she was."

Nathan's hand tightened on my knee, but he didn't contradict my assessment of his mother. I think we both knew her too well for that.

Dr. Banks stiffened but didn't say anything.

Fishy broke the silence. "Gee, will I be glad to go back to crazy science land, and no longer be sharing a van with the issues party," he said, amiably, and started down the hill toward SymboGen.

The buildings around us seemed cleaner somehow, like they had been cleared out before they could take anything more than superficial damage. I kept a tight hold on Beverly's leash, watching warily for signs of ambush. It wasn't until we were almost to the front gates that I realized the fizzing sensation in my head was gone. There were no sleepwalkers nearby, unless Dr. Banks was holding some inside the building for further study. If they were in airtight rooms—and they would have to be, to keep them from upsetting each other—I wouldn't be able to pick up on them. The thought was sobering. If he got me into one of those rooms, no one would ever find me.

I didn't have time to dwell on that new and disturbing idea. Fishy pulled up in front of the security gate. I was somehow unsurprised to see that it was still manned, although the two men who were waiting to check our IDs were wearing full

SWAT gear and carrying assault rifles—a far cry from their careful inoffensiveness of days past. Fishy rolled down the window.

"Afternoon, gentlemen," he said. "As you can see, we have your fearless leader captive. You want to go ahead and buzz us in?"

"Sir?" asked one of the men, sounding utterly baffled as he peered past Fishy to the handcuffed form of Dr. Banks. Confusion was an understandable sentiment. Fishy was pretty darn confusing when you weren't prepared for him.

"I'm their hostage, Kirk," said Dr. Banks, sounding more annoyed about the situation than anything else. "Go ahead and let us in."

The man—Kirk—blinked. "Do you want me to notify Security?"

"Uh, hostage-taker right here, remember?" said Fishy.

Both men ignored him. "It won't be necessary," said Dr. Banks. "I'm in no immediate danger. Just open the door."

"Sir, this goes against the protocols that *you* established—"

"I know full well who established the protocols, Kirk," said Dr. Banks. A hint of steel had crept back into his tone, stiffening and sharpening it. This was something he knew how to deal with: a disobedient subordinate was easy pickings. "Now let us in, or you'll have your termination slip by the end of the day. And you know what that means."

Kirk went pale. "Yes, sir," he said, and retreated to the booth with his companion. The other man flipped a switch. The gate rolled slowly open.

"Man was pretty terrified of being fired," observed Fishy, as he restarted the engine and rolled forward through the opening.

"Any staff whose family was able to survive the initial outbreak and survive the trip to SymboGen has been allowed to have that family stay here with them," said Dr. Banks. "Living space is tighter than we would prefer, but sheltering those people was the only humane thing to do."

"I bet it also made an excellent PR opportunity," said Nathan.

"Not as good as it should have. People kept getting distracted by the chaos on the streets." Dr. Banks sounded disgusted. How dare people die when he was trying to capitalize on showing some basic human decency? "Anyway, everyone who works here knows that space is limited, and that we're doing serious research to try to resolve the problem. Anyone leaving my employ will have a choice between heading to the official government quarantine facilities in Pleasanton, or being turned out onto the street to do as they will. It's remarkable how many have chosen the latter."

Fishy pulled into a parking space near the building and twisted to stare, openmouthed, at Dr. Banks. Nathan and I did the same in the backseat, neither of us quite able to process what the man was saying. Finally, Fishy managed, "You mean you're turning them out to *die* just because they don't work for you anymore?"

"Resources are limited," said Dr. Banks coolly. "Can you really tell me your precious Dr. Cale would do any differently?"

Fishy shook his head. "You are a piece of work. Let's get you back into your ivory tower so that I can go back to where the monsters are the only thing I have to worry about fucking me over."

It was strange to be climbing out of a vehicle in the Symbo-Gen parking lot like nothing had changed; like the world was still the way that it had always been before. The doors would open automatically at our approach, releasing a gust of perfume, while tinny elevator music played in the distance. And Chave would be there, my straight-laced, by-the-book handler in her impeccable business attire, ready to take me off to whatever tests and appointments they had scheduled for me...

But Chave was dead. She had been a double agent for Dr. Cale, and her implant had eventually decided to take her over.

I'd never known her well enough to really miss her, but I'd known her well enough to grieve for her. That would have to be enough.

Nathan took the hand that wasn't holding Beverly's leash and squeezed it firmly. I squeezed back, and together, the four of us started toward the doors to SymboGen.

The closer we got, the more apparent it became that the illusion of normalcy was just that: an illusion. The grounds were still being maintained at a minimal level, but none of the dead or dying flowers had been replaced. It was late November; the flower beds should have been a riot of poinsettias, and every hedge should have been dripping with tinsel and no-break glass balls. Instead, the early fall plants were still in place, being coaxed along to keep things looking as functional as possible.

I wasn't the only one who noticed. "Who are you keeping up appearances for?" asked Nathan. "Who could possibly be looking at your hedges right now?"

"It's been important to downplay staff losses and their impact during this crisis," said Dr. Banks. "The people we're working with want to look at us and think that we're weathering the storm without getting wet. It builds their confidence. You understand."

"Image is everything with you people," said Nathan. He sounded disgusted. I was just glad he was the one doing the talking. I wasn't sure I would have been able to shape the words.

"Son, image is everything with everyone, no matter what you try to tell yourself." The glass doors leading into the lobby slid smoothly open as we approached. The cool air that drifted out to greet us was perfumed—apple, orange blossoms, and fresh corn, a far cry from the sugary chaos of Captain Candy's—but the music wasn't playing. That was almost a relief. "Or are you trying to tell me you'd still be so interested in that little girl whose hand you're holding if we took her pretty chassis away and handed her to you in a jar? You love the woman, but you love the look, too. Don't think you're any different from me."

"I am different from you," snapped Nathan. "I didn't cut somebody's head open and shove a worm inside to get the look I wanted. I fell for a miracle, not a science project."

"Just keep telling yourself that," said Dr. Banks, and he stepped inside.

The lobby was empty: they must have been running on a skeleton staff. That, too, made me feel a little better. Anyone who wasn't here was probably either dead or in the quarantine facilities that Dr. Banks was using to keep his remaining staff in line. Either way, they would probably have been happy to return to work if it meant that their lives would also return to normal.

Dr. Banks stopped when we were halfway across the lobby. "Now's when you untie me," he said, a new serenity in his tone. "I'm home."

"I'm not seeing where this changes anything," said Fishy.

"Then you're a fool," said Dr. Banks. "I still haven't decided whether I'll let you have your girl. You'll be pleased to know that I'm leaning toward 'yes,' since she's useless to me now and you've given me something much better." The smile he slanted in my direction stopped just short of becoming a leer. I managed, barely, to suppress my shudder. "That does lead to the greater question of whether I'm intending to let any of you leave here alive."

"Dr. Cale thought of that," said Fishy mildly. "Or did you genuinely think she just went 'sure, I'll let my son and his girlfriend and my favorite handsome, dashing, suave assistant go off with the man who killed humanity' and pushed us out the door? I knew you were arrogant. I didn't know you were stupid."

For the first time since we'd arrived at the SymboGen gates,

Dr. Banks looked uncomfortable. "What are you talking about?"

"Get us to the elevator and I'll explain." Fishy nudged his elbow. "Unless you'd rather stand right here until the timer runs out?"

"Timer? What timer?" Dr. Banks started walking again. He was virtually stomping as we crossed the floor, but no one came rushing to his rescue.

I wasn't the only one to notice that. "Huh," said Nathan. "No one's coming to find out who we are or why we have you in handcuffs. I wonder why that is? I mean, everyone enjoys working for a heartless despot who treats human lives like tissue paper, right?"

"The timer I started when we left the boat," said Fishy calmly. He gave Dr. Banks another nudge. "It's amazing what you can do with C-4."

"You can't really expect me to believe that Surrey would let you blow yourselves up just to spite me."

"Not us: me, and you," said Fishy. "In case you haven't noticed, I'm not inner circle. That's cool with me, because I don't feel like taking on that kind of responsibility. But I'm totally down with grabbing hold of you while Nate and worm-girl run for the hills, and letting my explosive buddy"—he patted his pocket—"do the talking for me. I'm tired of this game, Doctor. I'm ready to log off and go home. I don't suggest you push me."

Dr. Banks gave him a startled look before pressing the call button for the elevator. "Son, I have serious concerns about your mental health."

"Suits me," said Fishy amiably.

I hung back, leaning close to murmur to Nathan, "Does he really have a bomb?"

"Not that I know of," replied Nathan, equally quietly. "He

was originally planning to stay on the boat. But I honestly can't be sure."

"Swell," I said.

The elevator doors opened. The four of us got inside. As soon as the doors closed, Fishy undid the handcuffs holding Dr. Banks's arms. The handcuffs promptly disappeared into Fishy's pocket, where they would wait until they were needed again.

"About damn time," sniffed Dr. Banks.

If there is anything in the world more awkward than sharing an elevator with someone who hates you and considers you to be less than human, I don't know what it is. Dr. Banks initially reached for the button that would have taken us to his office. I reached out and grabbed his wrist before I could think better of it, stopping him mid-motion.

"Tansy's not going to be in your office," I said. "She's down in the lab, isn't she? Take us there. That was the deal."

"That was the blackmail arrangement," said Dr. Banks. He yanked his wrist from my grasp and pressed the button for the lowest level of the labs. "Happy now?"

"No," I said. "I'm here. I'll be happy when I'm not here anymore."

Dr. Banks shook his head. "You'd think that after all this time, you might have finally learned how to be grateful."

"I don't think you're the man who's going to teach me that."

The floors slowly counted down as we descended. Beverly kept her nose pressed against the base of the door. She growled occasionally, not on every level, but on enough that I had a strong suspicion I knew which floors were being used for sleep-walker resource.

I tensed as we started to slow. Finally, the elevator stopped and the doors slid open, revealing the empty hallway. The drums in my head pounded harder than ever. The hall should have been packed with technicians bustling to and fro, their hands full of lab equipment and clipboards, while Sherman—the old Sherman, with his tailored suits and ready smile—waited for me to come into his care. This was supposed to be my home away from home, and instead it was just one more place that was never going to be the same again.

Nothing was *ever* going to be the same again.

Dr. Banks led us out of the elevator and down the hall, stopping at a door I had never seen open before. He produced a key card from inside his pocket and swiped it in front of the door, unlocking it. He grasped the handle, pausing to look at me gravely and say, "I'll understand if you want to stay out here, Sally. I'm sure your boys can keep an eye on me."

Something about his tone was hesitant, even tender, like he had dug through his false affection and his too-real scorn until he hit whatever deep bedrock of actual compassion he still had buried under the persona he had worked so long and hard to build. I lifted my chin, feeling the muscles in my jaw tighten, and said, "I go where they go. Tansy's my sister. I owe it to her to be able to do this."

"Suit yourself," he said, and opened the door, revealing a stark white operating theater. There was a narrow bed—more like a cot—in the middle of the room, and there, naked and strapped down, was Tansy.

Her head had been shaved, and tubes snaked out of her, carrying and delivering fluids. A large bandage covered the right side of her scalp, concealing whatever terrible incisions Dr. Banks had used to extract samples of her implant. She didn't react at all to the door being opened, but I could see her stomach muscles tightening and relaxing very slightly as she breathed. She wasn't dead yet. It was a fairly near thing.

"I'm going to kill you," someone said, and I was only a little bit surprised to realize that it was me.

Nathan pushed past me into the room. Dr. Banks followed

him. I stayed where I was in the doorway, one hand clutching Beverly's leash, staring numbly as they bent over the bed where Tansy was lying. I didn't know what to do. I wasn't a lab or medical technician, I couldn't help, and I couldn't kill Dr. Banks for what he'd done—not if we wanted to get out of here alive, with Tansy, and back to the ferry landing without Symbo-Gen security or USAMRIID forces landing on our heads. That was already going to be difficult and would depend at least partially on Dr. Banks's willingness to let our insult against his person stand—and whether or not he believed Fishy really had a bomb. I was deathly afraid we were going to be fighting our way out…and I was also looking forward to it. Maybe, in the chaos, I could kill him after all.

I had never been excited by the idea of killing someone before. I was surprised to find that I didn't really mind the emotion.

"All right, let's get her to the elevator." Nathan started rolling the cot toward the door. To my surprise, Dr. Banks was on the other side, helping him.

That surprise was short-lived. Dr. Banks opened his mouth: "You'll keep your end of the bargain, yes? Once you have my Anna stabilized…"

"We'll contact you and arrange her return. *If* we can stabilize her, which we may not be able to do. Yes, we will let you know either way." Nathan sounded disgusted. "I know you can contact your government buddies and make up some reason that they *have* to find us whenever you want to. So we're not going to give you cause to want to until we've had time to disappear."

"I'll be honest, son, I'm surprised you're willing to trust me."

"Don't ever mistake this for trust," snapped Nathan. "You want Anna back and stabilized, you'll leave us alone long enough for that to happen—which means you'll leave us alone long enough that we can disappear completely."

"What makes you think I'll wait that long?" Dr. Banks sounded honestly curious.

Nathan looked at him flatly. "My mother says you will. She's a better judge of character than I am in at least one regard: she knows how to spot a weasel before it starts biting. If she says you'll risk losing us now to get something better later on, she means it."

Dr. Banks laughed. "Good old Surrey."

Nathan didn't say anything. He just put his head down and kept pushing.

The elevator was a tight fit with four adults, a dog, and the cot Tansy was strapped to. They'd brought her catheter stand and three IV poles as well as the bed itself, and Fishy and I had to work quickly to keep them from getting tangled in the loading process. Then we were heading back toward the lobby, and we were finally home free; we had Tansy, and we were going back where we belonged.

Everything was going to be okay.

The elevator dinged. Dr. Banks said, "I really am sorry about this." And the doors slid open to reveal eight soldiers with USAMRIID patches on their upper arms, standing in a flanking position around Colonel Alfred Mitchell, their drawn rifles aimed directly at us.

"Colonel Mitchell," said Dr. Banks. "You're just in time."

The rest of us didn't say anything. There was nothing left to say.

*I'm going to kill him.*

—FROM THE JOURNAL OF DR. NATHAN KIM,
NOVEMBER 2027

*Forgive me.*

—FROM THE JOURNAL OF COLONEL ALFRED
MITCHELL, NOVEMBER 17, 2027

## Chapter 20
### NOVEMBER 2027

For a long moment, no one moved. It felt like no one even breathed, like everything had been put on hold while the world rearranged itself around us. Then, calmly, Colonel Mitchell said, "Hello, Sally."

In that moment, I understood. Understood what Dr. Banks had been trying to accomplish, and understood how it could be used to our advantage, if I was willing to do what I had already done once before. If I was willing to sacrifice myself in the name of saving the people that I loved.

*Please understand, Nathan,* I thought, and wished that there was some way I could explain to him what I was doing, and why I was doing it. It was the only option I had left, but that didn't make it any easier, and that didn't make it *right*. It didn't make it not hurt.

I dropped Beverly's leash, pasting what I hoped would look

like a sincere smile across my face in the same moment. Taking a half step forward—which was harder than I expected, thanks to all the damn guns aimed at me—I swallowed hard, and asked, "Daddy?"

Everything seemed to stand still. Then, smugly, Dr. Banks said, "I told you I could do it. It was simple, really."

"Sally?" Colonel Mitchell sounded like he was afraid of his own question, like he was afraid of asking it where anyone else could hear. "Is that really you?"

"My head hurts," I said, which wasn't an answer. That made it the perfect reply. I took another step forward, and still the men with guns didn't fire on me. "Where's Mom?"

The Colonel's shoulders sagged—in relief or sorrow, I didn't know, and my genuine fear that something had happened to Sally's mother informed my performance, making it easy to take another two steps with stumbling quickness, one hand half reaching for him. The guns didn't track me.

"Are you here for me?" I asked.

"Yes," he said, eyes flicking first to my outstretched hand, and then to the people still standing behind me in the elevator. I heard Beverly whine. Taking Colonel Mitchell's gaze as an excuse, I twisted to look back over my shoulder.

Nathan was holding Beverly's leash. He looked resigned, like he hated this as much as I did, but understood its necessity. That made my heart hurt, in ways I couldn't entirely name. I was hurting him, and he was letting me go, because we would never be able to fight our way out of here together. Somewhere along the line, I had managed to teach him—unintentionally— that it was all right to let me go. That was a lesson I had never wanted him to learn.

If Nathan was resigned, Fishy and Beverly were confused. My dog was straining against her leash, struggling to get to me, while Fishy was shaking his head slowly from side to side, a scowl on his face. He was smart enough not to argue when there were that many guns pointed at him, but that wasn't making him any happier with the situation. And as for Dr. Banks…

Dr. Banks looked proud of himself. That was the worst part of all.

I turned back to Colonel Mitchell. "You need to let them go," I said.

His eyes snapped to me. "What?"

"These people brought me here because they wanted to get that girl back; she's theirs, and Dr. Banks took her without permission. He came so that we could get me here safe. They don't have any part in this. Let them go." I took a deep breath. "And they have a bomb. They'll kill us all if you don't let them leave."

"It's true," said Fishy. "Boom, baby, boom."

Colonel Mitchell frowned slowly, and with every part of his face, eyes hardening and brows drawing downward until he was nothing but suspicion. I felt suddenly unsure, and wanted to run back to the elevator, where I would be safe, where I wouldn't have to pretend to be someone I'd never met. Would Sally have requested the freedom of a bunch of people she didn't care about? Joyce hadn't liked her very much. She hadn't been a very nice person.

I forced myself to keep looking at Colonel Mitchell. If I looked away, we were lost. "You have to let them go," I said, slowly and clearly. "I'm very fragile right now. Any shock could cause me to go away again. Getting blown up would be a *big* shock."

He narrowed his eyes. I held my breath. If he called my bluff…

But this was a man who had been willing to get into bed with the enemy on the barest chance of getting his daughter back. He wasn't going to let me slip away again. Colonel Mitchell looked away first, then said, "Your friends are free to go. Steven, you're with me."

Dr. Banks didn't try to argue. He was as trapped as the rest of us, even if he was the one who had originally built the cage. He crossed the floor to stand beside me, and we fell into step with Colonel Mitchell as he turned and led us away. I didn't look back.

*It's all right, Nathan,* I thought. *I'll find my way home. I always do.*

The broken doors were open. We had so far left to go.

# INTERLUDE IV: ANAPHASE

*I am so sorry.*

—SAL MITCHELL

*This is how it begins.*

—SHERMAN LEWIS (SUBJECT VIII, ITERATION III)

*November 2027: Ronnie*

It had been surprisingly easy for Ronnie to reach the reservoir. It was still under guard, of course; the soldiers supplied by USAMRIID and sent in with the doctors from FEMA were patrolling the borders of the area, rifles in hand and nervous sweat on their throats and temples. But Ronnie was quick, and lithe, and had nothing to fear from the sleepwalkers; they had long since learned what her (*his*) pheromone trail meant, and they stayed away, like worker ants avoiding the territory of a greater colony.

The water had been capped, of course, to keep seagulls from shitting in it and—more important now—to keep people from drowning and polluting the water supply of an entire region. This was the reservoir that fed the largest of the quarantine settlements. Some people drank bottled water, of course, but they were all higher-ups, people who could afford the luxury of worrying about contamination. For the average man on the street, crammed six to a bedroom in their shantytown containment, what came out of the faucet was the only option.

Some things could be filtered out of the water, and some things couldn't. Ronnie slouched along the reservoir's edge until he came to a small building, more like a hut than a pumping station, and slipped inside. There was a heavy lid, almost like a manhole cover, over the water access. That was easy enough to deal with. Crowbars were simple tools, and all you needed to operate them was pressure.

The lid slid open with a snarling rasp, like a file being dragged across concrete. Ronnie kept pushing until the opening was almost a foot across. Then he stepped onto the rim of the water access and pulled a small plastic bag from the inner pocket of his vest. Holding it over the water, Ronnie opened the seal and shook out the bag's white, crystalline contents. They vanished into the darkness. Some of the powder would stick to the walls of the input, going nowhere, serving no purpose. But most would reach the water. Most would begin the journey toward their eventual homes.

The war had changed.

Ronnie took a deep breath and stepped off the edge of the access hatch, and plummeted, and was gone.

TO BE CONTINUED…

# ACKNOWLEDGMENTS

By the time you read this, it will be public knowledge that my duology, like the tapeworms that inspired it, has reproduced: it is now a trilogy, and what you hold is the middle volume. I credit this largely to the amazing medical professionals, scientists, public health workers, and readers who responded to the first volume with questions, critiques, and suggestions about what I could do to make my world more complete. I have done my best to honor their input, and I can't wait for you to reach the broken doors.

Michelle Dockrey, Brooke Lunderville, and Diana Fox again contributed much of their time and expertise; I would be lost without them. Sarah Kuhn, Amber Benson, and Margaret Dunlap had a lot to do with keeping me from tearing my hair out: I owe them a great debt of gratitude, or at least a drink at Trader Sam's.

My new editor at Orbit, Will Hinton, was happy to discuss the challenges of a middle book, and met my own idiosyncratic approach to the writing life with an open mind and an eager pen. I look forward to many more books with him. Lauren Panepinto, as always, has provided an incredible cover that I can't wait to hang on my wall.

Once again, acknowledgment for forbearance goes to Amy McNally, Shawn Connolly, and Cat Valente, who put up with an amazing amount of "talking it out" as I tried to work through the back half of the book; to my agent, Diana Fox, who remains my favorite superhero; to the cats, for not eating me when I got too wrapped up in work to feed them; and to Chris Mangum, the incredible technical mind behind www.MiraGrant.com. This book might have been written without them. It would not have been the same.

If you're curious about parasites, check out your local library. There's a lot to learn, and some of it will really amaze you.

Finally, welcome to the world, Aislinn. You are so loved, and so wanted, and I am so delighted that you are here. I can't wait to introduce you to the Birthday Skeleton.

Be careful now, my darling ones.

Don't go out alone.